Tyson Anthony Presents
About Him

....Him

1 - Suspect

At the age of eighteen, Damien accepted the fact that he was gay. Of course the feelings were always there since he was young, but never did he act on them until the night his brother's best friend Vincent had stayed the night over at their dad's house.

Damien never liked Vincent, mainly out of envy. Vincent had brown skin, a trimmed low afro, a clean shaven face, a smile that made him approachable, and a little mole under his right eye that only enhanced his attractiveness. He was more than just good looks though, his personality made him impossible to not want to be around. Last year, Vincent was kicked off of the basketball team during his final year of high school mainly because he was always playing pranks.

Vincent's pure charm and amazing comedic timing wasn't the reason Damien envied him, it was because Vincent had such a close friendship with his brother, Marion. Vincent and Marion were so close that instead of going to college right after graduating, they took a year off to just chill and to decide on what career field they would focus on. In two months, they both would be heading to the same school to study business and splitting an apartment in North Carolina.

Unlike his older brother, Damien had yet to pick a college. He was too focused on his newly embraced lifestyle and it all had begun with Vincent.

The night it all began, Damien was in his room glued to his computer screen strolling through Tumblr gawking at naked men. Eric, their hefty, dark skinned father, was in the living room forcing Vincent and Marion to watch some old football games on ESPN Classic. While Marion sat on the floor with an attitude, his usual state, Vincent sat next to him making jokes about the old uniforms. Eric was trying hard not to laugh and focus on the game, but in the end Vincent's jokes got to him. After the game was over, Eric headed off to work, their father the night stock manager at a local grocery store. It was one of the two jobs the man worked since their mother had passed.

Their father gone, and the living room feeling less like a macho fest, Damien left his room and took over the empty couch.

Marion pepped up as he snatched the remote from the couch before Damien could pick it up; always glad to have his way. "We watching Fuse."

On Fuse, they were airing a Beyonce video marathon. The video playing had her doing a striptease on a chair.

Vincent stood up from the floor, "Beyonce be educating them strippers. I bet you all the girls be in the club trying to dance on chairs and shit, breaking their necks. I ain't knocking the strippers though, if times were hard my ass will be on stage too." Vincent pulled his basketball shorts up high above his narrow waist until they were wedged in-between his butt cheeks. He fell back on Damien and started to grind against him while laughing, "Go ahead, tip me," Vincent joked.

Already, Damien could feel his dick getting hard. He pushed Vincent off of him, "Dude, stop playing so much."

Marion shook his head and rolled his eyes, "Man, that's some suspect shit, Vince."

Vincent laughed as he dug his pants out of his butt. He sniffed his fingers and wrinkled his nose, "Ugh, I'm about to go shower."

Damien rolled his eyes, "Dude, stop digging in your ass in front of me."

Vincent shoved his sweaty smelling fingers into Damien's face, "This heat wave be having my booty rank."

Marion sucked his teeth, "Really Vince? You gonna say some nasty shit like that?"

"I'm just being real." Vincent started towards the bathroom, "I'm going to wash."

Vincent left the living room, leaving Marion and Damien alone. Already, Damien felt the mood turn awkward. He had nothing in common with his brother. All Marion was interested in was girls, hip-hop, and working out. Marion was dark skinned, had low hair with waves, and even though he was muscled built and chiseled like an athlete, he was too self-centered to play any team sport. On his arm he had their mother's name tattooed, and a negative attitude since the day she had died. He only seemed to be happy when Vincent was making him laugh or when some girl was in his face.

"Can I watch something?" Damien asked.

Marion shook his head. "Nope, all you do is watch whack ass reality shows or scifi shit."

Though a scrawny Damien could be easily squashed by his brother, he wasn't afraid to talk back to him. "It's better than watching videos for songs you've heard a thousand times."

"Man, Daddy was right, you always starting some kind of argument."

Damien didn't even bother fighting anymore. In this household, everybody was allowed to speak their minds except for him. Eric and Marion basically ran the show while he spent all his time in his room online, discreetly watching porn or on gay forum sites. He had no connection with his brother or father and the moment he decided on a school, he was packing up and leaving.

Marion stood up and tossed the remote at Damien, "Here, I'm going to sleep anyways. And keep the volume low, shit."

Marion slammed his room door behind him and locked the door.

Damien gladly changed the channel and mostly watched random shows until Vincent stepped out of the bathroom.

Vincent carried his shirt in his hand, his barely-there six-pack and biceps damp from the shower. “Marion sleeping?”

Damien nodded. “He just went in there, which means he’s probably already knocked out.”

Vincent laughed, “He’s like a bear in hibernation or something.”

Damien noticed Vincent wore the same shorts he had on before the shower. “Aren’t those shorts dirty?”

Vincent brushed at the red shorts. “And?”

“Why would you get clean then put dirty clothes back on?”

Without hesitation, Vincent dropped his pants to the floor revealing his soft dick. “Happy?”

Damien regretfully looked away too quickly, “Dude, put your pants on.”

Vincent rubbed at his dick, “Why? You can look. I know I almost had your dick hard earlier.”

“No, you didn’t,” Damien lied.

“Yeah, whatever. But anyways, since you're hogging the couch I'm going to go lay down in your bed. I'm tired as hell myself. Just wake me up when you're done out here."

Vincent left his shorts on the floor and turned away from Damien. Damien looked out the side of his eyes to catch a glimpse of Vincent’s firm ass before he slipped into his room. At this moment, Damien’s hard dick was doing all the thinking for him. He knew walking into that room would gain him another look at an exposed Vincent. All of that envy he had built up for Vincent was already wiped away just by the thought of his nude body under his bed sheets.

Damien turned off the TV, stood up and adjusted his hard dick in his pants. His nerves were at an all-time high as he walked passed his brothers room door and down to his own. Damien picked up Vincent's shorts and balled them up in his hand. He opened his room door to find Vincent in his bed jerking off. Damien just stood there, staring at Vincent's face who formed a smirk with his plump soft brown lips.

Vincent softly chuckled, "Oh my bad, I always jerk off before I go to sleep. You want me to move?"

"Um, no, you cool," Damien said as low as possible, not wanting his brother to wake up.

"Well, are you gonna just stand there? Shut the door."

Damien stepped into his room and shut the door, "My bad."

"If you want to get in your bed, I'll scoot over."

Damien nodded. "Alright."

"But I sleep naked, especially during this heat wave. And you gonna have to sleep naked too."

Damien shrugged, "Alright."

Damien exhaled heavily as he dropped Vincent's shorts to the floor and took his shirt off revealing his hood-fit, scrawny body. His heart started to race as he pulled down his pants revealing his hard dick for the first time to another man. Vincent lay back and kept pleasuring himself as if Damien wasn't even in the room, rubbing on his balls and moaning. Damien's dick wagged from left to right as he walked over to his bed and sat down on it.

Vincent sat up, "Man, your dick is thick. I'm impressed."

"For real?"

Vincent grabbed Damien's dick and stroked it, "You got a big mushroom head too."

Damien looked at Vincent's dick, the head pink. "Yours is cool too."

Vincent placed his hand against Damien's bird chest and forced him to lie down on his back. "Aye, I'm just going to suck your dick real quick."

Vincent started sucking on the head of Damien's dick. He went down all the way on the shaft, the warmth of his mouth sending Damien crazy. The second Vincent grabbed at Damien's balls, he started to bust in his brother's friend's mouth. Vincent kept the dick in his mouth no matter how much Damien pushed him away while he continued to bust. Vincent released Damien's dick, spit the nut on the bed, and sat softly laughing.

Damien lay sprawled out, his body numb, smirking. "Fuck," he breathed out.

Vincent smacked his tongue against the roof of his mouth. "Your nut is kinda sweet."

"Oh," That's all Damien had the strength to say.

Vincent got up from the bed. "Alright, I'm going on the couch to finish myself off."

"You're not staying in here?"

"I was just playing about that shit earlier. Don't be slow, Damien," Vincent said with a smirk, "Night, man."

Damien lazily waved as Vincent slipped on his shorts and left his room. This night went down in Damien's mind as the best night of his life. Already, he was thinking about a ton of nasty things he wanted to do with Vincent. Nearly an hour ago he envied his charm, but now he found a reason to like Vincent. After that head though, it was more than lust, Damien was feeling something deeper for his brother's friend.

The next morning Damien woke up feeling as if a giant weight had been lifted from his shoulders. After tossing on some shorts and a tank-top he headed outside of his room scratching at his trimmed chin hair to find Vincent on the couch wrapped in a blanket still sleeping. Damien was beyond disappointed, the normal person in him wanted to talk about last night with Vincent while his inner freak wanted some more head. As he made some cereal he tried to be as loud as possible to wake Vincent up, but instead his brother Marion came out of his room.

Marion stretched his muscled arms as he yawned, "Nigga, can you be quiet with all that noise?"

"Stop complaining," Damien said as he sat down at the table.

The fact that his brother was awake just ruined his morning. That greatly decreased the chance of him and Vincent getting any time alone this morning. Marion fixed himself a bowl of cereal and the two brothers sat in silence chewing, their idea of a healthy conversation between them. After last night though, Damien had a bit of confidence which he usually lacked.

"Why are you always so cranky?" Damien asked.

Marion kept eating his cereal. "Ain't nothing wrong with me."

"Be for real man, you always have a stink attitude."

"Because you always get on my nerves and you know how daddy can be. I can't wait to leave."

"We used to be cool," Damien said, "Me, you, momma, and daddy."

"Well, she gone now. Things different, grow the fuck up. Get off the computer and go do some shit with your life. I mean, daddy working two jobs and you sitting around doing nothing all day, whining about everything. I can't help much; I'm getting ready for school and about to leave."

"Marion," Damien said as he tried to stay composed, "You had an entire year off after high school and you didn't do shit but go to the gym. I graduated four weeks ago. Everything you just said to me, you should be saying to yourself."

"I help out though. Who got this cereal you eating?" Marion said as he pointed to Damien's bowl.

"Some chick you slept with who let you borrow her EBT card."

"Alright then, that's more than anything you do."

Damien laughed, "That's bullshit."

Into the house sulked their dad looking as if he just had all the life drained from him. Already, the man was starting to get grey hairs, he was gaining weight excessively, and dark circles were developing around his eyes. Though they never outright said it to each other, both Marion and Damien were concerned about their father's health. The man looked as if he could drop any second from a heart attack.

Eric opened the refrigerator and drunk from the milk carton, "What y'all doing today?"

"I have to go to Target to get some stuff for my new apartment and school supplies," Marion said.

"Shit, I forgot about that. I have to order you a bed before you go," Eric said as he put the milk away.

"Just give me the money and I'll buy a bed once I get to North Carolina," Marion said.

Eric laughed, "You crazy. You'll spend it on sneakers and shit. I'll get the bed."

Marion rolled his eyes, "Whatever, that's just more stress on you."

Eric looked to Damien, "You picking a school today right? The Financial Aid people called me."

"What did they say?" Damien asked.

"You're approved, but they need to know who to pay. Pick a damn school, boy."

"I'll look today. I've already narrowed it down to two," Damien lied.

When it came to picking colleges, his hidden lifestyle was coming into play. He wanted a school that was in a gay friendly area he could escape to, away from his dad and brother. At the same time, he wanted to attend a school that offered great culinary courses, Damien as of now having a slight interest in cooking. He spent a lot of time on gay forum sites asking guys where they went to school and asking how comfortable campus life was for them as openly gay men, every day the list growing longer instead of shorter.

Eric checked his watch, "Shit, almost time to go to my other job."

"Aye, daddy," Marion called out, "I'm going to try to see if Brenda will let me hold her EBT card again."

"Do that then cause groceries are too damn much," Eric said, "I'll see y'all two later."

As Eric made his way off to his second job, he punched a sleeping Vincent in the side.

Vincent's head popped out from under the blanket, “Damn, man.”

“Wake your ass up,” Eric said, “I’m starting to think you homeless, boy.”

Vincent rubbed his neck as he sat up, “You like my second daddy man, I come around for you.”

Eric rolled his eyes, “Two fucking kids are enough,” He said as he left the house.

Vincent looked back to Marion and Damien, “Who gone fix me some pancakes?”

Marion stuck his middle finger up at Vincent, “Yeah right. Be ready after I get out of the shower.”

“Where we going?”

“Target,” Marion said as he got up and went to grab clothes from his room and then shower.

Vincent looked to Damien, “What’s up mushroom?”

Damien plastered a big smile across his face, “I’m feeling reaaaaaal, good. You?”

Vincent nodded, “All good over here. Mouth still taste kinda sweet.”

Damien got up, turned on the TV and sat at the edge of the couch. “So, last night was cool.”

Vincent yawned as he pulled his feet back to make more room for Damien, “I hope I ain’t scared you or nothing. I was just feeling some type of way and had to make a move. I legit love this family man, y’all are good people. And you being a cute ass dude doesn’t hurt.”

Damien was used to being called cute online, but never to his face by another guy. “You okay looking," Damien joked.

“I see how it is,” Vincent said as he laughed, “So, you gay all the way?”

Damien shrugged, "I guess so, you?"

"Bi," Vincent answered, "You're the second dude I've only messed with like that."

"Who was the first?" For some odd reason, Damien was expecting Vincent to say Marion. He sometimes thought they were a bit too close.

"Some dude offline. Nobody relevant, he let me fuck and that was it."

"It feels good knowing I'm not alone," Damien said, "Your cool points went way up."

"Nigga, you nut in my mouth, my points better be off the scale," Vincent said as he laughed.

"Does my brother know anything about you being bi?" Damien asked.

"Nope, and he doesn't have to know. My sexuality has nothing to do with our friendship."

Damien nodded, "I just never expected last night to happen."

"Man, I wasn't thirsty or nothing, but I always had my eyes on you a little. And I always figured you were gay just from some of the times I would try to talk about girls with you. I think one time you said Beyonce was alright looking and in my head I was like...this dude gotta be blind or gay." Vincent lowered his voice as he heard Marion's shower stop running, "Man, once I felt your dick jump last night I just had to take the risk."

"I'm glad you did."

"You ever sucked dick before?" Vincent asked.

Damien shook his head as he admitted, "I'm a virgin...to everything."

Vincent looked over his shoulder, "I dare you to suck my dick right quick."

Right away, Damien's dick got hard and his heart started to race. This scenario could play out in so many ways, from Marion catching them or even Eric walking back in the door because he forgot something. Vincent raised the blanket he was covered up with, revealing his hard dick hanging out from his boxers against his thigh.

"Hurry up," Vincent whispered, "I'll give you ten dollars if you can do it before Marion gets out of the bathroom."

Damien was nervous for another reason; he had no idea how to give head or even if he wanted too. He didn't want to disappoint Vincent though and come off as scared. Quickly, Damien dived under the hot blanket and stuck Vincent's dick in his mouth. It tasted sweaty and Damien was doing his best not to bite Vincent's dick. The minute Vincent heard the bathroom door opening, he kicked Damien from under the blanket.

Marion stepped out from the bathroom brushing his hair, "Vincent, I told you to be ready?"

Vincent motioned downward at his crotch, "Aye man, morning wood slowing me down."

Marion wrinkled his nose, "Your nasty ass have been really testing the bounds of this friendship lately. Five more minutes and I'm leaving you."

Marion went inside his room.

Damien looked to Vincent, "So um, where's my ten dollars?"

Vincent got up from the couch adjusting his shorts, "I'll hit you up when I get paid."

"You don't have a job," Damien said as he laughed, "You crazy man."

Vincent shrugged and went into the bathroom to get ready. Damien couldn't really describe the emotions he was dealing with inside of him right now. Being around Vincent, talking openly about their sexuality, it was all just so refreshing to him. In his mind, he could only wonder if this was how it felt to love somebody.

2 - Advice

Vincent was constantly on Damien's mind. It had been a week since he had last seen him, both Vincent and Marion spending lots of time with friends and preparing to leave for school in five weeks. Damien didn't really have any other gay people in his life to chat about what was developing between him and Vincent. So he did what most gay man did, seek advice online.

He posted a long paragraph on a gay forum explaining what was happening between him and Vincent and where they should take things next. The responses varied from, cuff him to don't ruin things by making it serious. Damien understood that he was a gay man, but couldn't imagine himself walking around in public calling Vincent his boyfriend. Still, Vincent made him feel so good that he wanted to shout it out to the whole world that he think he found love. He logged off the forum after one poster decided to mock him for falling in love after some head.

It was more than about the head; the small conversation they had as gay men on the couch showed they could converse with each other without any awkwardness. Damien needed to get in touch with Vincent and after failing to stalk down his Instagram; he headed over to his brother's room.

Marion was in his room packing up some boxes with his belongings.

Damien knocked against the doorway and cleared his throat, "Yo, I need a favor."

"What?" Marion questioned with an attitude as expected.

"Can I get Vincent's number right quick?"

"What the fuck do you want with him?"

"I need to ask him something," Damien said, "Just give me his number."

Marion tossed a pillow across the room at Damien who knocked it away, "Stop acting suspect and fall back, Damien."

"How am I acting suspect?" Damien asked, wanting a legit answer, afraid he was coming off a bit thirsty.

"Beggin for some dudes number. Vince don't wanna talk to you."

"I'm not begging for his number," Damien argued, "I just needed to ask him about something we talked about."

"Alright, I'll ask him. What y'all talked about?"

"Uh...some stuff about this girl," Damien lied.

Marion started laughing, "When you start caring about girls? Nobody don't want your boney ass."

Damien could only smirk, knowing he was wanted by somebody, Vincent. "I've had girlfriends. I just don't talk about them with you because you think you're the only man on the planet who can get pussy. And I don't tell daddy anything because he's just out of the loop on everything. All he know is football."

Marion sat down on his bed, "Well, I'm listening. Tell me about this girl instead. What you need to know?"

After getting online advice all morning from men who probably had social lives only online like him, he figured getting advice from somebody who actually had a physical dating history wouldn't be that bad. "Well, this girl and I have mostly been friends. Then one night she just straight up started sucking my dick. Ever since then, I can't stop thinking about her. I mean, at what point should I try to take this to the next level."

Marion burst out laughing. He lowered his head, pinched his nose and kept on laughing.

"Why you laughing?" Damien said as he tightened his lips and crossed his arms.

Marion looked up. "You making this shit up, right?"

"I'm serious. If you don't have any advice, give me Vincent's number."

Marion held his right palm out toward Damien, "Alright, alright, I'll stop. As somebody who's gotten head plenty of times from bitches who think they're my friends, all I can say is that there isn't a next level. You want a girl with some standards, not some ho who was horny one night and decided to eat the closest dick next to her."

"But it's not like that. When we talk it's like magic."

"Maybe it's magic for you cause you still high off some head, but probably not for her. Man, this girl probably already giving some other dude head right now. You can't go falling in love with everybody who wants the dick. I would have about four...five wives if I had that attitude. Next time you talk to this girl, just be straight up and ask her what she looking for. Don't assume shit."

The idea of a relationship with Vincent was now on shaky ground as Damien calculated his brother's advice. He recalled Vincent saying himself, the night he sucked his dick he was simply feeling some type of way. Yet, Vincent had a crush on him but that didn't mean he was ready to play house, Damien weighed in his head. Damien was pissed at how cloudy everything had become so fast. In the end, he still needed to talk to Vincent to find out how he felt about him.

"Man," Marion said, "Are you about to cry?"

Damien shrugged, "I'm cool," He lied.

There was a knock on the house door. Marion got up from the bed. "Finally."

Marion brushed passed Damien and went to answer the door. Into the house entered Vincent.

He wore a pair of camo shorts and a black tanktop. "I'm late," Vincent said. "I had to get gas."

"Man you always got an excuse," Marion said.

"Be glad I showed up though. I don't even want to go to Ava's party. That bitch hates me."

Marion laughed, "You called her baby ugly, what do you expect?"

"Well it is. I saw that baby picture on my newsfeed and blocked her ass in a heartbeat."

"What's up, Vincent," Damien said as he joined them in the living room grinning from ear to ear.

Before Vincent could greet him, Marion spoke up, "Aye Vincent, Damien was looking for you."

Vincent smiled at Damien, "Really? What's up?"

Once again Marion took control of the conversation, "He wanted to ask you about some girl he told you about. Apparently, this bitch gave him some head and now he's in love with her. As a big brother, I'm ashamed I let him grow up in a house with me believing head equals a declaration of love."

Damien's body temperature rose as embarrassment ran through his veins.

Vincent laughed, "It doesn't work that way Damien. Maybe this girl likes you enough to suck your dick, but that doesn't mean she's looking for a relationship or something. You gotta smarten up and recognize what's real and what's just fun. There's a lot of dick hungry fish in the sea dude."

Marion nodded, "Yup, exactly."

Damien took Vincent's advice as his official response to him; sure Vincent was aware that this supposed girl was him.

Vincent elbowed Marion in the chest, "Are you dressed or what?"

Marion nodded over to his room, "Give me five minutes to change. I'll be back."

As Marion headed to his room, Vincent approached Damien. "You mad?"

"Mad about what," Damien said with a forced smile.

"You know." Vincent bit his bottom lip and grabbed at Damien's crotch. "Don't be mad, mushroom."

Already feeling his dick getting hard, Damien slapped Vincent's hand away, "I said I'm cool."

"Then why you slapping my hand away."

Damien looked over his shoulder, "Because I don't want Marion to see."

"Oh, I thought you were trying to keep the dick away from me or something."

"No, we just having fun, right?" Damien asked hoping for a different answer.

"Exactly. So if I end up sleeping here tonight you aint gonna be acting all weird, right? All emotional?"

"Nope, you set the record straight. No point to get mad or anything."

Vincent grabbed at Damien's dick again, "Want me to help you nut again, tonight?

Damien found himself stalling to answer. His emotions were still wrapped up in what could've been and he wasn't ready to simply just have fun with Vincent. He searched for a legit reason to say yes then remembered how good the head felt the first time. Before he could answer, Vincent quickly pulled his hand away as Marion exited his room.

"Alright," Marion said as he adjusted the collar of his polo shirt, "I'm strizzle."

Vincent turned away from Damien as if they weren't deep in a conversation and left with Marion. Damien took the moment alone to growl out some of his frustration and to get his mind together. He wanted Vincent bad but would just have to settle for some fun between them.

3 - Bathroom

The entire day, Damien watched the clock, waiting for Marion and Vincent to get back from the party. To waste time, he went online and searched topics like how to top or how to bottom, not knowing what to expect from tonight. Around eight, his dad came home early from work, a rare occurrence.

Eric plopped down on the couch. "Aye Damien, you picked a school yet?"

Damien joined him on the couch, "Not yet."

"Well, you know the deadline is coming up? Don't make me pick for you."

"How did Marion get to take a year off, but not me? I feel rushed."

Eric sighed, "Because I'm tired of working two jobs. Once you and your brother are gone I can quit one."

"You can quit now and I'll take care of myself until I go."

"No, I told your momma I was going to let y'all focus on school. I'll deal with the bills and shit, y'all are going to school." Eric kicked off his work boots, "I don't understand why you're making it so hard. Just do what your brother is doing, go somewhere your friends go. If not that, then go to your mom's alma mater. I'm giving you two days."

And then what, Damien thought to himself.

"After that I'll take you down to the nearest community college," Eric continued as if he could read his son's mind.

"Fine, in two days you'll have two sons packing and leaving for college."

"I better." Eric groaned and clutched his lower back as he stood from the couch. "Wanna help cook?"

If there was one thing Damien enjoyed, it was cooking. It was something they all used to do as a family, but since his mother died, it became a rare practice. Damien didn't hesitate to follow his father in the kitchen and help him make some spaghetti. While cooking with his father, conversation was easy. Sure they bickered over how much salt was too much, but that was better than talking about football. Once the meal was done, Damien was dreading sitting down for dinner because he knew the topic would be back on him picking a school.

As Damien finished setting two plates, into the house stumbled Marion and Vincent poorly rapping the lyrics of a Drake song. It didn't take a genius to determine the two nineteen year olds were drunk. While Eric was cussing up a storm, Damien added two more plates to the table. He had an extra pep in his step, giddy about his father and Marion going to bed so he could have some alone time with Vincent.

Eric sat down at the table, "Vince, did you drive here like this?"

"Nah," Vincent said as he fell into his seat, "We walked."

Marion managed to get in his seat without falling to the floor, "And got lost then found."

Vincent laughed, "I was like...nigga...where you live?"

"And then I was like..." Marion shrugged and slurred out, "Niggra whro dru arsking?"

Eric shook his head and sighed, "Y'all know y'all aint supposed to be drinking right?"

"We were celebrating," Vincent said, "It's our last month here."

"It's not like you two are never coming back," Damien said as he plated food.

"Not me," Marion said, "I'm done here. Moving on, y'all can catch a brotha on Skype."

Damien put the pan on the stove and joined them at the table, "Bon appetite."

Vince laughed, "Man, I think I'm hearing in French or something. I'm fucked up."

Eric slammed his right fist on the table, "Aye, both of y'all just need to shut up and eat."

The entire meal, Vince and Marion struggled to get the spaghetti in their mouths as if they were operating heavy machinery instead of forks. If they weren't struggling to consume food, they were laughing and spitting it across the table. It didn't take long for Eric to take his plate and go finish is food in his bedroom.

Damien didn't mind watching them both make fools of themselves. "I guess the party was fun then."

Marion shrugged, "I don't even remember who was there. Did I hookup with somebody?"

Vincent nodded, "Redbone with the braids. She was thick and had her hands in your pants."

Marion shrugged once again, "Don't even remember her name though."

"Yo, did you see that picture of Ava's baby in the kitchen? That I remember. Scary shit."

Marion stood up from the table and took his shirt off, "I can't stay up no more, I'm going to bed."

If Damien could, he would pick his brother up and toss him into his bedroom. "Yeah, go," Damien said.

Marion dismissively fanned his hand at Damien and headed inside of his bedroom.

Damien looked to Vincent and smiled, "You're a cute drunk."

"Look at you trying to sweet talk me."

"Just stating some facts," Damien said as he finished off his food.

"Yeah whatever." Vincent looked over to the couch. "I need to get over there."

"You going to bed already?" Damien asked, not expecting Vincent to turn in so soon.

Vincent lazily stood up, "I feel heavy man, from head to toe. I gotta sleep."

"But I thought you came back for...you know."

Vincent shrugged, walked over to the couch and crashed down face first.

As Damien sat in the kitchen alone, he realized he would get no action tonight and that he had to clean up the mess everybody left behind. He was close to just leaving the kitchen a mess, but didn't want to wake up to his dad yelling about roaches and wasted food. Once he was all done in the kitchen, he took a shower and went to bed.

While in bed, all he could think about was how good Vincent looked and especially without clothes. Damien found himself digging his hand into his boxers and playing with his dick. He shut his eyes as he imagined walking out into the living room and fucking Vincent on the couch. Damien was so horny he didn't care if his father and brother walked out; he was going to keep fucking Vincent. It was easy to think brave in his mind, Damien so cautious he barely made a moan while jacking his own dicks many nights.

Damien caught himself off guard as he started to nut on his stomach. "Ugh, shit."

He carefully sat up and used his bed sheets to wipe the warm nut from his stomach that was still a little bloated from all the spaghetti he ate earlier. He started the loathsome and lonely post-masturbation depression, scolding himself for even consider fucking a dude in the sight of his brother and father. Damien got up from bed and went over to the restroom to take one of the uncomfortable pisses after nutting. It stung for a second but once the pain faded he had to focus on peeing directly in the toilet, not on the floor.

Damien flushed the toilet, opened the bathroom door, and in slipped a tired looking Vincent.

"What are you doing?" Damien whispered. "Are you drunk sleep walking?"

Vincent softly laughed, "I'm looking for you. I told you I was gonna help you nut."

"Well, I already did. I thought you were too passed out for any of that."

Vincent did his best to stay balanced as he stripped naked, "Then you gotta help me."

Damien badly wanted to just wrap his arms around Vincent's lean body. "How?"

Vincent slid down against the bathroom door into a sitting position. He started playing with his dick. "Eat my ass."

Even though he just nutted, Damien dick was already getting hard again as he watched Vincent use one hand to jack off and the other to spread his ass cheeks. His tight, pink, hole had a bit of hair around it. Damien lay down the best he could on the cold bathroom floor and started to kiss on Vincent's hole. Vincent cringed as Damien dug his tongue deep into his hole, jacking his dick harder the deeper Damien went. Damien had never tasted anything so nice. Vincent wrapped his legs around Damien's head. He grinded his wet hole up against Damien's face until he shot a big load into the air, some of it landing on Damien's forehead.

Nut rolled down Damien's face onto his thin lips, his first taste. "Shit, taste like salt water."

Vincent laughed as he reached his lanky, toned arms out to Damien. "Help me up, I'm stuck."

Damien stood up and helped Vincent to his feet. Vincent noticed Damien's dick poking out through the hole in his boxers and grabbed onto it. Damien flinched, his dick sensitive. Vincent started to stroke Damien's dick and kissed him on the lips. Another first, Damien thought to himself. Never had he kissed before, male or female. Damien reached down and dug his finger into Vincent's warm hole that was damp with his spit.

Vincent wiped nut from Damien's face as he continued to get fingered, "Shit feels good."

"Can I fuck you?" Damien uttered out, not even sure he was ready to actually go that far.

Vincent laughed, "Dude, I'm a top."

Damien removed his fingers from Vincent's hole. "Oh, my bad."

"It felt good though. Maybe cause I'm drunk." He kissed Damien again. "I'm going back to sleep."

Vincent left the bathroom leaving Damien wanting more.

4 - The Pick

Damien hit submit on the college application. He finally decided on a school. He knew exactly where he wanted to be and who he wanted to be around. Sure, he had to compromise on his choice of major, but he was young. He could switch schools and majors at any point and start over without wasting anytime. Right now, he had something special going on, something pleasurable that he hoped could someday in the future grow into something other than just playing around. Damien had Vincent.

Marion and Eric sat on the couch waiting for Damien to reveal his school of choice.

"Dude," Marion said, "Hurry up and say it."

"The quicker you say it the sooner I can help you start packing," Eric said giddy for the news.

"I'm going to NC Tech," Damien proudly announced.

"What?" Marion shouted, "Nigga, that's where I'm going? Why you following me?"

Damien was actually following Vincent, but he couldn't out right say that to his father and brother.

Eric shook his head, "I'm surprised. At least I can come visit y'all together."

Marion punched his fist into his hand, "Yo, that's not cool though. I'm supposed to be out on my own."

"NC Tech is a big school," Damien said, "Plus I will be living on campus and you won't be."

"But I'll still have to see you though. It will feel like I'm still back at home," Marion said.

Damien shrugged, "I didn't pick NC Tech to follow you, it was a last minute decision," Damien lied. "Most schools weren't accepting any more applicants and I realized I rather be there than stuck at home being bored for another year. Plus, you're majoring in Business and I will be doing Hospitality, our classes are on opposite sides of the campus."

"I thought you wanted to cook?" Eric asked.

"The hospitality and culinary world are very close," Damien explained, "I can switch to a culinary school with ease."

Marion got up and shoved Damien, "You a shady nigga. I'm not cool with that."

Damien shoved his brother back, a built Marion barely budging. "Don't be pushing me."

Marion struck back, punching Damien in the face, "Try me, bitch."

Eric shot up from the couch and stood between his two sons, "Hell no, now I'm not going to have y'all fighting."

Already Damien could feel his jaw clicking a little. He seethed as he gently touched at it, "Shit. Fuck!"

Marion shook his head, "Daddy, you gotta admit this some shady shit? He coulda pick any other school."

"All that matter is he picked one," Eric said, "And that you both will be away from me. Your momma wouldn't like none of this fighting shit and you took it too damn far Marion. I want y'all last few weeks here to be peaceful. Especially since y'all cousin Kendall is coming for the weekend. I just talk to his mom; he picked a school up here and has to tour the campus."

Marion raised his hands to his shoulders and backed off, "I got shit to do, I ain't dealing with him or y'all."

Damien cringed at the mentioning of Kendall's name, the news of his visit more painful than getting hit in the face, "Man, he can't go anywhere else? He aint even our real cousin."

Damien and Marion's mom's best friend was basically like her sister, which earned her son Kendall the title of cousin.

"Don't act like that with your cousin, y'all grew up together," Eric reminded them.

Damien couldn't stand Kendall for more than one reason. Plus, Kendall was the lone person who knew he was gay.

"I won't be here, I'll stay at Vincent's mom's house this weekend," Marion said as he stormed off to his room.

Eric looked to Damien, "And I'm working. So take care of your cousin this weekend."

Damien rolled his eyes and groaned, "Yeah, whatever."

The week building up to Kendal's arrival was miserable. Firstly, they didn't have any food in the house so Damien had no choice but to eat nasty fast food that made him break out. Marion was busy hiding out at Vincent's house, which meant they never stopped by. Damien was going through a Vincent withdrawal and jerking off only seemed weak compared to being with him. The dreaded Saturday morning arrived and around noon Damien found himself answering the door to be greeted by Kendall.

"Waddup cuzzo," Kendall loudly greeted as he held his arms wide opened.

Kendall was about the same height and had the same amount of body mass as Damien, with brown skin, low-cut hair on his rounded head, and an upper lip mustache that refused to grow in full. He was dressed in high-top sneakers, skinny khaki pants that he barely could pull up pass his butt, a navy blue dress shirt that was buttoned up to his neck, and diamond studs in both of his ears. On his back, he wore a bag packed with his belongings. Kendall had always been one of the worst kids Damien had to play with while growing up. He always started fights and cheated on video games when he started to lose. And to top it all off, he was nosey and a snitch.

"Sup," Damien said, refusing to hug Kendall.

Kendall strolled into the house, "Where your black ass brother at? Nigga block me on Instagram, you know?"

"He's not here."

Kendall laughed, "I bet his ass hiding from me. Imma find him though. Where your trifflin ass daddy?"

"Why are you talking so much trash?"

"Damien, you know I'm just playing. I love y'all boys."

Damien shut the house door, "Whatever."

"Damien, you still act the same and got sexy as a motherfucker."

Damien narrowed his eyes, "What?"

He was used to Kendall throwing out little remarks like that one, but that was only the tip of the ice berg.

Kendall laughed, "I'm just trippin." He flopped down on the couch and rested his bag on the floor, "Man, that bus ride was crazy yo."

Damien joined him on the couch, already wanting him to leave. "Oh for real."

"Yeah, this white bitch was trying to sell head. If I had cash she was getting all this dick."

Damien didn't believe his story one bit. "Oh for real."

Kendall rubbed his stomach. "I'm hungry, what y'all got to eat?"

"Nothing until my dad gets off later. He'll bring some food from work."

"Alright, cool cool, so what you been up to?"

"Well, I'm gonna go to NC Tech. I heard you're going to school up here though."

Kendall burst out laughing, "Man, ain't nobody wanna talk about school. Who you fuckin? She got an Instagram?"

Damien was beyond frustrated. "Nobody."

Kendall pulled out his phone, "I got about four-seven bitches texting me."

"Oh for real."

"For real my nigga." Kendall playfully slapped Damien in the chest, "Aye, remember when I found that gay shit on your computer?"

Damien was surprised it took him this long to bring that up. "No."

"Don't lie; you had them videos hiding in your games folder. Man, niggas were getting fucked raw, sucking dick, eating ass, pissing on each other and all type of shit. Then you tried to play it off like your dick wasn't getting hard." Kendall grabbed at his crotch, "That shit was kinda getting me hard though."

"I don't remember that," Damien lied.

"It was a long time ago though." Kendall stood up, "Anyways, I gotta shit my dude."

Damien pointed across to the bathroom as he wrinkled his nose in disgust, "TMI, dude."

"Man, this house went down since your momma died though," Kendall said as he entered the bathroom.

The moment he was alone, Damien buried his face into a couch pillow and screamed. Kendall had only been here for less than an hour but it felt like it had been forever. Unlike Marion, Damien didn't feel as if he could be mean or avoid Kendall. The truth was that Kendall knew his secret and could flip the script on him at any moment if he mistreated him. Damien just had to be strong and deal with him.

Kendall poked his head out of the bathroom, "Aye, bring me your laptop right quick?"

"Why?"

“Cause I have to finish some apps for school. Might as well do it while I shit since it’s gonna take a while.”

Damien shook his head, “Nah, that’s nasty. Just wait until you get out.”

“It’s not like imma dodo on your laptop, man. Stop playing and go get it.”

Damien didn’t want Kendall using his laptop on the toilet, but found himself caving. He got up, went into his bedroom and logged on to the guest account. Damien carried his laptop into the bathroom and kept his head lowered to the floor as he passed it to Kendall. All Damien could see was Kendall’s khaki pants and American Eagle briefs around his ankles, his hairy thighs, and his thick dick resting a bit against the toilet seat. Damien quickly stepped out of the bathroom, a little disgusted at himself for getting turned on by one of the biggest turn offs in his life.

5 - Lady's Man

Damien stood watching as he watched his dad pack a suitcase. It was so weird how much his parents' bedroom had changed ever since his mother had passed away, ovarian cancer defeating the woman. It used to smell like her perfume, Pine-Sol, and stayed spotless. That was no longer the case; his father had the room smelling like feet, sweat, and had clothes everywhere. Damien didn't even know how the man could tell what was clean or dirty as he packed them into a suitcase.

"So, how long are you going?" Damien asked as he leaned in the doorway.

"A week or more," Eric said, "The stock manager in the other district had a heart attack. I'm going to be covering his shift and training somebody new. They're lucky my ass ain't got small kids cause they would be up shit creek. My other job wasn't cool with me leaving though, so I had to quit. I'll be alright since y'all boys going to college and I only need one job now. Plus, I'm getting paid double for working in the other district and they covering my hotel room fees."

"I texted Marion and told him you were leaving."

Eric nodded, "Yeah, I talked to him. He said he aint coming around as long as Kendall here."

“Cause Kendall is annoying,” Damien said in low voice, not wanting Kendall to overhear him while in the bathroom.

“He’s your cousin. Family stick together.”

“Fake cousin,” Damien corrected.

“You know what I mean,” Eric said as he zipped up his suitcase. “Now I gotta go before I miss the train.”

“Aye, call me and stuff, dad.”

Eric shook his head and laughed, “No the hell I ain’t. This is a lil vacation from being a daddy.”

Eric grabbed his suitcase, some chips and soda from the kitchen, and left for the train. For a moment, Damien was excited to have the place to his self until Kendall started singing in the bathroom, reminding him of his presence. Damien headed in the living room and turned up the TV so it could drown out Kendall’s voice.

Out of the bathroom stepped Kendall with a towel wrapped around his waist, “Your dad gone?”

Damien tried not to stare long, but noticed that Kendall had a tone v-cut and a body that easily surpassed his own. “Yeah.”

Kendall did a shuffle dance, “Hell yeah, call some girls, lady’s man, we gone party tonight.”

“No, we ain’t,” Damien said.

Kendall laughed, “I’m just playin dude, your daddy would kill us. Aye, you still coming with me to my campus tour right?”

Damien didn’t want to go, but his dad had already made him agree to it, “Yeah, I guess so.”

Kendall thumbed into the bathroom, “Well, let me put my clothes on right quick and we can roll.”

After a short wait, Kendall stepped out of the bathroom wearing a white dress shirt with a red bow-tie, khaki skinny pants that were too tight for him to pull up as usual, and red converse sneakers. Damien kept it simple, all black Jordan’s, grey sweat shorts, a white t-shirt, and a snapback with the logo of a team he knew nothing about displayed.

"We some sexy mothafuckas," Kendall boasted as he adjusted his bowtie, "I'm keeping it business casual."

"Yeah, you look nice," Damien carelessly complimented.

"Same to you cuzzo," Kendall pulled up his pants as much as he could, "We gone get all the bitches."

"Mhm, sure," Damien awkwardly said as he opened the house door.

Outside Marion was getting out of Vincent's used Honda that rumbled like a monster truck and was making his way up the walkway to their house. Marion's face turned sour as he reunited with Kendall for the first time since he had arrived here for the weekend. Though Marion managed to put a smile on his face, it was obvious it was one hard to maintain.

Kendall walked up to Marion and dapped him, "Cuzzo, you get blacker every time I see you."

"At least ain't dressed like a jackass," Marion said as he flicked his fingers at Kendall's bowtie.

Kendall burst out laughing. "Oh, you think you funny now. What's been going on with you my dude?"

Damien wasn't interested in hearing his brother talk about his so-called bitches and whatever else was going on in his life. He made his way pass Marion and Kendall and started over to the driver's side of Vincent's car. As they both met eyes, Damien formed a smile on his face that he couldn't contain.

Vincent lowered the window, "Yo, ain't that dude y'all fake cousin?"

Damien rolled his eyes, "Yeah that's him."

Vincent took a quick look at Kendall, "Aye, your cousin got a fat ass. His booty just hangin out. Dayum."

Damien had no interests in adding in on the conversation. "Anyways, what's up?"

"I'm doing all right, man, chilling with your brother. He's been hiding out at my house from your thick up cousin."

"I wish I could hide," Damien said.

"Just ignore him and watch his booty. So, I heard you following us to NC Tech?"

"I'm not following y'all," Damien said, though he was technically just following Vincent.

"Well anyways, at least we'll have a third driver for the trip there when we leave."

Damien noticed Kendall coming toward the car and Marion heading inside their house. Not wanting to come off a bit too excited to be in the presence of Vincent in front of Kendall, he quickly stepped away and simply waved goodbye to Vincent. Kendall tried to start a convo with Vincent but Damien directed him away from the car.

"Let's go," Damien said as he pointed toward the downtown and campus area.

Kendall looked over his shoulder as he followed after Damien. "I can't believe he still hang with Vincent."

"Yeah."

"He just told me they were going to the same school and shit. Dudes must be fucking or something," Kendall joked.

Damien didn't find the idea of Marion and Vincent doing anything sexual together funny. "Why would you say that?"

"I'm just saying if they move in together after college you and your daddy better get ready for a gay wedding."

Damien started to walk a bit faster, ready to get the campus tour over with. "Just come on dude."

At the campus tour, Damien was surprised at how well-behaved Kendall was. He didn't make any jokes or create any awkward moments for Damien. As for the tour itself, Damien didn't pay any attention to the busty, red haired, girl who was directing the tour and spouting out historical facts about specific buildings and classrooms. He was just ready to get out of the heat and back home. Once the tour ended and Kendall continued his mature and respectable behavior, they stopped at McDonalds and he went directly back to his old self.

"Man that bitch titties were so big," Kendall said before he ate a fry.

Damien did his best to focus on eating his dry chicken sandwich, "I know."

"I gotta get me some local pussy before I go," Kendall said as he looked around the packed restaurant.

Damien nodded, badly wanting his misery to end.

Kendall nodded over to a girl with dreds who ate across from them. "Aye, how about that bitch?"

"She cool," Damien said without evening looking.

Kendall laughed, "For real? Well you can have that then. Spit some game lady's man."

"Huh," Damien said, as Kendall finally managed to get his attention.

"Aye," Kendall said as he hollered over to the girl, "My cousin want your number?"

Damien looked over to the girl who smirked at him. He sat there staring at her, feeling as if he was about to vomit.

Her smirk faded and turned into a snarl, "Well fuck you then and with your dingy ass Jordan's."

Kendall burst out laughing along with some other people who were dining around them. Knowing if he sat there for another second he would hurt Kendall, Damien got up and stormed out of McDonalds. After that stunt, he was done with Kendall. No matter what, he wasn't putting up with him anymore.

6 - Free

Damien was done with Kendall. He walked from McDonalds alone; he didn't even care if Kendall got lost on his way back to the house. Damien had arrived to an empty house, his brother nowhere in sight and father probably still on the train. He went in his room, logged in online and vented using his account on the gay forum he used. Of course responses to his situation were mixed: get over it, fuck him, that's wrong, dude sorry to hear that. And there was always that one comment that forced him to log off in anger: if you weren't DL that wouldn't have happened.

The idea of coming out was one Damien wasn't ready for. Firstly, he didn't understand why it was necessary to tell others about his private life, but at the same time figured if they knew about his private life he wouldn't have to live his public one in constant paranoia.

Secondly, he didn't know how his father and brother would react, two of the most important people in his life even though they annoyed him sometime. He heard his father say crazy things about Michael Sam while watching ESPN. And his brother only talked about anything gay related when he was trying to do his best to crack a joke. On the other hand, his brother and father were out living their lives, doing whatever they wanted, with little to no care about how he would feel about their choices and behavior.

Lastly, even if his family accepted him, Damien didn't want to get stuck with all the stereotypes that came with being gay. He understood their lifestyle was heavily sexualized and a bit out there, but wished others knew how many other gay guys simply wanted somebody to love and a white picket fence. Plus, he was sure straight people lived as equally wild lives as some gay men.

Damien needed to do something to distract himself from the anger with Kendall he had boiling up inside of him. He decided to start packing for school and with the little bit of stuff he actually owned and could take to his dorm, he was done in under an hour. Damien lay back on his bed staring up at the ceiling wondering what his mother was up to in the afterlife, evening managing to shed a tear. His anger started to fade as he thought about how his mom would somehow spin the McDonalds moment into something positive. All that anger came rushing back when he heard the house door close.

"Yo cuzzo," Kendall called out from the living room.

Damien ignored him.

"Aye, I packed your food you left," Kendall said, "I'm putting it in the fridge."

Damien wasn't even enjoying the nasty food they managed to serve him at McDonalds.

"I'll be out here watching a movie," Kendall said, "Okay?"

Damien grabbed his pillow and put it over his face. He lay like that until he fell asleep. Damien woke up hours later, feeling a bit better, over the embarrassment of earlier. Still, he was done with Kendall. Damien got up and left his room to go use the bathroom. Out front, Kendall lay curled up on the couch, one hand down his pants, the other holding on to the remote, while he channel surfed. Damien avoided eye contact with him and went to use the restroom. After he was done peeing, he headed in the kitchen and started to cook.

"Aye, what you making?" Kendall asked from the couch.

"Chicken tenders," Damien said, not truly cruel enough to continue to ignore Kendall.

"Dinner for two?" Kendall asked.

And he wasn't that cruel enough to let him starve, "Yeah, I guess."

"Cool. Aye, Casper coming on? Remember when we used to watch that when we were little?"

Damien did remember. Kendall would recite the entire movie. "Yeah, you knew all the words."

"I still do." Kendall said with a laugh.

Kendall got up and joined Damien in the kitchen. He stood around making odd comments and watching Damien cook. The entire moment felt awkward to Damien. He didn't want to talk about their childhood; he wanted to talk about the McDonalds situation but didn't want to come off as bothered by bringing it up.

"Are you mad or something?" Kendall randomly said as if he did nothing wrong today.

"Hell yeah," Damien said responding angrier than he thought he would.

"Man, forget that girl. Her dreds were fucked up anyways."

"I'm not mad at her," Damien said as he stopped cooking and plated their food.

Kendall motioned at himself, "You mad at me? I wasn't the only one laughing."

"But you cause the entire situation. You made shit worse by laughing. I feel as if you did it on purpose, you knew I didn't want to talk to that girl. But you think you so damn funny that you just had to say something. I'm getting real tired of the way you treat me, you take advantage of my kindness. But that's my fault because I let you. Not anymore though, I don't care who you tell, I'm done letting you hold it over my head."

Kendall shrugged, "Hold what over your head?"

Damien truly wanted to be free from Kendall's grasp. "The fact that I'm gay."

Kendall laughed as he crossed his arms. "Dude, you ain't gay."

"Yes I am," Damien said, "And you know that. You been know that."

"How would I know? Dude, I'm not in your life like that."

"You always bring up that time you found gay porn on my computer, you always making lil sexual remarks to make me uncomfortable, and in McDonalds you tried to make me talk to that girl knowing it was a fucked up situation to put me in because that's what you do. I'm gay, there, you happy now?"

Kendall shrugged, "I don't care, dude. Gay or straight, you still wanna watch Casper?"

Damien had it in him to cry tears of relief right now, but knew Kendall would just drag him for even shedding a drop of water from his eyes, he was just that immature. "Yeah, but you better not recite the entire movie or I'm going to slap you in the nuts."

Kendall started to laugh, "Oh look at you trying to act all hard now."

Damien passed Kendall a plate of food, "I ain't acting. Here your food, man."

"Thanks, cuzzo," Kendall said as he grabbed his plate.

Together, Kendall and Damien ate dinner and watched Casper. Kendall managed to watch the entire movie without reciting one line. For the first time, in which felt like forever, Damien managed to be in Kendall's company without wanting to behead him. They were actually having fun talking about the old days, touching on the topic of Damien's mother's death various times.

"Hey, let's sleep head-to-toe tonight," Kendall suggested.

"Why?" Damien asked as he turned off the television.

"To keep up with tonight's theme. I feel like we're both kids again."

"Alright," Damien said, "But if you fart I'm kicking you out the bed like I used to do."

Damien dumped their plates and Kendall straightened up the living room really quick before they went to bed.

They lay head-to-toe that night spending hours still talking about the old days and cracking jokes about a time when Marion had poop his pants at Six Flags. Damien truly felt free being able to be himself around Kendall, feeling as if coming out tonight was one of the best decisions he's ever made. He wondered if he would be this way with everybody if he simply announced to the world that he was gay, only for them all to shrug and move on.

Yes, for years he disliked Kendall but for a reason he refused to accept, Kendall knew the secret Damien wanted to keep hidden. Tonight, the secret no longer stunted their relationship and the two little boys who enjoyed playing together so much could now pick up where they left off. And based on how tonight went, Damien found himself trusting Kendall to keep that secret. It was a risk, but one that removed a lot of hatred from Damien's heart.

Damien drifted off to sleep only to wake up in the middle of the night feeling somebody's hand slowly climbing up his thigh.

Damien did his best to pretend sleep and lay as still as possible as the hand continued to move up his legs. The only part of his body was moving was his dick that was slowly growing hard as the hand approached the shaft. Damien cracked one eye opened to see Kendall in the dark, lying on his side with his arm moving around under the covers. Not wanting this moment to get anymore awkward, Damien quickly shut his eyes and tried as hard as he could to fight off an erection.

He didn't expect coming out to Kendall would lead to this. First Vincent and now Kendall, it started to make Damien wonder how many men in his life were actually secretly lusting after him. He thought back to his senior teacher Mr. Allison, the man always gave him passing grades no matter how much he screwed up a math test. Was it pity or did Mr. Allison want the dick, Damien wondered.

He snapped back into reality as Kendall cautiously wrapped his hand around his dick. Damien had failed to get rid of his erection, his dick stiffer than a soldier standing at attention right now. Damien had to admit it; Kendall was a good looking guy. And Vincent was spot on about Kendall having an ass to die for. And Damien wasn't much of a dick guy, but from what he saw Kendall packing, he wouldn't mind seeing how it looked erect.

Damien pushed all those confusing sexual thoughts out of his mind. Kendall was his cousin, well not by blood, but still, they grew up together. They played with legos, cops and robbers, Mario Kart for hours, but now the only joystick Kendall was playing with was between Damien's legs. As Kendall started to slowly stroke Damien's dick, his heartbeat could be felt racing against the mattress. Damien couldn't let this go on; his mother was probably watching from above, he could not let his pretend cousin jerk him off.

Damien let out a fake yawn. Kendall quickly pulled his hand away and lay down flat on his stomach. Damien turned on his side with his back to Kendall, a bit traumatized, swelling with guilt, and pissed off at himself at the same time. He let a perfectly good handjob slip away; all because he and the person giving it to him used to eat fruit loops and watch Saturday morning cartoons together as a kid.

For the rest of the night, Damien fought off sleep, not wanting to wake up to Kendall doing something worse. Was Kendall gay, bi, or just a really good fake cousin, Damien questioned as he lay in the dark. Eventually his guard was let down as he drifted off back to sleep. He awoke the next morning to find himself in bed alone. Damien got up and in a pair of old gym shorts from high school and a tank-top went into the kitchen. Kendall sat in the kitchen in just a pair of red American Eagle underwear eating cereal.

Damien joined him at the table, "Lost your clothes?"

Kendall took a bite of his cereal, "It's hot. Y'all heatwaves ever end?"

Damien laughed, "Yeah, probably around Halloween. I'll be at school though; I hope the weather is better."

Damien couldn't believe they were discussing the weather after what he woke up to last night.

"Man, last night was beautiful," Kendall said, "Just chilling like kids again. It's crazy because that might take years to happen again, we both going off to college, starting our adult lives, becoming men. It's a new chapter. I'm going to miss picking on you and Marion."

“Marion won’t,” Damien said with a smirk, “I won’t either. Man, you have no idea how sickening you could be.”

“I’ve been punched many times, trust me I know. I'm surprised you and Marion ain’t hit me yet.”

“Because you our special cousin. My mother would have cut our ass.”

Kendall raised his brows, “Special? I might be annoying, but I ain’t retarded.”

Damien started laughing, “Then I guess you don’t remember that helmet you used to wear.”

“Nope,” Kendall said as he tried to resist laughing, “Now you makin shit up.”

“Don’t let me break out the shoe box of pictures, Forrest Gump,” Damien teased.

“I used to fall a lot,” Kendall finally admitted, “You wrong for bringing up that helmet.”

“Now you know how it feels to get tripped on all day long.”

Kendall nodded, “I guess you right. So, are you really gay?”

Damien nodded, “Yeah, you’re kind of the first person I’ve ever told.”

“Really? Wow, man. Listen, I won’t say anything to anybody. I swear.”

After last night, Damien wanted to ask Kendall the same question. “Thank you.”

Kendall rubbed the back of his neck, “Cause I’m kinda gay myself.”

“Kinda gay?”

“Well, gay-gay. I’ve known since we been kids. I didn’t really become attracted to you until that summer before I started high school. Ever since then, I would think about you in that way but at the same time understood you we’re kind of my cousin.” Kendall sighed heavily as he tried to choose his words carefully. “I’m going to be straight up, I’ve picked on you mainly cause I wanted you to think I was funny but also because I like you. Damien, let's fuck."

Damien sat there speechless. "I...but...you..."

"We both adults, not related, and I knew you were awake last night. Before I leave tonight, let's fuck."

Damien was up for this, but also trying to back out. "I've never topped and I don't have condoms."

"Well, I'm verse, so I bottom sometimes. So of course I travel with condoms."

"So, you came here wanting to fuck?"

"Not you exactly, but now that I know for sure we play for the same team, then why not?"

Damien found himself thinking about how Vincent will feel about this. "Um..."

Kendall stood up and stripped off his underwear, revealing his thick dick. "Yeah or no?"

Damien's dick was already to go and he and Vincent weren't dating, he didn't need to be faithful. He stood up from his seat and dropped his shorts, revealing the pulsing mushroom head of his mocha toned dick. Kendall kept his eyes focused on Damien's dick as he walked over to his side of the table. Without hesitance, Damien reached down and squeezed Kendall's bubble butt.

Kendall leaned his head back as Damien continued to massage his ass. "Let's go to your room."

Damien kissed him on the neck. "Alright."

Damien walked behind Kendall, his dicked pressed against his bubble butt cheeks, as he was led to his bedroom. Once in the room, Kendall grabbed a condom from his duffle bag. He sat on Damien's bed, grabbed him by the dick, and pulled him over to him. Kendall sucked Damien's dick before slipping the condom on.

Kendall laydown on the bed face first and poked his butt up. "Fuck me."

Damien only had porn as a reference when it came to topping. He spit in his hand and rubbed it around Kendall's shaved butthole. Easier than expected, Damien slipped his dick into Kendall and entered a new world of sex he'd never experienced before. He fucked him from behind, on his back, he let him ride him, and they even ended up fucking on the floor. Damien's dick was so hard that it was numb, making it hard to nut.

They ended up back on the bed. Kendall started to finger himself and groan, "You the greatest ever, man."

Damien was caught off guard by the comment, not aware he was mastering topping. "Um...thanks."

Kendall laughed as he started jerking off. "Nut in my mouth."

Damien pulled off the condom, climbed on top of Kendall, and started to jerk his dick. Damien legs stiffened up as he felt great pressure build around his dick. The greatest amount of nut Damien had ever seen come from his dick, spurted out, splashing Kendall in the face and mouth. Kendall grabbed Damien's dick and sucked the nut that continued to drip out.

His dick extra sensitive right now, Damien pushed Kendall's mouth away. "Ouch."

Kendall swallowed all the nut. "Dude, you drenched me."

"I've never nut like that before."

Kendall used his hand to wipe more nut from his face. "That's because that ass felt good."

Damien lay down beside Kendall, panting heavily. "I'm not gonna lie, it was."

"I can't believe we just did that. It's crazy."

"I think this is something else we should keep between us."

Kendall nodded, "I definitely ain't telling nobody I fucked my fake cousin."

Damien laughed, "Aye man, from now on I think we need to ditch that cousin part."

"Cool with me." Kendall sat up, "So you wanna fuck around some more before I have to catch the bus home?"

"Let me try sucking your dick; don't laugh though because I've never done it."

"Don't worry; I'll make sure you learn the basics," Kendall said with a wink.

After a quick breather, Damien started his head lesson.

7 - Regret

The word of the day was regret, because that's all that Damien was feeling after sleeping with Kendall. He couldn't believe out of all the people he slept with, he allowed his dick to trick him into topping somebody who was almost like family. Not only was he almost family, but he had a big mouth. Damien could only imagine who Kendall would tell about their night together. And to make things worse, he went as far as sucking Kendall's dick and badly doing so. So, not only did somebody possibly know he put Kendall's dick in his mouth, they also knew he failed at making him nut and had the bad habit using too much teeth and not enough tongue.

It was all taking a toll on Damien, the regret, the guilt, the disgust. Kendall even had the nerve to call him one night and Damien simply allowed it to go to voicemail. He was glad they were close again, but having sex together only gave Damien a new reason to distance himself from Kendall. All he wanted to do was rewind time and allow them to connect as two friends who were gay and not two friends who were gay and fucked minutes after rediscovering each other.

His dad returning home and asking a million questions about what they did while he was gone wasn't helping much either. Damien was just ready to get to NC Tech, start over, and keep his sex life between him and Vincent only. That moment wasn't long away, because finally it was moving out day. Him, Marion, Vincent and Eric were loading everything into Vincent's Honda.

"Man, I wish I could drive you boys down there, but I gotta work," Eric said as he took a break on the couch.

"Nah daddy, we cool," Marion said as he sat on the couch arm.

"We just gonna take turns driving," Vincent added as he joined Eric and Marion on the couch.

Damien was on the floor stuffing some last minute things into the one duffle bag he packed, "I can't wait to get there."

"In a way, me either," Eric said, "I'm going to like having the house to myself and not having to feed two kids and one who ain't mine. But I know next time I see y'all, everybody gonna be different. You gonna be a little bit older, focused, and using words I can't fucking understand. But that's life, everybody gotta grow up and you might as well do it with a nice ass degree and good job."

"And a cute ass girl to cook me dinner," Marion said as he rubbed his belly.

"Man, you'll end up marrying one of those women who gonna beat your ass," Vincent joked.

"I dare a woman to hit me," Marion boasted, "Yo, I hit back."

Eric punched Marion in the thigh, "You better not hit on no female. I'll be on the phone myself calling the cops."

Marion rolled his eyes and moved from the couch, "Whatever. You still taking me to the store right quick for road snacks?"

Eric got up and checked for his wallet, "Yeah come on. We'll be back y'all."

"Bring me some skittles," Vincent said, "Dump all the purple ones out the pack though."

Eric laughed, "Surprisingly, I'm gonna miss your bummy ass."

"Yo I ain't bummy," Vincent said, "I just ain't afraid to ask for what I want. Two blue Gatorades also."

“You mean Powerade,” Eric corrected as he opened the house door.

Vincent twisted up his face, “I mean damn if money tight like that, I’ll settle.”

Eric and Marion laughed as they left the house, leaving Vincent and Damien alone.

Damien finished packing his bag, “You should be a comedian.”

“I can make you laugh easily, tickle your dick with my tongue,” Vincent said as he stuck out his tongue.

“Damn, you might have to come over here and try that.”

“Man you always ready to mess around, sex fiend,” Vincent said.

“It’s not my fault you’re so good at what you do. It’s been awhile though.”

“I know, how you been surviving without me?”

Damien figured this was the perfect time to bring up the fact that he slept with somebody else. “I found a way.”

“How?” Vincent asked, intrigued, “You messing around with somebody else?”

“Yeah,” Damien nervously revealed, “Don’t be mad though. You still the best.”

Vincent burst out laughing, “Yooo, I’m not mad, I want details.”

Damien wasn’t expecting this reaction. He wanted to see Vincent care a little. “Never mind.”

“Dude, you can’t just say that and then stop talking? Who you fucking with, do I know him?”

“No,” Damien lied, not planning on saying anything about him and Kendall ever, “I met him online,” He lied.

“Those online niggas freaky, the thirstiest in the barrel, ready to give up some ass. So what happened?”

Damien shrugged, "Not much, I topped some guy and that's it."

"Looka you getting ass on the low," Vincent said, "I feel replaced."

"Well, you're a top so it wasn't going to happen between us anyways," Damien said.

"I know, but you could've at least invited me over so we could tag team a nigga. Hogging the booty, I see how it is."

Damien believed one on one sex was the best and most special kind. "I don't role like that."

"You saying that but when it happens, it happens." Vincent thought back, "This one time I was talking to this older dude online. He was a tall, bald, Michael Jordan looking dude. I show up to his house and his boyfriend is there butt naked on the couch looking ready for me. At first I was gonna leave, but they told me they both wanted to bottom and that's it. I tore those dudes up, they still be hitting me up trying to buy this dick."

"I thought you were only with one other guy before me?" Damien asked, sure of what he was told.

"I did? Well, three, I keep counting them as one and then also one other dude. Anyways, don't knock a threesome until you try it."

Before the conversation could go any further, Marion and Eric returned. Damien sat on the floor feeling lied too, clearly remembering Vincent mentioning he had only hooked up with one guy in the past from online and that he was the second. Somehow that number had magically grown into three. For now, Damien wasn't going to hold it against Vincent. He would talk to him later and try to determine if what they had now was strictly just between them, that he had no other playmates on the side.

They finished packing the car and while Vincent waited outside, Eric sat down on the couch with his sons before they finally left.

Eric kept his eyes focused forward, trying to fight back his emotions, "Marion after you graduated high school, I was pissed you took a year off before going to college because I knew your momma would be mad as hell. It's something I've never gotten over, but today I put that in the past. Both of my sons are goin to college, together, and they better make it out. Y'all momma was strong, fighting ovarian cancer until the day she couldn't fight no more. Leave this house with the strength that woman raise y'all to have, the strength of a fighter." Eric stood up, "Alright now, give me a hug before I get tired of standing my ass up."

Marion and Damien stood up and together hugged their father. It was awkward, but in a way a reminder of the true love they possessed for each other no matter how many arguments they would have. Damien and Marion left their father and left the home they grew up in for new ones. A new chapter of their lives were beginning, Damien hoping to start his with creating something a bit more stable with Vincent.

8 - Third Wheel

On the road to North Carolina Damien found himself feeling like the ultimate third wheel. Vincent and Marion only stopped at the places they wanted to eat, only listened to the music they wanted to hear, and instead of letting Damien drive a portion of the trip, they only swapped driving duties with each other. The fact that Damien was crammed in the backseat with all of their stuff while his bag was strapped to the roof of the car, at some point it getting rained on, only made this trip more miserable.

At one point Marion did drift off to sleep and Damien expected to at least have some type of conversation with Vincent. But instead Vincent spent the entire time on the phone sweet talking some girl and making jokes about their zodiac signs. Damien tried to waste some time on his phone but his 3G wasn't working and he didn't have enough battery life to torture himself with Candy Crush. He just sat there, squished in the back seat, having negative thoughts about what type of roommate he would have and if the school would serve good food.

Once they were only an hour away from arrival, Marion had woken up and was on his phone talking to some of their friends who had gone to NC Tech a year ahead of them. Apparently a big party was planned for tonight at Vincent and Marion's new apartment and then on Sunday they were going to a cookout before school officially started on Monday. Damien wanted to vomit each time his brother said the phrase 'make sure some hot bitches in the house' and at how Vincent would make him repeat that to whoever was on the other end of the phone.

As they arrived to their destination, Damien noticed they passed the road that led to campus.

"You missed the turn," Damien said over the radio, "I said you miss the turn," He repeated.

Vincent turned down the radio, "What turn lil man?"

Damien didn't remember Vincent calling him lil man when his dick was in his mouth, "To the campus."

"But school don't start to Monday," Marion added.

"I know, but I live on campus, remember? I'm tired, just drop me off."

Marion shook his head, "We'll take you in the morning, we late for our own party."

"I hope somebody got some beer, after this drive I need to get black out drizzle."

"Drizzle, drizzle," Marion repeated as he danced in the front seat.

Damien rolled his eyes, "What time in the morning?"

"Why you being so annoying, dude?" Marion snapped, "When I get up. Damn."

"Well, how am I supposed to sleep if y'all are having a party though? I'm tired," Damien said.

"Aye," Vincent said as he looked at him through the rearview mirror, "Just lay in my room. It's the furthest in the back and the walls are thick. You might hear the music bumping a bit, but not loud enough to keep you up all night. Alright?"

Damien was agitated, but Vincent's words chilled him out a bit. "Thank you, I guess."

"I'm just keeping the peace," Vincent said.

Marion got more hyped up as they turned into a low-budget apartment complex, "Yo, we home baby!"

Damien figured the apartment with the crowd outside and where the loud music emitted from was their apartment. Some faces Damien recognized from back home, but a lot of the girls looked like a lineup of Instagram groupies and a lot of dudes looked like cornballs pretending to be thuggish or simply church boys who were rebelling while away from their overprotective parents.

As they exited the car a heavy set guy wearing a fraternity t-shirt ran up and trapped Marion in a bear hug. "By time you fools got here." He set Marion free from his grasps. "I called every damn girl in my phone and Jamal got his uncle to get beer and some blunts. Welcome to college, bitch."

Within minutes, Marion and Vincent left Damien by the car and vanished into the crowd. All Damien cared about was getting some sleep. As he made his way into the packed apartment, it seemed as if every guy was trying to fight him and every girl was completely turned off by his presence. Marion was already racing some guy as buff as him in a pushup contest and Vincent was grinding with two girls to a Chris Brown track while sipping from a vodka bottle. Their party was even lamer than Damien could imagine.

Damien headed to the back of the apartment and opened one room door to find a guy fussing on the phone. Damien recognized the bed the guy was sitting on as the one Eric had ordered Marion, figuring this was his brother's room. He opened another door where two girls where sitting on the edge of the tub smoking weed while a dude was taking a dump on the toilet flirting with them. Damien quickly shut the door on the messed up scene.

He finally found Vincent's bedroom, ready to lie down after being squished in the backseat all day. Instead, he found some fraternity brother's playing cards and getting rowdy like a pack of wild dogs around a round table set up in the room. Nobody bothering to leave at his request, Damien headed back out front to wait for somebody to clear out one of the bedrooms. He ended up squeezed on the couch with two plus-sized girls who had on too much perfume and were calling every girl who passed them a skinny bitch. His cellphone rang and desperate for somebody to talk to he answered.

"Yo cuzzo, where you been," Kendall said.

"Oh...I thought we were gonna stop the cousin thing," Damien said, annoyed that he didn't check caller-ID.

"It's a habit, man. Where you at? I just came from your dad's house. School starts Monday."

"Yeah, I just got to school myself. Marion and Vincent having a party right now."

Kendall laughed, "And I know it's whack as shit. I hear Trey Songz playing in the back, yup, whack."

Damien smiled, "Yeah, you spot on about that."

Damien was already starting to enjoy their conversation; maybe answering was a good thing, he figured.

"I'm glad you answered though, its real nice hearing your voice," Kendall said.

"Yeah," Damien feeling too awkward to compliment him back.

"Hopefully I can come visit once the semester is over. We can watch Casper again."

To Damien, Casper was code for fuck. "Yeah, that was a fun night," Damien strictly referring to talks they had.

"I'm glad to hear you say that. Thought you were avoiding me or something."

"I wasn't," Damien lied, "I just got busy."

"Join the twenty first century and post on Instagram fool, share your sexy ass with the world," Kendall said.

Damien still couldn't find a way to compliment him back without feeling awkward, "I will."

"Or you can just text pictures to me," Kendall suggested.

Damien let out a fake laugh, not into the entire sexting thing. "Hey, I got to go."

"Cool, have fun at that whack party. And practice on that dick sucking...I'm just teasing you though."

"Oh...okay. Bye."

Damien hung up and sat there feeling awkward as ever. It sounded as if Kendall legit liked him, as if he was romantically pursuing Damien without any care of their cousin-like history together. Though Damien was willing to have sex with him before, he told himself not to go that route with him again. Damien was finding the subtle flirting more awkward than the sex though.

The never ending party went on until Damien ended up falling asleep on the couch. He awoke the next morning to a bright, sunlit, quiet apartment. A couple of the party guests were knocked out sleeping on the floor. On the couch beside him, a shirtless Marion was curled up sleeping. Damien didn't feel like waiting for him to wake up for a ride to campus. He knew if he woke him up, Marion would only give him attitude.

He decided to try to find Vincent, somebody who was actually kind to him. Damien yawned as he got up from the couch and carefully made his way through the sea of sleeping bodies on the floor. He arrived to Vincent's room door and after a soft knock let himself in. In his bed, Vincent laid butt naked along with two girls who also wore nothing. After witnessing this, Damien knew there was no chance of him and Vincent being exclusive together.

Vincent cracked his eyes open as he rolled over and looked back at Damien.

"Yo," Damien whispered, "Can I get a ride to campus?"

Vincent charged out of bed, his limp dick swinging, and sternly said, "Nigga, shut my door!"

He pushed the door shut, it slamming against Damien's face. Immediately Damien's nose felt clogged up and he noticed blood dripping on his shirt. Damien rushed into the bathroom that smelled like a zoo, looked in the mirror and noticed blood rushing from his nose. He grabbed some tissue and stuffed his nose. Damien just stood there, staring at his reflection, replaying what just happened over in his head, feeling like a fool.

Damien stormed out of the bathroom, outside to the car, and yanked his duffle bag down. "Fuck them."

Damien was seeing red as he sped walk until he found the nearest bus stop that would take him to campus. He sat on the bus bench, gently touching at his aching nose. Quickly, all the anger turned into frustration. That frustration turned into sadness as he realized he was done with Vincent and stuck at school that he had only picked because of him. All Damien could do was sit there with bloody tissue in his nose crying tears he was ashamed to shed, waiting on the bus.

****

9 - Batman

After a mind numbing morning of class, all Damien wanted to do was release some tension and then sleep the rest of his Friday away. He lay on his twin-sized bed, slowly stroking his dick to a video of two guys fucking on a desk. The plot of the porn was something a child could write, but Damien wasn't complaining. This was all he had and needed, sex was something that was pushed into the back of his mind. Ready to wrap things up and go to sleep, Damien rubbed the head of his dick until he nutted. Into their dorm room barged his roommate, Leon.

"Really dude," Leon said as he quickly covered his eyes and shut the door.

Damien quickly pulled his sheets over his nut drenched stomach, "You're supposed to be in class."

Eyes still shielded, Leon did his best to make it to his bed on the opposite side of the room. "It ended early."

Damien shut down his laptop, wiped his stomach with the sheets, and pulled his shorts up. "I'm all good over here."

Leon slowly removed his hands from over his eyes. "We need to create some kind of a system."

"Which you mean?" Damien asked as he sat up on his bed.

"Like, we need a 'do not disturb' sign or something. This walking in shit is starting to happen too much."

"Yeah, we'll figure something out though."

Two months ago, Damien had walked into his dorm room, nose stuffed with bloody tissue, preparing for the worst case scenario. Instead, he was given a roommate who was obsessed with all things related to basketball, sneakers, and who had a gay older brother back home who he never shut up about. After a month, Damien had little fear when it came to telling Leon about his sexuality and keeping it between them.

Leon, who always wore baggy clothes that made him look way thicker than he actually was, started using a hair pick to touch up his afro. He kicked off his Jordan's and sat back further in his bed against the wall. "Our professor had to take her kids to a costume party at their lil school or whatever so she let us go early. That works out for me though, because now I got time to do some homework, nap, and then hit a club up tonight."

No interest in doing homework, Damien shrugged. "I'll probably just sleep and mess around online."

"Fuck no," Leon said, "I'm tired of seeing you on your laptop. We going clubbing. It's Halloween, man."

All it took was Leon's positive vibes to pep Damien up, "Alright, I'll go. Imma wear my batman mask."

Leon laughed, "So, you already had a costume?"

"No, I just always had a batman mask. Who doesn't?"

"Niggas with lives. I have a hoodie with the super man logo on it. Batman versus Superman then?"

"Superman about to get his ass beat," Damien joked as he threw his pillow across the room.

Leon avoided the pillow as if it carried a disease. "Keep your nut stained shit on your side of the room."

Damien burst out laughing, "Aye, I do my laundry. You ain't changed sheets since the first day of school."

Leon brushed off his shoulders, "A clean nigga sheets never get dirty," Leon bragged.

"Yeah, whatever," Damien said as he chuckled and turned to his side, "Don't let me sleep long."

"Alright, sweet dreams, princess."

Damien stuck his middle finger up at Leon, got comfortable, and drifted off to sleep.

Later that night he woke up, legit excited to go out tonight. Leon was his only close friend on campus and that's all he needed. His roommate always brought the fun into any situation. Damien got dressed in all black, sporting a matching hoody and his plastic batman mask that covered the upper part of his face. He brushed his low-cut hair and trimmed down his goatee a little. As for Leon, after a long shower, he slipped on some khakis, Jordan's, and a royal blue hoodie with the superman logo in the center.

They left the dormitory around ten that night and joined the crowd of other students who were heading to house parties and the clubs. Most of the girls were dressed like strippers as expected, any guy with a body found a reason to go shirtless, and the dudes not blessed with abs settled for something more comedic or went as themselves. After walking a few blocks off campus, they arrived to Planet B to find a long line stretching out of the club.

"Fuck," Leon said, "Why everybody had to cop my plans for tonight?"

"Man, Planet B is always packed like this. We shoulda came earlier."

"Now you know anybody who shows up to the club before nine is whack. I ain't whack, Damien."

Damien laughed, "But you dressed like a ghetto superman though. He's the whackest hero of them all."

"Can Batman fly?" Leon asked as he raised his chin high, ready to make his point.

"He can soar," Damien said as he thrusted his arms forward.

"But can he fly though?" Leon asked.

"He's rich."

"No," Leon said, "Can Batman fly?"

"No," Damien admitted, "But Superman is still whack to me."

"I don't respect your opinion, but anyways. We need to find somewhere to go."

Damien shrugged, "No house parties, some girl always getting date raped. I don't wanna be around that."

"Let's go to Shane's," Leon suggested.

Damien wasn't sure he heard Leon correctly, "Shane's? The gay bar? Are you gay now?"

"No, but you are. If you were willing to party around us heteros tonight, I can party around you gays."

"Are you sure?" Damien didn't even want to go himself. He had never been around a group of gay men.

"My brother used to bring his friends around all the time and I'm comfortable with my sexuality. I'm cool."

Damien wasn't going to dampen the night. "Then let's go."

Once again, they started walking; Shane's was a bit further out from campus. Unlike Planet B, it wasn't that popular at all with students, most of those who went to Shane's being locals. They knew they were close when they could hear a mixed Rihanna track bumping. While the music got Leon more hype, Damien got more nervous. He knew how direct some gay men could be, he only hoped his outfit was up to par. Damien right away ditched the batman mask.

They made it into the parking lot of a redbrick building that was located in a low-budget shopping center that included a CiCi's Pizza and dog grooming shop. The sign that said 'Shane's' on the violet door of the club was missing a few lights around the border. No line or bouncer out front, Damien and Leon let themselves in. Inside, the club was jammed pack and more gay men than Damien had ever seen were packed on the dance floor.

A buff man dressed like a gladiator approached and with his deep voice said, "IDs."

Damien and Leon showed their IDs and with them both being under twenty-one they had to wear green wristbands before they were allowed to go any further. Once pass the bouncer, Damien and Leon found a spot on the wall and watched the night unfold. Compared to what they were wearing, the majority of the outfits were Rated M. So many dicks were swinging on guys who were simply wearing facial paint or splashed with fake blood. And so many asses were out on guys who were wearing colorful thongs and silly wigs.

Damien tried not to stare too hard, while Leon found himself playing on his phone a lot.

"This is insane," Damien said over the loud music.

Leon looked up from his phone, "Yup, a lot of dicks in here. Man, if only my momma could see me in here."

Damien laughed, "Two gay sons too much?"

"I think one is too much. She only likes my brother now cause he a lawyer and pays her mortgage."

Damien rolled his eyes, "Women, that's why I don't fuck with them," He joked.

"Wait until you try pussy, your tune will change."

Damien had a girlfriend back in the eighth grade; he had no desire of faking his way through that situation again.

The music stopped no matter how much the sweaty men on the dance floor protested. On to the stage walked a leggy, towering, dragqueen wearing a sparking green unitard and a bushy wig of red hair. She was accompanied by a scrawny light-skin guy, with fade cut hair that was curly at the top, and wearing a fitted grey suit. In their hands, they both carried mics.

The dragqueen spoke into his mic, "I'm sorry Tyler and I had to ruin your fun, but listen up bitches."

Tyler laughed, "I'm up here with Jay to announce the winner of the costume party."

Damien was surprised at the natural swag Tyler had, from his sexy country accent to the way he stood with one hand in his pocket.

"If I had worn my entire mermaid costume I woulda wiped the floor with you bitches," Jay said.

"But his ass was too big for the fin," Tyler quipped to some laughter from the crowd.

Damien laughed a bit too loud which caused Tyler and others to look in his direction.

Leon nudged Damien, "Damn, it ain't that funny. You acting like he's Katt Williams or something."

Damien composed himself and try to regain some of his cool back. "Aye, don't be hitting on me Superman."

Jay removed a sheet of paper from in between his breasts, "And the winner is Lavirio Winters."

Jay and Tyler started applauded as the biggest and buffest dude in the club who only wore white underwear, a captain's hat, and was covered in a lot of baby oil, made his way to the stage. He flexed to the crowd as they swooned over him and clapped. Lavirio took it even further when he whipped out his black dick and swung it around at the gasping crowd, a few not pleased with his stunt. Jay pretended to faint as Lavirio put his dick away and a red in the face Tyler handed the winner five hundred dollars cash from his pocket. The music resumed playing, the crowd growing crazy to some classic Missy Elliot.

"I'm going to the bathroom to pee and rinse the site of that gorilla's dick out of my eyes," Leon said.

Damien was tired of standing up, especially after walking here. "I'm going to go sit at the bar."

Leon and Damien separated, heading to opposite sides of the club. Damien grabbed a seat at the bar that was messed with spilled drinks and peanut shells. Instead of cleaning up, the bartender who wore nothing but body paint was trying to get a guy's number at the other end of the bar counter. Damien could only wonder if this much nudity was always involved or like most tonight, some were using Halloween as an excuse to go wild. There was a tap on Damien's shoulder.

He turned left to find Tyler sitting next to him. Damien smiled at him, "Oh, sup."

"So, you thought I was funny," Tyler said.

"Yeah, actually."

"What's your name?"

Damien motioned at himself, "I'm Damien."

Tyler looked around, "Where's your boyfriend at?"

Damien shook his head, "No, that was my roommate. He's straight."

"Oh, so you're in college. I'm done with that life, graduated with two degrees."

"Congrats, man. I'm just starting, already struggling."

"What are you in school for?" Tyler asked.

"Hospitality," Damien said with enough feeling in his voice to express how much he hated his major.

Tyler nodded, "That was one of my majors. I can help you out. Can I give you my number?"

Damien wasn't looking for a tutor and knew Tyler wasn't looking for a student. "Yeah."

Tyler pulled out his gold IPhone. "Alright, I'm just going to call you. What's your number?"

"555-2121," Damien said.

Tyler called him, Damien's phone rang, and Tyler hung up. "Just save it to your contacts."

"I will." Damien motioned at Tyler's costume. "What are you supposed to be?"

Tyler brushed at his suit, "Gay royalty. That doesn't change after midnight either."

"Cool," Damien removed the batman mask from his pocket, "I'm Batman."

Tyler grabbed the mask from Damien's hand it put it on for him, "Damn, you're a cute Batman."

"Hey, you're a good looking dude yourself."

A guy ran over and whispered something in Tyler's ear.

Tyler got up from his seat, "I got to go, my friend is somewhere in here being messy."

"Alright, I look forward to those lessons."

"All you gotta do is answer when I call cutie," Tyler said as he waved goodbye.

Damien watched Tyler as he followed his friend through the thick crowd. As he sat waiting for Leon to come back from the bathroom, his phone rang. Damien checked the caller ID already hoping it was Tyler but instead it was Kendall for what seemed like the one thousandth time. Without haste, Damien sent him to voicemail.

Leon rushed up to Damien, eyes widened, panicked, "Alright, we gotta go. I'll pee at the dorm."

"Why? What happened?" Damien asked as he stood up.

"First, some dude grabbed for my dick. Then, in the bathroom two niggas were fucking on the counter."

Damien laughed, "Aye, you wanted to come here."

"I was trying to be a good friend, but fuck that. Next time we come on gay Christian's night or something."

Damien followed a rushing Leon out of the club. "I got a number."

Leon chilled out once they got outside into the fresh night air. "From who?"

They started walking back towards campus.

"Tyler," Damien said, "The guy who was on stage."

"Oh the host dude. I thought you were DL. Why you gonna talk to somebody that known?"

Damien shrugged, "I don't know. He's cute."

Damien was sure nobody that mattered would care if he was ever seen out with Tyler or even if it would get that far. He was just excited to be back out there, with somebody who seemed legit interested unlike Vincent who just wanted to play around. As they continued home, a big crowd of drunk fraternity dudes passed them on the street.

"Batman and Robin, going to get some candy and shit," Somebody shouted from the crowd.

Within the crowd, Damien spotted Marion and Vincent drunkenly walking among the frat boys.

"I'm Superman bitch," Leon shouted back as they kept on walking.

"Ignore them," Damien said, "I can't stand the frat dudes at this school."

"Was that your brother and that Vincent dude I saw with them?" Leon asked.

Damien shrugged, "I don't know and I don't care," Damien lied. "Now, back to this dude Tyler though."

Damien was done letting others like Marion and his friends dampen his spirits. He wasn't that bloody nosed fool sitting at the bus stop crying anymore and refused to end up there again. When it came to Tyler, Damien was going to let him make all the moves and until he did, they were simply just friends.

10 - Finer Things

Damien sat at his desk in his dorm room reading his introduction to hospitality text book. In all honesty, it was all gibberish to him. From dealing with inventory to dealing with human resources issues, Damien had no idea what he was actually reading or even if he cared anymore. Behind him Leon was mixing up around the room digging for something.

Damien pushed away his textbook and faced his roommate. "You lost something?"

"Man, I had this red v-neck yo and now I can't find it."

"What you need it for?" Damien asked.

"This girl I study with in the library said I looked cute in it. I mean dude, she's the perfect woman. We both studying accounting, she thinks I'm funny, and most importantly she's a big girl who knows how to keep her shit together. She's like Jill Scott fine. You know, the lady from the Tyler Perry movie?"

"I know who she is," Damien said with narrowed eyes, "My mom was a fan."

"I gotta get this girl man. For real Damien, I think she gonna be my wife. Where in the fuck is my shirt?"

Damien shrugged, "Maybe somebody stole it from the laundry room or you left it in a dryer?"

Leon stopped searching and thought about it, "Yeah, you could be right, I'll be right back."

As Leon rushed from the room Damien's phone started to ring. He was expecting this to be his daily morning call from Kendall, but instead it was Tyler's name and number on the screen. Damien thought Tyler had forgotten about him, it being a couple of days since they had met at the club. But no matter how interested he was, he wasn't going to be the chaser anymore, the ball was in Tyler's court.

Damien answered his phone, "Yo?"

"Well, good afternoon," Tyler said in his seductive southern accent.

"Hey...Tyler," Damien purposely stalled, even though he clearly remembered his name, "What's up?"

Tyler laughed, almost sounding like a purring cat, "So, it's like that? You don't know my name?"

"Hey, I'm the one who feelin forgotten though."

"I'm sorry, I've just been working so darn much but I have this upcoming weekend free, how about you?"

"I'm in college," Damien said, "I'm always free."

"What about studying?" Tyler asked. "Don't tell me you ain't a good student."

Damien closed his textbook, "Oh, I get all my studying done early."

"Well, since you're all free how about we spend the weekend together. You can come stay with me."

Damien wasn't expecting a weekend away. "You sure?"

"It'll give us some time to get to know each other, see if the lord put you here for me."

Damien was sure the lord had more pressing matters on his hands, "Alright, I guess. I'll pack a bag."

"Now, I'm going to pick you up in the Shane's parking lot. My campus days are over and I refuse to come out there and even look at those buildings. Anyways, I'll be parked and waiting in a black BMW. I'm leaving my condo now and should be out there in an about half an hour. Don't be having me out there looking like a fool now and waiting."

Damien got up from his desk, "Nah, I won't. I'm packing my shit right now. I'll see you later."

"Bye sweetie," Tyler said with another one of his purr like laughs before he hung up.

As Damien started to pack, he replayed their conversation in his head. From some of the keywords mentioned, obviously Tyler enjoyed the finer things in life and instead of dragging out the introduction phase of meeting other men he handled it as a weekend long interview. Damien liked his style and him being a cute southern gentleman was only a plus.

Leon returned to their room, no shirt in hand. He noticed Damien packing clothes. "Where are you goin?"

"I'm spending the weekend with Tyler at his condo."

"Damn, already? I know y'all gonna be doing some nasty shit the entire time."

Damien laughed, "He doesn't come off as a freak though. Anyways, your shirt still MIA?"

Leon nodded as he plopped down on his bed, "Yeah, but imma catch the bus to H&M. Buy about five of em."

"So, while you're gonna be bus riding imma be cruising in a BWM," Damien bragged, "Aye, enjoy your weekend pedestrian."

Leon rolled his eyes as he chuckled, "Stop showing off, it ain't your BWM."

Damien slipped on his backpack full of clothes, "Typical pedestrian hater," Damien joked, "I'm out."

Leon threw up the peace sign, "Yeah, yeah, wear a condom and take selfies by the car, front for Instagram."

Damien nodded at Leon and left the room. He made his way off campus, his hoody keeping him warm while the autumn winds blew. He arrived to the parking lot of the club to find no waiting car. Damien decided to wait a bit longer before he started to feel as if he was being stood up. He didn't want to call Tyler and come off as desperate, but in the end nobody liked the feeling of rejection. Damien resisted calling and the moment he was about to start back to campus a shiny, black BMW pulled up.

The passenger's side window lowered revealing Tyler, "You look cute, the door's unlocked."

Damien slipped into the car, his body feeling relaxed on the leather seats. "I thought you forgot about me again."

Tyler turned down the classical music that was playing in his car as he pulled away, "I'm sorry, first I was at the salon getting a cut, then I stopped by J. Crew to buy a little something to slip on, and then I swear I saw a smug on the hood of my baby so I just had to get it washed. I'm sorry; I'll make it up to you. I'll buy you lunch."

Tyler wore black slacks, a pressed white dress shirt, and a silk vest that matched his pants.

Damien was already over him being late and free food was always welcomed, "I like Taco Bell."

Tyler shook his head, "Nuh uh, no sir. I don't do fast food. I know an upscale diner that sells lamb tacos."

"For a dollar? Because Taco Bell won't leave your wallet feeling light."

"Please," Tyler said with an eye roll, "I can buy an entire Taco Bell with the money in my wallet."

"Alright, Mr. Big Shot," Damien poked.

"Yes, I am," Tyler said, seriously accepting the title. "I'll get you lamb tacos, then we can go to my condo."

Tyler turned back up his music as he drove Damien downtown to a part of town he never even knew existed. Most of the shops were locally owned and the area looked like a mocked version of Rodeo Drive. The majority of the shoppers were either old or white. Damien felt out of place and really poor at the moment, while Tyler on the other hand seemed to be right at home. After picking up the tacos, which came out to the total of fifty dollars, they drove over to Grand Oaks condos.

They arrived at a front gate for the Grand Oak condos that looked like overpriced apartments to Damien. Tyler entered a number on a security pad that gained him access to the property. They got out of the car and made their way across the property. Tyler's condo was located in a brick building near a lake with a waterfall in the center, third floor. He unlocked his condo door and let Damien into one of the cleanest living spaces he'd ever been in. It felt as if he was walking into the lobby area of a hotel.

From the dark leather couches, to the sixty inch flat screen TV, the entire condo just looked and smelled like money to Damien. Tyler led him to the dining area that had a nice view of the lake outside and placed the bag of food on a thick mahogany table that looked as if it needed to be in a museum. Out of the kitchen, Tyler grabbed two plates that looked as equally expensive as everything else in the condo, and plated the food.

Damien sat down and bit into the rich in flavor taco, "It's amazing. Everything here is amazing."

Tyler took only small bites of his food, "Thank you, I should've told my maid to come in today."

"Wait, you got a maid?"

Tyler did his purr like laugh, "I can't clean this place and work."

"Where do you work and are you guys hiring?"

"No, we're not, sorry," Tyler said with a playful pout, "I'm in management."

"Your TV looks like a movie theater screen."

"That was actually a gift," Tyler said, "A lot of things in here are gifts from men who try to buy my love."

"You meet them at the club?"

"Yes, oldies night is when the ballers come out. I have no interest in being bought."

Damien thumbed at the TV, "Then why you have that on your wall?"

"Because sometimes I just show up and gifts are sitting on my porch. I wasn't going to trash it."

"I understand. Man, I bet any movie looks amazing on that," Damien said.

"I actually thought we could cuddle up and watch Dark Knight since you're an obvious batman fan," Tyler said.

"For real? Man, that'll be cool. You've seen it before, right?"

Tyler shook his head, "I don't watch TV. I'm either working or reading."

"Then you'll like it. It's the best one."

Tyler simply said, "Mhm," as he pushed away his plate of food that he barely touched.

After eating, Damien grabbed a spot on the couch while Tyler stood using the remote to order the movie directly on his TV set. For somebody who didn't watch TV, he was an expert at navigating the device Damien thought. Once the movie started playing, Tyler joined Damien on the couch and they cuddled up. Thirty minutes in, Tyler looked bored and started to talk about his life.

Damien wanted to listen but he was really enjoying the quality of the movie. All he could remember was Tyler going on and on about how much money his parent's made, how his brother was in medical school, and that his sister was a teacher in Africa and engaged to a prince. After he was done detailing his blessed childhood as he labeled it, Tyler started to strip Damien.

First, he got down and took off Damien's socks and shoes, "Just keep watching the movie," Tyler said.

"Um...okay," Damien said as Tyler started to remove his hoody and shirt.

Lastly, Tyler unbuttoned and removed Damien's jeans, leaving him just in his boxers. Tyler stripped off his own clothes and dropped them to floor, only wearing a really skimpy pair of white underwear that left his small, but bubble butt exposed. He sat back down on the couch, cuddled up closer to Damien, and stuck his hand into his boxers.

Tyler just sat staring forward at the TV as he played with Damien's dick as if it was no big deal. As for Damien, he was doing his best to focus on the movie but only to avoid nutting too quickly. Based on the way Tyler was aggressively tugging at his dick, it was going to be hard not to nut within the next few seconds.

Damien let out a groan, "Do you wanna-"

"-Shh," Tyler interrupted as he kept playing Damien's dick, "No, talking."

The pleasure too great, Damien started to nut all over Tyler's hand, staining his boxers.

Tyler raised his nut stained hand to his face and licked it clean. "It's sweet."

He leaned over and started to lick more nut from Damien's dick and even sucking it out the fabric of his boxers.

Damien put his hands behind his head and lounged back, "That felt so damn good."

"Taste better," Tyler said as he licked his thin lips, "I'm tired now. I just want to go lay in bed and I want you to hold me."

"Alright, I can do that for you."

Tyler got up, grabbed Damien by the hand and led him through his condo to his bedroom. The bedroom was as fancy as the rest of the place, the massive bed taking up most of the room. Together, they pulled back the heavy white blanket on the bed. Tyler stripped naked, his penis on the small side, crawled into bed, and lay in the fetal position. Damien removed his damp boxers and joined Tyler, cuddling him from behind. His dick was somewhat still hard and Tyler's moaning and grinding his ass against it was about to make him nut again. As Damien felt another load coming, Tyler stopped grinding and started snoring.

Damien was a bit agitated that he was left hanging, but he had already gotten a lot more than Tyler had offered. Plus, this was only the first night of their weekend together and Damien was sure the next few days weren't just only going to consist of expensive meals and handjobs. He held Tyler tighter until they both slept soundly.

The next morning, Damien awoke the next morning fully rested. Tyler's bed provided something no twin-sized dorm room bed could provide, comfort. As Damien rolled over he noticed that Tyler wasn't in bed with him. Damien slid out of bed and slipped on his stained boxers from last night. He made his way out the bedroom to find a dressed Tyler wearing a fitted tan suit, setting the table for breakfast.

Tyler carefully placed some pieces of fruit in a bowl on the table. He looked up at Damien, "Rise and shine."

Damien smiled as he rubbed the back of his neck. "You wake up kind of early."

Tyler did his purr like laugh, "Because I have a lot to get done today. But first, we have to eat."

Damien took a seat at the table, "Bacon and eggs?"

"Nuh uh," Tyler said as he poured some orange juice from a picture, "Fruit and oatmeal."

Damien ate a piece of watermelon from the bowl of fruit on the table, "It's fresh."

"And organic," Tyler said, "I don't mind spending a lot to be healthy."

"I guess." Damien shrugged, "I eat whatever they serve us in the cafeteria."

Tyler headed into the kitchen and returned with two bowls of oatmeal. He placed a bowl before Damien and sat down with his oatmeal. "Well, if you're going to be with me you're going to have to start eating better and dressing better. I went through your bag and did not like the clothes that I found. Before we get to the meeting I'm going to stop you by J. Crew and get you something nice to wear."

"You went in my bag?" Damien said shocked.

"I'm nosey. And I wanted to make sure you weren't carrying anything to hurt me."

"Why would I try to hurt you?"

Tyler shrugged, "Some dudes are just crazy."

"I'm not one of those guys then." Damien's mind rewound back a bit, "And what meeting?"

"Every four months along with my friend Howwy, we host a gathering of gay black men to discuss issues within our community. It's very discrete and every guy who shows up is given a twenty-five dollar VISA gift card. It's sad that we have to use money to bring our community together, but it's worth it. A lot of friendships originate out of our meetings and a lot of wounds are healed. I'm inviting you as my personal guest."

Damien's last experience with a group of gay men was pretty wild. "Will it be anything like the club?"

"No," Tyler said not amused with the comparison, "This is a serious event, not a dance party."

His words made Damien a bit more comfortable with going. "I don't mind. Will there be food?" Damien asked, the fruit and oatmeal not filling him up much.

"Of course and if you behave I'll give you something sweet to eat tonight," Tyler said as he seductively bit his lip.

"Then I'll be on my damn best behavior."

After breakfast, Damien took a shower in a bathroom that was nearly the size of his dorm room. He slipped on some clean clothes, but he didn't wear them long. Thirty minutes later, he was in the J. Crew dressing room being dressed like a human Ken doll. Tyler picked out some skinny, denim jeans, a blood red dress shirt, and some nice brown shoes for Damien. At the checkout, Damien found himself feeling guilty once he saw that the total was nearly two hundred dollars.

"I can pay half," Damien suggested though that was all he had on his debit card.

Tyler swiped one of the many cards from his wallet. "It's my treat. This total is nothing."

With the shopping all done and Damien's attire up to Tyler's standard, they took a drive down to a convention center. They arrived to a half-full parking lot and a variety of gay black men were filing into the convention center. Once exiting the car, Damien followed Tyler into the building. Nearly every person they passed seemed to know Tyler, excitingly greeting him or thanking him for inviting them.

Inside the room, folding chairs were set up and a table full of finger sandwiches, bottle water, and meat trays was available. Tyler pointed Damien to a seat while he went off and joined a towering man wearing thick rimmed glasses near a table of pamphlets. After chatting back and forth, Tyler and the man started to hand out the pamphlets around the room. Damien grabbed one from Tyler and flipped through, it mostly discussing AIDs awareness and places where you could get tested.

After handing out all the pamphlets, the man in thick rimmed glasses cleared his throat. "Hello, everybody."

Everybody settled down and found seats.

"My name is Howwy Matthews," The man continued, "And I want to thank all you for showing up."

Tyler took a spot next to Howwy, "And I'm Tyler aka the guy who most likely begged you to be here."

Damien's attention drifted as he started to browse around the room for any familiar faces. He ended up spotting one person from a campus, a football player. Their eyes connected and quickly both of them looked in the other direction. Damien wasn't nervous at all about the football player spilling his secret, because now they both were keepers of each other's hidden alternate lives.

A wide variety of issues were discussed, ranging from when to come out to who's the better performer Beyonce or Rihanna. A lot of emotions were shared, Damien laughing at some of the crazy sex stories shared, to feeling pain for many of the guys who discussed cases of sexual harassment at young ages. At times he felt like an outsider to the community, not knowing the definition of the word 'Trade' or what it meant to 'Read' somebody.

After all the talking was done, they were all free to mix and mingle, have some snacks, and collect their gift cards at the door. Damien knew he wasn't leaving anytime soon, nearly every guy trying to talk to or swoon over Tyler. Damien grabbed some food from the table and hung out, eavesdropping or doing his best to converse.

The football player from campus approached him, "Man, I came for the money."

"But, you're gay right?"

"I am who I am, so don't go around campus telling people that I'm gay."

"I won't and I expect the same from you. I'm Damien by the way."

"Max," He introduced, "Aye, I'm outta here though, a lot of these fem dudes making me uncomfortable."

"Alright man, see you around campus."

Max snarled as he looked him up and down, "No, don't see me."

"Relax," Damien said, "We both in the same boat."

"Yeah, whatever," Max said as he walked away.

Damien wasn't offended by Max's paranoia; he wasn't out himself so understood how it could be sometimes.

Damien turned around to go grab more food and ended up crossing paths with Howwy.

Howwy extended his hand out, "I saw you come in with Tyler, you must be his new sponsorship project."

Damien shook hands with Howwy. "What do you mean?"

Howwy shook his head, "Man, you'll find out. He's a complicated story."

"I think he's nice. And everybody else seems to think the same thing. Aren't y'all cool?"

"I'm the type of friend that doesn't fit into his world anymore. I'm surprised he still helps me host my event."

"I thought you two put this together?" Damien asked.

Howwy adjusted his glasses, "His newest story, huh? Go ahead and believe that bullshitter."

Damien didn't like the way Howwy was bashing Tyler. "I'm going to go get some more food," Damien said as he pointed over his shoulder at the snack table.

No matter what kind of vibes Howwy put out there, Damien's opinion of Tyler remained the same. He watched how Tyler interacted with the remaining guests and everybody was enjoying his company, while Howwy on the other hand was being brushed off or putting away folding chairs. The only time he saw anybody be friendly with Howwy was when he was handing them a gift card.

Howwy ended up leaving to take somebody home who was having car troubles, leaving Tyler and Damien to clean.

Tyler and Damien started to clean off the snack table.

"So, was the meeting informative enough for you?" Tyler asked as he trashed the meat tray.

"It was cool. I learned a lot. Everybody was nice, except for Howwy."

Tyler raised his right brow, "What did Howwy say to you?"

"Shit about you, calling you a bullshitter."

"He is bitter," Tyler said, "That's why you never work with an Ex. Bitter and messy."

"Oh, now his hate for you make since. You two looked like you were getting along though."

"It's called being professionals, but outside of these meetings we do not communicate often. We were together for a while; he supposedly loved me and wanted me to be his stay at home husband. I didn't so now he walks around telling people that I owe him. Do I look like I'm in debt?"

"Hell no," Damien said, "I ain't ashamed to say you're basically sponsoring me this weekend."

"I'm doing it because you're sweet."

Damien smirked, "For real? Thank you. I like you too Tyler. You've been nothing but kind to me."

Tyler stopped cleaning and started to rub up against Damien's chest. He forced Damien to lay back against the snack table. While chewing on his bottom lip, Tyler started to unbutton Damien's pants. A wide smile formed across Damien's face; sure he knew where this was going. Damien was already hard as Tyler pulled his pants down and whipped his dick out of his boxers.

Tyler removed a condom from his wallet, "You wanna know why Howwy is so bitter?"

Damien slowly nodded as Tyler slid the condom on his dick.

Tyler turned around and pulled down his pants, revealing his ass. "Because he can't get this pussy no more."

Tyler sat back down, slowly allowing Damien's dick to enter him. His ass cheeks jiggled as he slowly started to ride Damien. He was doing things with his ass that Damien never even imagined could be done. If Tyler stopped messing with him, Damien would be as bitter as Howwy.

Tyler looked over his shoulder and down at Damien, "You like that?"

"Man, your ass is magic."

Tyler slid off of Damien's dick, faced him and removed the condom. He started to suck Damien's dick and it was as equally good as the fucking. Everything he experienced with Vincent and Kendall could not compare to the skills Tyler was displaying. Damien felt as if he was crossing over into another dimension as he started to nut into Tyler's mouth. Tyler moan as he swallowed every bit of nut, not letting any of it go to waste.

Tyler pulled up his pants. "Beyond way better dick than Howwy's."

His body weak, Damien did his best to sit upright, "You did all the work."

"Only because I had the right tool to work with." Tyler said as he pulled Damien's pants up and kissed him on the lips.

Damien had to catch himself before he started falling for Tyler. There was still a lot they had to get to know about each other. The sex was amazing and Tyler wasn't shy about spreading his wealth and overall positive vibe. Damien reminded himself this was just a friendship, not setting himself up for any heartbreak. He feared a guy as good as Tyler was going to be tough to hold onto, especially with guys like Howwy trying to stir up drama.

11 - Peeping

It was Sunday morning, nearing the end of Damien's weekend with Tyler. All he could think, based on the amazing sex, food, and gifts, was that he was lucky stumbling into this friendship. He was confident in the fact that he didn't have any romantic feelings for Tyler; things were a lot more materialistic for him.

Once again, Damien found himself dressed in an outfit Tyler purchased for him to wear to the gym. He sported brand new running sneakers, shorts, and a fitted athletic shirt.

Damien slaved away on a treadmill, the last thing him needing to do was burn body fat.

From his treadmill, Tyler checked Damien's burnt calories amount. "Nu huh, you need to speed up."

"I'm tired."

"Next weekend I don't want you showing up at my condo with a gut."

Damien smirked, "Oh, so we already have plans for next week?"

"As long as you stay up to par, yes. You can easily be replaced."

"I can say the same about you."

Tyler rolled his eyes, "Please, you don't have the skills to snag another sponsor."

"Oh, so you legit see yourself as my sponsor? Nothing else, we not even just cool?"

"You're a cute dude with a nice dick and who knows how to shower me with compliments, my tool."

Damien powered off his treadmill. "I compliment you out of kindness, not because I want more free shit." Though Damien didn't mind all the clothes Tyler had given him.

"Oh boy, please don't tell me we're going there," Tyler said.

"Where?"

"Once a man finds out he's nothing more than a weekend play thing, he starts getting hurt feelings and acting as if the gifts and attention means nothing. First Lamario and then Trey. Please do not join that list of investments gone bitter. Yesterday you were all laughs and giggles, calling me your sponsor. But now that you know your role, it's not funny. As I said, I can easily replace you Damien, you see men flock to me."

The smugness was making Damien sick, "I'm going to go get some water."

Damien headed into the locker room and sat on a bench. He didn't feel disrespected; he just thought it was so funny that Tyler thought he was in control. From his side, Damien felt he was in control, easily fine with walking away from Tyler with some new clothes, not letting his feelings get hurt like he did with Vincent.

Into the locker room entered Howwy. He nodded at Damien, "Hey man."

"You work out here too?"

Howwy laughed, "Man, ninety percent of the man in here are gay, the other ten are questioning."

"Oh. I just found out what you meant about Tyler being complicated."

Howwy sat down beside Damien, "Ah, he broke the news to you, huh? It's funny, because four years ago he was in your place and I was in his. I used to see him down at the club working hard and then studying whenever he could. As a well off brotha, I felt I could afford to step in and help him, take care of him. At first, it was just money in exchange for sex and his attention. But I fell in love with his story, a young gay dude banished from his family, in a new state alone, struggling to build himself up. I wanted him to be my husband, but of course he started making his own money and needed his own power. He left me and then every weekend I started to notice him leading around young dudes like you. He became a sponsor. It's a lonely life, I try to tell him that but he's too busy enjoying the control."

"Well, I'm not looking for anything romantic. I just don't like how he thinks I'm helpless without him."

"And nothing will change that because he's in control. Either you accept it or you don't."

"Fuck that, I already got a daddy. Yeah Tyler buys me better clothes but he ain't in control of me."

"I take all the blame; guys like me pass that lifestyle on. It's not right."

"Yeah, I suppose," Damien said, "It was nice chatting with you man."

Howwy nodded, "Yeah, be smart out there."

Damien left the locker room to find Tyler flirtatiously showing another guy how to lifts some dumbbells and giggling with him. He started to walk over there, but Damien wasn't in the mood for Tyler to talk down to him. Damien decided to let things be and return to his first love, porn. He left the gym and caught a cab back to campus, no hard feelings against Tyler. The man was simply a product of a world of power and materialism.

He arrived back to his dorm to find Leon in bed watching basketball.

"I'm back," Damien said.

Leon kept his focus on the game, "How was your weekend?"

"Damn nice, good food, nice condo to chill in, and I walked away with some new sneakers and clothe."

"He treated you real nice; you must've done some nasty shit for the coins."

Damien laughed, "Shut up, I basically just stroked his ego and let him use my body."

"Oh, that's that 'gotta pay my rent' love. My mom dated a nigga who gave her anything for the pussy."

"I guess. I can't deal with the controlling you part though."

"Cause you ain't got four kids to feed or actual rent to pay. People put up wit that shit all the time."

"Yeah, I bet they do. Aye, you ever get that girl's number?"

"Man, I haven't seen her all weekend. It's some depressing shit, but it's a work in progress."

"All you need is your red v-neck and some Usher cologne and you can get her."

Leon laughed, his attention still on the game, "Yeah man, I'm gonna come correct."

Starting to smell his post gym funk, Damien stood up, "I'm going to shower, right quick."

"Hurry up then, we can go get some food from the cafeteria afterwards."

Even after his lavish weekend, Damien was glad to be back in his dorm room chilling with Leon. He grabbed some changing clothes and headed down to the showers. Like most guys in the shower, he did his best to avoid eye contact at all times. He didn't feel at ease until he pulled the curtain closed on his showering booth. Afterwards, Damien dried off, slipped on his clothes, and went to the sink area to wash his face with a cleanser.

After rinsing his face, he stood up to find Max directly behind him, breathing on his neck.

The football player wore nothing but a towel, revealing his dark-skinned, chiseled torso of muscles. "Sup."

Damien kept his back to him, "I thought we weren't supposed to see each other around."

"We just two dudes talking, that's it." Max checked over his shoulders, "We're alone anyways."

"Still, you should back up off of me."

Max smirked, "You right? I'm mad on that faggot shit right now."

"What do you want?"

"I just wanted to say that ass looked real nice in that shower."

"What? You watched me?"

Max chuckled, "Just a lil bit through the curtain. I told you, I'm on that mad faggot shit right now."

"More like creepy shit." Damien faced him, "That's not cool man."

"My bad. Anyways, imma hit the showers. This talk never happened."

Damien shrugged, "Yeah, whatever."

Damien left the showers turned-on but crept out all at the same time. He returned to his dorm room, still trying to shake off the strange encounter he had with the buff peeping tom. Leon slipped on his sneakers and they left for dinner. As they walked down the dorm hallway, Damien ended up spotting Max coming his way. Max avoided contact and simply brushed passed Damien like he was nobody, yet a couple of minutes ago he was in the shower dick watching. Damien could only smirk.

12 - Dirty Laundry

Damien had been looking forward to the Thanksgiving break for weeks. His excitement had nothing to do with getting to see his family or the food, but instead a break from classes and studying. Like every year, Damien was celebrating the holidays at his aunt's house in Columbia, South Carolina. The plan was for him and Marion to drive down there later tonight and their father would arrive in Columbia the next morning. Leon and the majority of students on campus were also heading away for the holidays.

Leon carefully placed hat number three of his into his suit case, "Man, I can already taste my momma's yams."

"My aunt always takes credit for cooking, but she mostly just runs her mouth," Damien said as he lounged in bed.

"Are you excited about road tripping with your brother?" Leon asked.

"It's gonna be awkward, as usual. I told you man, my brother treats me like I'm shit."

Leon sat on his bed, "Maybe he doesn't like gay people."

"He doesn't know I'm gay though."

"You don't know that. He might just be keeping quiet about it."

"Nah, he would tell my daddy. Anything to make my life miserable."

"I feel bad for you man," Leon said, "My brother and I cool as shit, even if he's gay."

"Gay or straight, it don't matter, my own blood shouldn't treat me like a dog."

"Call him out," Leon said.

"It's pointless, he'll dig deep for an excuse or just say I'm starting drama. I've tried this before."

Leon doubled checked his duffle bag, "What time are you leaving?"

"I'm going to do laundry downstairs first then catch a taxi to my brother's apartments."

Leon raised his right brow, "Why won't he pick you up in the car y'all driving to Columbia in?"

"Didn't I just tell you my brother is a dick?"

"No, that nigga is cruel. He's the laugh at your funeral type of dude." Leon cringed, "That's fucked up."

"I don't think he's that fucked up. Anyways, when you leaving?"

"Whenever Megan drives me down to the bus station."

"Megan, she's the girl you study with, right?" Damien noticed Leon wore a red v-neck, "You gonna make a move?"

Leon smirked as he proudly nodded his head and rubbed his palms together, "Yup, tonight is the night. I just feel as if the mood is all right and shit. Man, it's as if the man upstairs wants me to do it. When we were studying two nights ago, I mentioned catching the bus home and she offered me a ride to the station, cause she got a good heart and all. This will be our first time alone outside of the library, imma speak from my heart."

"That's cool, man."

"And how's your love life doing? When's the last time you heard from that Tyler dude?"

Damien shrugged, "I got a text from him last week. He was cussing me out, saying I owe him for shit he got me."

Leon laughed, "Man, he can't get salty when one of his hoes run off with the loot."

"I'm not a ho," Damien said, though he was aware in this case the label was sort of fitting, "You always joking."

Leon stood and up grabbed his duffle bag, "Hey, tops can be bought and paid for just like bottoms."

"Man, your knowledge of the gay world is vast, you sure you not at least bi?"

"My brother used to make me watch Noah's Arc with him, I learned something I guess."

"You leaving?" Damien asked.

"Yup," Leon said as he checked his phone, "It's time for me to go lay my heart out dude."

"Be safe; come back with a girlfriend and about twenty extra pounds."

"You be cool too and tell your sadistic brother I said fuck him." Leon opened the door, "Peace out."

Damien waved goodbye and Leon left the dorm room. After lying around dreading the upcoming ride with Marion, Damien finally got up and started packing his clothes and everything he would need while away from campus. He was going to wash clothes and immediately after he was done, call a taxi to pick him up from the dormitory laundry center. Damien kept his travel outfit simple, sneakers, grey sweatpants, and his black hoody that he wore so much that the drawstring was missing.

Damien started downstairs to the laundry center. The dormitory felt a lot more peaceful without all the busy and energetic students rushing through the halls. He arrived to the laundry center to learn that he was the only one there; glad he wouldn't have to wait to use a washer or dryer. Damien started to load his dirty clothes into the washer.

"Did you drop this?" A monotone voice asked.

Damien looked over his shoulder to find Max, his hair cut low and baby-face hairless, holding his dirty pair of plaid boxers. "Oh, yeah, thanks."

Max wore metallic grey gym shorts and a shirt with the school's name and football team's logo of a lion on the front.

Max waved the boxers back and forth as Damien failed to grab them. "Hold up," Max said with a mischievous smirk.

"What do you mean hold up? Give me my boxers, stop being creepy, man."

Max's dimples became more defined as his smirk expanded into a smile, "I'm trying to imagine how good you look in these."

"Well, you've already seen me naked so there's not much to imagine."

"Yeah, but still, sometimes clothes can make a dude look sexier," Max said.

"I guess so; now give me my boxers for I can start my load."

Max balled the boxers up in his hand. "I'm keeping these."

Damien formed an uncomfortable grin, "Huh? What you mean?"

Max shoved the boxers into his gym shorts pocket, "Exactly what I said, I'm keeping them."

Damien shrugged, needing to get his laundry started, "Fine, do what you want."

Damien closed the washer and took a seat in a waiting area on a tattered couch that smelled like fabric softener.

Max joined him on the couch, "Is your boyfriend gonna get mad about you giving out your boxers?"

"I don't have a boyfriend and technically you stole them."

Max rubbed his square jaw, "So you ain't fucking Tyler no more?"

"It was a weekend thing. He aint my type of dude really."

"Yeah, I fucked him and moved on quick." Max made a slicing motion across his throat, "I cut that faggot quick."

"Don't call him that, cause if he's a faggot then you're a faggot."

Max laughed, "I ain't though. I just like to fuck. Tyler was into all that faggot shit, wearing body oil and shit."

"Dude, you sound so dumb right now."

"Why you gotta play me? I'm trying to have a nice conversation with you."

It was hard to deny that Max was striking, but Damien didn't expect him to be so ignorant.

Nothing but waiting to do, Damien entertained him, "So, did Tyler try to buy you shit?"

"Yeah, but I never let another dude buy me shit. I left every lil thing in his condo, along with my nut in his ass."

Damien was a bit disgusted that he stuck his dick in the same place Max did. "Dude, has he fucked everybody in town?"

Max laughed, "Young and old. He a sexy ass dude, real talk, but he ain't nothin you take home to mom."

"What kind of guy would you take home to mom then?" Damien asked.

Max scooted closer to Damien, "The one I'm looking at now."

Damien couldn't believe this big buff guy had any attraction to a scrawny him. "Yeah, right, shut up."

"Don't act like you wouldn't like that, you blushing," Max said as he ran his hand down Damien's face.

"I'm not," Damien said even though he knew that wasn't the truth, trying hard to contain his smile.

"Whatever and I wouldn't take any dude home to mom anyways. That shit don't even sound right."

"Don't lie, you already said it. You like me. Man, you carrying around my stink ass boxers, you borderline obsessed."

Max laughed, "You a weird dude, but in a good way. I could tell that from the minute I met you."

"I didn't expect you to be the type to fall so hard. Am I your first overboard crush?"

"Why you gotta make it sound so gay though? You just a nigga I wanna suck tongue with."

"Suck tongue?" Damien said as he wrinkled his nose, "What the fuck is that?"

"Kiss," Max seductively whispered.

Damien checked out Max's moist, brown lips, he would kiss him back. "Too bad. Ain't happening," He teased.

"I got your boxers to hold me over then. You wanna do Thanksgiving together this week since we both here?"

"I'm going to Columbia right after my clothes are clean. You stayin on campus?"

Max nodded, "Yeah, I ain't up for no traveling. My family don't do holidays that much anyways."

"Mines always does, I'm riding to Columbia with my brother."

"Oh, he picking you up?"

Damien thumbed over his shoulder to outside, "Nah, I'm catching a cab to his apartment off campus."

"Oh, so your bro local? That's cool."

"He's a student here. Marion? Built? Dark dude? Usually with Vincent?"

Max snapped his fingers, "I know them, don't fuck wit em. They assholes."

"I agree with you on that one," Damien said.

"Your brother though, I would fuck him," Max said as he laughed and grabbed at his crotch.

Damien lightly punched him in his in muscled arm, "Aye, that's nasty man."

"I'm an honest dude though. Vincent could get this dick too, your brother first though. He fine, right?"

"He's my brother you idiot." Damien said as the washer dinged, signaling that his load was complete.

Max quickly got up, "Chill, I'll put it in the dryer for you."

Damien started to stand but sat back down, "Alright, but don't steal anything."

Max started to unload the clothes, "Nah, these already had all the stank washed out anyways."

"Man, your mind is on some other shit," Damien said.

Max put all the clothes in the dryer, "You remember what I told you in the bathroom? I be on that mad faggot shit sometimes. I see you and corny ass Leon always hanging out, and I would just kinda think about the shit y'all would be sayin to each other, sometimes wishing you would be talkin about me. When I saw your lil ass show up with Tyler at that meeting, I know I had to get at you, no matter who been calling you bae."

"To me you were just another cute straight guy on campus, so I kept my distance naturally."

"Man, shit would be so cool if we could just walk up to dudes and spit game, right?"

Damien shrugged, "But we can. We might get our asses beat, but that's life."

Max closed and started the dryer, "I'm untouchable."

The ignorance, the arrogance, Damien liked it the whole package. "Yeah, yeah, yeah, tough guy."

"Aye listen, imma have to leave you though. I'm tired and got shit I wanna do with these boxers."

Damien promised himself not to be the chaser, but he liked the entertainment Max provided, "You suck."

"Man, working out all day drains me. Is it cool if I get your number for we can text over the holidays?"

Damien figured it would be a nice distraction from his family, "Yeah, I can use a text buddy."

Damien got up and put his number in Max's phone.

Max bit his bottom lip as his face lit up with joy, "Imma text you about a million times."

"Of course you will, it's what you stalker bitches do," Damien joked.

"I ain't no bitch," Max snapped, missing the humor of Damien's words.

"I'm joking; you're Max, the boxers thief. Go to sleep meathead."

Max calmed down and smirked, "I gotta remember you like to joke. Anyways, night and I'll text you fo sho."

Max left the laundry center and immediately Damien sunk into boredom. Yes, Max was on the super discrete side of the gay picket fence, but underneath all the toughness, Damien loved his soft side. Already Damien was ready to get the holidays with his family over with so he could sit around and listen to more weirdness come from Max's mouth. Until then, he would just have to settle for texts that he was sure would be as equally as weird.

13 - Band

There was only one thing that could make a road trip with Marion worse, Vincent. Marion also thought it was a good idea to bring along his flavor of the month girlfriend named Shannon. She was one of those too proud light skin girls, who worshiped her long hair, light brown eyes, and shared her features with the world on Instagram all day. Damien counted her taking about ten selfies so far as she sat in the front passenger's seat. He didn't sense any type of genuine chemistry between her and Marion; they both just came off as the NC Tech resident Kim and Kanye.

When it came to Vincent, Marion wasn't even fazed by his presence one bit. He preferred him to not be there, but was over him enough to simply tolerate him. Every now and then Vincent would try to start up a conversation, asking questions about school and about what he was excited to eat for Thanksgiving. Damien kept his answers short and sweet and his attention either on the starry night sky or his phone texting Max, making sure Vincent knew he was being given the cold shoulder.

They arrived to Columbia and drove through a suburban neighbor of expensive brick homes. All the lawns were kept; you could see the fancy furniture and light fixtures and families gathering through some of the windows that had the curtains pulled opened. This neighborhood brought back so many memories for both Damien and Marion, the boys spending most of their holidays here with their mother and father. They pulled into the parking lot that was crowded with two BMWs, a Range Rover, and two rental cars.

Shannon pointed at the Range Rover, "Baby, I want one of those for Christmas."

"Alright," Marion said as he powered off the car.

Damien rolled his eyes as he gladly exited the car and broke away from Marion and his crew. He grabbed his duffle bag from the trunk of the car, Vincent grabbed his, and Marion grabbed both him and Shannon's bags. They made their way up the pebble stone pathway that led to the front door of the home. Damien knocked and a woman with braided hair, spotless brown skin, a curvy figure, and wearing a flowing red dress answered the door.

This was a bitter sweet moment for Marion and Damien. The sweet being that they were staring at the face of a woman who had so much of their mother's features, her sister, and the bitter being that their aunt was a self-absorbed woman who loved to tear her own family down to raise herself up. They both just stood there with forced smiles on their faces, wishing their dad had arrived with them to combat the woman.

"I knew you boys were going to take forever to get here," She said.

"Hi Aunt Bernice," Marion greeted as if he didn't want to speak her name.

"Hi Marion," She looked over his shoulders, "Vincent again? And who's this little girl?"

Vincent waved, "Hi Mrs. Bernice."

"Hey," Shannon said, her eyes mostly focused on her phone. "I'm Shannon."

Bernice ignored their greetings and looked to Damien, "And you can't speak young man?"

"Hi Aunt Bernice," Damien said, "It's nice to see you," He lied.

She looked Damien up and down as if she knew his word weren't genuine. "Alright, better. Come on in."

Bernice stepped aside and let them inside her lavish home. She was Marion and Damien's mother's only sister and the success story of the family. Not only was she a doctor, but on a popular reality show that focused on the lives of African-American woman in the medical field. Damien never watched an episode, seeing her during the holidays was enough.

Her five bedroom home was decorated from corner to corner with expensive furniture and she wasn't shy about price dropping how much she had spent. A few other family members had already arrived early in the evening including their grandmother, their two uncles with their young kids and wives, and Bernice's stay at home husband was in the kitchen cooking. Bernice led them to the den to catch up and to allow them to put down their bags.

Vincent, Marion, and Damien put down their bags and along with Shannon squeezed on the couch together.

Bernice rested her hand on her hips and stared them down. "How's school?"

"It alright," Marion answered.

"You mean 'it's alright'," Bernice corrected, "I don't want you boys speaking like street thugs in my house."

"Sorry," Marion said.

"Marion, you're majoring in business, correct?" Bernice asked.

"Yes' ma'am," Marion answered, "Both Vincent and me plan on opening up a chain of luxury barber shops."

"That's nice, but how are you going to have business meetings if you can't form proper sentences?" Bernice asked.

Marion softly chuckled, "I know how to speak proper when needed."

"It's a skill you should display at all times," Bernice said.

Damien's cellphone beeped and he checked it to find a text from Max. It was a shirtless selfie of him trying his best to look seductive. Damien rated his attempt a ten out of ten.

"Please put your phone on vibrate," Bernice said, "I can't tolerate all that binging."

Damien put his phone on mute, "Sorry."

"And how's school going for you?" Bernice asked.

Damien shrugged, "Decent."

"I know I wasn't going to get a full answer from you, you're the mysterious one, but that's how your mother was, always keeping to herself. She went to her grave with the same attitude, hiding her cancer from us for no reason. It still hurts me. I could've possibly saved her, but that's the past." She looked to Shannon, "And how's school for you?"

Shannon looked up from her phone, "Yes ma'am," She responded, obviously not paying attention.

"Where's Big Mike, Aunt Bernice?" Damien asked, pretending to show some sort of interests in the whereabouts of his cousin.

He loathed Big Mike, Bernice's only son that she treated like royalty.

"He's in Paris," Bernice boasted, "He's doing Thanksgiving abroad with some classmates from NYU."

That was the best news Damien heard all day, "Aww man, I wanted to see him," He lied.

"Maybe for Christmas," Bernice said, "Anyways, I've already assigned rooms. Marion I suppose you and Shannon here can have Big Mike's room, I wasn't expecting you to bring her. Damien, you'll be sleeping right here in the den, I have blankets that I just ordered from Madrid that I'll bring down in a few minutes. Vincent you're also in the den and when Kendall and his mother shows up later tonight, he'll be joining you two."

Damien's faced dropped, sure Kendall's mom was coming but not expecting him to show up with her. Not only would he have to see Kendall, but also sleep in the same room with him and Vincent. Already, he felt awkward; rooming with two of the men he'd had sexual encounters with. Tired from all the driving he did tonight, Marion and Shannon headed up to their room, while

Bernice rejoined her husband in the kitchen to prep for tomorrow's big dinner.

Vincent took out his cellphone and lounged back on the couch, "I'm not sleeping on the floor."

"I don't care, take the couch," Damien said.

"Why have you been treating me so bad?"

"Don't you remember slamming the door on my face?"

"I was hung-over though," Vincent said, "I'm sorry."

"You could've said that months ago, instead you were too busy being a jackass around campus."

"Classes, girls, I don't have a lot of free time," Vincent said, "I guess you don't want to play around anymore?"

"Hell no, I can find much more committed guys. I'm not catching one of your STDs."

Vincent softly laughed, "So you done move on, what his name is?"

"I'm not with anybody; I'm just enjoying the single life."

"Aka fucking around, yet you talkin about I'm the one out there catchin STDs."

"Shut up," Damien said, "I'll be back. I'm gonna go talk to my uncles and brush my teeth."

Damien headed out and made his rounds, greeting and joking around with his uncles. Each of them prodded him about his dating life, but he stuck with the typical 'I'm just focusing on school' act. After brushing his teeth, he returned to the den to learn that Bernice had already brought in the blankets. Vincent was on the couch covered up messing around on his phone.

Damien made himself a bed of blankets on the floor and lay down. "Are you jerking off?"

"What?" Vincent asked.

"You told me once, that you always jerk off before bed. Or was that you just playing mind games."

"Mind games. I usually fuck a nice bitch every night though at school," Vincent bragged.

"No more dudes?"

"On campus? Nah. I was fucking with this dude I met online though," Vincent said, "I know you be on A4A and BGC and don't lie. I always wonder one which profile is yours."

"It's the one that'll block you after you unlock your pics," Damien quipped.

Vincent laughed, "Can we just be somewhat cool again? Minus the gay drama?"

"I guess. But the minute you start showing off, I'm one hundred percent done."

"Aye, that be your bro starting shit with you."

"Has he ever told you why he hates me? Damien asked.

"He doesn't, your brother has just been cold sense your mom died. He's that way with me sometimes too."

"But I get it the worst."

"Don't stress about it," Vincent said, "He'll open up. Night man, I'm tired."

Damien hoped Vincent was right, at some point he wanted his brother to show him some type of love. He dozed off, but awoke in the middle of the night to catch the den door opening. Into the moon lit room slipped Kendall carrying his duffle bag and using his cellphone screen as some added light to guide him to a spot on the floor.

He shined the light directly on Damien's face as he joined him on the floor. "Yo cuzzo," He whispered.

Damien squinted his eyes until Kendall turned off his phone screen, "Hey, what time is it?"

"About four AM. My mom and I just got here. Man, your crazy ass aunt has your daddy and my momma sharing a room. I think she tryin to get them to fuck or something so she can have a reason to cut my momma out of the family. You know she can't really stand her." Kendall said.

"My aunt can't stand anybody but your momma is at the top of the list."

Bernice always felt as if Kendall's mother Monica stole her sister away from her.

Kendall found his set of blankets and made a bed next to Damien's. "I've been callin you."

"I've been busy. With school-"

"-And dude's," Kendall whispered as he interrupted, not wanting Vincent to overhear.

"No, just school."

"I left voicemails, hit you up on Instagram, I think you avoiding me. Cuz, I thought we were good."

"Just call me Damien, man. No more of that cousin shit. And you know why."

Kendall reached his hand under Damien's blanket and reached for his dick, "I remember. I'm always thinking bout it."

Damien scooted away a little as his dick got hard, "Dude, somebody's on the couch."

Kendall moved closer to him, "I don't care. Man, I wanted to see you bad. I want some dick again."

Damien told himself not to go there again. He wasn't going to do it. "It aint happening."

"Just let me give you some head."

"Why are you being so thirsty?"

Kendall laughed, "I got feelins for you Damien. Deep ones. I want to please you all the time."

"But don't you think it's sort of wrong. We have history."

"That history only adds to why I like you. I know we connect on many levels emotionally and sexually."

Just because Kendall liked him, that didn't mean he had to like him back Damien figured. If giving him some dick was all that Kendall wanted, Damien didn't mind giving it to him. But there was no way Damien wanted any type of romantic relationship with Kendall. It didn't feel right to him.

"Alright," Damien said, "But you have to be quiet."

Kendall started to strip under his blanket, "I got you dude."

"Why are you getting naked, I just thought you wanted to give me head?"

Kendall playfully rolled his eyes, "I was just playin, I wanna fuck."

Kendall started kissing Damien as he climbed on top of him. As Damien remembered how good it felt last time he fucked him, he didn't protest to the idea. Damien found himself getting more into the moment, shoving his tongue deep into Kendall's mouth. He couldn't help himself, at his core he liked sex, and it was even better with somebody as attractive as Kendall. Damien grasped at Kendall's bubble butt as he slowly slipped his dick into him.

Vincent sat up and both Kendall and Damien froze like statues. "If you two gonna fuck, can I at least jerkoff?"

Damien wasn't into the idea, feeling as his dark secret had just been uncovered.

"Fuck yeah," Kendall answered for them.

Vincent started to jerk his dick. Accepting this was going to happen even if Vincent was there, Damien thrust deep into a whimpering Kendall. As if they were a band, Vincent and Damien stayed in rhythm with their strokes. Damien started to pull out, about to nut, but Kendall will not let his pulsating dick leave from inside of him. Vincent started to nut and with no other choice, Damien nutted into Kendall. As he was being filled with warm nut, Kendall leaned over and kissed Damien once again, breathing heavily.

"I'm sorry," Damien whispered, "I couldn't hold it any longer."

Kendall smirked, "It's what I wanted though. Shit feels good."

"That was hot," Vincent said as he used his shirt to wipe up his nut, "Y'all some freaks. Night."

Kendall slipped off of Damien's wet dick and lay down on his side. "I miss you so much, man."

Damien kept staring up at the dark ceiling, not wanting to say it back. "Good night."

A silence fell upon the room, until they all feel asleep.

Damien awoke the next morning to find a shirtless Vincent staring down at him as he slipped on some slacks.

"What?" Damien said as he yawned and stretched his limbs outward.

Vincent zipped up his pants and pointed over to Kendall, "Your cousin's ass is thick."

Damien looked over to Kendall to find him laying butt naked, only one of his legs covered up safely.

"Shit," Damien said as he sat up and quickly covered Kendall, "Did anybody see him?"

"Nah, he just rolled over like that," Vincent said, "But I'm about to wake him up with this dick."

"Shut up, stop being such a ho."

"At least, I ain't a cousin fucker."

"He's not my real cousin," Damien said as he got up off the floor.

Vincent grabbed at Damien's dick, "Morning wood. And what a lovely morning it is."

Damien slapped Vincent's hand away as he adjusted his dick in his boxers. "Don't ever touch my dick like that again."

Vincent grabbed at Damien's dick again, "Stop it, you know you miss me."

Kendall coughed as he woke up to find Vincent with his hand in Damien's boxers, "What the fuck?"

Damien lightly pushed Vincent away, "I said stop touching me."

"Yeah," Kendall said as he sat up, "You gay all of a sudden now Vincent?"

"Aye, mind your business, thickums," Vincent said.

"How you gonna jack your dick to us fucking last night and then say mind my business? You crazy," Kendall said.

Vincent seductively rubbed at his jaw, "That was sexy last night. You should let me get some ass too."

"You don't want nothin from him, Kendall" Damien said, "He likes to use people. I know from experience."

Vincent looked to Damien, "So, first you gonna cut me off and now you cock blockin, I thought we were cool."

"We are cool," Damien said, "But not that cool."

"Yeah," Kendall said as he started to crawl over to Damien butt naked. He grabbed Damien's dick through his boxer hole. Kendall made eye contact with Vincent as he started to suck on the head of Damien's dick. Damien just stood there, the morning head sending tingles throughout his body. Kendall kept eye contact with a snarling Vincent as he deep throated Damien's dick. He pulled his lips from Damien's dick and gently kissed the head. "Only I can do that to him."

Vincent stuck his middle finger up at them and smirked, "Fuck y'all." He slipped on a shirt, "I'm going to watch football."

As Vincent left the room, Kendall resumed sucking on Damien's dick until he nutted down his throat.

Damien quivered as he released a sigh of ecstasy, "Kendall, you give some damn good head."

Kendall stood up and slipped on his underwear, "Because you inspire me. I'm only like this with you."

"What do you mean?"

"Drinking nut, fucking raw, I never do that shit. Man, your spirit makes me go beyond."

No matter how much Kendall admired him, Damien could not get into him romantically. "Oh, interesting."

Damien and Kendall finished getting dressed and joined everybody else, officially starting their Thanksgiving Day. Eric had arrived earlier and after catching up with his sons, joined the majority of the other men watching football. Bernice, her husband, and all the women cooked. The entire time all you could hear from the kitchen was Bernice making snarky comments to Kendall's mom, Monica. Kendall and Damien kept most of the younger kids entertained, playing football with them in the yard and just joking around until the food was finished.

The time everybody around the country was waiting for finally arrived, dinner time. Around the table family and friends gathered and Damien somehow ended up sitting between Vincent and Kendall. Too busy trying to stock his plate with food and listen to the various conversations around the table; he didn't know which one of them thought it was the right time to keep trying to play with his dick through his pants every other minute. All he could do was stay focused on the dinner and keep adjusting his sitting position in his seat.

"Bernice, "Eric said, "Now which one of these dishes did you pretend to make?"

Bernice, who sat at the head of the table in the biggest chair, rolled her eyes, "I made the beans."

"You mean you washed the beans," Monica, Kendall's heavyset mother, corrected.

Everybody around the table laughed, Bernice not finding any humor in Monica's words.

"I think Christmas should be strictly blood family this year, no pretenders," Bernice said.

"Oh the shade," Shannon said. She looked at Marion, "Baby, your auntie don't play."

Marion just shrugged off her comment and kept stuffing his mouth with food.

"Now why you gonna say shit like that, Bernice," Eric called out, "That shit ain't cool."

Bernice rolled her eyes, "Then spend Christmas with Monica, Eric. We all know you rather it be just you and her."

"Excuse me," Monica snapped.

"Don't play dumb Monica, everybody knows you want my sister's husband," Bernice pointed out.

"I never had the thought," Monica argued, "Don't try to slander me because you're jealous."

Bernice brushed back her braided hair, "Jealous of what? Your apartment? Your associates' degree?"

"No, the fact that your own sister told me that she was dying before you," Bernice pointed out, "The fact that your sister wanted me to walk her down the aisle at her wedding in place of y'all father, not you. The fact that your sister watched my son every summer but barely could tolerate your brat for a weekend. Oh, and maybe because on her deathbed she reached for me and said, 'sister, I love you'."

Bernice sat, doing her best to look unbothered, "Well at least my son isn't a faggot."

It was as if a bomb just went off in the room and everybody around the table was shell-shocked.

"What?" Kendall uttered out, "I ain't gay."

Bernice chuckled, "Monica, my dare sister told me how you called her crying because you found naked pictures of men on your son's phone one night. How you opened an app called jacket or jacked and saw him butt naked, claiming to be versatile or oral friendly. Now, if that's not enough proof that he's a faggot, then I don't know what to say."

"Versatile," A confused Eric said as he looked at Kendall, "What the fuck does that mean?"

"He tops and bottoms," Shannon blurted out, "Don't act like none of y'all don't know what that means."

Tears started to rain down Kendall's face. Damien, feeling mortified for him, couldn't even bring himself to make eye contact with Kendall. It was just a frightening moment, Damien imagining himself being next on Bernice's hit list. Kendall got up and stormed from the table.

His mom Monica followed behind him. Everybody sat in silence as Kendall cussed and yelled at his mother, who could only tearfully apologize for sharing her discovery with anybody. Kendall grabbed his things and stormed from the house. After grabbing all that she could of her belongings, Monica followed her son out the door, begging for him to stop walking away from her.

Bernice took a bite of her turkey, “And Eric don’t let me get started on your kids.”

“My sons ain’t gay,” Eric said. “They better not be.”

His word stabbed Damien like a knife. Damien tried to stay composed and not shed a tear.

Bernice turned her eyes to Marion, “This morning my neighbor told me she saw Marion and his little girlfriend last night, sneaking out in my backyard to smoke some weed. I trust my neighbor’s words, so I don’t even want to hear any excuses. And Damien, he’s quiet, too quiet, which means he’s hiding something and doing his best not to slip up and say what it is. He adopted that behavior from my sister. She raised her boys to be just like her, conniving and irresponsible. Everybody was blinded by her innocence, not me. I knew of the devil she hid inside.”

Marion shot up from his seat, “Bitch don’t be talkin about my mom like that!”

Bernice motioned at Marion, “See, she raised a thug. He’s going to grow up to be nothing.”

“And you raised a punk ass bitch,” Damien said, not letting her trash his brother and mom, “Big Mike is a big ass punk.”

“Y’all calm down now,” Eric said, “We don’t act like this around family.”

“Daddy how you gonna let this bitch trash momma like that,” Marion argued.

“Cause I know they lies,” Eric said, “I know Bernice’s game; she can’t make me act out.”

“I’m just being real,” Bernice said, “Anybody wants more wine?”

"Fuck this," Marion said, "Y'all get your bags, we leaving right now. Daddy, stay if you want, we out."

"If that's what y'all gonna do, I respect that son," Eric said, "Bernice ain't going to ruin my holidays though."

Damien agreed with his brother, it was time to go. "Be good daddy," Damien said as he got up.

"I will. And aye, call your cousin Kendall. He need some support. Verse this, top that, what the fuck."

"Yeah, I will," Damien said, knowing he would want the same if the roles were reversed.

Damien, Vincent, Shannon and Marion grabbed their bags and left. Marion first to get inside of the car. Everybody else joined him in soon after, Shannon in the front already texting away about what had happened, and Vincent in the back with Damien looking as if he was the one who just had his sexual life spilled out in front of everybody. Damien knew exactly what Vincent was feeling, and they both feared to encounter what Kendall had experienced today. No matter what it was, nobody liked a spotlight shone on their secrets.

Marion started the car but immediately cut it back off, "I need some air first. I'll be back."

He got out of the car and started to walk down the block.

"I'm going to go talk to him," Damien said as he got out of the car and followed after his brother.

Marion looked to Damien as he caught up with him, "I can't stand her."

"Nobody can. I wish I was as strong as daddy to put up with her," Damien said.

"Man, daddy sat in there like a bitch though. I had to speak up. Blood shouldn't treat blood like that."

Damien hated to make this about him, but the moment was fitting, "You treat me like that."

"When?" Marion said as he stopped and got in Damien's face, huffing and puffing.

"Right now, every time I try to talk to you, ever since momma died."

Marion aggressively poked Damien in the chest, "Because momma told me to take care of you before she died, she told me to make sure you were alright, even though I was losing her too. She was always babying you, even making us lie to you when she first found out she was sick. Always, she lied to you but made me deal with the truth. I knew when the lights were disconnected, but she told you we were just playing a spooky game. When we didn't have food, I knew we were starving, but she would just tell you we were playing who couldn't eat for the longest."

Damien remembered those childhood moments. "Yeah, and?"

"She wasn't preparing you from the real world, so I have too. I'm not goin to baby you, treat you like some innocent lil kid. We both men now and we gotta be tough, especially with an aunt like Bernice who want us to fail cause she got issues with our momma. I'm not gonna hold your hand, this call tough love, nigga."

Damien understood his brother's point, "Still, I feel as if I was getting jumped, you wouldn't help me."

"Nah, but I would teach you how to fight so you can kick some ass next round."

"But I would jump in to help you."

A tear streamed down Marion's face, "I know that. Cause you got a soft heart, like momma had for you."

Damien hadn't seen his brother cry since their mother's funeral, "Why is that a bad thing?"

"It' ain't. But it does mean I gotta toughen you up even harder."

"Can you at least say you love me? Once as men."

Marion wiped his face clean of tears using his hand, "Ain't that a lil gay?"

"We brothers, our love is different, you know that. Stop making excuses."

Marion took a moment and in a hushed toned said, "I love you."

"I love you too, Marion," Damien said as a big smile formed on his face.

Marion lightly smacked him in the face, "Come on with the smiling shit, you makin this awkward."

"I'm sorry, I'm happy. I thought you fucking hated me."

"No, you okay. I hate Kendall, but guess we gotta help him out of his situation too now."

"You cool with him being gay?" Damien asked, looking for a little room to come out to his brother in the future.

"I mean, gay niggas gotta love too. We good though, we normal. Kendall still annoying, but different now."

Damien didn't want his brother to think of him as abnormal. "Yeah. You good enough to drive now?"

Marion nodded, "Yeah, let's get back to NC. I'm ready to ditch Shannon, bitch pussy got a scent, you know?"

No, Damien didn't know and most likely never would. "Ew, now imma keep tryin to smell for it on the ride back."

Marion shook his head and chuckled as he started back to the car. On the ride back, Damien did find himself trying to sniff for Shannon's stench, but couldn't pick up on it. As they got back in NC, Vincent started to loosen up a bit, getting back to his regular self by calling which ever girl he was going to hang with tonight. Marion surprisingly didn't make Damien catch a taxi back to campus, dropping him off for the first time at his dorm.

The first thing Damien did when he got in his room was call Kendall, but it went directly to voicemail. Damien felt safe back in his dorm room, his secret once again not in danger of being exposed to anybody in his family for now. He realized that this was a security Kendall no longer had. It made him feel so bad for him that he called again only to get sent to voicemail once more. Damien could only hope that Kendall was fine and not thinking crazy.

Damien needed a distraction, something to get his mind off the grim subject of Kendall's outing. He knew exactly what person could cheer him up a bit. Damien scrolled through his phone contacts and listed under the letter 'M' was the one and only, Max. He sent him a text simply stating, 'I'm back'.

14 - Guidance

Marion was throwing a big welcome back party to wrap up the end of the Thanksgiving holiday break. Soon, everybody would be glued to their text books studying for the semester finals. NC Tech had a zero tolerance policy when it came to students not successfully passing all their courses each semester, the school infamous for its high dropout rates. The school had no choice to initiate this policy, making sure only those confident enough to pass all courses enrolled into their school.

But before buckling down, some students were letting loose at Marion's party including Damien who was surprisingly invited by his brother. He wanted Leon to come with him but his roommate hadn't returned from holiday break yet. Instead of sitting around an exchanging weird, but entertaining text with Max, he went to the party. Damien didn't feel like an outcast this time around, feeling as if his brother told his friends to be cool with him.

Not only did Damien get to participate in and lose a pushup contest, he also played truth or dare and ended up making out with a girl who mouth tasted as if she chewed cigarettes for a living. It was a big change seeing his brother look at him with a somewhat smile, instead of his usual snarl. As for Vincent, he was being himself, the center of the attention and walking around with body paint on his chest.

Damien went to use the bathroom. As he started to pee Vincent joined him.

Vincent sat on the edge of the tub. "Are you having fun?"

Damien did his best to pee without Vincent seeing his dick. "Yeah, why are you in here?"

"I need to chill out for a minute."

Damien finished peeing and zipped up his pants. He sat on the sink counter. "You do need to calm down."

"I'm on some kind of pill now that has me feeling like I'm floating."

"A ho and drug addict?"

Vincent laughed, "Damn, you just described my parents. I'm not though, I like having fun."

"Nah, you're spoiled. People throw themselves at you, I fell for it myself."

"I can still get you though, but for now looks like you into your cousin."

"He's not my cousin," Damien corrected for the millionth time, "And we're not together."

"Oh, well have you heard from him since your aunt fucked up his life? Shit, left me traumatized for a bit."

Damien shook his head, "Nope, I tried calling him but no answers at all."

Marion poked his head inside of the bathroom, "Aye, what y'all doing in here?"

"Talking about Bernice," Damien said.

"And just chilling," Vincent added.

Marion nodded, "Alright, I ain't gonna let her name ruin my night. Imma go try to get some bitch naked."

Vincent laughed as Marion left and shut the door. He looked to Damien, "Man, girls love your brother."

"He's with a new girl all the time though, he's been like that since high school," Damien said.

"Cause he has that dark mysterious thing going on and I heard he got a big dick, so that could be it."

Damien covered his ears and laughed, "Come on with that man, I don't want to know that about my brother."

Into the bathroom stumbled a short, built guy with low-cut hair. "Sup," he leisurely greeted.

Vincent pointed at him, "Damien this is frat brother Noah, Noah this is Marion's lil bro Damien."

Noah nodded at Damien, "Sup lil dude."

Damien found himself a bit intimidated by Noah's presence, the guy handsome. "Hey."

Noah looked to Vincent, "Wait, this the lil dude, right?"

Vincent nodded, "Yeah it's him."

Noah whipped his dick out and started to pee, "I heard you got a mushroom dick head, lil man?"

"What?" Damien said, caught off guard by the question.

"He's cool Damien," Vincent said, "Noah, one of us. You know..."

"Oh," Damien said, still uncool with the question, "You told people about me?"

Vincent rolled his eyes, "Don't pretend like you don't tell people about me. And I just told Noah, cause he cool."

"I don't tell people about you...well, Leon knows," Damien said, giving up on his argument.

Noah finished peeing but kept his dick out, "I'm drunk ass fuck, you dudes wanna fuck?"

Vincent bit his bottom lip as he stood up and locked the bathroom door. Noah dropped his shorts and briefs to around his ankles, revealing his toned muscled thighs and ass. Vincent unzipped his pants, pulled out his dick, and as if they had done this plenty times before, he started to slowly fuck a smiling Noah.

Vincent looked to Damien as he kept stroking, "See, Noah is my fav Fratboy."

Damien just sat there watching, his dick hard.

Noah looked to Damien, his eyes rolling with each stroke into him, "You want me to suck your dick?"

"Or you can get back here and eat my ass," Vincent said.

Damien wanted to say yes to both offers, but knew this was only a one way ticket back into Vincent's world of games. He was cool with Vincent, but wasn't going to cave to his sexually spoiled commands. Damien slid from the sink counter, adjusted his dick in his pants, and slipped out of the bathroom leaving them to finish alone. He heard the bathroom door be locked as he walked away.

Marion walked up to Damien, "You okay?"

"Yeah, I had to get out of there. Vincent and that Noah guy are getting high," Damien lied.

Marion shook his head, "I aint the mood to sit up in no bathroom smoking, I got a room for that."

"I'm going to try to find a ride to campus."

"Nah, chill out in my room. But your ass ain't sleeping in my bed. I'll drop you off in the morning."

"Alright, cool."

Damien decided to withdraw himself from the party and headed into his brother's room. Even though his bed was nearly big enough to fit four people, Damien chilled out on the floor, sure this was just more of Marion's tough love treatment. He played around on his phone, until he drifted off to sleep. He awoke the next morning being lightly kicked in the side.

Damien opened his eyes to find a shirtless Vincent standing over him. "What," He yawned out.

Vincent sat down on the floor, "Sorry, about last night. You know, for fucking Noah in front of you."

"He's sexy ass fuck, but that's not my thing. Don't apologize for being you though."

"I want to change that about me though, cause I sort of like Noah, legit like him."

"Stop lying," Damien said as he softly chuckled, "No way you'll stop having sex with everything."

"Hell no, I'm too young for that shit. But still, I want Noah to be down with me once I'm over it."

"I don't think it can work that way. Unless you guys have like an open relationship."

"I know," Vincent nodded, "But I don't like the idea of him being with others dudes besides me."

"Yet, you basically wanted a threesome last night."

"But I was there," Vincent said, "I'm cool with that."

"Man, you're confusing."

Vincent shrugged, "All this shit is confusing, being bi or whatever is a lot. There's nobody I can ask for advice."

"I go online, some of them were right about you. They told me not to fall for you, I did, then I learned my lesson."

Vincent smirked, "For real? Man, fuck those basement living niggas."

"Most of them are men just like you and me, with nobody out there to guide them through this gay jungle."

"Yeah," Vincent nodded, "Aye, want me to take you to campus? Your brotha knocked out in the front."

"That'll be cool. Can you buy me some breakfast too?"

Vincent chuckled as he stood up, "Dude I ain't your man."

Damien got up off the floor, "Nah, you just cheap."

Vincent playfully punched Damien in the arm, and they played fight back and forth. Damien liked where his relationships with Marion and Vincent now stood. He could actually party with them without feeling revolted. Being around them was starting to remind him of the days when his mother was alive, it was a great feeling.

15 - Real

It was the final week of Damien's first semester of college and he'd never been so happy. For the next few months he wouldn't have to attend mind numbing classes or type an essay. He was completely free from the world of hospitality. As for exams, he hadn't received his scores yet and hoped he made enough C's to move forward into the next semester. He awoke this morning to find Leon packing up his side of their room. Damien saw Leon a lot less, especially since he started officially dating his once study buddy, but now girlfriend, Megan.

Leon looked over his shoulder at Damien, "Wake up dude, you gotta start packin."

Damien sat up, "I will, but first I have to meet with my advisor and then thou who shall not be named."

"Oh, your secret love interest. You whack for not telling me who he is."

Damien promised Max he would keep their odd friendship super discrete. "I have to keep my word on this one."

"But I tell you about Megan."

"Too damn much," Damien joked, "Megan rolled over, Megan breathed, Megan took a shit."

Leon laughed, "Shut up, man. Imma miss rooming with you. Hands down, best dude I know on campus."

"Are you sure you and Megan are ready to share an apartment next semester?"

Leon faced Damien, "We bonded. The entire holidays I texted her twenty-four seven. We'll be traveling the entire summer together too. She's the one."

"Do you see yourself marrying her before graduation?"

"I would like that," Leon said as he got back to packing.

Damien was happy for Leon, but couldn't see himself getting into that mindset again. He was doing fine with this 'just friends' motto. Of course Max was making that very hard to maintain, he was coming on very strong. Damien couldn't even imagine how Max would behave later when they would meet up for a date. Max picked KFC as the location and no mattered how hard Damien mocked the location, he refused to change his mind.

After a shower, change of clothes, and a stale donut for breakfast, Damien found himself sitting in the office of his advisor. The woman, who looked like a retired WNBA player, chatted on her phone behind her desk as if Damien hadn't been sitting there for the last ten minutes waiting for her to address him.

She finally hung up her phone, "Chile, my sister is crazy. Have you seen the show Diva Doctors?"

Damien didn't but sadly knew one of the stars, his aunt. "Nope."

"Well, my sister swears she's the look-a-like of one of the doctor's. Bernice?"

"Never seen it, Miss Leslie."

"Not even a commercial?" Leslie asked as she adjusted her red framed glasses.

"I don't watch TV," Damien lied.

"Well, with these grades it seems like that's all you do," Leslie said as she clicked opened a file on her desktop computer,

"Damien, you didn't pass one single course. It's just ridiculous, because based on your placement tests you're a smart young man. Not even a C, you've got D's all across the board. Your GPA is just abysmal."

Damien was at least expecting to pass one class. "Are you for real?"

Leslie nodded as she double-checked, "My eyes don't deceive me." She looked to Damien, "I've invited you here to inform you that you're officially being placed on academic suspension. It simply means NC Tech is going to give you the next semester off to rethink your educational goals and possibly enroll in a college that'll better fit those goals."

"I'm being kicked out?" Damien asked.

"Technically, yes. Ninety percent of those on academic suspension rarely return. I'm sorry but this school is really serious about maintaining our graduation rate after nearly a decade of poor numbers."

Damien was almost glad to be free from college; he just wasn't looking forward to telling his father. "Damn."

"If you have any questions about the process I can answer them for you."

Damien stood up, "Not really. I mean, what's done is done. I failed and this is the result."

"Thank you for not crying, I've had to give out a lot of tissue today."

"Nah, I'm cool. Bye, I guess," Damien said as he waved at Leslie and left her office.

Damien knew he should be upset, in tears, disappointed in himself, but he wasn't. He was glad he would not have to come back to NC Tech next semester, because he never wanted to be here in the first place. The only good thing about coming here was becoming friends with Leon and expanding his list of sexual partners. He just kept walking to KFC as if it was an ordinary day, his educational failure an afterthought.

As Damien arrived to the parking lot, a car horn sounded. He faced the car to find Max in the driver's seat.

Damien entered the passenger's side of the red hooptie. "Nice car," Damien sarcastically said with a smirk.

Max gripped the steering wheel and stared him up and down, "Man, you look so amazing."

"I'm wearing jeans and a hoody," Damien said, "I always look like this."

"And to me you always look amazing. I just wanna lick your lips."

Damien smiled, "You always manage to say something creepy, but cute. So, are we going inside?"

"Hell no, I'm not eating no damn KFC, especially with anotha nigga."

"People might think we just homeboys."

Max rolled his eyes, "Please, you mad clockable."

"Why, because I don't look like I'm on steroids. Don't be an asshole, man."

"Let's get off that topic, because we not even here to eat. I wanted to show you something." Max pointed forward through the windows of the KFC. "I want you to keep your attention on the register area. You'll see why we're here once you see him. Then, we gonna have a talk."

"See who?" Damien asked.

The second he finished his question, Tyler, wearing a KFC uniform, approached the register to ring up a customer.

Damien narrowed his eyes, confused, "Um, are we stalking Tyler?"

"No," Max said, "I want to show you the life of a fake, dishonest, man. Yeah, Tyler drives a nice car, but he works at KFC, is the manager at Khols, and some weekends work at that gay club Shane's. Ain't nothin wrong with his hustle, I just don't like that dudes like him only tell half the story to lure dude's like us into their lives. It's easy for them to get a dude, cause they hide all their flaws and cover them up with exaggerated truths."

"Oh, yeah that's not cool but there are no hard feelings between Tyler and me. He was sorta just a hookup."

Max started the car and drove away, "That's not the point I'm trying to make. Just listen, instead of coming at you with a bunch of exaggerated truths I want to give you the real me. I love to play football and it's all I ever wanted to do, the idea of doing something else strikes fear into my heart. My dad is a pastor for a struggling church, my mom babysits kids for free, so I grew up poor and I'm still poor. My fifteen year old sister has a baby and doesn't know the father and my six year old brother has the vocabulary of an infant. I think you cute, I like the sound of your voice, and I sleep in your boxers I took some nights. I refuse to offer you a fake story. This is all real."

Max turned down a dirt trail into a wooded area as Damien contemplated all that was just poured out to him. He now understood the comparison Max was trying to make between himself and Tyler. Damien respected what he just did and that he liked him enough to do that. It was enough for Damien to put down his walls, get rid of that just friends motto, not expecting Max to pull out any surprises or intentionally hurt him emotionally.

"It takes a lot to be that honest, especially in the gay dating scene," Damien said.

"I'm telling you, it's the only way you weed out the fake dudes, by sharing your raw truth."

Max stopped the car as they arrived to a clearing in the woods that had a couple of picnic tables.

"Well, your truth doesn't scare me," Damien said.

Max breathed a sigh of relief, "You serious?"

"Yeah, it's not like I'm from the Hamptons or some shit. So why are we out here?"

Max got out of the car and Damien followed after him.

"Because I'm DL," Max said, "And places like this, in the middle of nowhere allow me to escape and be myself for a few hours. I hope that's another truth you'll accept about me. We not going to be kissin and holding hands in public, I'll tell my homeboys you're my tutor, and my parents won't even know you exist, because I don't want to be a gay football player. I just wanna play ball. But still, I want to date you, know your truth."

"My roommate Leon is my only friend, I hate Love and Hip Hop, I suck at giving head, and I'm on academic probation aka officially kicked out of school," Damien revealed, followed by a heavy sigh as he got all of that off his chest, "There, now you know a bit about me."

"I want to know more of your truth."

"And you will learn it. Because I like the idea of possibly dating you."

"The same," Max said as he approached Damien, "So, you got kicked out of school?"

"Yup, but I'm fine. I'm cool."

Max hugged his arms around Damien, "Shut up, no you're not. Nobody's fine with something like that."

As Max held him, this is when it all hit Damien. He messed up and failed out of college. "My dad is gonna kill me."

"Do you know what I'm going to do to make it a lil better though?" Max asked.

Damien shook his head, "No."

Max leaned forward and kissed him on the lips. Damien kissed him back, already feeling a little better.

****

16 - President

All it took was a morning shift to actually make Damien miss attending college, but his academic suspension was a mistake he now had to live with. Instead of going back home after being put on academic suspension, Damien found a job at the first place to hire him. He spent two months living with Marion and Vincent until he could find a place of his own. It was much easier explaining to his father why he wouldn't be returning to school over the phone, simply removing the phone from his ear when the man started to cuss and mention how much his mother would be disappointed with his failure.

And his job wasn't that bad, he got to work alongside a staff and customer base that was dominantly male at Aerostyle. Being in a relationship meant all the beautiful men around him were hands off, but that didn't stop him from checking out some of the gay men who would spend hours trying on clothes or some of the straight men who were dragged into the store by their significant other. The pay was decent and unlike college, he actually exceled at what he did here, customer service.

A man with ginger red hair approached Damien in the denim section, "Hey, are these jeans too tight?"

Damien stopped organizing jeans and did a double-take at the man's butt without appearing to be staring directly at it. "Um, are you going for the skinny fit?"

"Yeah, but at the same time I don't want to attract the wrong type...you know...dudes."

Damien softly chuckled, "Come on, everybody likes attention."

"Yeah, but I don't want the ladies to think I'm not trying to get there's."

"Understandable, I would go one size up. And actually, if you sign up for the store credit card you can walk away with two pairs for half the price. Just grab the pairs you like, go up to the register and let the cashier know that Damien sent you and you want a store membership card. Trust me; it'll save you a lot of money when you come back in the future. And imagine the ladies you'll get wearing our brand."

The man shrugged, "Alright, that all sounds good to me," And walked away to find a better fit.

Unlike some of his co-workers, Damien was actually good at selling membership cards. Plus, it was an extra ten dollars on his paycheck for every one sold. Being actually good at his job was bitter sweet, the sweet being that he made a lot of money and got a lot of hours. And the bitter being that he had less time with Max and more hate was thrown his way from his uptight co-workers. There was one co-worker who didn't openly hate him, but who Damien couldn't stand, the store manager Lincoln.

Lincoln, tall and narrow and wearing dark slacks, a sweater vest, and tie, approached Damien, "Excuse me."

Damien forced a smile as he stopped folding jeans, "Yeah, what's up?"

"Did you read the schedule?"

"Of course," Damien said, "That's why I'm here."

"You're supposed to be working the register only today."

Damien shrugged, "I switched. I work better on the floor and sell more cards."

"And? In the end, you're still disrespecting me, your boss. You work where I tell you to work."

"I'm not a child, so don't talk to me like that," Damien said, trying not to come off too angry.

"If you start respecting me, I'll start respecting you, understand?"

Damien didn't feel like listening to his manager-talk anymore. "Fine, I'll go work the register."

"And before you do that, I thought you should know that Aerostyle has started this whole second chances program, hiring reformed inmates for tax credits. I just got a call from corporate confirming one new hire under this program. He starts tomorrow and as my best employee, I'm putting you in charge of training him."

Damien just felt as Lincoln was pawning off this new hire all on him. "Are you sure?"

"I'm sure. Figuratively speaking I'm the president here and you're all members of my cabinet. Think about it Damien, do you think Obama will train every new person hired at the EPA or Homeland Security, no; it'll be one of the underlings in his cabinet. In this situation, that's you." Lincoln said as he poked Damien in the chest.

Damien did not understand Lincoln's obsession with Obama and all things politics. "Fine, I guess."

"And don't mess this up, it'll make me look bad and ruin my chances of becoming store manager in Charlotte."

"I said fine, I'll train the inmate. But if he shanks me I'm suing this company."

Lincoln let out his fake laugh that he usually displayed when he was attempting to fit in with the other employees and walked away. Not wanting Lincoln to come back and nag him later, Damien took his spot at a register and worked his shift there until it was time to leave. He drove home in the piece of car that he had managed to purchase from a seller in a trailer park that rattled and had a broken speedometer.

Damien pulled up to the neighborhood he called home, West Town Apartments. The complex was mostly occupied by single moms, the elderly and struggling families who had six to a two bedroom apartment. There was about one violent crime every two months and luckily for Damien, he wasn't a victim of any of them.

Damien parked and to avoid talking to his neighbors, he played around on Instagram as he walked to his apartment door. On his former roommate Leon's page were mostly pictures of him and his girlfriend celebrating their one year anniversary. Kendall's page only had a few updates, one simply a selfie of him staring directly into the camera with the hashtag '#harshtimes'. Over the year, Damien tried getting in contact with Kendall, but it felt as if the roles were now reversed. Kendall seemed to be ignoring Damien, Marion and even their father.

Damien arrived to his one bedroom apartment and entered. He didn't have much furniture, but he considered this an upgrade from living with Vincent and Marion who threw parties almost every other night. Plus being so far from campus now only made him think less about his failed college life.

Damien entered his bedroom and jumped a little when he discovered Max sitting on his bed reading a textbook and only wearing black ankle socks.

"What if somebody was with me?" Damien said with a smirk, "You would be lookin real suspect right now."

Max closed his book and put it away revealing his soft dick, "Nobody else should be comin inside your room."

Damien started walking towards his bed, "I missed you today."

Max held his hand up, "Wait, take your clothes off first."

"Why? I really want to lie down, my legs are hurting."

"Please," Max said with a pout as he reached into his backpack that was placed beside the bed.

Damien slowly started to strip naked, "Alright, but only because you cute."

Max pulled a red jockstrap out of his backpack. "Put this on," He said as he tossed them at Damien.

Damien caught the jockstrap, "These again? Where's the football jersey?"

"I forgot it, I left it at the dorm," Max nodded at Damien, "Now put them on and get over here."

After remembering which holes to put his legs through, Damien slipped on the jockstrap. As he slowly climbed on the bed, doing his best to be seductive, Max's dick started to get hard. Max lay back and put his hands behind his head, his muscles flexing. Damien climbed on top of Max and hugged his butt cheeks around his dick, no desire of allowing actual entry into him. Max's eyes rolled back in his head as Damien slowly started to dry hump his dick.

Damien did his best to appear as if he was enjoying this, but on the inside he was feeling little pleasure. This is what his sex life had become, frustrating. Max didn't bottom and he didn't either, but at least Damien gave head when in the mood, unlike Max who never even bothered. Max just loved his dick to be worshipped while Damien got nothing but a gorgeous man to stare at. Max started to moan and Damien could feel his warm nut draining down his legs. Damien leaned forward and kissed him on the lips.

Damien was still entertained by Max, but not in the bedroom. He forced himself to accept that in a relationship there had to be compromise, but he wanted Max to at least budge a little in the bedroom.

The next morning, Damien arrived to work not looking forward to training an ex inmate. Lincoln gave him an hour long run down of what training aspects he wanted Damien to focus on and company policies. Damien figured Lincoln was better off simply training the new employee himself instead of making him sit through all of this policy talk again.

After he was free from the presence of Lincoln, Damien roamed the sales floor until he was approached by a guy who was tattooed down from his face to his wrists. He wore some black, sagging sweatpants, a white tanktop, and unstrung, dingy combat boots. Damien figured the guy roamed into the wrong store, but his Aerostyle name tag was a dead giveaway of who he was.

Damien tried to read his nametag, "So uh...you're-"

"-Zyan," He said as he pointed at his nametag, "You the Damien nigga...I mean dude."

Damien tried not to laugh, "Yeah, that's me."

"The tall manager dude said you're training me or something. You want me to fold shirts or some shit?"

"His name is Lincoln."

"Yeah, him," Zyan said, "I got bored listening to him talk, I couldn't even remember his damn name."

"I like you already, he's a legit boring ass dude but can fire us, so just pretend he's the shit."

"I got you my dude," Zyan said, "So um, we folding shirts?"

"That's the basics, but we gotta do more than that. If somebody looks lost, we ask them if they need help or something. We find what they need, try to sell them a membership card, and then point them in the direction of the register," Damien explained even though Zyan didn't seem to be paying attention, "Got it?"

"Yup," Zyan answered as he snapped back into reality, "I ain't gonna be doing all of that."

"I was that way at first, but you'll start. For now, simply try to sell them what you would wear."

Zyan tugged at his tanktop, "I don't wear shit from here though."

"Then lie. Just point out whatever the mannequins are wearing."

"Man, I just thought I would be folding and stocking. I ain't really into selling shit from China to people or dealing with dumbasses."

Damien nodded, "I understand that, people are idiots. Why did you decide to work here then?"

"I had too, it was one of the reasons I got released early. I promised to work and then get my own place."

"Well being here is just a lil bit better than being in a jail cell."

Zyan laughed, "You a funny dude, Damien. I like that."

"Nah, everybody else here is just boring as hell. Anyways, let me show you around the store."

As Damien gave the tour, he could tell Zyan didn't care. Zyan just kept accidentally knocking things over, mean mugging shoppers, or day dreaming. Damien was into more clean-cut guys, but found himself getting into Zyan's whole tattooed and rough around the edges look. All of a sudden, training Zyan wasn't all that bad especially cause he had a cute face and his butt looked nice in a sagging pair of sweatpants.

At lunch, Damien and Zyan ate across the street at a Subway.

"Dawg, I'm so damn bored at that store," Zyan complained.

"That's why I like it when it's busy, time flies," Damien said.

"I can't take it. And that Lincoln nigga just seems like the type to fire you for even breathing too hard."

Damien laughed, "I think he knows nobody likes him, so he tries to scare us into respecting him."

"I ain't scared of him; I'll beat his ass with a hanger."

"Aye, if you don't mind me asking, why were you in jail?"

Zyan shrugged, "Cause cops are bitches."

"No, why were you really in jail?"

"Same ole same ole, selling weed outside a club. It helped my mom pay the bills and kept clothes on my back. I made more money doing that. Now I'm folding fucking shirts and catching the bus to and from everywhere. A life like this makes you wanna get high. I don't know how you do it."

Damien felt sort of bad for him, "Where do you live? I can drop you off?"

"In those townhouses behind that old Target."

Damien knew the area; it was mostly occupied by hood folk who could afford not to live on Government assistance.

"I'll save you the bus ride and take you home."

Zyan reached across the table and dapped Damien, “Because you my nigga, cool, cool.”

Damien didn’t know why he liked Zyan so much, he was just glad to have somebody at work who wasn’t either intimidated by Lincoln or one of his henchmen. They returned to work and instead of focusing on training, they spent a lot of time making fun of customers and trying to avoid a lurking Lincoln. Once it was time to go, they headed out and got into Damien’s car.

“Yo, this is a nice car,” Zyan said as he played with the broken buttons on the dashboard.

“No it’s not,” Damien said as he started his rattling car and pulled off.

“Trust me dude, compared to a bus full of broke niggas, this car is a lambo.”

“Alright, alright, I’ll take your word for it.”

Zyan lounged back in the passenger seat, “So, you got a girl?”

“Nope, it’s just me. You?”

“I ain’t got no car and live with my mom and sis, no bitch would want me.”

Damien was close to saying being cute and funny should be enough. “You’ll find the one.”

Zyan shrugged as he sat up, “Aye, let me tell you where to drive before we end up in the wrong part of the hood.”

Zyan directed Damien through an area with a lot of low budget shopping centers, abandoned buildings and failing infrastructure. The place where Zyan called home, his mother’s townhouse, was located in a neighborhood near a trailer park and an abandoned Target. It was one of the nicer homes Damien saw in the area.

Damien pulled into the parking lot of the townhouse. “If you ever need a ride from work, just ask.”

“Definitely,” Zyan nodded toward the townhouse, “Don’t be rude though, come meet the fam.”

“For real?”

"Yeah, they good people. Just don't be lookin at my lil sister."

Damien laughed, "I won't, I'll keep my eyes on the floor."

"Nah, I mean she's just fourteen, so that shit would be fucked up if I caught you lookin."

"Oh, I'm not into that shit at all."

Zyan got out of the car and Damien followed his lead into the townhouse. A young girl was on the couch watching Teen Mom as if it was the most interesting show in the world. Zyan introduced Damien as they kept walking through the neatly organized townhouse, but the girl didn't even acknowledge them. Damien followed Zyan into the kitchen to where his mother was cooking baked chicken and prepping some mac and cheese.

"Mom," Zyan said, "This Damien, from the job. He's the dude training me."

The woman, who had freckled dark spots on her cheeks, greeted Damien, "Hey, sweetie."

"Nice to meet you, it smells good in here," Damien said.

"Enough for two only, I'll start cooking for Zyan when he follows the rules."

"I'm a twenty-four year old man momma; I ain't following no damn curfew."

"I understand that but three in the morning is too damn late to be strolling in my house and to make matters worse you always bringing somebody in here with you. I told you, no company unless you ask me, and no more smoking weed in my house. Your sister went to school one day smelling like I ain't raised her right," His mother said.

"They called me Snoop Dogg," His sister shouted from the living room.

"Cause you got a dog ass face," Zyan snapped backed.

"Your sister looks just like me," His mom pointed out, "And I ain't no dog."

Zyan nodded upstairs, "Come on Damien, they being sensitive."

Zyan started upstairs and Damien followed him to his bedroom. As Damien entered Zyan's bedroom, his nose was hit by the scent of weed. And judging by the cannabis plant poster on Zyan's wall, he was a big fan of smoking. Zyan kicked off his boots, grabbed a shoebox from on his dresser, and sat on his bed.

Zyan used the materials from the box to roll a blunt. "You smoke?"

"Nope, I don't mind if you do though. I lived in a dorm; I've been around it a lot."

Zyan nodded as he lit the blunt and took a puff, "So, you a college dude?"

"Not anymore, I basically failed out."

Zyan laughed, "Dumb ass."

"Fuck you, it was torture."

Zyan fanned his hand at him, "I'm just messin with you. Man, you know what smoking does to me?"

"Makes you hungry? Too bad your mom ain't cooking for you, you're grounded man."

Zyan laughed, "Nah, I can feed myself. But smoking makes my dick hard as fuck."

Damien never heard of weed making that happen. "Oh."

"Aye, no gay shit, but you wanna jack off together? It's more fun with yah nigga."

His sex life a bore, no way Damien was going to pass on this. "Alright."

Zyan put out his blunt and nodded at his room door, "Make sure that door lock, then come on over here."

His dick already hard in his pants, Damien locked Zyan's room door. As he started back to the bed, Zyan whipped out his own dick and used some spit to lube it up. Damien was more of an ass man, but he was impressed with what Zyan was packing. It was one of the biggest dicks he'd seen in person and its veins were so defined.

Damien lay back beside Zyan and did his best to pretend not to be that interested in watching Zyan play with his dick. After unbuttoning his pants, Damien started to jack his own dick and unlike him, Zyan wasn't too shy about watching him. Zyan started to smirk and laugh as he continued playing with his dick.

At one point Zyan ended up reaching his hand over, and jacking both of their dicks at the same time. This was enough to make a sexually frustrated Damien nut a river that went flowing down Zyan's hand. Zyan nutted seconds after, it spurting from his dick and mostly landing on his neck and face. They both just lay there, staring at the ceiling, breathing heavily, feeling closer than ever since they'd met.

17 - Blackness

It wasn't cheating, Damien told himself. There was no actual sex involved, just mutual masturbation, he justified. It wasn't a moment of passion, but instead just some cheap pleasure to fill the void of his dull sex life with Max, He declared. In Damien's heart, Max was still number one, especially after being together for nearly a year. But in his pants, Zyan lit a spark that had gone dull. It would've been much easier to calm his flame if he didn't have to work around Zyan today.

Just a day after their masturbation session, Damien found himself confined to the dressing room area of the store training Zyan. He had already taken him through all the rules and regulations, and the remainder of his dressing room training session was all hands on. Luckily, it was a slow day and they found themselves doing their best not to go insane from boredom.

Zyan started browsing a rack of clothing that needed to be sorted, "I'm going to try some stuff on."

"I thought you didn't wear Aerostyle."

Zyan shrugged, "Yeah, but that nigga Lincoln said I better start soon. He ain't firing my ass."

"I like the clothes to be honest, try some shit on and I'll tell you if it fits your personality though."

Zyan grabbed a handful of clothes and went inside the dressing room in the rear, one of the policies employees had to follow on or off the clock. Damien waited at the front fitting room desk area until he heard snickering coming from Zyan's dressing room. After making sure no customers were coming to interrupt, Damien made his way to Zyan's dressing room door.

"What are you laughing at?" Damien asked through the door.

"Man, I think I'm wearing these skinny jeans wrong."

"Let me see, you might need a bigger size."

Zyan opened the dressing room door. He stood there with the jeans pulled up to his knees, no underwear on, his dick freely hanging out. Zyan kept on laughing as he hopped around in the tight dressing room, struggling to pull the jeans up past his knees, his dick flapping around.

Damien tried not too hard to stare, but was sure after yesterday Zayn wouldn't mind. "Man, where your drawers at?"

"I had to freeball today; momma stopped doing my damn laundry."

"And you trying on clothes? That's unsanitary."

Zyan brushed at his dick, "My nuts clean yo, don't stress."

"Well anyways, you most definitely need a looser pair of jeans."

Zyan struggled to strip off the pair of tight jeans before returning them to the stack of clothes he brought into the dressing room. He took off his shirt, now completely naked in front of Damien, and started digging through the stack of clothes for something else to try on. Damien eyes traced the series of tattoos on Zyan's body and his eyes ended up on his firm, perfectly mocha toned ass. Zyan bended over so far that Damien could see the little hairs around his hole.

"Damn," Damien whispered under his breath.

Zyan slipped on a snug t-shirt, "I ain't makin you uncomfortable right?"

"Huh? About what?"

"Being butt ass naked, being in jail I got used to changing in front of dudes. And after yesterday, I know you ain't acting shy about seeing my dick. You can't have your nut running down my hand one day then get shy the next day cause you see some dick." Zyan slipped on a pair of black jeans, "We cool are not my nigga?"

"Yeah," Damien quickly answered, not wanting to come off as bothered, "Oh, and those jeans fit much better."

"Damien," Lincoln shouted as he entered the dressing room area, "What are you doing? Where's Zyan?"

Damien stalled to answer, more concerned with whether or not Zyan was wearing enough clothes.

Zyan stepped out of the dressing room while slipping on a t-shirt, "He helping me pick jeans, why?"

Lincoln stopped before them and eyed Zyan up and down, "You look nice, like a true employee."

"Too bad I can't pay for this shit though, I got bills. We got layaway?"

Lincoln rolled his eyes and let out a snotty laugh, "Um, no, but you'll get your employee discount."

"Fuck it," Zyan said as he shrugged and went back into the dressing room to change back into his clothes.

The minute he shut the dressing room door, Lincoln pulled Damien away and whispered, "How is he?"

"He's good; customers get intimidated but they're just prejudging him."

"Alright, I guess. Keep an eye on him though; make sure he doesn't steal anything."

Damien was offended for Zyan, "That's not cool, brotha," Damien said with extra emphasis on the word 'brotha'.'

"Oh please," Lincoln said, "Don't try to test my blackness. I stood in line for eight hours to vote for Obama."

"And?"

"And I'm not saying he might steal because he's black, I'm saying that because he's an ex-inmate, remember?"

"Reformed," Damien defended.

"Remember that I'm your boss, Damien. I don't know how you two have bonded so quickly, but don't put yourself in his corner especially against me. Because if I do catch him stealing or breaking any type of rules, I don't care how many membership cards you sell, I'm terminating you both. Now, think on that...brotha," Lincoln smugly said before shuffling off with his head held high.

Zyan stepped from the dressing room dressed in his clothes. "Was Lincoln out here bitchin?"

"As always."

"He say something about me, I know he did. What he say?"

Damien was still getting to know Zyan and didn't know how he would react to what Lincoln had just said, "Nothing."

"Oh, I thought so. I can't stand his ass. A bitch like him could suck my dick."

Damien laughed.

"For real though," Zyan said, "Nut all in his throat, have him walkin around here gargling instead of bitchin."

"He'd still find a way to drop a lecture on somebody. Anyways, let's restock the shit from the dressing room."

After a work day of joking around with Zyan and pimping out membership cards, Damien found himself once again taking his trainee home. Today, he didn't have enough time to hang out with him after work, because apparently Max was back at his condo with a surprise. As Damien got close to home, he realized this would be his first time being around Max since his masturbation session with Zyan. As he entered his apartment he told himself once again, it wasn't cheating, yet he was nervous.

In the kitchen, Max wore nothing but a cooking apron and was stirring a pot of tomato sauce.

"Alright, I'm starting to think you don't own clothes," Damien joked.

"This apartment is my freedom zone, no clothes, no stress, no judgment, just me and you."

Damien playfully smacked him on his muscled butt, "You're cooking? Is this the surprise?"

Max tensed up, looking obviously uncomfortable with having his butt slapped, "Yup, because you're my heart."

His words made Damien feel appreciated, but at the same time like the worst person on the planet. Max was nothing but kind to him and even supported him constantly following his academic suspension. All Damien had to do was support his football dreams and return the same kindness, but as he stood in the kitchen with Max, Damien felt like scum. He needed to set things right, restore some good karma.

Damien forced Max to turn away from the stove and got down on his knees, "I have a surprise too."

Max turned down the pasta sauce, "Really? What are you doing?"

Damien raised the front of the apron, revealing Max's soft dick. After replaying some porn clips in his mind for guidance, Damien took Max's dick and shoved it into his mouth. As Damien sucked slowly and carefully, Max's dick started to stiffin in his mouth. Damien wanted to pull away, but forced himself to get this right; he had to restore some good karma.

Damien focused, ignored his already aching jaw, and sucked Max's dick as if their entire relationship depended on this one session of head. Max moaned and groaned and started to use his strong hands to force Damien's head back and forth, making his mouth slide up and down the shaft of his dick. His grip on Damien's head became strong and Max quickly pulled his dick away and nutted all over Damien's neck.

The warm nut drained down Damien's neck and stained his shirt as he stood up, panting for air.

Max's body trembled as he exhaled heavily, "You delivered on your surprise."

Damien wiped some spit from his lip as he looked to the pot of tomato sauce, "Hopefully you do the same."

Damien left Max to finish cooking as he headed into his room to slip into something more comfortable. He took a seat on the edge of his bed. After his attempt to restore some good karma, Damien found himself still feeling the exact same way, like a cheater. He needed some guidance when it came to dealing with the title of being a cheater.

Damien couldn't rely on his own advice or even of those online. He needed a straight shooter to tell him exactly what he needed to do when it came to his relationship. Unfortunately this person was straight and unaware of Damien's sexual orientation, Marion. Damien had already rehearsed how he would tell his side without mentioning Max's name or the fact that he was referring to another man. The next day he headed over to Marion and Vincent's apartment.

Marion opened the door, "I hope this is about my money."

It was a big shock for Damien that his brother had let him stay with him following his academic suspension. The fact that Damien basically had to pay him one hundred dollars each month he stayed wasn't surprising though. He was jobless at the time so basically now had a giant debt he owed his brother of about six hundred dollars.

"I'm working on that, but I need some brotherly advice."

Marion rolled his eyes and stepped aside to let Damien in, "I should charge for this shit too."

Damien entered the messy apartment and took a seat on the couch. "I said I got you."

Marion stood over Damien with his arms crossed, "I got class in ten minutes, talk."

The feeling of being rushed made Damien a bit scattered brain, "Um, well, basically, I'm dating this girl right. And all she likes is me eating her pussy, that's it. She doesn't fuck, give head, or nothing. So, I was hanging with this other girl I know and we sort of hooked up. She gave me a handjob. Now, I feel like shit. As if,

I've just cheated on the chick I'm with now, but sexual frustration led me to that."

Marion shrugged, "Just don't tell one bitch about the other. Nigga, why you always make life difficult?"

"But I feel so bad about it though."

"Another result of momma babying your ass. Toughen up and do what I say."

In the apartment scrolled Vincent accompanied by Noah the frat boy.

Marion turned his attention to Vincent, "By time my dude, gimme the keys. I gotta go."

Vincent tossed Marion the car keys, "My bad, I had to go scoop up Noah."

Marion rolled his eyes, "Noah, you ain't got shit else to do but hang around here all the time?"

Noah laughed, "I can't tolerate my new roommate."

"Yeah, I told your cheap ass to move off campus," Marion said as he started for the door, "I'm out."

Damien sat with his mouth opened in shock, "So, he's just gonna leave while we talking?"

Noah nodded at Damien, "Sup, mushroom."

"Sup Noah," Damien said, still pissed at Marion for abruptly leaving.

Noah crashed on the recliner, kicked off his shoes, propped up his feet, stuffed his hand in his pants, and watched TV.

Vincent joined Damien on the couch, "Did we interrupt your brother to brother moment?"

"No," Damien said, "I'm just sorta pissed he walked out like that as if we weren't talking."

"Hey, you work at Aerostyle, right?" Noah butted in.

Damien nodded, "Uh, yeah, why?"

"Is Lincoln still the manager?"

Damien nodded, "Yeah, why, you know him?"

Noah sucked his teeth, "He was in the frat when I joined in my freshman year. He was a cunt, man."

"Yeah, I put up with his nonsense all the time. He swears he's the next president of the country."

"Is he cute?" Vincent asked.

Noah laughed, "Your mind always in different zones man. He's alright looking, a square though. He used to be really into dating fat bitches he met online. It used to be so funny watching this skinny dude walk around with these big girls who would just boss him around. I just think it's funny he talks down to dudes, but used to let girls play him."

"He's not my biggest problem though," Damien said, "I think I cheated on my boyfriend."

Vincent laughed, "What do you mean, you think? Either you did or didn't."

"That's what I was trying to get Marion to clear up before he just left," Damien said.

"And let me guess," Vincent said, "Marion basically said keep quiet."

"Who's your boyfriend?" Noah asked. "Do we know him? Is he a student at NC Tech?"

Damien was sure they knew of one of the school's top athletes. "Nope," He lied.

"Well, do we know the person you cheated on him with?" Noah prodded even more.

"Is mutual masturbation cheating though?" Damien asked.

"In an open relationship like mines and Noah, nope," Vincent declared.

Ever since Damien had first met Noah a year ago he was aware that he and Vincent messed around with each other. But he didn't know they had branded what they had as a relationship.

"Well, we have a normal relationship," Damien said, "So I guess I cheated."

He hated accepting that.

Vincent elbowed him, "Aye, don't try to play us, our relationship is normal. We understand what each other want."

"But I'm sure Vincent would prefer me not messing with other dudes," Noah said, "He desires a 'normal' relationship, but only for me. Vincent still can't stop trying to sleep with the entire campus; I can stop at any time though. Damien it sounds like your boyfriend and I are with men who aren't ready to settle down."

"I told you after I graduate I'm all yours, but feel free to stop messing with other dudes now," Vincent said.

As they debated about their relationship back and forth, Damien realized he had ruined his. "I can't tell him. I'm scared."

Noah focused back on Damien, "Then don't, just stop cheating and try to spice up you guys' sex life."

"But he's a very strict top," Damien said, "I'm a top also but at least I try other things. I'm sexually frustrated."

"As in you haven't had head in days?" Vincent asked.

"No, months," Damien revealed.

Noah and Vincent gasped in unison.

Vincent scooted close to Damien and put his hand on his thigh, "Dude, for your sanity, let me suck your dick."

Damien pushed Vincent's hand away, "Hell no, I'm definitely not doing anything with you. I'm not a cheater."

"But you are," Noah pointed out, "You've already done the dirty deed. To me it sounds like you're stuck in a sexless relationship with a very nice guy. Damien, you're nineteen, right? This is the start of your sex life. I don't think you want to spend the rest of your life being some strict top's plaything, especially if you're a top." Noah got up and forced Damien to his feet. He grabbed at Damien's hardening dick, "See, even your dick knows it true."

Vincent stood up and nodded back to his bedroom, "Because we cool, I'll allow Noah to suck your dick."

"Even if he didn't approve I would do it," Noah said, "I feel bad for you man. I'll let you fuck too."

"Whoa, hold on," Vincent said, "I didn't say all of that."

Noah looked to Vincent, "You're one who doesn't want to keep things strictly between us. This is your doing."

Vincent thought about giving up an open relationship. He couldn't. "Alright then, shit. Damien, it's cool if you fuck, Noah."

Damien knew he would feel bad after this, but he needed it. "I'm down."

Vincent smirked and led the way back to his bedroom as Noah walked with Damien, massaging his dick through his pants. Once inside the room, Vincent locked the door and started to help Noah strip Damien. They pushed a naked Damien down on the bed and started to take off their own clothes. A short and buff Noah joined Damien on the bed and started to suck his dick. A tall and lanky Vincent just stood bedside playing with the head of his dick, looking like he was missing out.

Damien rolled his eyes at Vincent, "Dude, just come on."

Vincent bit his plump bottom lip as he joined them on the bed. As Noah worked the head of Damien's dick, Vincent licked the shaft. Damien just lay back enjoying the pleasure that had been absent from his life. Vincent grabbed a condom from his dresser and once Noah stopped sucking, he slipped the rubber on Damien's dick. Noah mounted Damien and started to ride his dick in the reverse cowgirl position.

Vincent lay back beside Damien as he watched Noah ride him. "That shit feels good, right?"

Damien nodded.

"Amazing ass for some good dick," Vincent said, "I remember the first time I saw your dick."

Damien was more focused on Noah's tight ass, not Vincent. "Uh huh."

"It had been raining that day," Vincent recalled, "And you came in the hospital wearing those light blue shorts you always wore to school on gym day. I was chilling in the waiting room, while Marion and your daddy were upstairs with your momma. The nurse told you to sit and wait until she could walk you upstairs. You sat across from me, I was too bored to even start a convo. Through your damp shorts, all I could see was your dick print. After you went upstairs, I went into the bathroom and busted the biggest nut."

Damien remembered that day, it being the last week of his mother's life. The heart aching memory was quickly wiped away as he yanked his dick from Noah's ass, tore off the condo, sat up, and nutted all over a moaning Noah's back. Damien crashed down into the bed, feeling so relaxed he could just fall asleep. Vincent and Noah started to sixty-nine with each other, and Damien just lay there watching.

Max was nice to playhouse with, but Damien couldn't resist the lure of sex any longer.

18 - Client

It had been a few days since Damien accepted that he cheated on Max. Still, he hadn't found the guts to tell his boyfriend about what he had done with Zyan. Especially after hooking up with Vincent and Noah, Damien knew it was time for him and Max to end. All it took was for him to open his mouth and say it was over, but he would get there when he could. He just focused on work, today training Zyan on the register.

Instead of working as usual, they were just making jokes.

Lincoln joined them at the register, "I just received a customer complaint."

"Who snitchin?" Zyan asked.

"A woman was shopping with her son and overheard one of you use the B word while snickering," Lincoln said.

"We were just talking," Damien explained, "We can't help that she overheard us."

"But you should be training Zyan to use the POS, not discussing your personal lives," Lincoln pointed out.

"Four eight hours straight?" Damien argued, "That's impossible. We train and chat."

Lincoln pointed at Damien, "If he hits a wrong button or anything, it's your fault. Remember that."

"I'll make sure he doesn't, I can train and talk to him like a normal person. It's called multitasking."

Lincoln crossed his arms, shook his head at Damien and stormed away.

Zyan laughed, "Alright, that nigga aside, I need a ride somewhere before you drop me off."

Damien would go anywhere except for back home where Max was most likely hanging out. "Oh yeah, where?"

"Well, you know I used to sell weed, right?"

Damien nodded, "Yeah."

"I'm out of that business, trust me, I'm done. I learned my lesson, but this one regular client I had still owes me. He hit me up on Facebook asking for some weed, knowing I just got my ass outta jail. Anyways, he dropped his new address thinking I'm gonna bring some weed over, but imma just confront him about the money he owes me. I'm not gonna get violent, I won't put you in a situation like that. I just know I can get my money out of him easier face-to-face."

Damien never saw any sign of misbehavior from Zyan since meeting him, he trusted his word. "Cool, I'll take you."

"Cause you my nigga." He faced the register, "Aye, I forgot how you told me to do refunds."

Later that day, they left work, Zyan decent on the register but not yet close to being ready to work alone on the POS. Using GPS on his phone, Zyan led Damien to a suburban neighborhood. All the brick houses looked the same, it sort of reminding Damien of where his Aunt Bernice lived in Columbia. Zyan made Damien park in front of a vacated house that was for sale and they walked down the block to another. Zyan knocked hard on the door and a dark-skinned man, with a bald head, and wearing khakis and a yellow polo shirt, answered.

The man nervously looked over Zyan's shoulder at Damien, "W-w-w-who's that?"

"Shelton this Damien, Damien this Shelton," Zyan introduced, "Damien works with me."

"Don't tell him my name," Shelton panicked, "Are you crazy?"

"Man stop being a scary bitch," Zyan said, "Damien's cool. Only nigga I trust."

"Are you saying you don't trust me?" Shelton asked.

"I mean, somebody pointed the cops in my direction. And you aint even visit me in jail."

"My wife would flip if I told her I had to go visit my weed man. No fucking way man. And I didn't snitch on you."

Zyan pushed his way into Shelton's home, "Just let me in."

Damien followed Zyan inside the nice home, smiling at Shelton to at least let him know he was friendly and had no reason to be afraid. Zyan walked through the home as if he owned it, taking a seat in Shelton's lavish living room. Around the living room were pictures of Shelton along with his wife and two kids. Damien sat beside Zyan on the couch as Shelton stood before them.

"Do you two want anything to drink? A beer? Wine? Water?" Shelton asked.

"Beer," Zyan said, "Get my nigga here some water. He's driving."

Damien laughed, "I don't think one beer will get me tipsy."

"I figured, but I ain't trying to go to jail cause you got pulled over for swerving a bit."

Shelton vanished into the kitchen and returned with their drinks, "My wife took the kids to her sister's this weekend and I figured I might as well let loose and smoke some of the good stuff. I didn't know who in the hell to call, so I decided to get in touch with my favorite weed man, you." Shelton sat down on the couch across from them, "How much did you bring? I'll buy it all."

Zyan sipped his beer, "I don't sell that shit anymore, I came here cause you owe me."

"No I don't. I'm very good with money, I have good credit."

"But you have bad credit with me," Zyan said, "Last time I sold some shit to you, you claimed you didn't have any cash. So I told you to just pay me later, I ended up getting arrested the next day so I never got to collect. You were the only person who owed me money, $150 to be exact. I don't forget shit like that."

"I can't just give you that. My wife and I combined finances, she'll ask questions."

"Then lie," Zyan said, "I'm not leaving until I get my money."

Damien knew Zyan was bluffing, he hoped he was bluffing.

"Listen, how about we do what we did last time?" Shelton suggested.

"Man, you still chasing dick behind your wife's back?" Zyan asked.

"I've stopped for a while, I love her, but since I can't pay you I have no choice to do this, right?"

Zyan stood up, "Y'all still got that soft ass bed?"

Shelton nodded as he rose to his feet, "Of course, it was built to last."

Zyan thumbed down at Damien, "And you also gonna suck his dick."

Shelton looked Damien up and down, "He's clean, right? No STDs I can pass on to my wife?"

"Does it look like he's dirty, nigga," Zyan said.

Damien stood up, excited to get some head. "I'm clean, don't worry, sir."

Shelton rolled his eyes, "Alright, and don't call me sir."

Damien smiled, "My bad."

Shelton led them upstairs to him and his wife's bedroom. Zyan and Damien took their seats on the bed. Damien looked to Zyan excited, while Zyan looked as if he was not into this idea at all and was just ready to nut and get on with his life. Still, as they were both getting ready to get head from another man, Damien didn't know if Zyan was gay or straight, he just stuck him with the bi label. The mutual masturbation, the careless nudity, and now this should've made it easier to determine if Zyan preferred men or women. If he preferred men, Damien didn't understand why Zyan treated him strictly like his homeboy with benefits. He in a way, wanted Zyan to like him on a deeper level.

Shelton got down on his knees before them, unbuttoned their pants and whipped out their dicks. Zyan's dick was as big as Damien remembered, almost a bit envious of the size. Shelton dived for Zyan's dick first as if he was anticipating the moment for a while. Whenever Shelton would suck Damien's dick, he would only do it for a second and then switch back to Zyan's. As if Zyan picked up on Damien's feeling of annoyance, he would yank his dick from Shelton's mouth and make him suck Damien's.

Shelton stopped sucking, "Zyan, come on man, just fuck me this one time."

Zyan furrowed his brows, "Nigga are you crazy? I ain't fuckin you. Hurry up and catch this nut."

"Sweetie," A female voice shouted as the downstairs door closed, "I left Jason's asthma pump. Can you believe we had to turn all the way around?" Shelton's wife could be heard making her way upstairs, "I was just going to go to CVS and see if I could pick up his prescription, but the doctor's office was closed so nobody could put in the order."

Shelton quickly signaled for Zyan and Damien to get up and shoved them into the bedroom closet.

"I'll help you look," Shelton said as he rushed from the bedroom and shut the door.

In the darkness of the closet, Damien and Zyan were crammed together, their hard dicks still out.

"I'm so nervous," Damien whispered, his heart racing.

"Nigga, this shit kind of funny," Zyan snickered. "Can you believe his lil gay ass asked me to fuck?"

"So, you're not into that?"

"Hell no, it ain't my style," Zyan said.

"Oh, okay," Damien said, still confused about what was Zyan's style.

Zyan grabbed Damien's dick and started to stroke it, "Damn, your dick brick as hell."

Damien was so nervous they would get discovered, but turned all the way on, "Yeah."

"Come here," Zyan said as he pulled Damien closer and started kissing him and stroking his dick.

Damien didn't know what Zyan wanted, but was just going to enjoy it. He gripped onto Zyan's ass for balance as he started to nut. Zyan kept stroking Damien's dick until the last drop. Even though he was done nutting, Zyan kept on kissing him and letting Damien rub against his ass.

"She's gone," Shelton said as he opened the closet door. He gasped, "Is that nut on my wife's dress?"

Zyan stopped kissing Damien, pushed Shelton out of his way and sat back on the bed. "Just come get this nut."

Shelton surveyed the damage done to his wife's dress for a quick second before rushing over and continuing to suck Zyan's dick. Damien just stood in the doorway of the closet watching as Zyan stood beside the bed and aggressively made Shelton deep throat his dick. As he started to nut on Shelton's face, Zyan smirked and kept his eyes locked with Damien's.

19 - Forgiveness

Damien usually always looked forward to a Saturday off. Those were usually the days him and Max would just hang out all day watching movies and eating junk food. It was final exam season and Max sat on the couch with his face buried into a textbook while Damien sat next to him channel surfing. The day was extremely dry, Damien wondering what kind of craziness Zyan was getting into as he kept on browsing through the channels.

He landed on the reunion show for Diva Doctors. It was his first time actually seeing the show outside of a trailer. His Aunt Bernice was sitting on a long couch with other cast members wearing a lavish gold gown that was fit for royalty. In her typical fashion, she was controlling the entire show, over talking the host and asking her cast mates inappropriate questions. She was even trying to force one lady to admit her medical license had been revoked.

Bernice started to bug another cast member about her husband being a gold digger and DL. Damien couldn't stomach her any more. The moment he started to change the channel, one of the other cast members charged across the couch and punched Bernice in the face. The woman managed to get in a couple of more face punches, kicks, and pulled off Bernice's wig before security showed up. Bernice tried to get up and fight back, but she was so winded after being punched in the face a couple of times, she ended up stumbling backward over the couch. Damien burst out laughing, vowing to find Bernice's attacker on Twitter and thank her for putting his aunt in her place.

Max looked up from his textbook, "Are you gonna watch shit like this all day?"

"Actually, I'm going out with Leon and his girl later, you comin?"

"Man you must be trippin. What I'm gonna look like hanging with y'all?"

Damien shrugged, "My homeboy. Only in your head it's something else."

"That's some fag shit man. I don't do double dates especially with some female, bitches talk."

"They don't even know we together. You're overthinking everything."

"If they see me with you, a gay man, they'll know what's up."

"Man, that's kind of insulting. But whatever, you stay inside tonight hiding. I'm going."

"So, you just gonna leave me like that?"

Damien stood up from the couch, "Exactly, I'm leaving you tonight." If only he could say forever, Damien wished.

Damien stormed off; tired of Max always making it feel as if being gay was a bad thing. He felt as if men like Max were one of the many problems with the gay community. Every guy like Max was a number, a voice, a new representation of what it meant to be gay, but society would continue to believe and be subjected to all the stereotypes of what a gay man was, especially a black gay man. Damien stayed in his room searching online for easy ways to end a relationship. All the results were basically the same, open your mouth and say it's over. No point of searching for the same answer over and over, Damien just watched porn on mute until it was time to get dressed and head out.

He ended up meeting Leon and his girlfriend Megan down at TGIS Saturdays. The place was packed as always with a lot of faces from campus, thugs who were dragged out on dates with their girlfriends, married couples who wished they could afford somewhere better, and teenage girls who were all glued to their phones texting. Damien made his way inside and joined Megan and Leon at their booth.

"Long time no see," Leon said.

"I know," Damien said with a wide smile, "I've actually missed you too damn much."

"Damn, you tryin to fuck," Leon joked. He thumbed at Megan, "Mah dude, my girl right here though."

Damien laughed, "Shut up, nobody wants your ass."

"I do," Megan, who was already tearing up some spinach dip, piped in.

Damien motioned at her, "Besides you and maybe his parents might still tolerate him."

Megan was a beautiful girl, but was the size of a house compared to Leon who was just the garage.

Megan brushed back her micro-braided hair, "Baby, where's the waitress? I want some more appetizers."

Leon searched the crowded restaurant, "I'll let him know when he walks by."

"Are you two married yet?" Damien asked.

"We're in the process of getting commitment rings," Leon said. "Are you still secretly boo'd up?"

Damien nodded, "Unfortunately yes. Long story short, in my head it's over but I can't break his heart."

"He's a grown ass man; he'll be fine, unless you dating some dude fresh out of high school."

"I know, but he's sort of a big ass dude and mentally in his own world."

Leon laughed, "One of those niggas with that retard strength, who might rip your dick off and toss it?"

"Him actually touching my dick would be a different story."

Damien sort of forgot Megan was at the table, noticing they were talking a bit too freely about his sex life around her. She didn't seem to mind, especially as she was licking her empty bowl of spinach dip. The waiter eventually resurfaced and everybody ordered. Leon got chicken fingers, Damien got steak and shrimp, while Megan got what they both ordered, plus the lobster pasta, and put in her order for dessert early. Leon seemed completely fine with his girlfriend eating the same portion of three diners. They waiter left with their orders.

"So," Leon said, "Who's your side piece?"

Damien laughed, "Why would you assume that?"

"Because I know you dude, you always sleeping with some crazy, random ass dude."

"Alright, alright, it's this guy from work."

Leon nodded, "Sounds normal, but keep going. What's wrong with him?"

"He's sort of a blank slate, but in a good way. Every time I hang with him it's a new adventure."

"And still, what's wrong with him?"

"I don't see this as a flaw, but he recently just got out of jail but it was just for selling weed."

"Oh you got you some...um, what's the word? Trade?"

Damien laughed, "Okay, mister gay man expert."

"Speaking of gay, his brother can cooooooook," Megan butted in, "Best cake I ever had."

"It did look good," Leon said to her, "To bad you ate all before I could get any."

"Baby you know I eat a lot when I get agitated."

Damien figured she was one constantly agitated woman. The waiter returned with their food and the conversation shifted to many different topics, from Megan's list of favorite burger places to the Diva Doctors reunion show slaying of Aunt Bernice the big mouth dragon. Overall, it was a fun night and Damien was glad to get to see Leon again. His mood died down as he returned home to find Max where he left him.

Max put his textbook on the couch, "I'm sorry."

"For what?" Damien asked as he closed the door.

"For not coming. I'm sorry for being like this but I warned you, I can't be out."

Damien had little care for this conversation, "It's okay," He lied, "You're right."

Max got up and slowly made his way over to Damien. He smirked, "Tell me to beg for your forgiveness."

"Um, beg for my forgiveness."

Max stopped before Damien and pointed to the floor, "Tell me to do it on my knees."

"On your knees," Damien said as if he was reading badly from a movie script.

Max got down on his knees and started to unbutton Damien's pants. Damien didn't know how to react. Max pulled out Damien's soft dick and for the very first time, put it in his mouth. It was a moment Damien wanted for a while, but found himself not into at all. He ended up closing his eyes and thinking about Zyan to get hard, but that wasn't enough to get him into this head session. Max kept awkwardly and poorly sucking until Damien couldn't take it anymore.

Damien forced him to stand up and formed a phony smile, "Alright, you're forgiven."

"Do you want me to finish?" Max asked as if he was begging for a no.

"Maybe after exams, study. I can't have you failing out of school."

"Alright, cool," Max said relieved as he went back to the couch to study.

Damien didn't know how long he could keep this up. He needed to get out of this relationship.

20 - Blue Room

Damien could honestly say a work day with Zyan was more appealing than spending anytime with Max. Not only was Zyan simply fun, he didn't overly sexualize their friendship. It wasn't all about sex jokes, flirty stares, or pointless convos until their next sexual encounter. Damien could have legit fun with Zyan, just like he used to have with Leon all the time. Their two sexual encounters only made this new friendship more interesting. After a work day together, Damien dropped Zyan off at home.

Before getting out the car Zyan turned to him, "Aye, you wanna go out tonight?"

"Yeah, where?"

"There's this club a few miles out called the Blue Room. It's the club I got arrested selling weed outside of. Man, I've been banned from the club since then but my old boss allowing me back in. Not only do I need a ride, but I think you would have fun and can meet some of the people I used to hang wit."

As long as Zyan was there, Damien was sure it would be fun, "Cool, what time should I pick you up?"

"Eleven and just text me when you pull up. Don't honk man, my moms would trip."

"Oh yeah, your curfew," Damien teased, "I'll text, don't wanna watch a grown man get his ass cut with a belt."

Zyan laughed and playfully shoved Damien, "Man, get the fuck out of here. I dare her to try."

"Talk is cheap, man. I'll catch you later."

Zyan got out of the car and Damien pulled off excited about later tonight. He arrived home to find Max there, still studying away for his final exams. Damien made up some grand lie up about having late night inventory tonight, which he had to work before, as an excuse to be leaving out of the house so late. When that time came, Damien tried not to overdress, simply wearing black jeans, a white v-neck, and Timberland boots. He gave Max a throwaway kiss on the lips and left to go pick up Zyan.

As instructed, Damien texted him upon arrival instead of blowing the horn. Zyan was dressed similar, but in all black and had on a hat. He also wore a gold chain around his neck and a pair of matching grills in his mouth. After dapping each other, Damien and Zyan started the nearly hour long drive to the club that was in a country town that mostly had old apartment buildings, fields, and liquor stores. Zyan nervously rubbed his palms together as they pulled into the crowded parking lot of the Blue Room.

Damien could hear Beyonce playing and mostly men filing into the club. "Is this a gay bar?"

"To me it all bout dat money, gay niggas tip good. This place will get me a car quicker than Aerostyle."

Damien shrugged, "Yeah, I suppose. This is my second gay bar visit ever."

"Man, they all the same."

If that statement was true, Damien knew he was in store for a wild night. Instead of going through the front entrance, Zyan led Damien to the back of the club to an employee entrance. Once his identity was confirmed through a sliding peep hole in the door, Zyan and Damien were let inside by a bouncer. After traveling through a narrow hallway, lit by a flickering light, they entered a room that was crowded with half naked men walking around while getting dressed in elaborate costumes.

"You're a stripper?" Damien whispered to Zyan.

"I was a bartender nigga, but I've hit the stage once or twice, not really into niggas grabbing on me though."

One of the dancers spotted Zyan and made his presence known. Soon, Zyan was rushed by these chiseled, oiled up, half naked men who greeted him with daps and some with hugs. It was strange for Damien seeing all these towering or built men walking around half naked, some wearing nothing at all, as if it was no big deal. Two guys were in one section of the dressing room practicing a dance routine together.

They all just came off as worked focused but fun loving guys, like a basketball team getting ready for a big game. Zyan introduced some of them to Damien as his homeboy before leaving him alone to go meet with the club manager. Damien just found the one spot not covered with clothes or baby oil and sat waiting and enjoying the eye candy. Zyan eventually returned looking a bit upset.

Damien stood up, "Did you get your job back?" Expecting the answer to be no.

"Yeah, but first this fat ass nigga gonna make me dance tonight before he puts me back on the schedule."

"Oh, well, are you going to do it?"

"Man, working at Aerostyle is good for my reform program and shit, but without selling weed anymore, I'm not making shit. I need to be back here working weekends again. So I ain't got no fucking choice but to do it. Aye, at least you'll be out there in the crowd supporting me. Imma keep all my focus on you; just don't make no silly ass faces. I can't be out there giggling and shit."

"I won't," Damien said as he laughed, "I'll just throw my last two dollars at you."

"Nah, that'll lower my value. Let them other niggas throw the twenties. Anyway, let me go prep."

Damien looked over his shoulder, "Alright, I'll find my way out to the club."

Damien separated from Zyan and made his way through a dark hallway that led to the crowded club area. As expected, the bar and dance floor were packed with men. Unlike the Halloween party at Shane's, the men in this gay club were actually wearing clothes. Damien found him a spot at the bar and just sat there on his phone, blowing off any guy who even attempted to flirt with him.

The first dancer to hit the floor wore a leopard thong that came off halfway through his performance. The dancer did all types of splits, flips, and even dried hump a lucky club goer on the dance floor. Of course things got a little out of hand when the club goer tried to put the stripper's dick in his mouth. Two more dancers followed, the dance floor getting shinier from all the baby oil following each performance. A mix of a Kanye West track started to play and finally Zyan hit the floor.

He wore nothing but a black thong, his gold chain around his neck and grill in his mouth. The sight of his oiled up tattooed body instantly got Damien hard. Damien got up from the bar and forced himself to the front of the crowd to get a clear view of Zyan's show. Once again, something new was discovered about the guy that was simply supposed to be Damien's trainee. Not only did Zyan have a nice bubble butt, but could actually dance.

Half way into his performance, he snatched Damien from the crowd and whispered to him, "Just roll with it."

Zyan ended up getting Damien to lay flat on his back onto the oily floor. He took his position over Damien as he started to roll his hips and slowly dig into his thong. Zyan removed a condom and the crowd went wild. He dropped down onto Damien and started to unzip his pants. Damien noticed more money started to hit the dance floor as Zyan whipped out Damien's dick. The crowd got even more amp as he slipped the condom onto Damien's dick. Damien just lay there, rolling with it as Zyan told him to do so.

Zyan returned to his feet, danced out of his thong, and tossed it into the crowd. He dropped back down onto Damien and pretended to ride his dick, simply grinding against it while he caught twenties. The music started to change and the crowd cheered Zyan's name as he stood up and helped Damien up from the floor. A staffer rushed onto the floor and started to collect Zyan's earnings for him.

Damien, his dick still out, was dragged to the back by Zyan. The moment they got in the dark hallway that led to the dressing room, Zyan pushed Damien down onto a folding chair. There were no words between them, just stares, but Damien felt as if he knew exactly what Zyan was thinking. Zyan straddled Damien, slipped his dick inside of him, and started to ride him. A set of dancers passed them in the hall as if nothing was happening. Tonight, this moment, it was all so exhilarating to Damien. It was as if something inside of Zyan drew him in and made him do crazy things.

Damien wrapped his arms tight around Zyan's oily body as he started to nut. His dick still hard, Zyan kept riding.

21 - Pure

Damien couldn't get last night off his mind. The sex was amazing and the adrenaline rush had made it tough for him to sleep next to a snoring Max that night. His night out led to him having a bad morning. He now had some strange rash on his back, probably from laying on the dirty dance floor and he was running nearly three hours late for work. He checked his phone to see his manager Lincoln had been calling him all morning. Damien took the fastest shower he'd ever had and rushed off to work.

As he rushed into Aerostyle all his co-workers were whispering and pointing fingers like high schoolers. He expected the sight of Zyan to make his horrible morning a little bit better, but he didn't spot him as he headed into the back to clock-in. The minute Damien managed to clock-in Lincoln popped up and motioned for him to join him in his office.

Lincoln sat down at his desk, "Three hours, really?"

Damien took a seat in a chair placed at the desk, "Yeah, I overslept."

"For three hours? Are you kidding me?"

"I'm here now," Damien said, "It's not like I didn't show up."

"This isn't you, Damien. You're never late."

"Mistakes happen," Damien said, "Can I please get to work? I have training to do."

Lincoln rolled his eyes, "Your trainee called out sick, allegedly. I was expecting the same stunt from you."

"Why would you expect that?"

"Because apparently you were at some club last night dancing butt naked along with Zyan."

Damien eyes widened, not expecting Lincoln to know his business. "You were there?"

"Hell no, I would never be in a place like the Blue Room. I've got respect for myself."

"Don't act like that, Lincoln. And I wasn't naked on stage, that's a lie."

"Well, I was so disgusted I didn't really listen that much. You must've forgotten many of the men on staff here and our customers are homosexual. I heard them gossiping about you and Zyan this morning and hoped none of it was true. You've allowed this trouble maker to corrupt you. I mean, there was nudity involved in whatever was going on last night, what if he has AIDs? Have you thought about that?"

Damien laughed, "Nothing I did last night could lead to me catching AIDs. I practice sex safe."

"Are you sexually involved with him Damien?"

"Why would you care? Are you jealous?"

Lincoln curled his lips as an attempt to suppress his anger, "I'm asking as your manager, get over yourself."

"I don't see what my private life has to do with my work life."

"I can't have a couple working shifts together in the same store. What if you two breakup? That'll create drama."

"I'm not dating Zyan."

Lincoln paused as he tried to calm himself, "I don't like this at all. He's corrupting a once good employee."

"I've been late once. I can walk out of this office and still sell more membership cards than the entire staff."

Lincoln, "I agree. You're right about that. Damien, I just want you to stay focused. Soon, they'll be selecting new managers for the store in Charlotte. I know in my gut I will be selected and will have to name a successor to my position here. Damien, I would want you to replace me. I believe in you so much that this weekend, I've selected you to accompany me to the corporate meeting in Charlotte. We'll leave Saturday morning, the meeting takes place that day, and then we'll depart on Sunday morning."

Damien couldn't imagine being trapped in a car and hotel with Lincoln. "Is it mandatory?"

"In this case, yes. Because I won't let you become a failure. Now, get to work. You're working denim today."

Damien was already thinking up excuses to avoid the trip to Charlotte. He then thought about the alternative of sitting around all Saturday with Max. In this case, the trip away from his boyfriend wouldn't be so bad. Plus, he could use the time away to clear his head and possibly figure out a way to breakup with him.

While out on the floor working, Damien texted Zyan to make sure he was okay. As Lincoln predicted, Zyan wasn't so sick after all, just hungover from the night before. Nobody to entertain him, Damien focused on work. As he folded jeans he noticed two guys whispering, snickering and looking in his direction while they shopped.

"Do you two need anything?" Damien asked. "Or are y'all just gonna keep acting like kids?"

The skinniest out of the duo pointed at Damien, "You from the club? The Blue Room?"

"Not really."

"Don't lie, you were there last night."

"I'm not denying it," Damien said.

"My friend think you gotta big dick," The chubbier one out of the duo said.

Him and his friend bickered back and forth and laughed as they rushed away from Damien like two school girls.

"Idiots," Damien said under his breath. Yet, at the same time he kind of enjoyed his five seconds of fame.

The never ending workday finally came to an end. All Damien wanted to do was get home and sleep. Of course before he could leave, Lincoln trapped him in another lecture and gave him a bit more details on the trip to Charlotte. On the drive home, Damien nearly fell asleep at a red light twice and was so out of it didn't even notice he somehow was driving with his trunk popped opened for a few blocks. He pulled up to his apartment and thought his tired mind was playing tricks on him as he spotted Kendall sitting on his porch.

Damien got out of his car, "Kendall?"

Kendall, who wore black slacks and a white dress shirt, stood up and smirked. "Hey, Damien."

"What are you doing here? How did you find my apartment?"

"Well, your father directed me to your bro, your bro directed me to you, and now I'm here."

Damien knew something was different about Kendall. He spoke different and his entire vibe was more relaxed.

"Is it okay if we talk inside," Kendall asked.

"Yeah, sure."

Damien opened his apartment door and let Kendall inside. It was a big convenience Max was out taking exams.

Kendall sat on the couch, "This is a nice place, I see God has blessed you."

That sentence was all it took for Damien to know what was up with Kendall.

Damien sat down beside him, "You're a church boy now, huh?"

"Church is just a building, I'm saved, a renewed soul, cleansed. And my mother has joined me in this new life, also renouncing her sins and living her life for the one and only almighty." Kendall smiled, "I know you think I'm just talking crazy, but respect that fact that I'm happy for the first time in my life. And I'm not here to convert you, I'm here to apologize. I led you further into a lifestyle that I no longer live anymore, a life of homosexuality. "

"Oh, so you're like straight now?"

"I'm committed to becoming a better man. No simple label can define me."

Damien wasn't religious but never aimed to mock those who were. He did have a problem with the gay-be-gone act. This was not the real Kendall. He was free to get saved, but Damien wasn't cool with him denouncing who he really was deep down inside, a gay man. Damien felt he needed to take things a step further and test Kendall.

Damien formed a mischievous smirk, "So, you have no desire to sleep with me or any other men?"

"No, not anymore. I'm good with G-O-D."

"Alright," Damien said as he stood up and unzipped his pants, "Are you sure?"

Kendall fidgeted around in his seat, "What are you doing? Don't let evil influence you, man."

Damien pulled out his dick and started to play with it until it got hard, "So you don't want this?"

Kendall turned his head away, "Damien, stop. This is pathetic."

"I'm not the one lying to myself."

Kendall stood up and did his best to hide his erection, "It's a process, Damien. What happened to me at Bernice's house was mortifying. I felt as if I was a freak and nobody tried to side with me, not even you. I wasn't expecting you to out yourself, but you could've at least defended me. I don't want to be gay because I don't ever want to experience that feeling again, that feeling of being an outcast. I'm not lying to myself, I'm protecting myself. And it's a struggle, but one I will overcome no matter what temptations are put before me." Kendall grabbed Damien's dick and started to slowly stroke it, "This once made me have so many un-pure thoughts, but now I feel nothing."

Kendall released Damien's dick and stormed from the apartment. Damien found himself wishing he could rewind a bit and handle this differently. If he could, he would apologize to Kendall for not standing with him. The truth was that he was afraid as he watched Bernice out Kendall, but unlike Kendall he had more courage to continue living the way he was born and not tuck it away out of fear.

22 - The Fight

While Damien saw it as a chamber of torture, most would call it a car. He stood outside of Aerostyle beside Zyan staring at the silver, four-door, rental car he would have to travel with Lincoln in for the next few hours. Yes, this was better than an awkward day with Max, but not by much. While Damien wanted to run away and go hide, Zyan couldn't stop cracking up.

"It's not funny," Damien said.

"Man, you gonna be bored ass fuck," Zyan said.

"I need some advice, quick, how can I make this trip less miserable?" Damien asked.

Zyan shrugged, "Get high, ditch Lincoln's bitch ass, and find your type to kick it with."

"I don't smoke, I'm sure Lincoln will be on my back the entire time, and I'm not that good at just finding dudes."

"Ain't they got those apps and shit, Jack'd?"

Damien shrugged, "Most dudes on there are just catfish."

"Ass is ass, dick is dick, find any gay nigga to fuck wit."

Even though they had officially had sex, Damien still didn't know what to think of Zyan's sexual orientation.

Lincoln exited the store and joined them, "Zyan, what are you doing out here? Get back to work."

Zyan laughed as he looked Lincoln up and down, "I was just getting a lil tan," Zyan joked, "Don't worry; I'm goin in right now. Y'all be safe."

As Zyan walked back into work, Damien only wished he could hide him in the trunk and bring him with them.

"I'm driving," Lincoln blurted out, "And I pick the music. No more stalling, let's burn some rubber."

Damien rolled his eyes and gagged on Lincoln's corniness. That was only a preview of what his boss had to offer. The entire ride he only played P Diddy, Macklemore, and Nick Cannon songs. Every word out of Lincoln's mouth was worked related. He even spent an hour talking about past employees that Damien didn't know and didn't care to know anything about. Damien tried to distract his self with Instagram. Leon was posting loads of pictures of him and Megan out to eat, Vincent was getting new followers by the second as he kept posting shirtless photos, and Kendall's page was drowning in bible quotes and photos of himself playing the drums at church.

Bored with Instagram, Damien decided to try to change the subject, "I know one of your frat bros."

"Oh, really?" Lincoln said as he kept his eyes on the road. "Which one? I have many frat brothers."

Damien decided to have some fun with this, "Man, saying his name will only start drama."

"Why? Am I being disrespected behind my back? If so, I deserve to know by whom."

"Not really, he was just telling me about the women you date."

"I don't date," Lincoln said, "I have female acquaintances that I have sexual encounters with and that is all. I made the decision a long time ago to focus on school and work only. Yes, I'm a man and I have needs but I can easily please myself or get one of my acquaintances to come over. It's done wonders for my life, I consider myself a success."

"You manage a men's clothing store, you don't own it."

"Maybe someday I will," Lincoln said.

"Man, you're such a robot. Do you even have friends?" Damien asked.

"No time for friends, I work. And as a black man, I work twice as hard. Now, what else has this frat bro said?"

Damien tried to have fun, but Lincoln just ruined it with his too serious response. "Nothing."

"Alright, then. May I ask you a question regarding your personal life?"

Damien shrugged, "Sure, go ahead."

"Now, based on rumors around the store, you're in a relationship but not with Zyan."

"Uh huh."

"Well, it's obvious there's something going on between you and Zyan. Are you cheating on your boyfriend?"

"It's complicated," Damien said, "In my head, I'm single and Zyan is just a friend. Never believe work rumors."

"My advice, get out of your head and live in reality. End things with your boyfriend for his sake."

"I don't need your advice," Damien said, "I plan on doing that very soon."

Lincoln nodded, "Good. In my eyes, that'll improve your status as a man."

Damien loathed how Lincoln spoke as if he was Bill Cosby and he was Theo. He didn't need any advice from him; he knew exactly what he needed to do to repair his personal life. He just wanted Lincoln to focus on the road, but they ended up getting lost anyway. By time they arrived to Charlotte, there was no time to check-in. They headed straight to the meeting that was being held in the same hotel they were staying in.

At the meeting, Damien was introduced to many other Aerostyle corporate figures. The best part about the meeting was all the great food, while everything else was a bore. They watched training videos and even got to witness a mini fashion show that featured some upcoming clothes. Damien found himself getting trapped by a district manager named Bob.

"So," Bob, who barely could fit in his suit and looked like a Caucasian walrus, asked, "Is Lincoln a good boss?"

"He's a good boss, but that's it. Lincoln runs the store with fear, employees don't respect him, they fear him. To me, he's more of a nag than somebody to be feared. But, I think he does a good job following the rules and handing down whatever corporate sends our way. He's very by the book. It's not my style. I would actually try to be a real person with my workers and spend time on the floor working, not in the back watching us on camera."

Bob burst out laughing as he waved Lincoln over.

"What's the joke?" Lincoln said as he joined them.

Bob motioned at Damien, "I think he just basically called you a soulless corporate shill."

Damien wasn't expecting Bob to reveal that. He just stood there with an awkward smile.

"Damien just doesn't understand a hard day's work," Lincoln said, "He's a bit of the store jokester."

Bob aggressively patted Lincoln on the back, "Then next meeting make the right choice and don't bring a fucking jokester."

Bob walked off laughing. Lincoln remained composed, but the minute Bob was far away a snarl formed on his faced. Damien had seen Lincoln upset many times, but this was a new level. Lincoln looked as if he was simply disgusted with Damien and wanted to tear his head off. The entire night Lincoln avoided Damien, up until they were trapped in their shared hotel room together.

The only sound in the room was the TV.

Damien, who lay on his bed, couldn't take the awkwardness, "I was trying to talk you up."

"Shut the fuck up," Lincoln shouted from his bed, "Don't you fucking dare talk to me. I'm done with you."

"It was a mistake dude. I was telling him how good you were and shit. He made it negative."

"Bob is the man who decides who manages the Charlotte and you basically painted him one big negative picture of me. I can't fucking believe I brought you. I figured you were one of my best employees, but deep down inside you're just the typical messy little nigga. A straight up nigga bringing down good black men like me."

"Whoa," Damien said as he sat up, "Lincoln I think you need to chill the fuck out."

"Talk to me again and I'll show you a side of myself you don't want to know. Damien, shut the fuck up."

Damien sized Lincoln up and down. He could handle him, "No, you shut the fuck up."

Lincoln charged from his bed and tackled Damien. He used his body weight, pinned Damien down, and started swinging on him. Damien tried to throw in some punches, but Lincoln hands were quick. Damien realized Lincoln was legit serious about this fight after he got hit in the nose twice. That only forced Damien to fight back harder, punching Lincoln in the side. Damien managed to flip things, getting Lincoln on his back and trying to restrain his arm as they struggled on the bed.

Damien pressed his knee down on Lincoln's crotch area only to realize is dick was hard.

Damien let loose off Lincoln's arm, "What the fuck?"

"I swear you're so fucking dumb, Damien," Lincoln spat out, "How in the hell did you just throw me under the bus like that? But if Bob asked you about a stupid ass nigga like Zyan you would've defended him. Smart dudes like you always falling for the wrong types. Yeah, I was at the Blue Room when Zyan's dumb ass was up there grinding on your dick. That dirty ass nigga can't do it like I do though."

Lincoln sat up and yanked at Damien's pants until they came loose. He pulled out Damien's hard dick and started to suck it like it was a source of air and his lungs were running dry. Damien didn't try to stop him; a guy liked Lincoln deserved a dick in the mouth to shut them up. Lincoln stopped sucking Damien's dick and started to take off his own pants. He didn't even manage to get his pants all the way off before Damien flipped him over and started to fuck him raw. For Damien, there was no passion in his stroke, but anger.

Not a single thing about his attitude towards Lincoln had change, even as he was nutting deep inside of him.

23 - Assistant

Damien hoped that things between him and Lincoln would've change following what happened on their trip to Charlotte, but it seemed as if things had gotten worse. Lincoln was a lot more open about his dislike of Damien and Zyan's relationship, no matter if it was platonic or romantic. Damien's role of training Zyan was passed onto somebody else and he rarely saw Zyan at work anymore. It was hard to hang out with Zyan outside of work now with Max on break from school and constantly around.

Damien was expecting to clock-out and go home directly after his shift but found himself in Lincoln's office.

Damien sat down at Lincoln's desk, "Hey man, what is it?"

Lincoln sat back in his chair, "So, are you still with Zyan?"

"I'm not with him, get over it. He's my friend, we have fun together. Stop with the envy shit dude."

Lincoln laughed, "You think I'm jealous? Of that street rat? Nah, come on."

"Well, obviously you want me. Don't pretend I didn't fuck you."

"You did and I regret it. It was a moment of weakness for me. It's been awhile since I've tried a guy. And after our little time together, I still prefer woman. So, please don't sit here thinking

I'm secretly lusting after you. I'm just tired of idiots like Zyan giving black men a bad name. Black children don't look up to black intellectuals like me, but instead of rappers and low lives like Zyan. Even you have fallen for it."

"Zyan is cool because he's real; he doesn't walk around talking down to people."

Lincoln's desk phone rang. "Give me a minute." Lincoln answered the phone and his face lit up with a smile as he kept on nodding. Half way into the call that smile started to fade and Lincoln's face dropped. "Alright Bob, thanks for the call. I'll be sure to share the news. I look forward to hearing from you again." Lincoln hung up the phone.

"Was that Bob as in the district manager?" Damien asked.

Lincoln nodded. "Yeah."

"What did he want?"

"He was calling to let me know that you officially fucked me."

Damien eyes widened, "Why would Bob know about that?"

"Not in that way. Damien, I didn't get any of the manager positions in Charlotte. And I'm sure your little conversation with Bob had something to do with that." A tear streamed down Lincoln's face, "I fucking hate you. I can't even believe I let you put your dick in me. I want to fire you. But I can't."

Damien shrugged, "Why? What do you mean?"

Lincoln stalled and revealed, "Because Bob has made you my official co-manager."

Damien wanted to laugh; he was free from Lincoln's control. But at the same time he understood Lincoln's dream had just been crush and he was most likely responsible. Instead of showing any sign of excitement, he got up and left Lincoln alone. The moment he was out the store, Damien finally released his smile. He immediately wanted to share the news with one of the most important men in his life, Zyan. Right away, he drove over to Zyan's mom's house.

Upstairs in Zyan's room, he lit a celebratory blunt for Damien, "I wish I coulda see that nigga's face."

"Man, I saw a tear. It was heartbreaking but fucking funny at the same time."

Zyan took a puff of his blunt as he sat down on his bed, "Man, I gotta give you a gift."

Damien shook his head, "Keep your money, I know how much you make."

"I'm talkin about some ass, my nigga."

That was a gift Damien wasn't going to deny. Zyan put out his blunt and Damien started to unbutton his pants until his cellphone rang. Zyan started to strip down as Damien checked his phone to learn it was Max calling. A ton of guilt was starting to set in as Damien stared at Max's picture on his phone. He didn't know why, but he answered.

"Max, what's up," Damien said.

"Where are you?"

"At work," Damien lied. "But I'm just leaving."

"Good, good, because man, I fucked up. You gotta come home and fast."

"What do you mean, you fucked up?" Damien asked.

"I can't even explain this shit over the phone; you just need to come home now, alright?"

Damien looked at Zyan who looked so fuckable in his boxers right now. "Aright, I'm coming now."

Damien hung up the phone, kicking himself for being in this situation.

Zyan stuck his hand in his boxers, "Man, don't tell me you leavin?"

"I have to, but I can come back by."

"Nah, my sis gettin out school soon and my mom will be here."

Damien started to leave, "Then let me know when you free again man, I really gotta go."

Zyan relit his blunt, "You lame for this, my nigga."

Damien agreed with Zyan, he was not cool with his decision, but needed to get home to Max. As he drove home, he was hoping whatever Max did he could use it as a way to finally end their relationship. He just hoped it wasn't anything that could end his football career early. Damien arrived to his apartment and barged in to find Max sitting on the couch with two duffle bags.

Damien shut the apartment door, "What's wrong?"

Max stood up and formed a smirked, "I fucked up and did some fag shit, I fell in love with a man."

Damien narrowed his eyes, "What?"

"Damien, I love you." He motioned down at the two duffle bags, "Imma grow some nuts and move in, officially."

In his head, Damien was screaming for Max to leave. "That's....that's what's up. I...love you too."

Max rushed over to Damien and kissed him, "You ain't had to say it, I know you do. You put up with my DL shit."

Damien did not want to be here, he did not want to be in Max's arms. Still, he found himself helping Max unpack, cooking dinner with him, watching a movie, and cuddling as they fell to sleep. Damien was far too depressed to sleep all the way through the night, he badly needed to speak up at any moment and end things with Max. But he didn't think it was possible to confess your love, and then break up the next morning. He was going to put up with this relationship for a bit longer and then force himself to set a break up date.

The next morning Damien woke up to a text from Marion stating, 'dad is in town'. After exchanging a couple of text with his brother, Damien let Max know he was heading out to go see his father, but mostly just wanted to get away from him. Damien was nervous about seeing his father, not seeing the man in person since Thanksgiving. He did figure the news of his promotion would make up for him failing out of college. After a shower and mind numbing breakfast with Max, Damien drove over to Marion and Vincent's.

He knocked on the apartment door and Vincent answered, "He's here," Vincent announced.

Damien entered the apartment to find his father and brother in the kitchen. "Hey Dad."

"What took you so long to get here?" Eric asked. "Some girl?"

"Nah, I had to stop by work first," Damien lied.

"Y'all had a meeting about shirts or some shit," Marion joked.

"Actually, I was getting told about my promotion. They made me co-manager."

"Well damn son," Eric said, "You actually doin some shit with your life. This is good, one of my boys in college and the other one is taking over the retail world. I real proud of both of you. Man, I know your momma just lookin down beaming. I wanna celebrate, tonight, we gonna drink and have a lil party. But I left my damn wallet all the way back home, so Marion you gonna have to pay and go to whoever be hookin y'all youngsters up with liquor."

"Then we gotta go to the store now," Marion said, "The dude who be sellin to us only works morning shifts."

"Alright then," Eric said, "We gonna go to the liquor store in my car. Vince and Damien go buy some food."

Marion and Eric left for the liquor store, leaving Vincent and Damien alone.

Vincent laughed, "Y'all daddy don't want a party for y'all, he tryin to get some college pussy."

Damien laughed, "Shut up. You have money for food? I just paid rent."

"Hell no, but I'll just call a pizza dude I know when the party starts tonight. He'll hook us up."

"Oh, cool. How are you doing anyways? Where's Noah?"

Vincent laughed as he rubbed the back of his neck, "Oh, we on a break. Forever."

"How did you manage to screw up an open relationship?"

"It's funny that you ask, because it involves you. One night when we were fucking, I called him Damien."

Damien burst out laughing, "Stop lying? You always trying to get in somebody's head."

"I'm serious. Noah is everything, but you more. I think we should give each other a try again."

"Nope, I'm already in a relationship that I don't even want to be in."

Vincent raised his right brow, "You ain't dump that nigga yet?"

"I'm working on it."

"Then how about I give you a lil kiss of courage, to end that shit."

Damien rolled his eyes, "Yeah, cause I'm sure you're an expert at leaving dudes."

Vincent walked up to Damien, placed his hand on the back of his head and pulled him in for a kiss.

Marion stormed into the apartment, "I left my wallet."

Vincent and Damien's lips parted. Damien looked to his brother who was stewing with rage, like an angry bull.

****

24 - Dallas

Dallas, Texas was far away from NC and especially far away from home and that's the way Damien liked it. Moving to Dallas came with one big flaw, Max. Actually, it was the entire reason Damien found himself living further down south, besides it being an escape from his family. Max had been offered a football contract for a professional team and the opportunity to finish school in Dallas while training. It was the perfect opportunity for Damien to end things, a long distance relationship most likely not lasting.

Instead of ending things, Damien took an extended leave from Aerostyle, simply stating family issues, and ran away to Dallas, away from his father and brother. Marion had completely blocked Damien from all his social media pages and Eric would call every now and then, leaving voice messages begging Damien to talk about his sexuality. Damien was not ashamed of who he was, but feared that his own father or brother were.

With Max's rent covered by the team that signed him, Damien spent the last eight months being a stay at home boyfriend. He mostly watched TV, chatted with gay men online in secrecy, and did his best to stalk down Zyan online. He had lost touch with Zyan, only the memories of the great sex and times they had to hold on to. Damien sometimes could only laugh at himself after spending hours Googling Zyan's name and browsing Facebook profiles in the NC area.

When he wasn't searching for Zyan, he was glued to Instagram while lounging away on the couch, like today. Leon had posted an invitation to him and Megan's wedding. A lot of the comments were congratulatory, while others mocked them for tying the knot so early. Damien didn't care; it was just nice to see two people in a happy relationship. Another interesting Instagram he kept up with was Vincent's.

All of Vincent's pictures had become a lot more x-rated. Though in some he smiled, Damien could see the sadness and loneliness in his eyes. Damien hadn't talk to Vincent since the day Marion had walked in on them. At first he blamed Vincent for what happened, and now was too ashamed to speak to him after having that idea in his mind for so long. The strange thing was, Vincent never tried to contact him either, so Damien wondered if he was blaming him back.

A sweaty Max entered the apartment carrying a duffle bag. "I'm sore."

"Oh, for real?" Damien said trying his best to sound interested.

Max dropped his bag to the floor and joined Damien on the couch, "I might need a little massage."

"Please, do it yourself," Damien said with a bit of attitude.

"What's wrong with you?"

Damien realized he allowed his true feelings to show. He forced a smile, "Nothing, I'm cool. Just hot."

"It's Texas, it's always hot. Imagine doing what I do out there."

"Playing tackle with a bunch of sexy dudes, I wish."

Max bit his bottom lip, "But you got the sexiest one right here. Soon, I'll be all over ESPN and magazines."

Damien could honestly see that happening. Max was indeed a good looking man, but so damn boring to him. The promise of the fame and fortune to come wasn't enough to keep Damien interested. He had no idea when he was going to simply break up with Max, because that would mean making an actual decision about his future.

Max nodded at the kitchen, "Can you please cook?"

"What do you want?"

Max kicked off his sneakers, lounged back, and shut his eyes, "To wake up to something good."

Damien didn't find his comment funny at all, but he kept his composure and went inside the kitchen to make turkey burgers and cheese drizzled broccoli. Thus began their nightly routine, they ate, then he watched a mind-numbing episode of some show on USA Network that Max was obsessed with, and then they ended up in bed together.

This was the most awkward part about their relationship. They were two horny young men who didn't know how to please each other. Max started to kiss on Damien's neck and play with his soft dick. Getting an erection with Max was a challenge. Damien was not turned on by simply being kissed anymore. As for giving each other head, it was a onetime deal for both of them, mutual masturbation dominating their sex life.

Max licked his thumb, slid his hand under the sheets and slowly started to play with Damien's hole.

Damien quickly jerked away, "What are you doing?"

Max laughed, "I'm trying to open you up."

"Why?"

"Cause I wanna fuck you, that's why."

"I don't bottom," Damien said.

"Try it before you knock it," Max said.

"But I have no interest in trying it, how about you try it," Damien snapped back.

"Hell no, you ain't gonna be having me walking funny," Max said, "I'm a masc top."

Damien hated how he always had to add on the masc part, "I'm a top too."

“Well, you gonna have to compromise if I’m going to be supporting you.”

“I can support myself. I’m not turning into a bottom just because you keep the lights on.”

“And pay the rent and keep the fridge stocked. There’s nothing wrong with being a bottom,” Max said.

“I know that and I love bottoms and so does my dick. But I’m not a bottom so stop trying to force it on me.”

Max sucked his teeth as he scooted away, “Don’t fuckin talk to me for the rest of the night.”

“No, don’t talk to me,” Damien said as he turned his back to Max.

Damien was legit upset with the entire situation, but at the same time saw it as the perfect opportunity to dump Max. The reality was that he needed Max, not willing to go back home and face his family yet.

The next morning Damien and Max were giving each other the cold shoulder. Damien was actually glad for a break from Max’s annoying voice. His silence was a gift. It was Thursday, which Damien considered his favorite day of the week. Because not only did Max have class and practice, he would have to attend a pre-season game for the team who signed him and watch from the stands. Damien considered this his club searching night.

The minute Max left for the day; Damien broke out his laptop and started searching the area for gay bars. The scene was mostly dominated by white gays, Damien had nothing against them, he just lacked an attraction to them. After a lot of searching, he found the Facebook of a new bar named Toochi’s. The majority of men in the pictures that were taken inside the club were black.

He spent a few more minutes just researching the place and the operating hours, the doors not officially opening until nine. Max usually got home around midnight, so that gave Damien a couple of hours to have fun while his dull boyfriend was away. He spent the majority of his day doing his stay at home boyfriend duties of lounging around on the couch, Instagramming, and cyber stalking Zyan. But once the sun went down, Damien slipped on some sneakers, black jeans, a red polo shirt and hit the club.

Walking into Toochi's was a breath of fresh air, even though the club smelled like sweat, liquor and a combination of hundred colognes. The vibe of the club was attached to many great memories for Damien. He always thought back to the night he and Leon went to Shane's or when Zyan took him to the Blue Room. If they both were here today, Toochi's would be a lot more fun but Damien had to settle with what he could get.

Not much of a dancer, Damien took a seat at the bar and just watched the clubbers enjoy themselves. Being around these joyous gay men reminded him that their life style wasn't so doom and gloom. Sure, they had to deal with issues many straight people wouldn't have to, but in life good and bad things happen. In the end, you had to make your own happiness no matter how dark your past was. Damien knew at some point he would have to face his family and tell them to either love him or forget him, in time; he would have that courage to do so.

The shirtless bartender who had dredded hair approached Damien, "You ain't gonna dance?"

"Nope, I'm actually sorta here to just clear my head, you know? Escape reality."

The bartender looked him up and down, "What's your reality stranger?"

"My name is Damien actually."

"I'm Romeo. So...your reality...wait, let me guess."

Damien smiled, "Alright Romeo, do your best?"

Romeo looked him up and down, "Married young to some fat girl, but you really like the bussy."

"Wrong, wrong, wrong," Damien said, "Try again?"

"Bitch just tell me, I'm intrigued."

"Alright, well I'm in a sexless relationship and hiding from my family after basically stumbling out of the closet."

"Then find somebody else to have sex with and man up and tell your family to fuck off."

"I know," Damien said, "But it's not as easy as it sounds. I kind of need my boyfriend financially also."

"How old are you?" Romeo asked.

"Twenty."

Romeo laughed, "You are too damn young to be living like this. Don't let that nigga you with trap you because he got money. Damien, this ain't a gay issue, this is a man issue. You need to get up and go fend for yourself. Find a nigga in here who will let you sleep on his couch or something, but get away from this boyfriend. As for your family, just accept that you might have to start a new one. I haven't talked to my mother in years, but I know plenty of dragqueens who look out for me and even love me better than that woman has ever had."

"I don't think my family situation is that drastic. My dad calls me, but I'm not ready to face him yet."

Romeo rolled his eyes, "You need to stop being stupid then and answer the phone."

"I'm just afraid of what he's gonna say," Damien said.

"But you don't even know, so answer the phone and find out. If he calls you a fag, so what, you are, right?"

"I prefer the word gay, but I guess you right."

"I'm a fucking bartender," Romeo said, "I'm always right."

"Are you over here distracting my employee?" A familiar southern voice said.

Damien looked over his shoulder to find Tyler, dressed to impress in a fitted black suit. "Yo, I know you."

Tyler fanned his hand at him, "Why are you in my club talking instead of buying a drink?"

"I'm still underage and Romeo gives good advice. He's a good bartender."

Tyler looked at Romeo, "Please go wash out some glasses Dr. Phil."

Romeo laughed as he grabbed a washcloth and walked away.

Damien had to know the truth, "Is this your club or are you just really like the manager or something?"

"It's mine. I worked my ass off and called in a lot of favors to get this. You want a tour?"

Damien shrugged, "Yeah, okay."

Tyler toured him around the club, showing off the features, and going into more detail about how he got the place. Damien didn't know how much to believe, but he just went along with the tour and kept his eyes on Tyler's ass. The tour ended in Tyler's office where he had some licenses hanging on the wall for the club with his name actually printed on them. That was more than enough proof to convince Damien that Tyler wasn't lying or just good with Photoshop.

Tyler sat on the edge of his desk, "Don't forget to tell people about my club, support my business."

"I will, most definitely. So the business is going good, but how are you?"

"Oh I'm perfect honey, brothas in NC still hitting up my phone but that's my past."

"Don't be ashamed of it though, they hittin you up because you know how to put it down on a dude."

Tyler laughed, "Shut up."

"I'm serious, some of the best sex I've ever had."

Tyler got up and grabbed Damien's crotch, "For real? Well, you had some of the best dick."

Damien's dick started to get hard, "It remembers your touch."

"Let me see," Tyler said as he got down on his knees and pulled out Damien's dick.

Damien wasn't expecting himself to ever be putting his dick in a man so many had been with again, but he was desperate. His desperation combined with the fact that the head Tyler was giving was masterful, led to him nutting a bit too quick. Making sure he didn't mess up his suit, Tyler cleaned up every bit of Damien's nut with his mouth.

Tyler stood up laughing, "That is not a club service, so don't go telling everybody about that."

"I won't," Damien said as he zipped up his pants. He checked the time on his phone, "Shit, I gotta go."

"Alright, come buy tomorrow then around lunch, maybe I can show you my new place."

"Alright cool," Damien said not sure if he wanted to go that route again with Tyler.

It nearing midnight, Damien had to rush home in order to beat Max back. As he pulled up to their apartment, Max's car was already there. Damien took a minute to come up with a lie and just settled on the easiest, a late night trip to Wal Mart. His story set, Damien entered the apartment to find Max butt naked on the couch with another man getting some head.

"What in the fuck?" Damien said, instantly not feeling as guilty about his cheating ways.

Max's guest kept sucking as if Damien wasn't there.

Max looked over to Damien, "This is Omari. I've been messin with him for a couple of months since we've been in Dallas. After last night I accepted you won't bottom for me and I won't bottom for you, so I've invited Omari to be a part of our relationship. I feel as if having a bottom will keep us together longer."

Damien could not believe the stupidity of this idea. "No, fuck this. Max...if he's in...I'm out."

Damien was taking the bartender's advice, he had to man up.

Max shrugged, "Together, we both crumble. We need Omari."

"Fuck this," Damien said as he stormed from the apartment.

He got in his car and just started driving. Tears were rolling down his face, his heart not broken but freed. Damien knew where he had to go, NC. It was a scary thought, but he only hoped the longer he drove, and the closer he got, he would find that same strength he just had back at the apartment and man up.

25 - Fatherhood

It had been the moment that drove Damien away from everything he built; the moment that led to him living a life in Dallas with a guy he had zero care for; it had been the day he felt as if he had lost his family. A moment so unforgettable, yet all it had involved was him standing there speechless.

While Vincent had simply tried to pass it off as one of his many joking moments, Marion knew what he saw. His best friend was kissing his brother. As Damien had stood there numb, he had only hope none of the rage coming from Marion was coming his way. He had been far too stricken with fear to move, yet to defend himself. As Marion took, slow heavy steps towards Vincent, he had kept trying to pass it off as a joke, but his excuse hit a brick wall as Marion's fist collided with his face.

"Don't even say shit to me," Marion said, "Get the fuck out right now."

Vincent cupped his aching face as he stood to his feet, "Nigga, who do you think you are hitting me?"

"Man, I don't want to hear any of your shit right now Vincent. I'm disgusted to my inner core with you."

"I don't care how you feel, I'm not gonna let you hit on me," Vincent argued back.

Damien had just stood there as they exchanged harsh words back and forth, preparing his own defense.

"I feel betrayed man," Marion said, "This shit just ain't right. Vincent, get the fuck out."

"I live here too; my name is on the lease."

Eric entered apartment, "Boy what's taking your ass so long, Marion come your ass on?"

"Not right now, daddy," Marion said, "I'll leave right after Vincent packs the fuck up and go."

Eric rested his hands on his hips, "Why the hell y'all two fightin?"

Damien did not want the question answered, but he knew it was coming.

"This sneaky bitch was in here kissing on Damien," Marion revealed.

Eric raised his brows, "The hell?"

"Why not the other way around?" Vincent said, "He could've been trying to kiss me."

Damien couldn't believe Vincent just threw him under the bus like that.

"There wasn't no trying, I saw what I saw," Marion said, "And I mean what I say, get the fuck out."

Vincent threw his arms up in surrender, "You know what? Fuck this, I'm getting my shit and leaving."

As Vincent stormed off to his room to pack, all eyes turned to Damien.

Damien faced Marion but could not speak any words. Marion simply turned his back to him and sat on the couch.

"Damien," Eric said.

Damien faced his father, still unsure of what to say in a moment like this.

"Damien talk to me son, what the fuck," Eric said, "Say what's on your mind."

Damien couldn't find the words. He stormed forward, brushed past his father, and left Marion's apartment. Besides taking a leave from Aerostyle and sharing goodbyes with Zyan that moment was his last memory he had of his life in North Carolina. And as he officially pulled back into town, he felt as if it was time to pick up where he left off. First thing first, he had to go back to his old apartment complex and work out the details of his suspended lease.

As Damien was walking into the leasing office, he bumped into an unexpected face, Kendall.

Kendall's face lit up, "Well God works in mysterious ways, my mind was just running on you."

Damien was not expecting this blast from the past, "What are you doing here?"

"I just moved in two months ago with my fiancé. We havin some maintenance issues."

"Fiancé," Damien repeated.

"Yeah, her name is Shantell. Maybe you can meet her someday, come on down to one of my sermons. I don't have my own church yet, I actually do these weekends sermons at this hall downtown that I rent. I fell in love with the good people of NC when I came to visit you last time. It's also where I met Shantell. So, instead of settling up north, I decided we can stay here, close to her family." Kendall checked his watch, "Anyways, I gotta get going. I have to take Shantell down to the hospital to get checked out; I might be on my way to fatherhood."

Damien tried to find some source of enthusiasm, "Oh, good luck."

Kendall shuffled passed Damien like he was the happiest man on the planet. When it came to his fake cousin's new life, Damien had little care. As long as Kendall was his idea of happy, that was all that mattered. Right now, Damien had to focus on resuming his lease. Luckily, the landlord made his return easy, but gave him a smaller and more outdated apartment. Damien returned to NC with nothing and had no furniture for his empty apartment, but considered it all a step in the right direction.

As he stood in the center of his empty apartment, his cellphone started to ring. He checked his cellphone to realize it was his father calling. Damien felt as if the universe was giving him that extra push when it came to taking his life back. Easily, Damien could send the call to voicemail as always, but there was no more running away. He had to be a man and face his father.

Damien answered the call, “Hello?”

“Damien? Tell me it’s really you.”

“Yeah dad, it’s me.”

“Boy, where in the fuck have you been,” Eric asked.

“Dallas.”

“And you couldn’t tell nobody. Your brother kept telling me to find you on Insta-something, I don’t what that shit is.”

“Instagram. How is Marion?” Damien asked, mainly wanting to know how his brother felt about him.

“Oh you know how he is. He don’t even like to talk about you, but he’ll be alright.”

It crushed Damien hearing that, “So, he basically hates me.”

“Nah, he just mad. But I ain’t callin about him, I’m callin about you. How you doin?”

Damien sat on his empty living room floor, “I’m back in NC. Might go back to Aerostyle, I gotta pay rent.”

“Well, I know you would end up back on your feet. But I wanna talk about you and Vincent.”

“There is no Vincent and I,” Damien said.

“Then why were y’all kissin?”

“It’s a long story dad.”

“So...um...so you gay now?” Eric asked.

“I’ve always been gay. I’m still the same ole Damien though.”

Eric cleared his throat, "Yeah, I guess. Plus ain't much I can do, you grown."

"So, you're not mad at me?"

Eric laughed, "Nah, just don't let Bernice find out. She'd never shut up about that shit."

Damien smirked, "I don't even talk to her."

"I got another question though."

"Yeah?"

"Now, I see all these fancy gay men on TV, why in the hell you kissin on dumb ass Vincent?"

Damien was finding this conversation to be hilariously awkward, "Those guys on TV are rare."

"Well, you find one of them then tell your aunt Bernice. Let that bitch hate."

"I will."

"Anyways, I gotta go. It's nice knowing you not in a ditch somewhere."

"Alright, by dad," Damien said before hanging up.

Damien could only laugh at himself, the one call he'd been avoiding was one of the best he ever had with his father. It wasn't all so pleasant, learning that his brother was not a fan of what he discovered about him and Vincent. After replaying the conversation repeatedly in his head, boredom set in. Nothing to do in his empty apartment, Damien could only wonder, where in the hell was Zyan?

26 - Income

Damien felt a bit desperate hunting for Zyan, but he missed him. It wasn't just the amazing sex or the wild adventures, he just enjoyed his personality overall. And now that he was free from Max, Damien was looking forward to trying to take things to a higher level with Zyan.

He started his search for Zyan at his mother's townhouse only to learn that he no longer lived there and had moved out on his own. Damien figured things were going pretty well at Aerostyle for Zyan if he was able afford his own place. The woman pointed Damien in the right direction and gave him the name of the apartment complex, Midland Apartments, where Zyan resided.

Damien already knew where the apartments were located; it was one of the nicer ones in the area. He applied once but got denied because of his low income, the apartments costing two times more than the place he was staying at now. He arrived to the complex that had a beautiful pool and gym area that made Damien sort of envious. He parked and walked through the maze of apartments until he found door 6N. Damien knocked on the white door.

A shirtless, tatted, Zyan answered and started laughing, "No fuckin way. I must be so high I'm seeing things."

"Nope, it's me."

Zyan stepped aside, "Man, get your ass in here. Where you been at?"

"Dallas. I'm back now. I dumped my boyfriend and everything."

Zyan shut the door, "Nigga, I don't even know why you followed his ass down there."

Damien was a bit awestruck by how nice Zyan's apartment was. All the furniture was new and his TV was nearly sixty inches. The place didn't seem affordable on an Aerostyle salary. Damien slowly turned around as he took in the beauty of apartment.

"Man, this is nice."

Zyan proudly nodded, "Yeah, thanks. So, how did you end up finally leaving that dude?"

"He wanted a three person relationship because I refused to bottom and so I just left."

"You ain't never let him get in that ass, huh?"

Damien shook his head, "The closest he ever got was when I would dry hump him in jockstraps or thongs and shit."

"And you turn down a three person, relationship? Man that shit sounds sexy ass fuck."

Damien laughed, "I wasn't sharing a bed with two dudes, fuck that. So, how are you?"

"I'm living the fucking life, besides that shitty ass Aerostyle job."

Damien would call the store sometimes, hoping Zyan would answer but it never happened. "How is it shitty?"

"Man, Lincoln got me doing some overnight shift, unboxing shit. He hates me, but I need that lil job. If I lose it, it'll fuck up my reform program shit. I think Lincoln is trying to do anything to get me back behind bars. I've tried asking the niggas who run the program to relocate me, but you know if you commit one crime in your life people treat you like second class shit. They don't care how much I complain, I'm stuck with Lincoln's skinny ass."

"So, do you get paid more or something because this is a really nice apartment?"

Zyan took a seat on his couch, "Nah, I'm back at the Blue Room and doing some other shit."

Damien joined him on the couch, "Selling drugs? I thought you were done with that."

"Fuck that drug shit, I'm doing some escortin."

Damien already started to look at Zyan as overused goods, "Dude, why? That's dangerous."

"It's cool; I meet most clients at the Blue Room, not that online shit. And a lot of them don't even want sex, one dude just likes to talk, one likes going to the movies, and there's another who just likes to watch me clean up his house butt ass naked. You got the freaks though who like me to piss on them. I'm telling you, they love this whole thug shit, and they pay a lot for me to act like the hardest nigga from the streets."

"Well, how much do you make?"

Zyan burst out laughing, "Why, are you trying to cut in on my business?"

"No, not at all, I'm just curious. Because this is a really nice apartment."

Zyan did some math in his head, "About seven hundred a week."

"Jesus, I made that in two weeks at Aerostyle working eighty hours."

"Exactly," Zyan said, "And most of these dudes only get me for about an hour. It's a good job. But, you gotta know how to keep these niggas in their place. There's always that one gay nigga who tries to turn me into a wifey, asking me to stay over or spend the weekend in ATL or some shit. I always be like, yeah I'll stay but I charge by the hour nigga. Overall, it keeps my stomach full and phone on."

"I've been calling your phone too, no answer. I can't even find you on Instagram."

"I lost my old phone and Instagram for pretenders, I live in the real world, my nigga," Zyan said.

"Well, make sure I get your new number before I leave out here."

Zyan nodded, "I will, I will, and you might as well come to the Blue Room tonight. I'm bartending."

"Fine, I'll be there. I just have to eat something before I go out."

"I'll make you something. And while I do that tell me what in the fuck has been going on with you."

Zyan got up and headed into his kitchen to make Damien something to eat.

"Well, as I said, I dumped my boyfriend and now I'm back in NC. I'm back at my old place, but only a smaller and shittier apartment, no rent adjustment, but I can't complain. I was glad she even went as far as suspending my lease. I'll most likely end up back at Aerostyle and I hope Bob will let me return as co-manager. I know Lincoln will fight against that though, but they can't demote me because I had a family emergency for some months."

Zyan laughed, "Nigga, you ain't had no family emergency," He said from the kitchen.

"Kinda, my brother caught me kissing his best friend and my dad just happened to be in town that day."

"Oh shit," Zyan said with more laughter, "They whip your ass and sent you runnin to Dallas, huh?"

"No, my brother did hit his friend though. I sorta just walked out. I talked to my dad and based on our convo everything is good. As for my brother, my dad said he's not cool with it. I figured he would be cool with me based on how he reacted to this guy we know being outted. I guess it's different when it's your brother."

Zyan walked out of the kitchen carrying a plate with two sandwiches and a bag of chips. "Man, I don't even fuck with that label shit. Sometimes I like pussy, some time I like dick, I just happen to mostly be into some dick. But I ain't gonna let nobody try to get up in my face and call me a faggot and shit. I'll beat their ass." He handed Damien his plate of food. "Who's the nigga you been kissin anyways?"

"Vincent," Damien said as he grabbed the plate. He used his other hand to pull up Vincent's Instagram. "Him."

Zyan grabbed and scrolled through the phone, "Man, that's a pretty ass nigga. Aye, you gotta give me his number?"

Damien grabbed his phone back, "He's alright, but not a lick of loyalty in him. I used to be really into him."

"Damn, I wish I was into that nigga right now. He got a tight booty?"

"He's a top."

Zyan rolled his eyes, "Man, you niggas with these labels. We young, fuck and do whatever."

"Yeah, yeah, yeah, whatever mister free spirit."

Zyan stood up and dropped his pants and boxers to the floor, "Imma go shower, then get ready for tonight."

"Oh, alright, I'll be right out here," Damien said as his eyes were glued to Zyan's bare ass.

As Zyan walked away, Damien kept all eyes on him. He was glad to have him back in his life.

Later that night, Damien once again found himself at the Blue Room. It was nice seeing Zyan doing a job he seemed to actually enjoy. Zyan was behind the bar flipping bottles, filling up shot glasses in style, and making every customer laugh. Damien loved all the charisma he displayed. Zyan even made those more uptight clubbers breakout of their shells and crack a smile. A lot of his charm reminded Damien of Vincent's. Damien started to realize how similar both of the men were, except for the fact that Zyan seemed to be a believer in loyalty. Damien was sure Zyan had other friends and men in his life, but when he was around Zyan he felt as if he was the center of his universe.

Zyan took a break from serving drinks and checked on Damien, "You ain't bored, right?"

"Nah, I'm just watching you work man. Where did you pick up these skills?"

"Google and Youtube, shit we don't even need college anymore cause of them."

Damien shrugged, "College gives you that hands-on experience though."

"I'm not gonna let a dropout educate me on college," Zyan teased.

"I'll go back at some point."

"You better," Zyan said, "For you can get a good ass job and hook me up."

"Man, you doing better than me and some college grads out there."

Zyan rolled his eyes, "I ain't gonna be sexy forever though."

"I don't believe that."

"Stop flirtin my dude, you actin like one of these thirsty ass customers," Zyan said as he laughed.

"I'm not flirtin, plus I already had a taste of you anyways."

"Only cause I let you, don't think you sweet talk me out of my boxers. I choose who I fuck wit."

Damien stuck his tongue out at Zyan, "Stop lyin. I had game."

Zyan pinched his fingers together and smirked, "A little, but let's just call it fifty-fifty for now, lemme go work."

Zyan walked away to go chat up a plump man at the bar who was sweating as if it was a hot summer day in the Blue Room. Damien liked Zyan, on more levels than one, romantically was one of those levels. His issue was that he didn't know how to convert their friendship into a romance. Damien was used to men approaching him, to guys wanting to be with him, but it wasn't often when he played the chaser. Besides the gifts he was blessed with that attracted men to him, Damien realized he didn't actually have game.

Zyan rejoined him, “Aye man, imma give you a chance to make some money.”

“I know nothing about bartending.”

Zyan laughed, “No, listen...you saw that sweaty nigga I was just talking with?”

Damien nodded, “Yeah, what’s up?”

“He just gave me his address and wants us to break into his house tonight around one AM.”

“Huh?” Damien said as he furrowed his brows.

“Man, these dudes love this whole thug shit. He saw me talking to you and wants to drop five hundred dollars on us if we break in his house tonight and go straight street on his ass. Ain’t nothing illegal, nigga even let me know where the spare key to his crib is hidden. All we gonna do is fake break in, act street as fuck, and then do the opposite of whatever he tells us not to do. I’ll give you three out of the five, but just this one time.”

Damien could use the money to furnish his apartment, “Man-”

“-You my nigga, my ride or die,” Zyan begged, “I wouldn’t put you in no messy situation.”

Damien wanted to be all of those things, hoping one meant boyfriend. “Alright, I guess.”

Zyan jumped up and down and dapped him, “See, that’s why I fuck wit you. When my shift over, we out.”

Damien was nervous about the idea, but he was desperate to do anything to make Zyan like him even more. His nerves high and still underage, Damien snuck a couple of abandoned drinks to calm himself. It wasn’t long until Zyan’s shift was over and they were pulling up to the client’s home, the name on his mailbox reading Peterson. The home was located in one of those well-off suburban neighborhoods, these types seeming to be big fans of Zyan.

Zyan parked in the man’s parking lot, “Remember, do the opposite of what he says. I’ll lead, you follow.”

“I can do this, especially since I’m kinda tipsy.”

Zyan laughed, "I don't blame you, for shit like this a buzz is needed. Now come on."

In the night, Zyan led the way to Mr. Peterson's porch. He grabbed a key from under a miniature figurine of a frog playing a bongo and opened the man's front door. Most of the lights were on downstairs, a rerun Simpson's episode was playing on the TV and it smelled as if Mr. Peterson had just got done cooking.

Zyan slowly snuck upstairs as if this was an actual robbery and Damien followed, his heart about to jump out of his chest. Zyan led them down a hallway, checking each door until they found Mr. Peterson in his bathroom applying a facial mask and wearing just a towel wrapped around his waist. Mr. Peterson started screaming as if he was starring in a bad horror movie. The drunk in Damien wanted to laugh, but he did his best to keep up the thug act.

"Get the fuck down," Zyan shouted.

Mr. Peterson dropped to his knees, "Please don't step on me, please!"

Zyan pushed Mr. Peterson down to his bathroom floor and stepped down on him, "Shut the fuck up!"

"I'm a good man," Mr. Peterson pretend cried out, "You thugs are careless."

"Bitch you the careless one," Zyan said, "Leaving your damn key under a mat like some dumb bitch."

"Oh lord," Mr. Peterson exclaimed, "Why did I do that lawd? Please don't shove your ass in my face."

After that line, Damien was indeed glad he got drunk for this. He found it to be beyond weird.

Zyan pulled down his pants and shoved Mr. Peterson's face in his ass, "Sniff my ass bitch."

Mr. Peterson grabbed Zyan's butt and inhaled deeply, "No, why, I just can't."

Zyan stepped away and pulled up his pants, "Where in the fuck do you keep the money?"

"I'm not saying. Please don't piss on me."

Zyan looked to Damien and whispered, "Do it."

"Why me?" Damien whispered back.

Zyan softly laughed, "My bladder dry."

"You lyin."

"We ain't getting shit if he don't get pissed on," Zyan said, "Nigga, you came this far. Just do it."

Damien was starting to feel all those drinks he had coming down, "Alright, damn."

Zyan made sure he was out of the bathroom to avoid any splashing before Damien whipped out his dick and started to pee on Mr. Peterson. The man rolled around on the floor and massaged himself all over as Damien peed on him. Damien could not believe he was doing this and that some people actually enjoyed this.

"The money or your life," Zyan threatened.

Damien finished peeing and just stood there with his dick out, shocked, drunk, and confused.

"It's under the center piece on the kitchen table, you good for nothing thugs," Mr. Peterson revealed.

Zyan softly hit Damien in the chest, "Alright nigga, put your dick up. We out."

Damien snapped back into the moment and put away his dick. He didn't know if it was proper to say goodbye or not to Mr. Peterson, but just figured it was less awkward to just walk away. Damien caught up with Zyan downstairs in the kitchen. He was counting a stack of twenties and handed Damien his cut.

Damien checked the amount, "Four hundred?"

Zyan nodded, "Yeah man, you just had to pee on a nigga. You deserve it."

Damien put the money in his pocket, "That was-"

"-fun?" Zyan interrupted, "Eww, you a freak."

"I was gonna say fucked up," Damien said.

Zyan just started laughing, the smile on his face luring. Damien went in for a kiss.

Zyan quickly pushed him away, "Nigga, what you doin?"

"A celebratory kiss...I guess."

"Nah, we dap," Zyan said, "Stop actin funny, nigga."

"Oh." Damien started to feel as if he was being played with.

"Now let's go before that piss up ass nigga come downstairs."

Damien left behind Zyan, not sure if them becoming legit romantic partners was even possible.

27 - Solo

Damien found himself doing something that he hadn't done in months, seeking advice online. He was completely cool with him and Zyan being friends, but felt there could be more, especially after some of the things they had done together. Most online said don't let sex ruin a friendship, but they had already had sex and things were still pretty good between them. Others made it clear that there was a difference between fuck buddies and boyfriends. If they were fuck buddies, Damien would suck up his feelings and accept that. But Zyan was a man of no labels, Damien wanted labels.

After their odd but profitable night, Damien stopped by Zyan's place again to check in on him.

Zyan answered the door coughing, his eyes swollen, not looking so good, "Man, I'm sick."

"You should've called, I would've brought you something," Damien said as he entered the apartment.

"My phone is dead and I was just too lazy to get up from the couch and charge it."

Zyan shut the door, sulked over to the coffee table and grabbed his phone to charge it.

"I spent my four hundred dollars online last night; I bought a bed and kitchen table," Damien said.

"I'm glad I could help," Zyan said as he coughed and plugged up his phone.

"Still, I went to sleep feeling weird as fuck. All of that last night wasn't me."

"It ain't me either, just a role I play to survive. As I said, I ain't gonna look this good forever, might as well use it."

"So, what's next?" Damien asked.

Zyan's phone powered on and he checked his messages, "Antwan. He's next."

"Who's that?"

"Man, he used to be this dealer until he got this girl pregnant and settled down. Oh yeah, and he likes the dick."

Damien nodded, "And what else kind of freaky stuff is he into?"

Zyan shrugged, "He likes to talk, chill, and hear the sound of his own voice and shit."

"How much does he pay?"

Zyan checked his phone, "He offering three hundred, but I'm way too sick to meet up with him."

Damien needed a living room set, "I can go."

Zyan shrugged, "If you want to wit your ole ho ass."

Damien laughed, "If I'm a ho, you're the master ho."

Zyan typed something on his phone, "I am who I am."

Damien rolled his eyes at Zyan's avoidance of another label, "So where does he stay?"

"I just texted you the address and the time. He's a day client, his bitch works in the day and kids are at preschool."

Damien checked the address and time, "Damn, that's thirty minutes from now. I gotta leave now."

Zyan crashed to the couch and curled up in the fetal position, "Alright, bring me some OJ when you get back."

"I will."

Damien left and put the address in his GPS when he got in his car. He wasn't as nervous as he was last night, mainly because it was daylight, he sort of knew what to expect now, and Antwan's home was located in a decent neighborhood. Him being a former dealer was the only negative about this situation. Instead of parking in front of Antwan's house, Damien parked around the corner, walked and knocked on the door.

A well-built, dark-skinned man with a mini afro answered the door, "Yo."

"Are you Antwan?"

"Why?"

"Um, Zyan sent me," Damien whispered.

"And you came knocking on the front door like we homies. He ain't tell you, back door only?"

Damien shook his head and was preparing himself to step back and go walk around to the back, "No, he was sick. My bad."

Antwan nodded over his shoulder, "Just come on in and hurry up before somebody see you."

Damien entered the home that was messed with toys and had walls with crayon markings on them.

Antwan shut the door, "You want some kool-aid or something? I think we got a couple of lunchables."

"I'm cool."

"Alright then, come on to my room."

Damien followed Antwan through the house and into his bedroom. It was clear one side of the room was his area and the other belonged to his girlfriend. They were even a couple of family photos placed around them room including Antwan, his girlfriend, and children. Damien felt a little bad being here, feeling like a homewrecker, but decided to leave all of the guilt on the conscience of Antwan.

Antwan sat down on his bed, "You different from Zyan, where you from?"

"Up north."

"You a real clean-cut dude, college boy?"

"Former, but I'll go back eventually."

Antwan nodded, "Yeah, I like that. An educated nigga. Don't do the drug game shit, it's stressing."

"Is your family the main reason you stopped dealing drugs?"

"Yeah," Antwan said, "And disloyal niggas." He patted the bed, "Come sit down, I ain't paying for you to be shy."

Damien sat down as he was told, "So, what do you do now for income?

Antwan put his arm around Damien's shoulder, "Give me a lil kiss."

Damien was expecting to talk and listen only, like Zyan foretold, "Huh?"

"Zyan the type I like to smoke and jack off with, but I'll throw in an extra hundred for some ass from you."

"I'm cool with the three; I didn't come here for sex or anything."

"Five hundred," Antwan said.

"Still no."

"Then how about if I try to take that ass," Antwan said as he forced Damien down on the bed.

"Yo, get the fuck off of me," Damien said as he tried to wrestle free.

"Nigga you gonna let me fuck first," Antwan said as he started to laugh.

Damien couldn't get free; he didn't know what to do but to feel like an idiot. He wasn't raised to be doing stuff like this. He was taught to work, go to school, make his money the hard way. Antwan was nearly out of his pants as he did his best to try to turn

Damien over. A door slammed and a woman's voice and two kids could be heard.

Antwan quickly pulled up his pants and set Damien free, "Nigga, get out," He whispered, "Go out the window."

Damien had it in him to scream and let Antwan's girlfriend find them, but he wasn't starting a feud with a former dealer. As he quickly got up from the bed Antwan tossed some twenties at him, Damien needed money but not that bad. He simply turned from Antwan and rushed out of the home through the bedroom window.

Damien found himself sitting in his car in silence, still shaken up about what almost happened to him. After getting his mind together, he drove off and over to Zyan's. Damien tried to stay strong on the ride over, but shed a tear. He parked at Zyan's complex and made sure there was no sign of his crying as he made his way back to his apartment door. Damien let himself in to still find Zyan wrapped up on the couch.

Zyan cracked his eyes opened, "Yo, where's the juice?"

"Fuck that juice," Damien said, "Antwan tried to fuck me."

Zyan laughed, "Yeah, they try to go overboard sometime."

"It's not fucking funny, he tried to rape me."

"What you mean rape? Why you talkin like a female? You shoulda beat his ass, I would."

"Man, rape is rape dude," Damien said, his eyes welling up with tears.

Zyan rolled his eyes, "Man, go ahead out here with that crying shit. I told you, escortin ain't always a cake walk."

Damien couldn't understand how Zyan could be so insensitive. He was mad at him, but at the same time didn't want to be. Damien wasn't in the mood for this emotional rollercoaster, so he just left. All of today was just bad, from almost being sexually assaulted to seeing a heartless side of the man he wanted to be with.

28 - Criminal

Damien forced himself to get over it; he couldn't stay mad at Zyan. Still, he saw him in a different light. Zyan was selfish, all about making money and looking out for himself. Damien never considered that a flaw until he needed some sympathy and Zyan couldn't give up any. Since the beginning of their friendship, Damien trusted Zyan and saw him only in a positive light, those days were over, still he consider him his closest friend today. Damien decided to quickly refocus back on his life, vowing to pick the men he pursued more wisely.

His first mission had been to go back to work and after some calls with Lincoln and District Manager Bob, he was awarded a full-time customer service position but would have to wait a few more months before possibly becoming co-manager again. His amount of power at the store was decreased, naturally, but so was his pay and that bothered him most. He had his own self to blame, he was the one who tossed aside his stable foundation to go hide away in Texas.

Damien arrived to his first day back at Aerostyle and went directly to Lincoln's office. He knocked and entered, "I'm back."

Lincoln lounged back and formed a smirk, "I know that, I wrote the schedule, genius."

"Man, you haven't changed at all."

"I like who I am, I have no reason to change."

"Eh, this version of you is okay, I like you better with my dick in your ass," Damien joked.

Lincoln sat stoned faced, not amused with the memory, "And now I already want you to leave."

Damien sat on the edge of Lincoln's desk, "Anyways, what's changed around here?"

"Business has improved, a couple of new hires, and we added a baby's section."

"And what about the drama? Who's fucking who?" Damien asked.

"I don't know, hopefully not you and that crack baby."

"Who?"

"Don't be an idiot," Lincoln said as he rolled his eyes, "Zyan, that illiterate fool."

It was obvious Lincoln's hating ways towards Zyan had not changed. "Maybe you should get to know him before you judge him."

"He's a drug addict, ex-con, and herpes having stripper, trust me, I know him. I can judge all I want."

"But you're leaving out all the positives. Yes, I'm very aware of the bad things about him, his selfishness, and I can go on. But I can easily list bad things about you, mister perfect."

Lincoln laughed, "I don't put my business out there."

"You don't douche before fucking," Damien said with a smirk, "You left my dick a lil bit funky."

"Stop bringing that shit up."

"I can't help it, it's funny," Damien said.

"No, I'll tell you what's funny. What's funny is that when Zyan comes in a bit he's going to lose his job here."

Damien narrowed his eyes, "Why? To get back at me? Because of a joke?"

"Damien everything isn't about you my brotha. We've been missing inventory, Zyan does night stocking, he's a suspect."

"You can't fire him because you think he stole something," Damien argued.

"I'm also letting go the entire stock team. Bob's orders. You and a crew will work nights until we get new hires."

"Lincoln, come on man, you know Zyan needs his job," Damien said.

"I'll consider letting him stay only if you're upfront with me. Why do you like him so much over guys like me? You know...gentlemen."

Damien shrugged, "There's nothing wrong with men like you. Yes, you annoy the hell out of me and jokes aside, you were a good fuck. But when it comes to Zyan, I'm just drawn to his charisma...his looks....his attitude. He's not perfect though; he's driven mostly by financial gain, a pothead, and has little concern for others' feelings just like I said. It took me awhile to see that. Still, just because he's flawed like everybody else on the planet, doesn't mean you should fire him just because you think he took something. The other night employees should be spared also."

"I'm not firing them," Lincoln cleared up, "This is Bob's doing."

"Bob's supplying the bullets and you're shooting the gun."

Lincoln laughed, "Overdramatic, but sure."

"It's not right."

"Yes it is. We're protecting the company from thieves like Zyan and the other low lives."

"He could end up back in jail. This job is required for the reform program."

"He can tell them about his stripper job. I heard he's really good at twerking. His parents must be so proud."

"It's a shame to see another black man bringing down another," Damien said.

"Oh, don't play that shit with me. Zyan's the one bringing other brother's down."

"Lincoln, seriously, reconsider this."

Damien wondered if Zyan would've care enough to fight this much for his job.

Lincoln stood as he checked the store parking lot camera, "I know this car parking, it's our boy Zyan."

"I'll ask him face to face who's been stealing," Damien said, "He won't lie to me."

"Then you better beat me to the parking lot because I'm ready to let him know I'm no longer his boss."

Lincoln left his office and Damien trailed after him.

Lincoln raised his hand to Zyan as they met him at the front door, "Wait, wait, wait a minute."

Zyan stood outside the door way of the store, "What do you want?"

"Who's been stealing?" Damien blurted out before Lincoln could say anything."

"That fat nigga with the braids," Zyan said, "I saw him take some shorts once. Why?"

Lincoln got in Zyan's face, "Why didn't you say anything? Wait, let me guess, snitches get stitches?"

Zyan shrugged, "Snitch or no snitch, it ain't my job to play store security."

"Zyan," Lincoln said as he if was warming himself up to hit the trigger on a bomb of hurt, "You're fired."

"Nigga, what?" Zyan shouted. "For what?"

"For helping another employee steal shorts. You not saying anything hurt the company's profits."

Zyan looked to Damien, "You couldn't even warn a nigga? But you up here with him questioning me?"

"I just found out," Damien said.

"I thought we were boys," Zyan said.

"I said I didn't know Zyan, stop making me try to feel like the bad guy," Damien explained.

Lincoln started laughing, "A lovers spat."

Zyan focused back on Lincoln, "Nigga, I ain't nobody's lover."

Not aware of the two cops leaving the shoe store next door, Zyan punched Lincoln in the face. Lincoln took things overboard as he fell to the floor and started screaming as if he was just shot. Both of the cops made their way over, Zyan started to run but simply stopped and threw his hands up in air.

"He's a thief and uncontrollable," Lincoln said to the cops as he stood up caressing his face.

"Seriously," Damien said as he looked to Lincoln, "He barely tapped you."

"This some fucking bullshit," Zyan said as one of the cops cuffed him. "Damien, let my mom know I'm in cuffs."

"I'll call her man," Damien said as he got out his phone.

"On your lunch break," Lincoln said, "You're on the clock."

"I didn't even clock in yet."

Lincoln started walking towards the back of the store, "So it's even worse, you're running late."

The cops had already got a struggling Zyan halfway to their patrol car that was parked near the shoe store.

Damien couldn't do much, so went after Lincoln, "This is some foul shit. Unreal."

Lincoln looked over his shoulder as he kept walking towards the back, "I didn't force him to hit me."

"Still, you didn't have to let them arrest him. That could end up fucking up his life big time."

Lincoln arrived back to his office, "No, it'll teach him not to act like an animal."

"He got fired for a shit reason, he was upset," Damien said as he entered the office behind Lincoln.

Lincoln shut the door and lowered his voice, "Please, you're just mad because you won't get to fuck him tonight."

"I knew this was all about me." Damien whipped out his dick, "Here, shit, you happy. You can have it."

Lincoln laughed, "Man, I don't want you and your weak ass dick game. I don't fuck with dudes like that anyways. Pussy is my vice."

Damien put his dick away, "Then what can I do to convince you to tell those cops to let Zyan go."

Lincoln sat down at his desk, "Nothing. He's going to pay for what he did. Now clock in and go work the register."

Damien couldn't do it. He would rather starve than work with Lincoln, "Fuck this, I'm out."

Lincoln shrugged, "Good, I don't care. Go get your mind together and off of trade dick. You're pathetic."

Damien wanted to hit Lincoln, but didn't want to end up in a patrol car like Zyan. He had to find the little bit of civility in him right now and just leave.

29 - Desperate

Damien couldn't allow himself to fall into a depression. He was jobless and his closest friend was now behind bars. Damien kept in touch with Zyan's mother mainly to get updates, only family allowed to visit Zyan at the moment. The woman kept the conversations short, as if she had little care about her son being in jail. Damien just assumed this was nothing new to her and he would have to be patient until he was allowed to visit.

Damien used the positives in his life to drive him. Apparently his father was dating, Vincent finally found some respect for himself and deleted his Instagram, and Leon had a great wedding based on the pictures Damien saw online, him not able to make it down to Georgia for the wedding. As for his brother, he actually sent Damien a happy birthday text, it was a dull one, but made his twentieth birthday a better one. He wasn't doing much to celebrate at all, just having dinner later with Kendall and his fiancé out of boredom and because he wanted a free meal.

Until then he focused on job searching the old fashioned way by going around and asking for applications. He didn't qualify for all the high paying jobs and all the minimum wage jobs were fully staffed. Damien reached a new low as he headed down to a gas station in the hood, the place infamous for its constantly changing staff. The line at the counter was nearly out the door but Damien finally reached the front.

“Hey, I was just wondering if you guys were hiring,” Damien asked.

The nearly toothless woman at the register shook her head, “Um...no, next in line.”

Damien wasn’t sure if she was telling the truth or too lazy to grab him an application. The people in line behind him were getting impatient and the cashier was acting as if he wasn’t standing there, simply repeating ‘next’ over and over again. Damien just decided to get out of the way before he was jumped from behind. He made his way out to the gas station parking lot.

“Hey, young dude, hold up,” A male voice called out.

Damien turned around to find a man with vibrant caramel skin, a bushy dark beard, and a built body following him.

Damien pointed at himself, “Me?” Surprised a man this beautiful was in this part of town and talking to him.

“If you’re looking for a job, yeah you,” The man said as he extended his hand out to Damien, “I’m Ford.”

Damien gladly shook his hand, “Damien, and yes I am looking for a job.”

“Well, I’m looking for an assistant. A young dude like you can do better than a dead end gas station.”

“What kind of assistant?”

“I’m opening up a set of gyms with a buddy of mine. I could use somebody to run errands for me.”

Damien considered anything a step up from his current position. “That sounds cool. What’s the details of the job?”

Ford crossed his arms and stroked his beard, “How about we discuss it over a business dinner tonight? On me.”

Damien couldn’t believe this opportunity was being given to him. “See, I already have dinner plans.”

“It’s Friday, that’s understandable. Are you taking your girl out?”

“Actually, it’s a birthday with a friend of mine and his fiancé.”

"Happy birthday, how old are you turning?"

"Twenty. I'm starting to feel old right in my lower back."

Ford laughed, "Now you're making me feel ancient."

"Nah, we ain't that far apart. Let me guess, twenty-six?"

Ford laughed, "Fourteen years ago."

Damien couldn't believe it; the man looked as if he was just finishing grad school. "Man, what's your secret?"

"Sleep, it's nature's fountain of youth. Anyways, how about we do a Sunday business brunch?"

"Yes, sir. Do you want my number?

"First, don't call me sir. I'm not that old. And we can most definitely swap numbers."

Damien and Ford typed each other's numbers into their phones.

Ford sent Damien a winking smiley, "I'm just making sure it's working. I'll see you Sunday."

"Most definitely."

Damien watched as Ford made his way over to the nicest car in the parking lot, a black mustang. Compared to his former boss Lincoln, Damien felt as if he would have a great work relationship with Ford. Already, he wanted to know so much more about this man and hopefully start to work for him. Damien wasn't blind either, Ford was breathtaking.

On that note, Damien ended his job search and headed home to get ready for dinner with Kendall and his fiancé. After a shower and grabbing some sodas that he said he would bring over, Damien headed over to Kendall's apartment to have his birthday dinner. He arrived, knocked and Kendall answered the door.

"Cousin," Kendall, who was dressed like a skinny Bill Cosby, greeted, "You came."

"After the way you talked about your fiancées food, I had to show up."

Kendall laughed as he let Damien in, "Man, tonight you'll have to settle for my cooking though."

"Why?" Damien said as he surveyed the apartment, a crucifix almost everywhere he looked.

"One of our church sister's took sick and my wife is going to sit with her tonight and look over her."

"Man, that's really nice. You found yourself a good woman."

Kendall shut the apartment door, "I had to dig through a sea of sin to find her."

"Am I one of those sins?"

Kendall hunched his shoulders, "Sometimes, I don't know."

Damien sat the sodas down on the kitchen table, "What does that mean?"

"I love my wife Damien; I know God wants me to be with her. But...you're still in my heart."

Damien believed Kendall was overall a good person, but simply confused. "My bad...I guess."

Kendall laughed, "It's not your fault, it's wickedness man."

"Could be...or it could just be the truth."

"But that's not me anymore."

Damien shrugged, "Alright then, get off the topic. Are we going to eat or what?"

Damien wasn't in the mood to play counselor, he wanted to get through this dinner and then have his interview with Ford. Kendall snapped out of his oddness and went back to his joyful self as he served some burnt chicken and bitter greens. The entire meal they just rehashed their childhood. But of course at some point they had to reach who they became as men.

"I want to forget what we've done," Kendall said.

Damien pushed away his plate of food, "Stop doing this, stop acting crazy."

"No, I'm just-"

"-Horny," Damien said, "I'm sorry, I had to say it."

Kendall lowered his head, "But I think you're right. Damien, how can I get over this?"

"Listen, being a Christian is cool but maybe you just need to accept you're a gay Christian. It's a thing."

"But how do I even know if I'm really gay? It could just be a wickedness in me."

Damien stood up, "The wicked shit is you just avoiding the truth. I know you know it, you're gay, we're gay."

Kendall looked up at Damien, "Why?"

"Because the God that you love so much made you that way."

"But why would he make me this way?"

Damien walked over to Kendall, forced him to stand up and kissed him, "For you can enjoy shit like that."

Kendall touched his lips, "How can something so wrong, feel so damn good?"

"It's called happiness, another thing your God wants for you. Fuck people, especially those like Bernice."

Kendall wrapped his hands around Damien's neck and pulled him in for another kiss. Next thing Damien knew was that he had Kendall out of his slacks and penny loafers and was fucking him on the kitchen table. With every thrust into his tight bubble ass, Damien felt as if he was knocking some sense into a moaning Kendall. Damien knew this fuck session was going to be one he would regret, but it would be the only way to hopefully wake Kendall up and save his fiancée from a dead end marriage.

As Damien nutted deep inside of him, Kendall moaned out, "God forgive me."

His words instantly turned this moment into an extremely awkward one for Damien.

Damien pulled out and zipped up his pants, "What the fuck was that?"

Kendall sat up and started to cry, "I'm so fucking weak," He cried. "You got in my head."

"Kendall, stop this shit right now. Your outing has seriously messed you up."

"I can't do this," Kendall said.

"Do what? Lie to yourself?"

Kendall grabbed a fork from the table and jammed it deep into his neck. Damien immediately stumbled backward against the wall as crimson sprayed from Kendall's neck until it slowly started to drain and stain his clothes. Kendall shed a single tear as he kept his eyes on Damien before collapsing from the table to the floor.

30 - Roots

Funerals are supposed to be sad, for Damien this was the easy part. The hard part was watching a human he knew for the most of his life bleed to death. Damien had tried to do his best to bust out his Grey's Anatomy skills and stall the bleeding, but by time the ambulance had arrived, Kendall was just a body. All the confusion, all the pain, all the hurt, no longer matter to him; his life was over.

Now, it was time for everybody to mourn him, from his mother to his fiancée. It was basically a family reunion for Damien, seeing his brother and father for the first time since they had caught him kissing Vincent. As always, Marion had some random girl on his arm who thought it made sense to wear a bright red dress to the funeral. Eric on the other hand looked as if he had just lost one of his own sons. It wasn't until after the burial at the funeral reception Damien got to catch up with everybody.

He took a seat next to Eric, "Hey dad."

Eric sighed heavily, "Man, why you let that boy do that to himself?"

"I couldn't stop it. He just did it."

"But why? Who kill themselves like that? Leaving behind all his people."

"He was lost dad."

"Why?" Eric asked, "Cause he was gay, we all knew."

"Still, the way you all found out and the reaction really drove him to the deep end."

"But, he was getting married? Going to church? He was happy, right? It had to be something else."

"Dad, a lot of guys suffer like this in the dark. I did."

Eric quickly looked over to Damien, "You tried to kill yourself? Why?"

"I never tried, but I always had that thought. It sometime seemed easier than being out."

"But I thought gays were all loud and proud. Like um...the Michael Sam fella?"

Damien smirked, "Dad, not everybody is lucky enough to come out and be accepted with ease. People deal with ignorance and hate. I mean, even you said some stuff that made me never want to come out. But if I knew you would act the way you did, I would've came out a long time ago. It's so many different scenarios though dad, Kendall is just one of the bad ones. But they're plenty of good ones like mines...sort of."

"Why do you mean by sorta? Who messin with you?" Eric asked.

"He's not messing with me, just avoiding me. Marion."

Eric nodded, "Oh, yeah I guess. I did make him text you on your birthday though."

"Knowing he was forced to do so only makes our relationship seem even more doomed."

Eric stood up, "I ain't gonna have it. Marion," Eric shouted across the room, "Marion!"

Marion rushed from the crowd and over to his father, "Damn daddy, why are you being so ghetto?"

Eric pointed at his seat, "Man sit yo ass down and talk to your brotha."

Marion looked to his seat, “I’m a grown man, I don’t have to do nothing.”

“If you so grown then pay for your own classes, cause you won’t be getting any money from me,” Eric said.

“Daddy it ain’t even that serious,” Marion said. “You know I use the Pell for rent, I need you man.”

Eric stared Marion down, “Boy don’t make me start actin a fool at this lil dead boy’s funeral.”

Marion sat down in the chair, “Fine, damn. You happy?”

Eric snapped his fingers at them, “Talk.” He turned his back to his sons.

Damien looked to Marion; it was almost as if he was staring at a stranger, “It ain’t fair.”

“What?” Marion snapped.

“You were okay with Kendall being gay but now you don’t even talk to me.”

Marion rolled his eyes, “Nigga, this ain’t about you being gay. That’s not even surprising, momma raised you soft anyways. My thing is how are you going to be sneaking around with my best friend? I don’t even know how long this shit been going on. Was Vincent my real homeboy or just at our house to fuck with you? That shit makes my skin crawl knowing that you were dumb enough to mess with ho ass Vincent. He sleeps with everybody, so him fucking niggas on the low wasn’t surprising either. But him being on my brother, that shit right there was a betrayal. Both of y’all did me wrong, I’m the one who needs to be sitting around saying it ain’t fair. So that’s that. I’ll speak to you on my terms, for now, I have to do my best to get images of you and Vincent kissing out of my mind.” Marion stood up, “There, I talked.”

Damien looked up at his brother speechless. He didn’t even see himself as the bad guy in this situation.

Eric turned around and looked down at Damien, “So, you got more to say?”

Damien just shook his head from side to side.

"Of course he don't. I'm going home. Where my date? Yo Brandy," Marion called out as he stormed off.

Eric patted Damien on the shoulder, "You forgot your brother got feelings too, huh?"

Damien stood up, "I need to go get some fresh air right quick."

Damien walked as fast as he could out of the community hall. He wasn't the victim. True, his brother put him through a lot of mess but he had become so used to being the victim he didn't even know when he was wrong. Damien started to think back on his life and was having a tough time figuring out which moments he was truly the victim or simply a naïve fool or selfish.

As Marion was leaving he simply brushed past Damien, dragging his date who carried a plate of food along with him. Marion got in the car with his date, turned up some Drake, and drove off. Damien stood on the stairs of the community hall in silence, staring blankly as he thought about where to go from here. He still had his interview with Ford, but he didn't even know if that was still going to happen, after he had to push it back a week because of Kendall's death.

"Man, this is awkward," A familiar voice said, "Are you about to cry?"

Damien looked left to find Vincent wearing a cheap suit arriving to the reception, "Why are you here?"

"I missed the funeral and thought I should show my face."

"Do you know that Marion is mad at us? He just left, blasting Drake, so he's deep in his emotions."

"Yeah I know for sure he's mad, duh," Vincent said with a smirk, "I was messing with his lil bro behind his back, I was dirty. It's something I regret doing but at the same time I'm glad I did. It's just sucks that I'm a loser either way; I don't have you or Marion now. All I have is myself. Even stacking up my Instagram followers couldn't help me feel noticed. Life is a bitch."

"True, but now as I look back on it, I've made my own life hard you know? I've done some stupid shit, especially after being outted. I stayed with a guy I didn't like, I was fucking around with this thug who was all about getting money...from stripping to escorting, I lost a good job but not before putting my dick in my boss, and I think I fucked Kendall to death."

Vincent laughed, "Nigga what?"

"I fucked him, he went on a guilt trip, and then killed himself."

"It ain't your fault he was fucked up. We both got outted and didn't go all preacher."

"Still, I knew deep downside he didn't cure the gay away...that if I pushed hard enough I could fuck him."

"Damn, you need to chill out on life man. I miss the old days, back at home, watching videos and shit."

Damien looked to Vincent, "I know right. It was all so fun and simple when we were sneaking around."

"And now we grown, don't have to sneak around, now we need to go back to our roots."

Damien nodded, "Let's be friends, Vincent, legit friends."

"I'm cool with that, but first we gotta apologize to Marion."

"We'll get there, but for now, let's iron out our kinks together, then go on an apology tour."

"Is sex involved?"

Damien thought about it, "I don't know, that's a kink we gotta iron out. We both get around...a lot."

"I'll behave, I miss that mushroom dick."

"And you gave some damn good head and I loved eating your ass."

Vincent laughed, "Better than Kendall's?"

"God rest his soul, but yeah, better than him."

Vincent looked at the community hall, "Wanna come with me as I go pay my respects?"

Damien nodded and stood at Vincent's side. He needed a new start and decided to start at the beginning.

31 - Origins

Damien sat in the visiting room as Zyan was carted out by an officer. He wore an orange jumpsuit and a smile as a pair of handcuffs was being removed from his wrists. Of course Damien still liked him, but he made the decision to not pursue Zyan romantically. His goal was to start fresh and that meant retooling some of the complicated relationships he had developed.

Zyan sat down at the round table, "Aye, first let me say that I'm sorry."

"Sorry about what?"

"For tryin to say you were working against me with Lincoln. I know you wouldn't do that, you hate that nigga."

Damien shrugged, "It's alright man, you were getting fired. That ain't nothin easy to deal with."

"I'm glad you came to see me. I was worried about you and shit. How's your money? Life?"

"It's tough, but I have an interview later with this fine ass dude I met at a gas station."

Zyan nodded, "Cool, so you done with Aerostyle?"

"I walked out the day Lincoln fired you."

"And you ain't tryin no more escortin?"

"Hell no," Damien said, "Especially after what nearly happened to me."

"My bad about that too, I have to remember we aint from the same background. You aint grow up fightin niggas."

Damien laughed, "You trying to say I can't fight?"

"Man, you the one who almost got your ass raped, I would've snap Antwan's dick off."

"Whatever," Damien said as he kept on laughing, "So, how long are you in here for?"

"Not long, I'm being offered another deal. They starting to recruit guys like me with petty crimes into military."

"Really?"

"Our pay is reduced and we gotta attend boot camp longer, but I'm taking the deal. I can't fuck with these rusty ass niggas in here no more. Plus, at least I got a chance to make some good money without breaking the law. And the big plus is that them military niggas sexy ass fuck."

Damien just had to know, "Are you gay, bi, or straight?"

"Man, I'm just a fan of pleasure, all that label shit don't matter to me."

"Alright, times up," An officer announced.

"Zyan man, you changed my life, I had a lot of fun."

Zyan stood up from his seat, "Yeah, you cool. When I get out of here or whatever, I'll hit you up."

The officer led Zyan back to his cell and Damien left feeling much better about the state of their friendship. He hoped that everything worked out for Zyan, knowing he desperately needed to get away from the nightlife and needed the more disciplined military life style to reign in his free spiritedness that was sometime just reckless.

As Damien got in his car, his phone rang; he answered the unknown number, "Hello."

"Hey Damien, it's me Max."

Damien didn't know what they had to talk about, "Oh, sup?"

"Man, this Omari nigga tryin to wreck my life. He's talking about outing me to TMZ if I leave him."

"That's some dirty shit," Damien said.

"Yeah, I wish I had kept things between us only. All that shit about bottoming and shit was just silly."

Damien decided to take a new approach to Max, "I wasn't right for you though, I was cheating on you."

Max laughed, "I sort of figured that but that's why I was cheating on you myself. I had to get some ass somehow."

"Damn, I guess we both should've been more upfront with each other."

"I was scared to say anything hurtful, cause I honestly liked you. I thought Omari could really save us."

"He couldn't, but I was wrong for leaving without trying to work things out. But I didn't want to be with you."

"Understandable," Max said. "I was calling to try to get you back, but I guess this is a wasted call."

"Don't say that. This was a good call; we got to be real with each other. You were a good dude, but not for me."

"Thanks," Max said, "You were good to, but was real strict on giving up some ass."

Damien laughed, "Yeah. Anyways, how are you gonna handle Omari? I suggest just coming out."

"Maybe, but for now I'll just keep fucking with him until I'm ready to come out."

"Well, good luck with that Max. Good luck with everything. I have to go, I have a job interview."

"Alright man, follow me on Instagram, keep in touch."

"I will."

Damien ended the call. The guilt of cheating on Max was still there. Damien wasn't afraid to admit he was wrong and it didn't make it any less wrong because Max was doing the same thing. They both weren't man enough to speak up and express their true feelings about their relationship. Damien pushed that aside now, he had to focus forward and do great at this interview.

He arrived at his interview that was being held at one of the many Starbucks in town. The moment he entered the coffee shop he spotted Ford sitting alone looking as gorgeous as ever. Damien did his best to think with his mind and not his dick; he really needed this job and was lucky to still have this interview after pushing it back so far.

Damien sat down at the table, "Am I late?"

"Not at all," Ford said, "I just came a bit early because I was already in the area. It's nice to finally see you."

"Yeah, a friend of mine passed so I had to deal with all of that before getting back to you."

"It's okay," Ford said, "I've got a feeling I'm going to be letting you get away with a lot of stuff."

"I promise you that I'm a responsible person."

"It's okay, don't try to sell me anymore, I've already hired you."

"Really?"

Ford nodded, "I like your attitude, your look, and your presence. I'm good at reading people."

"I can say that same about you. Most importantly, when do I start?"

"How about next Monday? I'll pay you two hundred a day, supply you with a smart phone that I'll cover all the charges for, and you must be able to work long hours and sometimes travel weekends with my business partner and I to other states. The gyms I'm opening are specifically for the elderly, so you would also have to be respectful and good with them."

"Trust me; I'm at the point in my life where I'm looking to keep busy."

Ford slid a business card across the table, "Be at this address, Monday at nine. Dress nice and bring that smile."

Damien grabbed the card from the table, "I will, whatever you say boss man."

Ford stood up and shook his hand, "See you Monday."

Damien was excited, especially about getting to travel. It would be nice to get out of North Carolina some days. He ordered a latte just because and headed home. The first thing he did was attempt to cyber stalk Ford, but didn't find much about him, just a blocked Facebook. His profile picture was old based on the way he was dressed. A knock on his door tore Damien away from his stalking.

Damien answered the door to find Vincent holding a puppy, "Why? Just why Vincent."

Vincent cuddled the bulldog puppy close to him, "I figured this could cheer you up."

Damien laughed as he stepped aside, "I can't afford a puppy."

Vincent entered the apartment and sat the puppy down on the floor, "This is me being a good friend."

Damien shut the door and sat down on the floor with the puppy, "What's its name?"

Vincent shrugged as he joined them on the floor, "I've been callin it Buster."

"That' so corny, but it'll work I guess."

"So, you gonna keep him?"

Damien shook his head, "For the weekend, but after that he's all yours."

Vincent wrinkled his nose, "Hell no, weekend here then he's going back to the shelter."

Damien didn't have time for a puppy, no matter how cute it was. "I guess so. So, what's up?"

"Nothing, about to go to the campus book store. How was your interview?"

"Perfect I got the job. My boss is really nice but I'm getting the feeling he wants to fuck."

Vincent rolled his eyes, "Man you think everybody wants the dick."

"Because that's how it usually plays out. I mean, even you want the dick."

"And you won't even give it to me."

Damien wanted a fresh start; he figured Vincent deserved a reset, "If you want it, come get it."

Vincent laughed, "Stop fucking with me."

Damien lay back down on the floor, "I'm not, go ahead. Get naked for me."

Vincent stalled, not sure if he was being messed with. He took off his shirt and tossed it on the puppy who started to play around with it. Vincent stood up and dropped his pants, revealing his rising dick. Right away, Damien got hard, making a tent in his pants. Vincent lay down beside Damien and started to kiss him as he dug his hand into his pants.

Vincent pulled Damien's dick out, went down and started to suck. Damien shut his eyes and went back through the list of men he'd been with since Vincent. After all of them, it felt nice to be back with the man who started it all. Damien slowly started to fuck Vincent's mouth. He thrust deeper and faster until he nutted.

Vincent coughed and gasped as he did his best to swallow. "It's still sweet."

"And all for you," Damien said as he started to sit up.

Vincent pushed him back down, "Nigga, we just getting started. Eat my ass."

Damien smiled; he'd been down there before and was excited to pay Vincent's ass a revisit. "Definitely."

This was happiness, ecstasy, pleasure, and Damien was enjoying every single bit of it.

****

32 - VIP

Damien stared at his reflection in the hotel bathroom mirror as he buttoned up his all black dress shirt. He took a moment to flex his toned arms, finally seeing the results of months of eating right and hitting the gym religiously. Damien found it hard to believe he was once a scrawny teen whose workout routine consisted of working eight hour shifts at a clothing store. Ford entered the bathroom, stood next to Damien, and started to mess around with the buttons of his red Henley shirt.

Damien looked to him, "Baby, just button the first two buttons. Show off your chest."

Ford continued fidgeting around with his shirt, "I feel exposed, man."

"Trust me, you look nice."

Ford sighed heavily, "Do we really have to go to this thing?"

"Of course, I go to events with you all the time."

"Those are business events, you have to be there, you're my assistant."

"And you're my boyfriend," Damien said, "Are you really going to let me go around a bunch of gay men alone?"

"Fuck no," Ford said, "On that note, I'm definitely going. Who's this Vincent guy again?"

Damien smirked, "Don't pretend you don't know of him, he was my first and the last guy I fooled around with before you. Actually, you're the reason him and I are probably not together. I got so busy working and traveling with you that I didn't have time to keep up with him. Then I started giving you the dick and he completely became an afterthought."

Ford playfully shoved him, "Don't say it like that. Giving me the dick? Is that what you call it?"

"I'm teasing," Damien said, "What we do is extreme love making."

"That sounds better. So Vincent, he's opening a gay bar, right?"

"No, do you remember how I told you he managed to start that barbershop slash strip club?"

Ford nodded, "Yeah, back home. He's opening a second location here?"

"Yeah and unlike the one back home, this one in Charlotte is for gay men."

Ford shrugged, "It's not a business I would start, but I get it."

"If he asks you to invest in it, would you?"

Ford shook his head, "I can't afford it. Gym funding, two kids in college, and a needy ex-wife, it's not in the budget."

"You forgot to mention a boyfriend who needs a new PS4."

Ford winked at him, "I'll surprise you with that."

Damien checked his self out once more in the mirror, "Cool, now let's go support Vincent."

Ford did all the driving while Damien used his GPS to guide him towards Vincent's newest business venture. At first, Damien thought the entire idea was a bad one and ignored every little ad Vincent would post on Instagram about the first location. After a few months sex sells proved itself to still be a good marketing plan and Vincent was ranking in decent money. They arrived at the barbershop slash strip club that was named Cut Up. A line was out the door, but Damien had passes that got him and Ford in without a wait.

Inside Cut Up, one side was a barbershop that had two barbers on duty who wore black speedos with the company's name written on the back. A couple of men were waiting to get haircuts, but as expected the majority of attendees were crowded on the other side of the snug building watching the strippers. Out of the crowd appeared a well-groomed Vincent wearing a black fitted suit and holding a bottle of vodka.

"Damien," Vincent exclaimed, "You made it!"

Damien dapped him, "I had to be here man. This is nice."

"Yeah, this is my true vision," Vincent said, "I love it much better than the first location, no titties, all dicks."

Damien motioned at Ford, "Hey, this is my boyfriend Ford."

Vincent looked a buff Ford up and down, "Man, you got yourself a sugar daddy."

"I'm not a sugar daddy," Ford said, not cool with the label, "I'm his boyfriend, his equal."

"Relax," Vincent said as he raised the bottle of liquor, "I'm drunk, imma say stupid shit tonight."

"Anyways," Damien said, "It's nice to see finishing college paid off for you."

"Yeah this was Marion's and I's dream, well I'm sure he wouldn't like the male strippers though."

"Still, he's missing out on all of this. You're doing all of this and he's managing a Burger King back up north."

Vincent shrugged, "Hey, we did our part and apologized, he's the one still being a bitch."

A stripper wearing nothing but a pair of sneakers and a backwards hat approached them. Damien already started to feel his body wasn't up to par as he eyed the chiseled stripper from head to toe. It was obvious Damien wasn't the only one impressed, Ford eyes were also locked on the stripper's body.

"Mr. Vincent," The stripper said, "Are these your VIPs?"

Vincent looked to the stripper, “Yeah they are, Flexx. Damien, Ford, meet Flexx. My main money maker.”

Flexx rolled his eyes, “I’m also the accountant here, not just a master at shaking my ass.”

Vincent thumbed back at a black door with a V on it, “Flexx is going to give you two the VIP show tonight.”

“I’ll be waiting,” Flexx said before grabbing the bottle of vodka from Vincent and heading to the room.

Damien looked to Ford, “We can always reject this.”

Ford smirked, “He’s fine though.”

“And clean,” Vincent butted in, “He doesn’t perform on stage, only for VIPs in private, fifteen hundred a session.”

“Damn,” Damien said, “That’s a pricey piece of ass.”

Vincent smirked, “Exactly, so you two better get your money’s worth and wear a condom. Enjoy.”

Vincent step aside and motioned back to the VIP room. Damien had no intentions of sticking his dick in a stripper, no matter how clean Vincent claimed he was. They made their way into the VIP room to find Flexx lying on a leather bed that had a golden silk sheet. Ford and Damien joined Flexx on the bed and he started to dance and grind against both of them.

After doing more than enough to get them hard, Flexx started to play with his asshole. “Don’t be shy.”

Ford and Damien took his advice, pulled out their dicks and started to jerk off. Flexx took things a little further and started to strip Damien and Ford down to their underwear. He forced the couple together and Ford and Damien started making out while Flexx played with his own dick. The stripper took things even further as he managed to get the couple out of their underwear and butt naked.

They kept kissing as Flexx took turns sucking their dicks. “I wanna feel some nut on my ass.”

Flexx lay down flat on his stomach and raised his butt in the air, revealing his clean shaven hole. Damien and Ford got on their knees and aimed their dicks at Flexx's waiting ass. They kept their focus on each other; the stripper's lure no match for the feelings and attractions they had for each other. Ford moved his thick, light-skinned, dick closer to Flexx as he started to nut. The scene hot, Damien started to nut immediately afterwards.

Damien and Ford continued to makeout some more, so into each other, they didn't realize Flexx making his exit.

33 - Budget Cut

Though Damien enjoyed working for the man he loved, he knew he didn't want to spend the rest of his life simply being an assistant. He had his own goals and wanted to have his own assistant someday. Damien knew exactly what he wanted to do with his life, cook. He was just having the toughest time finding a decent culinary school in NC or even the free time to take up some classes if he wanted to. But cooking made him happy, it bought back old memories of when his mother was alive and they would all cook as a family, even Marion.

Damien kept browsing schools while pretending to work in Ford's office. His office was located at the first elderly gym he had opened up that was only a few blocks away from NC Tech. So far Ford only had two locations, the gyms named Golden Age Gyms. Damien liked the idea, but felt Ford was a bit too kind when it came to the members paying their monthly fees. They all had excuses about their social security checks being late or having to spend extra on their medication. Ford would always fall for their sad stories and let them continue to work out for free.

Ford entered his office while talking on his phone, "I'll transfer five hundred to your account, okay?"

Damien didn't have to guess who was on the call, either Ford's ex-wife or one of his kids.

Ford ended his call, put away his phone and sat down on the leather couch in his office, "Damien."

Damien glanced away from the laptop placed on Ford's desk, "Yes Mister Piggy Bank."

Ford smirked, "What does that supposed to mean?"

"Oh, nothing," Damien said with a smirk.

"What are you doing over there?"

"Browsing culinary schools, while on the clock," Damien said.

"Remember if you find one, I'll help with your tuition."

Damien shrugged, "I can always get grants. You have other people lives to fund."

"Are you talking about my family? Is this what that piggy bank comment was about?"

Damien nodded, "You know I love you and that's why I'm honest."

"I have to support my kids."

"The eldest, kinda, the college student, yes," Damien said.

"Alright then."

"But," Damien said as he raised his index finger, "Is your ex-wife considered one of your kids?"

Ford laughed, "No, but she's my ex-wife. I have to support her also. I left her remember."

"Have you explained to them that you'll go broke if you don't stop giving them everything?"

"But I'm not going broke. The gyms are doing fine. I'm making a profit."

"Buddy," Damien called out, "I need your accounting expertise right quick."

Into the office strolled Ford's business partner Buddy who desperately needed to hit one of the treadmills.

Damien smiled at Buddy, "You handle the accounting, right?"

Buddy's neck jiggled a bit as he nodded and adjusted his glasses, "All fucking day, what's up?"

"Is Golden Age Gyms making a profit?" Damien asked.

Buddy sucked his teeth, "Shit, if you want to call it that. I might have to get me a second job."

"In the business world you have to make sacrifices," Ford said, "I do."

Buddy looked him up and down, "Sacrifice? Man, you need to tell that shit to the members who don't like to pay their fees every month. Matter of the fact, I see about two of them out there that I need to turn over and take their pocket change. And while you're at, tell your grown ass kids to get jobs cause you ain't no Will Smith. Oh, and yah wife can definitely be cut out of the budget and then we'll be making a profit."

"You two don't understand, I have to support them, I owe them," Ford said.

"Owe them for what?" Buddy argued, "Your problem is that yah guilty."

"Guilty?" Ford questioned as he narrowed his eyes.

"Ever since you came out, you've been bowing to them," Buddy said, "Doing your best to make sure they still love you by giving them everything they want. That's some cliché shit right there man. You a smart dude but you stuck in your emotions. I don't feel like I'm out of line saying this shit either, we business partners. This both of our money being thrown away. When you came out, you ain't change, shit between us aint change either, it's your kids and ex-wife that have changed. They should love you the same way you keep loving them, for free."

Damien agreed one hundred percent, but knew he couldn't talk to Ford the way Buddy could.

Ford kept nodding, "I got you Buddy, but give me some time to adjust, alright?"

"Brotha you gotta do it fast before we start having to shut these places down."

"Actually, an investor up north wants us to open a new location. The meeting is this weekend."

"That's what I'm talking about," Buddy said, "You focus on that and I'll be doing shake downs."

Buddy left the office and returned to work.

"You didn't tell me about this third investor," Damien said, "That's a good sign."

"I just got the call before I came here. He's actually located in your hometown. We're going this weekend."

Damien lounged back in his seat, "I'll get to see my family then. I can finally meet my dad's girlfriend."

"Are you actually excited about seeing your brother?"

Damien nodded, "Always, because I hope he would feel the same about seeing me. You can meet them also."

"I thought we said no family meetings so soon."

"We've been saying that for two years. I'm ready for you to meet mines."

Ford shrugged, "I suppose. But don't expect me to be bringing you around mines so soon."

Damien didn't want to meet Ford's kids who were around his age, the thought was awkward. "I won't push it."

Ford stood up from the couch, "I'll have to get a fresh cut before we go though."

"You just wanna go see some strippers at Vincent's place, your hair looks fine."

Ford laughed, "Nah, I'm going to my usual barber. Vincent's barbers looked so lost cutting hair."

Damien motioned at himself, "Do I look presentable? Are my naps coming in?"

Ford licked his pink lips, "Man you know you always look good to me, especially how you sitting in my chair thinking you run shit." Ford locked his office door, "So, I'm going to have to come over there and show you who really runs this shit. Remind you who the boss is."

"Oh for real?"

Ford walked over to Damien and got down on his knees, "Get that dick out for me."

"Damn, no please?"

"I own that dick; I don't have to beg for it."

Damien unzipped his pants and pulled out his dick, "You own my dick now?"

"Hell yeah."

Ford started sucking on the head of Damien's dick slowly. Damien loved how he kept eye contact with him the entire time, the act so intimate to him. He had gotten head many times in his life, but it was so much better coming from a man he loved. Ford kept sucking and licking Damien's dick. As the tension started to build, Damien started to jerk his dick until he nutted on Ford's face. Like it was a fine sauce, Ford wiped Damien's nut from his face and beard and sucked it from his fingers.

Damien definitely knew Ford was the right man to take home to his father, for more reasons than one.

34 - Memories

Damien had never been so nervous taking a simple ride home to the house he was raised in. Having Ford at his side eased his nerves a bit, but at the same time was the main reason for them. He rarely discussed his sexuality with his father even though when they did the man was very open about everything. His family knew he'd been working for Ford, but not that they were an actual couple. Damien wasn't that concerned about his father's reaction, but wasn't looking forward to Marion trying to act out.

The taxi arrived at the house; they got their bags from the trunk and headed up to the front door.

Damien looked to Ford before knocking, "Excuse any crazy shit you hear."

Ford smiled, "I'm legit excited to see where the man I love came from."

"For now, just wait."

Damien knocked on the door and a stout woman with braided hair and glasses answered.

Damien forced a smile, "Hi...is my dad...here."

"You must be Damien," The woman said, "Heck, I know you're Damien cause you look just like your daddy."

"Oh, you're Katrina, right?"

"Now don't act like your daddy ain't tell you about me. Yes, I'm Katrina." Katrina stepped aside, "Welcome home."

Damien entered the home to find Marion posted on the couch watching football, looking as if he slept in the gym, and his father was in the kitchen cooking. The house felt exactly the same, but much cleaner and with a little bit more décor. He figured this was Katrina's doing.

"I'm here," Damien announced.

Marion looked up at him, "I see you."

The last time Damien and Marion were in the same room, Vincent was there and they were apologizing for messing around behind his back. Marion accepted the apology but still kept his 'I'll talk when ready' attitude. Time passed, Marion never talked and just moved back home and got a job as manager at a Burger King, putting that business degree to work as much as he could. Damien didn't pity him; Marion was responsible for his own poor decisions.

Damien motioned at Ford, "And this is my boss, Ford."

"It's nice to meet you," Katrina said as she hugged Ford.

Marion rolled his eyes, "Man, we know you fucking this dude. Why you still being sneaky?"

"I'm not being sneaky. He just happens to be my boss and boyfriend."

"Then why not introduce him as your nigga then?" Marion argued.

"Because I don't want you acting stupid."

"I told you before; I'm cool with the gay shit. You know why I was mad."

Damien didn't want to argue, "Fine, this is Ford, my boyfriend. Happy?"

Marion fanned his hand at Damien and sucked his teeth, "Man, whatever."

Damien pushed his brothers' negativity aside and joined his dad in the kitchen, "Katrina's nice."

Eric looked up from the sink of chicken he was cleaning, "Thank you, thank you. So, that's your boyfriend?"

"I guess you heard all that."

"I ain't deaf yet, plus I already knew. Why else would you bring him over here? He looks rich."

Damien shrugged, "He does alright, he owns some gyms."

"At least he ain't Vincent. He looks kinda grown too from a distance."

"He's forty two," Damien revealed.

"Damn, you out there lookin for a father figure. I ain't did enough for you?"

"Dad please, you're perfect. He just happens to be older, nothing more to it."

Katrina led Ford over to the Kitchen, "Mr. Ford here owns some gyms."

"I heard," Eric said as he shook hands with Ford, "I hope you like baked chicken. I do it the best."

"If you cook as good as your son, I'll enjoy it," Ford said.

Eric proudly smiled "I taught him everything he knows, I'm a master chef."

"Is it alright if I help you cook dad?" Damien asked.

"Like old times, I don't mind," Eric said.

Ford thumbed over his shoulder, "I'm going to go sit down and watch the game. I have no kitchen skills."

"And I'll be in the room," Katrina said, "I'm taking some online classes. I'll work on those."

The group split up as Damien washed his hands and started to help his dad, "Where did you meet Katrina?"

Eric started to season the chicken, "I met her at an oyster roast. Man, she the first woman I've ever been into since your mother has been gone. I'm glad we both have found somebody; your brother on the other hand is into the same mess. Hiring those young girls and messin with their heads. He always bringing a new one home."

Damien glanced back and noticed Ford and Marion were actually talking on the couch and seemed to be getting along. Marion was even cracking some jokes and had Ford laughing. This was the exact opposite of what Damien was expecting when it came to Ford meeting his family. Everybody was on their best behavior.

Dinner went well also. Ford and Marion talked a lot about business and how they were fans of the same football team. When Ford mentioned having to find a hotel later, Eric was cool with having him sleepover with Damien in his old bedroom. Katrina shared some insight about the therapy classes she was taking. Damien knew the woman could never replace his mom, but was glad his father had her. After dinner, Marion and Damien worked on dishes while Eric went to bed and Katrina talked Ford's ear off in the living room.

"He's a cool dude," Marion said, "He ain't nothing like you."

"Thanks, I guess," Damien said as he dried some plates, "Have you talked to Vincent?"

"Fuck no."

"He has two barber shops now, one has a straight strip club and the other has a gay one."

Marion shrugged, "My barber shops will be better. I'm trying to get a loan."

"Or you can also reconnect with your best friend and continue with the original plans y'all had."

"I ain't ready to talk to him yet."

"It's been two years," Damien pointed out.

"I don't care if it was six," Marion finished off the final dish, "Anyways, I like Ford. He makes you tolerable."

Damien smirked, finally feeling forgiven, "Coming from you that actually means a lot."

"Yeah, whatever. Night lil bro."

Marion headed off to his room and Katrina took that as a sign that it was bed time. She left for bed and after outing all the lights, Damien and Ford did the same. They lay in Damien's bed, cuddled up together and staring up at the ceiling. All of this day was just unbelievable to Damien.

"My dad is happy, my brother talked to me mainly because he likes you, this has been great."

Ford smiled, "Damn, I might take you home to my family much sooner. I hope it goes this well."

"I'm ready when you're ready," Damien said, though he was not ready at all.

"It'll happen. So, have you had sex in this bed?"

Damien nodded, "My first time with Vincent was in this bed. And my friend Kendall, who passed away."

"Oh. Good memories or bad memories?"

"They were lessons learned type of memories. Do you want to make a good one?"

Ford laughed, "Sex in your dad's house? That's kinda risky."

Damien started playing with Ford's dick, "I mean...just a little head. It's my treat for you being on point today."

"I ain't complaining."

Damien slid beneath the sheets and pulled Ford's dick out of his boxer hole. He was once horrible at giving head, but with practice he became perfect. It was also a lot more fun giving it to a man who he thought deserved pleasure. Damien took it slow, just the way Ford liked it. He played with the head of his dick a lot, and just for fun fingered him a bit. They both did their best to keep quiet, Ford softly moaning. Damien picked up the pace, sucking up and down the shaft as deep as he could go. Ford grabbed at Damien's neck, a sign he was about to nut. Damien kept sucking until he could taste Ford's warm nut in his mouth. He swallowed it all, the flavor of Ford's nut something he found himself starting to enjoy.

Damien crawled from under the sheets and shared a kiss with Ford. “I love you.”

“I love you,” Ford whispered back.

Damien was glad to make this new memory in his old bed.

35 - Surprise

Usually when Damien woke up to morning sex, he knew Ford was about to surprise him with something that he would not be excited about. Before the bad came along to ruin his day, Damien decided to simply enjoy the good morning sex he was being treated to right now. He was still half awake, unlike his dick that was deep inside Ford who was slowly riding him in the reverse cowgirl position.

Ford taught Damien many things in the bedroom, including that sometimes taking it slow was the best thing to do. He also taught him that having anal sex or even performing oral sex on another man didn't make you any less masculine. Damien still had yet to bottom, but when the day would come, Ford would definitely be the guy. Fortunately for Damien, Ford really enjoyed anal stimulation and he wasn't complaining.

Ford started to ride Damien's dick a bit faster, his butt muscles tightening and moans becoming louder the faster he went. This was enough to wake Damien up a bit more. He sat up, grabbed at Ford's waist and started to pound him. Ford begged him to stop, but Damien knew that was his way of just telling him to nut already. Damien let loose some nut into Ford's tight ass and crashed back down to bed. Ford slowly eased off Damien's dick, nut rolling down his leg.

Ford panted heavily as he cuddled up next Damien, "Morning."

"That was amazing...as always. Now what's the bad news?"

Ford laughed, "What do you mean?"

"Every time we fuck in the morning bad news follows."

"Damn, I'm that predictable?" Ford asked.

"Yeah, but don't stop. I like the sex part. What's the bad news though? Are you filing for bankruptcy?"

"Nah, in about two hours you're coming over to my place to meet my kids. I asked them to make breakfast?"

"What?" Damien said, trying not to sound as unhappy as he was on the inside.

"No complaints, you have to say yes especially cause I have your nut in my ass at the moment."

"Yeah, I'll go, but damn a little more warning next time. Two hours?"

Ford nodded, "Don't be nervous, I'm sure you'll like them and have stuff in common with them."

"Of course I'll have something in common with them; we're all from the same generation."

Ford laughed and kissed Damien, "You're funny. That's why I fucking love you. Now let's go shower."

Damien had to take this punch in the gut and just roll with it. He got up from bed with Ford and they both took a shower. Damien was treated to some shower head even though he had no nut left to spare. After they got through their morning routine, they left Damien's apartment and drove over to Ford's place.

As expected, Ford lived nowhere near Damien. He lived in a different part of town where they had gated communities, private schools, yoga clubs, and cops who shot the criminals, not the innocent civilians who they deemed suspicious. Damien hoped to afford to live in an area as nice as this one day.

Damien looked to Ford who was driving, "How did they react when you told them I was coming over?"

"My kids are very nonchalant, their responses were very neutral I suppose."

"Hopefully this will go as well as your meeting with my family."

Ford nodded, "It's the entire reason I'm doing this. I plan on taking Buddy's advice and cutting my family off financially. With you around, I hope my kids get inspired to branch out on their own or to see what hard work looks like. Plus, just like my presence bettered things with your brother and you, I hope your presence can better things between my children and me."

"I didn't work hard for this job; you sort of basically wanted to fuck."

"True," Ford said with a smirk, "But you work hard every day to keep it."

"Please, as if you'll ever fire me."

"I'm a strong believer of having one worker in a relationship. I would love a stay at home husband."

"Hello no, I sorta played the role before, it was depressing."

"Oh yeah, you and the football guy, I forgot about that," Ford said.

"I love us just the way we are."

Ford pulled into the parking lot of a two story home. "Well prepare to add two more additions to us."

Ford and Damien got out of the car. Damien took a deep breath as he followed Ford to the front door. Ford opened the door to the lavish home and Damien entered behind him. The hardwood floors were so clean Damien could see his reflection in them. Damien felt like he was on a TV show because of how nicely built and decorated the home was.

Ford looked into the kitchen, "They haven't even started cooking."

Damien went into the living room and took a seat.

Ford stood at the bottom of the stairs and shouted, "Yo Matt and Bianca, come down here!"

"What?" A female voice whined from upstairs, "I'm fixing my hair."

"Yo pops," A male voice said as a room door opened.

Damien stood up from the couch as he heard a set of feet coming downstairs.

A young light skin dude who had Ford's eyes joined them. He had low cut hair and wore a shirt with Andre 3000 on the front and flannel pajama bottoms. All Damien could think about as he stared the young guy down was that if he wasn't fucking his dad, he would most definitely try to get at him.

Ford motioned at his son, "This is Matt."

"My friends call me Matty," Matt said, "But we ain't friends, so just Matt."

"I'm Damien," He introduced.

"Dad, this dude could be in my class, that's kinda nasty," Matt said as he wrinkled his nose.

Ford squeezed the back of his son's neck, "Don't be an idiot right now. Where's the breakfast?"

Matt jerked away from his father's grip, "Bianca ain't told me about no breakfast. I can make waffles."

"Do that then," Ford said.

Matt looked to Damien, "You want blueberries or any of that shit, bro?"

"Plain."

Matt nodded, "Just the way I like them." He elbowed his father, "I'm easily impressed, I like him."

"I'm glad to hear that now go cook. And throw in some eggs and bacon."

Matt headed off into the kitchen.

"Bianca," Ford yelled upstairs once again, "Come help your brother in the kitchen. Now."

"I mean damn, excuse me for trying to fix my hair," Bianca argued as she came downstairs.

Once again Damien was impressed with Ford's baby creating skills. Bianca had mocha skin, the body of a model, flowing long dark hair that obviously wasn't hers and wore a ton of makeup even though it wasn't noon yet. The pajama shorts she wore left little to the imagination and her baby-t did a great job of showing off the rest of her body.

She jerked her lips to the side as she pointed at Damien, "Is this him?"

"Damien, this is my daughter Bianca," Ford introduced.

"Didn't you go to NC Tech?" Bianca asked.

"For one year."

"I remember you, you were a freshman. I was a sophomore. You were at one of Marion's parties."

"He's my older brother."

Bianca laughed, "Ew, I slept with your brother and now my dad is sleeping with you, that's fucked up."

Damien agreed, it was very fucked up, as Bianca said. He forced out an uncomfortable laugh, "It's a small world."

Bianca looked to her dad, "If you loved me, you would dump him. His brother is a player; it might be in his blood."

"I love you both, he's not going anywhere. Now get in the kitchen and help your brother."

"I'm busy, deuces," Bianca said before heading back upstairs.

Ford shook his head in shame as he approached Damien, "She's the difficult one."

"Most girls who date my brother usually are." He pointed to the kitchen, "I can help Matt cook."

"Are you sure?"

"Yeah, plus he seems to like me so at least I can create a bond with one of them."

Ford kissed him, "Man, you're perfect. I'll be in my office updating some stuff on my computer."

"I'll let you know when everything is ready."

So far, Damien felt as if he could handle Ford's kids, Matt was just your typical eighteen year-old who was ready to leave and go to college, Damien learned while they cooked together. Bianca on the other hand would be a bit more of a challenge, especially since Damien was a year younger than her, but he was confident in making it all work.

36 - Family

The fact that he was meeting Ford's children wasn't Damien's only surprise. After spending the day at work together, instead of being dropped off at his apartment, Damien was surprised to learn that he was spending the night at Ford's house for the very first time. He was used to Ford sleeping at his apartment, Damien didn't really know how to behave at his place.

They had dinner together and Damien found himself hesitant to just go into the refrigerator when he wanted to get a refill of his drink. And when they watched some TV afterwards, Damien didn't know if it was okay for him to control the remote or not like he usually did when they stayed at his apartment. And the most awkward part came when they had to get ready for bed. Damien didn't know if it was proper for him and Ford to shower together, especially with his children only a few feet away from them.

After being convinced it was okay, they showered and climbed into bed. Outside of the room, Bianca could be heard out in the hall talking and laughing on the phone. Every now and then Matt would be heard opening and closing his room door, heading downstairs to gather food before returning to play video games in his room. Damien hoped in time he would get comfortable being around them and spending the night over, because he planned on being with Ford for a long time.

Ford turned on the room television and turned to ESPN, "Alright, what's your honest opinions of my kids?"

"Matt's nice, he made me feel welcomed."

"He takes after his mom, just like her, he just goes with the flow," Ford said.

"Are you saying Bianca takes after you?" Damien asked.

Ford laughed, "No, she takes after some demonic force. But yet, she can sometimes be an angel."

"I think she rolled her eyes at me about one hundred times today."

Ford shrugged, "She's that way with everybody. Don't be offended."

"I can't believe she was with my brother, it's crazy."

Ford pointed at the television, "And I can't believe you were with this guy and left him."

Damien glanced at the television to spot football star Max giving a post-game press conference. Not only was he the number one draft pick of his first season, but he was also one of the most famous gay athletes now. Max actually coming out was a surprise to Damien and of course the rest of the nation, who couldn't comprehend the fact that a homosexual man could throw a ball. Omari was no longer in Max's life though, all power over him lost the moment the baller came out.

"I left him because I was unhappy and I was cheating on him anyways."

"Do you still have his number?" Ford asked.

Damien laughed, "Yeah, why?"

"Can you imagine the clients we'll get if Max endorses my gyms?"

"No deal," Damien said, "All he gets are Holiday texts from me."

"That was my inner businessman trying to network." Ford turned off the TV, "I'm going to sleep; I have an early morning planned."

Damien cuddled up close to Ford, "Like what?"

Ford yawned, "A family meeting, you're invited."

Damien didn't know exactly what role he could play in a family meeting, but he sure wasn't excited to find out. He held on tight to Ford until he drifted off the sleep. Damien awoke the next morning to find himself hugging onto a pillow instead of Ford. He turned over and nearly jumped from his skin as he discovered a woman with a head of bushy curly hair sitting at the edge of the bed. She wore yellow jogging tights, a pink tank top, and enough beaded jewelry to start her own shop.

She formed her plump lips into a smile, revealing her mouth of pearly whites, "Bianca was right."

"Huh," Damien groaned out.

"She said you were pretty. Not as pretty as me, but you're damn close. I'm Nia."

"Um, Damien. Are you the maid or something? Do you need me to get up?"

Nia burst out laughing, "The maid?"

Bianca strutted into the bedroom, "Momma, what's so funny?"

Nia thumbed over to Damien, "He asked if I was the maid."

Bianca started laughing.

Matt slipped on his t-shirt as he joined them in the room, "Aye, I wanna laugh? What happened?"

"He asked mom if she was the maid," Bianca said still laughing.

Matt shook his head at Damien and laughed, "Dude, you trippin."

Nia patted her hand against the bed, "I actually used to sleep in the exact same spot."

"Oh, you're his ex-wife." Damien said as he tried to cover his shirtless body with the sheets, "I'm Damien."

"It's nice to meet you Damian," Nia said, "Are you joining us downstairs for this silly family meeting?"

Damien nodded, "I guess, even though I'm not sure if I'm really family."

"Please, Ford has been with you for two years," Nia said, "You're basically family. We'll see you down there."

Damien waited for them all to leave the room, before getting up and washing up in the bathroom. He couldn't believe what he had just woken up to. The good thing was that Nia seemed to be nice and accepting as Ford had told him, unlike her daughter. Damien headed downstairs to find the family gathered in the living room on the couch and Ford standing before them.

Ford smiled at Damien, "I told her not to go up there."

"I obey no man," Nia said.

Damien took a spot on the floor, "It's okay, its nice waking up to beautiful faces."

"Damn, he got game," Matt said.

"Just like his fake ass brother," Bianca added.

Nia snapped her finger at her children, "I raised you two say thank you when complimented."

In unison they mumbled out, "Thanks." Bianca adding a roll of the eyes with hers.

Ford cleared his throat, "Alright, I need to make this quick because I have to be at work. I've been talking to Buddy and he's basically told me financially we need to tighten our belt. Matt, I know you're going off to school soon, but this summer you have to work to get anything from me. We're hiring at one of the gyms for a front desk clerk and that could be you. Bianca, you're a registered RN, use that and get a job already."

Bianca motioned at herself, "Emotionally, I'm still dealing with this divorce."

"For the sake of my business, that I want to pass on to you and your brother someday, deal faster," Ford said. "And Nia, you're a teacher, you make decent money. I can't fund your yoga, shopping sprees, and lunch with your girlfriends anymore. I'm going to have to cut down on what I give you."

Nia raised her head high, "You left me, remember? For men. I'm still adjusting to not having a husband."

"Do you want a broke ex-husband?" Ford asked. "Do you want your children living with you?"

"Fine, I'll sacrifice, but only for six months," Nia agreed.

"Thank you," Ford said, "I have a lot bills to pay and debt to clear. Luckily, Damien will officially be moving in here and instead of paying rent on his apartment, he can now help out with bills around the house. And I'm sure you guys won't allow me and Damien to carry the entire load, especially because you were born into this family."

Damien raised his hand, "I was never made aware of this moving in thing."

"Then I forgot to tell you, my fault," Ford said, "So, I'm asking now, do you want to move in?"

All eyes in the room landed on Damien. He was sure the majority wanted him to say no, but Ford mattered most.

"Sure," Damien answered.

Ford's face lit up as he cupped his hands together, "Alright then, its official and meeting adjourned."

Unlike with Max, Damien felt it was time for him to live with his boyfriend. The only thing that clouded the decision was his children and wife who seemed to have little boundaries when it came to Ford's life. Damien was sure that dating Ford meant he was also dating his children and oddly enough his ex-wife.

37 - Father's Son

A lot of Damien's time was dedicated to Ford or at least working for him. Still, he always made time to hang out with Vincent. Even without sex, their friendship had been growing strong over the years. Damien never expected after all the years he knew Vincent that he would be calling him his closest friend, not Marion. They were chilling at Vincent's house mostly watching Netflix and just talking about life.

"Did your daddy call looking for you yet?" Vincent asked as he lounged on the couch.

Damien, who lounged with him, looked away from the TV, "Nah, I call my dad more than he calls me."

Vincent started laughing, "I'm talking about Ford."

Damien rolled his eyes, "Ha, ha, not funny. Try harder."

"I think it's fucking depressing man, you and him."

"I'm the happiest I've ever been in my life, even if his family is really evasive."

"Still," Vincent said, "All that good dick is being wasted on some old dude."

"Let me guess, I should be giving it to you?"

“That’s a possibility. I’m surrounded by strippers all day and you still the sexiest dude out there to me.”

“Are you blind?” Damien said as he laughed, “That Flexx dude is a ten out of ten.”

“I know that’s why I hired him, but he’s your typical vain fag.”

“Don’t use that word, that ain’t cool.”

Vincent shrugged, “Whatever. So, when you gonna leave Ford?”

“I have no plans on doing so; I’m growing something with him. Can you please get over me?”

“I have my days when I don’t even think about you, but then I have days when I can only think about you.”

“Stop talking, you’re embarrassing yourself.”

Vincent ran his hand down his face, “True, you’re right. I stop. Aye, I spoke to your brother.”

Damien’s eyes widened, “Hell has frozen over.”

“It was a short convo. Man, it was awkward as shit, we ain’t had nothing to really talk about. It took two years of being a part to sink our friendship of nearly a decade. I still love him like a brother and sent him the little money I had to spare to start his own barbershop.”

Damien nodded, “I’m really glad to hear that. Man, life is just perfect right now.”

Vincent thought about it, “Besides being single, yeah it pretty much is. We can only go forward...or back.”

“I can’t see myself going back to the lost dude I was.”

“I’m glad I’ve gotten my sex drive under control.”

“Yeah right, I can have you butt naked in a heartbeat," Damien teased.

Vincent smirked, “That’s because I got those never-ending feelings for you though.”

“But then again I rather see Ford naked.”

"Man, fuck Ford and his old man nuts," Vincent teased.

"He's not old for the one hundredth time."

Vincent held up two fingers, "Man, he could literally be your daddy. He got two kids older than you."

"Just his daughter, his son is eighteen. You might know his daughter, Bianca? She used to talk to Marion."

Vincent thought about it, "Damn, Marion done been with so many girls. They were two Bianca's."

"Anyways, she's the only one I know who don't like me for sure."

Vincent twirled his finger in the air, "Rewind back, how the son look?"

"As good as his daddy."

"Tell lil man Cut Up is hiring. Eighteen is old enough to be a dancer. Niggas tip well."

"Well, he is unemployed but I will not encourage anybody to be a stripper."

Vincent dismissively fanned his hand at Damien, "Don't act like dancers are below you; you were fucking one, right?"

"Zyan? Yeah. They're not below me, but try being a doctor or anything first before stripping."

"Nah, I'm sure you still make better money stripping and the hours are shorter."

Damien checked the time on his phone, "I'm gonna go. I got work in the morning."

"Yeah, yeah, yeah, you ole square. Hit me up if you ever need a free cut."

Damien stood up from the couch, "I will and keep me updated on you and Marion."

Damien lefts Vincent's and started his drive back home. Even though Vincent was constantly throwing himself at him, Damien had no urge to do anything with him. Actually, the longer he stayed with Ford, the less he even checked out or fantasized about other men. He didn't feel as if he was being a square, but loyal.

He arrived to an empty house and texted Ford right away to learn that he was working late into the night. Damien decided instead of grabbing something to eat alone he would try to invite Matt and Bianca to join him. He headed up stairs, knocked on Bianca's door, and after waiting, he slowly opened the door to learn she wasn't there. Her entire room was covered in clothes and half a bottle of wine rested on her messy bed.

Damien moved on down the hall to Matt's room. He knocked, waited a bit once again, and slightly opened the room door. On his bed, lay Matt jerking off, while wearing nothing but a pair of headphones. Right away Damien noticed he was watching gay porn. Matt started to nut and turned his head towards the door to find Damien. Quickly, Damien shut the door, and started to walk away.

Matt rushed into the hallway using his pillow to cover himself up, "Please, don't tell my dad."

Damien stopped walking and faced Matt, "Huh?"

"Don't fucking tell him what you saw, okay?"

"I'm not, I'm sorry. I should have not walked in the first place," Damien said.

"You fucking got that right, but you did. Listen, I don't want him to know...that I'm like him."

"Matt, there's nothing wrong with being gay and I'm sure if you tell him he'll understand."

"I know that," Matt said, "But him being gay has changed our family enough. It'll only cause shit to change more."

"I promise I won't say anything then, okay?"

Matt nodded and let out a heavy sigh, "Cool, now why in the fuck were you coming in my room anyways?"

"I swear I just wanted to invite you and Bianca out to eat."

"Well, Bianca went out. I can eat though. Just let me put something on, alright?"

Damien nodded, "Yeah, sure, take your time."

Matt slipped back into his room and Damien finally felt free to smack himself against the forehead. He had remembered when his mom caught him jerking off and how awkward things had become between them. Though he wasn't Matt's parent, Damien felt super awkward in his presence after what he had just witnessed. To make the situation worse, now he had to keep such a big secret for Matt away from Ford.

A dressed Matt slipped out his room, "Alright, where do you wanna go?"

Damien, who could barely make eye contact, shrugged, "Um, wherever you want."

Matt narrowed his eyes at Damien, "Really dude? You gonna act like this all the time now?"

"Like what?"

"As if I'm a different person now. Be normal. I should be the one freaking out."

Damien motioned at himself, "I'm not freaking out, I just don't want you to think I was watching you."

"But you with my dad, why would I think that? Relax and prepare yourself to answer a lot of shit though."

"About what?" Damien asked.

"Being gay. Why use the internet when I got somebody to talk about shit with now?"

Damien wished he had an actual person to get advice from when he was Matt's age. "I didn't think about that."

Matt chuckled and playfully hit him in the arm, "So, what's better...eating ass or sucking dick?"

Damien wasn't expecting the questions to start so soon and be so extreme, but he would do the best he could to guide Matt.

38 - Buddy

Damien's work day would've been a lot easier if Matt wasn't texting him every two minutes. Matt actually texted Damien more than Ford now. The texts were always the most random things: pictures of sexy guys from tumblr, profiles of guys from online dating sites that Matt wanted Damien's approval on before chatting with or just random small talk that always turned into a retelling of Damien's sex life. Damien felt more like a gay big brother to Matt, but he supposed in this case he was his gay step-father.

Damien put his phone away as Ford entered his office.

Ford looked happier than a child in a toy store, "You won't believe it."

"Believe, what?"

"Well, do you know how Florida is a retiree hotspot?"

Damien nodded, "Yeah."

"I've been calling a bunch of elderly living communities down there pitching the idea of Golden Age Gyms."

"That's smart."

"I know," Ford exclaimed, "And it just paid off. Four elderly communities want me to build a Golden Age Gym in their area."

"Have you just dug yourself out of debt forever?" Damien asked, excited about the development.

"Actually, more into debt, but overtime these new locations will pay for themselves."

"And what about the one in my hometown?"

"That's opening at the end of the summer," Ford revealed.

"That means you're going from two locations to seven, that's a lot of gyms to manage."

Ford paced back and forth, "I know. Buddy and I agreed on one of us moving to Florida. I mean, I'm more settled here in North Carolina but Buddy isn't that experienced when it comes to the managing the openings of the new gyms. He's the money guy; he can count all the numbers here. I just want to know if I do decide to go, if whether or not you'll be by my side?"

Unlike Ford, Damien didn't really have any roots established in NC, "Sure, but what about your family?"

"I can still support Nia from a distance, Matt is going to college, and Bianca will be forced to move out."

"Unless she latches on to your leg and comes down to the Florida with you."

Ford shook his head, "No, I won't let her do that. This move will be all about you and me."

"Can we live by the beach?"

"Man, with all this money coming in eventually I can buy a beach."

"Thank god I dated up," Damien joked.

"Yeah, yeah, now get your butt up from my desk, I need to scout locations."

Damien stood up and Ford swapped spots with him. "You need me to do anything or can I cut out early?"

"Actually, I was wondering if you can take Matt to find a suit for graduation," Ford asked, "He said he's cool with you taking him."

"Are you sure? That seems more like a father son moment."

Ford shrugged, "I'm sure. Plus, it shows how much he's starting to like you. Just say no if you don't want to do it."

Damien knew it would make both Matt and Ford happy if he agreed to do it, "I don't mind, I'll take him."

Ford started typing at his computer, "Thank you best boyfriend in the world."

"It's what step-fathers must do I suppose," Damien said as he stuck his tongue out at Ford and left.

As he left the gym, he spotted Buddy walking around smoking a cigar as if he was already a millionaire. Damien could only laugh at the sight, glad the men's business was gaining some steam. As he got in his car he gave Matt a heads up text that he was heading over to take him suit shopping. Matt was already outside waiting for Damien as he pulled up to the house.

Bianca was getting dropped off by one of her friends. "Where are you two going?"

"I'm going to get a suit for graduation," Matt said as he got in the car with Damien.

Bianca eyed Damien up and down as she approached the driver's side, "Well aren't you two just buddy-buddy."

"You can come with us," Damien offered, even though he preferred she didn't.

"I'm not going to the mall with my father's rent boy."

"I'm not a rent boy," Damien said.

Bianca flipped her hair over her shoulder, "Uh oh, somebody needs a reality check. Later rent boy."

Damien waited until Bianca turned around before he let his dislike of her appear on his face, "She's really...the worst."

"Nah, that mean she's just jealous when she's mean like that."

"Why would be she jealous of me?" Damien asked.

Matt laughed, "Man, you are really unaware of your reality. You jacked our daddy from us."

"But you don't treat me like she does."

"Because I'm not a dick and I think you're sorta cool. Anyways, you ever slept with a rent boy? Don't lie."

"No," Damien said as he reversed out of the parking lot, "And neither has your father."

Matt laughed, "I think you let Bianca hurt your feelings, toughen up man."

Damien's feelings were not hurt, but that didn't mean he was fine with being called a rent boy. Yes, all his money came from Ford but he worked for it. And it wasn't his fault that Ford wanted to take care of him and let him move into his home. If Damien wanted to, he could've called Bianca a freeloader, but he wasn't going to stoop to her level.

A trip to the mall with Matt was a difficult experience. Firstly, Matt had a dangerously wandering eye. He had a really bad habit of staring some dudes down for too long or saying a bit too loud how sexy they were. Damien wasn't as brave as him when he was that age, all his fawning done mostly online. And when it came to trying on clothes, Matt wasn't shy about stepping out the dressing room in just his boxers, obviously enjoying the attention from some shoppers in the fitting room line.

Damien was glad when Matt finally picked a suit and they got out of the mall.

On the drive home, Matt's fawning didn't stop as they drove through the hood.

"Damn," Matt exclaimed as they drove past some dudes on the corner, "That dude in the hat was sexy."

"Um, Matt," Damien said as he kept driving, "Are you just discrete at home?"

"Huh? What do you mean?"

"I mean there's nothing wrong with being out, it's great, but I thought you were more discrete."

Matt laughed, "What am I doing wrong?"

"You can't just kept pointing out and staring down dudes, especially if you're tryin to stay discrete."

Matt shrugged, "Man, just being around another gay dude brings it out more. I'm comfortable with you."

"I guess so. At your age I was a lot more closed off. I didn't have anybody else to feed off."

"You mean you didn't have anybody else to back you up if some straight dude ran up in your face."

Damien laughed, "You think I was going to back you up if somebody came swinging at you in the mall?"

"Man, don't tell me you're that type of friend who dips out when the going gets tough."

"I'm the type who knows how to pick his battles," Damien said, "And you were picking some big battles."

"Ain't my fault all the fine ass dudes were built like wrestlers."

Damien and Matt joked back and forth on the entire ride home. By time they got back, Ford was already home from work and was relaxing in the living room on the couch. Matt took his suit inside the living room to show his dad while Damien headed upstairs to finally get out of his work clothes. As he passed Bianca's door, she stepped out of her room and blocked his path.

"How was your date?" Bianca whispered out.

"What?"

"I swear you're a master at playing dumb, just like Marion." Bianca said as she poked him in the chest.

"Why are you fucking with me?"

"Listen, I know my brother is gay...he started wearing headphones will watching porn for a reason."

After seeing Matt in action, Damien wasn't surprised his sexuality wasn't such a big secret, "And?"

"If you try to fuck my brother, I'll make sure my father knows, okay?"

"I'm nothing like my brother," Damien said,

Bianca rolled her eyes, “Sure, whatever you say.”

Damien knew this was all just envy coming from Bianca. He was close to her father and now her brother, she was on a fast track to being the odd woman out in the house. Still, Damien didn’t know how conniving she could be and decided to tread easy around Matt. He knew that would be difficult especially because Matt was always around him every opportunity he could get.

39 - Snake

Ford had been in an exceptional mood since his deal for the Golden Age Gyms in Florida was officially signed and sealed. The question of who would be moving to Florida, Buddy or Ford, still went unanswered. That decision would come later, but right now all the focus was on Matt's fast approaching graduation. Ford and Damien came together to surprise the household with some steak, eggs, and toast for breakfast. Ford funded the meal and Damien cooked.

Matt bit into his steak, "I didn't believe it at first, but Damien you can actually cook."

Damien, who sat across from Matt at the table, formed a smug grin, "And that's without classes."

Ford raised his fork, "I paid for the groceries."

"Man daddy that's like your only talent, paying for stuff," Matt said.

"Don't act like you don't enjoy it," Ford pointed out.

Bianca strolled into the kitchen, her hair messed and face puffy, "Ugh, I feel like death."

"What's wrong with you?" Ford asked. "Are you drinking again?"

Bianca took a seat at the table, "It's the best way I can deal with this divorce. It's your fault."

Ford didn't even bother to focus his energy on her this morning, "Matt, you gotta get a fresh cut."

"Let me drive your car to the barber shop then," Matt suggested.

"Noooo," Ford said, "You ain't wrecking my car. I can take you after I have a conference meeting later."

"Or," Bianca butted in, "Damien can take him. They seem to enjoy each other's company."

Damien forced a smile, "Because Matt isn't always grumpy."

"Good idea though," Matt said, "Damien, can you take me? My barber is quick."

"Say yes already," Bianca said.

Damien stalled on his words, "Yeah...I'll take you, Damien."

Bianca did a slow clap, "Surprise, surprise," She sarcastically said.

Ford raised his right brow as he looked to Bianca, "Are you still drunk or something?"

Bianca staggered as she stood up from the table, "You're so blind father. I'm going back to bed."

Ford thumbed at her as she walked away, "Matt, what's up with your sister?"

Matt shrugged, "I don't even try to care anymore." He looked to Damien, "I'm ready when you're ready."

Damien finished the last bit of his food, "Yeah, the earlier we get there the sooner we get out. I might get a cut too."

"If you're looking for me, I'll be down at my office all day," Ford said, "Matt, don't get no crazy Kanye type cut."

Matt laughed as he brushed at his hair with his hand, "Nah, I'll keep it low. Laters."

Damien flashed Ford a quick smile before he followed Matt outside and into the car.

Matt buckled up, "Why was Bianca trippin like that?"

Damien didn't even want to talk about it, "I ignore her. So, where's your barber?"

"Charlotte, Cut Up," Matt said with a wide smile.

"Stop playing, where is your real barber?"

"Come on Damien," Matt begged, "It can be my secret graduation gift. I've seen how tight that place looks on its Facebook. Plus, don't you know the guy who owns the place. The money I was going to use for a haircut I can put in the tank and then you can get your friend to hook me up. I promise, I'll never mention it or ask for anything if you take me to Cut Up."

"Man, your parents will kill me if I take you to a strip club."

"I'm eighteen, it's legal. Please, I won't ever mention it."

"If I do it, you have to promise me that'll you stop being so nice to me when your sister is around."

"Why?" Matt asked.

"Because she's trying to start drama, saying we sneaking around behind your daddy's back."

"I figured she said something to you. So, she does know I'm gay? That's what happens when you don't mute porn."

Damien nodded, "Yeah, she knows. So, if I take you there, can you do that for me and tone it down."

"Hell yeah, as long as I get to go to Cut Up!"

"Alright then," Damien said as he started the car.

Damien felt as if he was killing two birds with one stone as he started the nearly two hour drive to Charlotte. He was making Matt happy with this trip to Cut Up and taking some ammo away from Bianca when it came to her starting petty drama.

They arrived to Cut Up a bit after noon and it wasn't close to as crowded outside as it was during the grand opening. Matt was giddy as they got out of the car and he was led by Damien into

Cut Up. Inside, the vibe was a lot different. Flexx was sitting in one of the barber chairs and only about three men were watching a stripper lazily dance around on stage in a jockstrap.

Matt wrinkled his nose, "Is this it? Man, it looked more fun on the Facebook."

Vincent stepped out of his office, "Damien, what are you doing here?"

"I came to get a haircut along with my bud here, Matt. He's Ford son."

Vincent seductively bit his bottom lip as he dapped Matt, "Damn lil man, the cut is free for you."

"And what about me," Damien asked.

"Nah," Vincent said as he kept his eyes on Matt, "Business is tough, you gotta pay. Flexx will hook you up."

"I thought Flexx was the VIP dancer?" Damien asked.

"He just got trained to cut," Vincent said. He refocused on Matt, "You wanna meet the dancer?"

Matt shrugged, "I guess."

Vincent nodded toward a set of couches near the stage, "Go have a seat lil man, I'll be over in a minute."

As Matt walked away, Vincent bit down on his thumb and watched him.

"He's off limits," Damien said.

"Nu uh," Vincent said, "Five minutes and I'll be eating his booty. I need something to cheer me up."

"I didn't bring him here to get molested."

"Please," Vincent said, "If I can't have you, I'll take the next best thing."

"Dude, seriously no. He's not supposed to even be here. And why the hell is it so depressing in here?"

Vincent rubbed the back of his neck, "Man, shit has really died down since opening night."

"And that's why every customer matters," Flexx interrupted as he stood up, "Are you getting a cut or what?"

Damien started walking over to Flexx, "Yeah, just touch it up a bit."

Vincent thumbed over to where Matt sat, "I'll be over here keeping your son company, step daddy."

Damien flipped Vincent off, "I'm not saying it again, he's off limits."

Vincent walked off and joined Matt while Flexx started Damien's haircut. Not only was it the most painful, but one of the longest haircuts he had ever been subjected to. Damien was surprised when Flexx finally showed him the finish product that everything turned out right. He got out of the seat, paid Flexx, and realized he couldn't find Matt or Vincent even though he swore they were just sitting by the dance stage when Flexx started his lineup.

Damien rushed across the club and barged into Vincent's office to find him kissing on Matt. "Really, Vince?"

Vincent stopped kissing Matt and slipped a card into his pocket, "Aye, call me later, okay?"

Matt smirked and nodded at Vincent, "For real? No doubt."

Damien thumbed over his shoulder, "Matt, we're leaving now. I'm taking you to another barber shop."

"What you mad for?" Vincent said, "Let him get his free cut."

Damien led Matt out the office, shut the door behind him and ran up on Vincent, "I told you he was off limits."

Vincent laughed, "Why? You trying to fuck with him or something?"

"No fucker, he's just eighteen. You won't do to him what you did to me."

"Oh, so you're just jealous. Ain't my fault you fucking some old man while he's in the same house."

Damien resisted hitting Vincent, "Why do you always have to be such a snake? We were doing good."

"I'm not the one overreacting and cock blocking. Sixty more seconds and I would've had him on his knees."

Damien couldn't help it, he smacked Vincent upside his head, "Stop thinking with your dick man."

Vincent laughed, "Man, you did not just hit me? Don't get your ass knocked out."

"Aye, fuck you Vincent. Call me when you stop trying to fuck everything, dumbass."

Damien stormed out the office and bumped into Matt.

"What did I do wrong?" Matt asked, "He's fine as shit and nice."

Damien couldn't be mad at him, he fell for the same trap, "That's not always a good thing. Let's go."

Damien barged from Cut Up with Matt trailing him. Though he stopped things from going further between Matt and Vincent, Damien felt it was already too late. Vincent's venom was already flowing through Matt's veins.

40 - Hands On

The moment Damien saw that Matt was following Vincent on Instagram, he knew he had failed as his go-to-gay. Matt liked almost every picture Vincent would post. If he wasn't glued to Vincent on Instagram, he was asking Damien endless questions about him. Damien stayed honest; he told him the entire story of him and Vincent's history, the good and the bad parts. He could tell by Matt's reaction that the good parts stayed in his mind while the bad went in one ear and out of the other.

Damien felt as if he had done the best he could to keep Matt away from Vincent, but had a gut feeling Vincent would get what he wanted. He wasn't completely washing his hands with Matt when it came to Vincent. Damien was preparing himself for the moment he would have to tell Matt that he told him so.

As days passed, the less and less Damien interacted with Matt. It kept Bianca out of his hair, but at the same time Damien knew Matt wasn't out focusing on graduating or hanging with friends, but was most likely with Vincent. Damien ended up getting really busy at work, especially with five new gyms opening up soon. He didn't really zero back in on Matt until the morning of his graduation.

Nia thought it would be a good idea to surprise Matt with an early morning graduation gift and cake. Of course Ford paid for the gift, a PS4, and Damien baked the cake while Nia simply dictated the flavor of icing, cream cheese. Bianca was tucked away in her room sleeping in late like she did most mornings while everybody was in the kitchen putting the final touches on Matt's surprise.

"I can't believe I spent six hundred dollars on a video game system," Ford said as he patted the box.

"Please, stop with the tight pockets," Nia said, "Splurge for once in your life."

"I wish I could splurge," Ford said, "On myself, not you and the kids."

"Well if you had slept with men like you knew you always wanted to, you wouldn't have us to deal with," Nia said.

"I was young and confused when I met you."

"And then remained confused as you married me and put two children inside of me," Nia quipped.

"How about we just focus on the now?" Damien asked. "As in, your youngest child and his graduation."

Ford checked the time on his watch, "I figured he would be awake by this time. It's a big day for him."

"He was probably up all night stressing about his future," Nia said, "Today, the training wheels of life come off."

Damien raised the plate the cake was placed on, "I'll carry the cake."

Ford picked up the video game system box, "I got this expensive shit."

Nia deeply inhaled and exhaled, "Alright then, let's go surprise my baby."

Nia led the way and Ford and Damien followed her upstairs to Matt's room. She softly knocked and whispered out Matt's name as she slowly opened the room door. After no response at all or sign of Matt's presence in his bed, Nia pushed the room door all the way open to learn Matt wasn't there. Nia pulled up and looked under his blanket as if that would've made him suddenly appear.

Bianca popped out of her room yawning, "He's not here."

Nia looked back to her daughter, "What?"

"Last night I caught him sneaking out. I guess he and his friends went out to have one last hoorah."

Nia snapped her fingers at Bianca, "Call your brother and tell him to get his ass home."

Bianca went into her room and returned with her phone, "No answer, it rings until it hits voicemail."

"Keep trying," Nia said.

Ford took out his phone, "I'm friends with one of his friend's dad. I'll call and see if I can find him."

Bianca and Ford made their calls, both leading to nowhere. It wasn't long until Matt's absence started to make everybody nervous. They contacted his friends via their Facebooks and simply just had to sit and wait for responses or for Matt to show up home. After a couple of hours, the panic increased. The graduation was starting very soon and most of Matt's friends had already responded with no information about his whereabouts. Once he was confirmed not to be with any of his friends, Damien knew exactly who to call.

He snuck away and called Vincent, "Please tell me Matt isn't at your place."

"He is," Vincent said with a soft chuckle, "Lil man is hung over as shit though."

"Do you know he's graduating in less than an hour? His family is panicking."

"Well, he didn't tell me that. What am I supposed to do?"

"Um, well, you should've never messed with him in the first place you sex addict."

"We didn't do anything," Vincent said, "We talked, kissed a little, and I taught him how to take shots. That's it."

"Oh how sweet of you," Damien said sarcastically, "I guess next date you'll try to fuck him."

"Nigga, I'm hanging up, fuck you."

"Yeah whatever," Damien said, "Just wake Matt up, I'll be over there to pick him up."

Damien hung up his phone and joined the family in the kitchen.

Bianca was on her laptop surrounded by her parents, "There, found him. The lost phone GPS tracker app on his phone is active. Being nosey and knowing his password that he uses for everything since middle school like an idiot has finally paid off."

Ford looked at the address, "Who would he know that lives in that area?"

"Let's go get him right now," Nia said, "He could be hurt or something."

Ford and Nia left while Damien stayed behind sweating bullets. He knew he would be dragged into this once Ford tracked down Matt at Vincent's apartment. Damien sat down at the kitchen table as he tried to call Vincent back to let him know what was coming his way, but of course his feelings were still hurt and he was not answering his phone now. Bianca looked away from her laptop and over to a panicking Damien.

She formed a sinister grin, "What have you done?"

"What are you talking about?"

"It looks as if you're about to have a heart attack. Do you know who my brother is with? Is it a boy?"

"Mind your business," Damien snapped.

"Fine, I'll just wait until they all get back. I'm pretty sure I'll find out then."

Instead of sitting in a panic, Damien was trying to figure out the right way to exclude himself from all of this. He had tried to warn Matt that Vincent would only mess things up, but he never expected it to be something this major. Matt's graduation was officially under its way. Instead of being there, he was at Vincent's sleeping away a hangover and his parents were on the way.

The wait ended as Nia and Ford finally returned with Matt who looked like death and his face was damped with tears. Nia rested her hands on her son's shoulders as she led him upstairs.

Bianca followed her mother and brother and they all went into his bedroom. Ford on the other hand joined Damien in the kitchen, his face red.

Ford glared down at Damien, "You took him to Cut Up? What the fuck were you thinking?"

Damien wasn't going to try to lie his way out of this, "He begged me."

"He's eighteen, he's still a kid. And how could you keep so much from me?"

"It was our secret."

"Damien, you don't fucking keep secrets with my son. And why didn't you tell me my own son was gay?"

"I promised that I wouldn't," Damien said, "I wasn't going to betray him."

"So instead you betrayed me? I feel so fucking blind right now. All of this shit was going on and I didn't even know. You didn't think once about even bothering to tell me my kid was messing around with some dude who owns a strip club or even that he's gay like myself? He said in the car that you've been giving him all kinds of advice and shit, telling him which guys were good for him or not. That's my responsibility. I mean damn, have you been teaching him other shit I don't want to even imagine?"

Damien narrowed his eyes, "Excuse me?"

"Like about sex? Damien, be honest, have you done anything sexual with my son? Any hands on shit?"

Damien couldn't believe it. After two years, two years of building a trust worthy relationship, he couldn't believe Ford would even think he would do something like that. He could go on and on about how he was actually trying to protect Matt from guys like Vincent, but he was far too insulted to even look at Ford. Damien just stormed out of the house.

41 - Severance

All Damien wanted to do was fuck, but for some reason this guy he met on Jack'd was trying to talk him into moving in with him. They had only had about two conversations over the app and this was their first meeting in person. Damien figured since they were both butt naked in the man's bed he would be getting what he actually wanted, but instead of he was being cuddled and treated to endless conversation.

"I just feel as if we can grow into something," Michael, who had a scruffy beard, said, "I feel a deep connection with you."

"I'm not really trying to date anyone; I'm still in a complicated relationship."

Complicated as in he was still too upset at Ford for the last two months that he didn't bother speaking to him.

Michael rolled his neck and snapped his fingers, "Then why the fuck are you here?"

"Honestly, to get a nut."

"I'm more than just somebody you can fuck though," Michael said, offended.

"Listen, I'm not the one who messaged a picture of my asshole though."

"It's the only way you can get men's attention, you know how it works."

Damien sat up, "Listen, maybe we can do this another time. I'm gonna go."

"Just like that. I swear y'all niggas are all afraid of commitment."

Damien got out of bed and started to put his clothes on, "Please, you don't fucking even know me."

"Well I'm trying to get to know you but you're just trying to fuck."

"I wasn't gonna lie to you because I'm not that type of dude who would do that. I wanted a nut, but whatever."

Michael grabbed his phone from his end table, "Boy bye, I'm already on to the next one."

"Yeah, good luck finding a husband on Jack'd," Damien sarcastically said as he left.

As he drove through his hometown, Damien realized how much he was starting to miss having stability in his romantic life. He felt as if the dating pool in the area was deadly, most dudes only worth a quickie and that's it. He had yet to encounter anybody as luring as Ford. He arrived home to find Katrina cleaning up the kitchen.

Damien grabbed a bottle water from the fridge, "Where's everybody at?"

"Um, your father is sleeping, Marion stepped out for a minute, and I'm about to study. How's your night?"

Damien shrugged, "The same as every other night I've had since coming back home."

"Well, I've liked having you here, a much warmer personality than Marion."

"Oh, yeah, but that's just Marion. His horribleness grows on you."

Katrina laughed, "You're so funny Damien. Are you still searching for culinary schools?"

"Yeah, I've narrowed it down to one down south, close to Atlanta. I'm just trying to get some financial aid."

"It's nice to see you're trying to do something you love. I can't wait until I can call myself a therapist."

Damien softly patted her on the back, "It'll happen. I'm going to lay down, okay?"

"Going to bed this early? Well, alright."

Damien headed into his bedroom and plopped down on his bed. This had become his usual routine. No job, no boyfriend, so he just laid around waiting for funding of his culinary education. Damien was growing so impatient waiting on some aid; he was close to calling his Aunt Bernice to borrow some money. That was how desperate he wanted to be back on track in his life. Damien eventually drifted off to sleep out of boredom and was awoken by the sound of some familiar laughs from the living room.

He stepped out of room to find Marion and Vincent sitting on the couch drinking beers.

"What is he doing here?" Damien asked.

Marion looked over to Damien, "Oh, he's wake."

"What's up Damien?" Vincent asked.

"I like how you're acting as if you didn't just fuck up my last relationship."

Vincent laughed, "I didn't do anything to cause you to leave old dude, forgive and forget."

Marion put his arm around Vincent's shoulder, "Exactly, my nigga. I mean, it took me awhile but it's time to stop playing. Ever since that Ford dude told me how he was running gyms with his homeboy, I knew me and Vincent would have to reconnect at some point." Marion removed his arm from Vincent's shoulders and motioned at some documents on the coffee table, "Man, Vincent and I are finally gonna get on track and start a luxury barber shop. I'm tired of burgers and fries and watching daddy and Katrina kiss up on each other."

"And Cut Up is a dying brand," Vincent said. "We're both going into work mode only."

Damien couldn't imagine them both not fucking the entire world to simply focus on work, "I have to see it to believe it."

"Man, you're seeing it right now with your hatin ass," Marion said as he dapped Vincent.

Vincent laughed, "Nah, leave him alone, just no free cuts for him."

Marion burst out laughing.

Damien couldn't believe the two of them were actually not only friends again, but business partners. He felt if Marion could forgive Vincent, he could do the same with Ford. Sure, the love had been for him was damaged a bit, but Damien missed his job, having his own, and simply having Ford in his life. That upcoming weekend, Damien took a road trip down to North Carolina and stopped at Golden Age Gym.

The first face he spotted as he entered the gym was Matt's who was working at the front desk.

Matt's face lit up, "Damien, you're back!"

"I'm just stopping by to talk to your dad. I miss it here and my job."

Matt twisted his lips, "Man, he got Bianca doing your old job and me out here answering phones and shit."

"Why haven't you started school?"

Matt shrugged, "Man, after coming out and everything and feeling as if I caused you to leave, I felt bad. Instead of going to school, I decided to wait and just work for my dad. I'm going next year though for sure. Hey, I'm glad you're here also because I was wondering if you could talk to Vincent for me. He's been ignoring me."

Damien couldn't believe Matt was still under Vincent's spell, "I haven't seen him in a while either," Damien lied.

"Oh," Matt said, sounding disappointed, "Well, my dad is in his office."

"Alright, man."

Damien walked off and bumped into Buddy. "Sup, Buddy?"

Buddy stepped back and looked Damien up and down, "Aye, listen here, don't come in here all disgruntled trying to shoot up the place."

Damien laughed, "No, I left on my own terms, remember? I didn't get fired. I'm here trying to get my job back."

"Oh, that's cool then. Bianca can't get shit right. She's never even here. Hell, she ain't here now."

"Hopefully, I get my spot back then."

Buddy winked at Damien, "Aye, if you need a reference, shout for me."

"Most definitely."

Damien continued to Ford's office and knocked on the door.

"Yeah, come in," Ford said.

Damien entered the office to find Ford behind his desk on his laptop. "It's just me."

Ford stopped typing, "Well damn, I thought I was never gonna see you again."

"I felt the exact same way."

"Well, I'm glad I'm seeing you because I want to apologize."

"Really? Why?" Damien asked.

"For accusing you of what I accused you of," Ford said, "Listen, at that moment I was embarrassed, upset, and overall felt like a bad father. My son was seeking advice from a man half my age, about stuff I as a gay man myself could've easily answered for him. It made me wonder about my parenting skills. Instead of throwing money at my family, I should've at least done more to let them know they could be honest with me."

"Still, I should've let you know what was going on."

"I think you did the right thing, Matt trusted you and you didn't betray him. Things are different now."

"How so?"

"Well, both Nia and I are realizing our divorce is still affecting our children. Bianca is a mess, Matt basically stayed in the closet because he didn't want to make things worst between Nia and I. He felt as if she would've gotten mad at me and blamed me for him being gay. Of course Nia didn't, but still, he kept that secret to simmer any possible tension between his mother and me. We've both stepped up as parents. And one decision I've made is that I can't date somebody their age...no matter how much I want to. It's not right."

Damien took that as Ford saying they were over, "And I suppose me working here will complicate things."

"Especially since I'm moving to Florida to manage the new locations. So far, Matt's joining me and Nia and Bianca will stay up here in the house. I don't think hiring you and taking you down there with me will help the situation. Plus, you can do so much more with your life. You have a gift for cooking."

"Thanks, I've been trying to get into a certain school, but financial aid is a mess to deal with."

Ford shrugged, "Well, you never got your final pay check. I can throw on some severance to cover your tuition."

Damien laughed, "Nah, you don't have too."

"I want to though. I'm going to do it no matter what you say." Ford took out his check book.

"Well, I do need my final pay check," Damien said with a smile.

Ford held out the check, "This is a thank you for our wonderful past and a down payment on your future."

Damien took the check from Ford. In his hand, he held a five thousand dollar start to his next step in life.

****

42 - Brunch

There was a sole reason why Damien liked doing it in the missionary position when he slept with Mateo, it made it easier to cover his mouth. The bed creaked as Damien thrust into Mateo as hard as he possibly could. His goal was to keep Mateo moaning in order to stop him from talking during sex, one of his worst habits. If he wasn't so cute or close to campus, Damien would've dropped him long ago. Truth was, he enjoyed having a sex partner with no emotional investment required. They were both simply two culinary students who were focused on school, not their romantic lives.

Damien removed his hands from Mateo's mouth as his body muscles flexed and he nutted.

"Damn papi," Mateo said as he gasped for air, "I couldn't breathe towards the end."

Damien lay down flat on his back, panting heavily, "My bad."

"And can you stop fucking me as if I stole something. I won't stay tight if you keep trying to split me open."

Damien just nodded, wishing he had some ear plugs. "Okay, okay."

Mateo tried to get out of bed, "I don't think I can even walk at the moment."

"It can't be that bad."

"Have you ever bottomed?" Mateo asked.

"No."

He slapped Damien against the chest, "Then how in the fuck would you know if it hurt or not."

"I'm sorry, okay? I only do it that hard because I'm enjoying it so much," Damien lied.

"I just think you're trying to hospitalize me so I can't outdo you on the winter exam."

Damien rolled his eyes, "Please, you can't even make an omelet."

"At least I can bake a cake without reading the directions," Mateo said as he playfully stuck his tongue out.

"That's a low blow. You hurt me on that one."

"You started it, my mouth is my greatest weapon."

And his worst trait, Damien thought to himself. "Shut up and kiss me."

Mateo cuddled up close to Damien, "Why are you so horny this morning?"

"I'm trying to get as much stress out of me so I can focus solely on exams. This benefits us both."

"Like normal people, I studied to prepare for my exams. I'm ready."

"I did that too, but this helps also."

Damien forced Mateo to kiss him. He dug his tongue deep into Mateo's mouth and started grabbing at his ass. Damien found himself to be already hard again. As he continued to kiss Mateo, he slipped two fingers in him and started to slowly massage his insides. Mateo started to moan, a sound Damien liked. Before he knew it, his dick was back into Mateo and round two had started.

After round two was done, Damien went for his own personal record and they had round three in the shower. He was legit stressed about his winter exam. All this sex wasn't helping as much as he wished it would, but still, it was better than sitting around wondering if he was on the verge of failing out of school again. After they were done in the showers, they both left Mateo's apartment in their own cars.

A few blocks away, Damien arrived to the lavish campus of Arts & Craft Institute of Tomorrow. The school was located in Tomorrow, Georgia, nearly an hour away from Atlanta. It was the learning place of future chefs, fashion designers, models, and artists. Damien made plenty of friends, the closest being those he shared some culinary classes with. He spotted his friend Harris leaving Baking 101.

Harris dapped him, "Man, I just baked the mother fucker out of a cake."

Harris was built like a brick house, had a bushy beard that covered up his square jaw, and was a tall glass of chocolate milk. Damien was surprised to learn the chef in training was ex-military, having serving some time in Iraq. He was even more surprised to learn Harris was gay after spotting him at a gay club. Harris became distant at first after being discovered at the club, but he was just starting to warm up to Damien again.

"I get to tackle that shit in an hour," Damien said, "Come have brunch with me and the dudes."

Harris shook his head, "Nuh, I ain't in the mood for them right now. Plus, I have to go to practice. They've officially named me team captain so it's my responsibility to whip these lil limp wristed dudes into shape. Man, some of them dudes can't even throw a football. I think they signed up for the team just looking for tops. Gay niggas so damn thirsty."

The Gay Football League was a local organization, Harris the captain of the team he played for. Damien had little interest in adding sports to his busy schedule.

Damien dapped Harris again, "Have fun with that then, I'll see you later."

Damien parted ways with Harris as he continued through campus. He still had a lot to learn about Harris. One thing he knew for sure was that Harris avoided gays who weren't up to his masculinity standards at all cost. Damien didn't let that attitude dampen their friendship, but wished it wasn't such a task to get Harris to hang with him and his other friends in public.

He arrived to the state of the art cafeteria to find Kyle and Sean waiting for him at their usual table.

Kyle, whose cute face was constantly plastered across Tumblr, looked up at Damien, "You smell like Mateo."

Damien laughed as he sat down beside Kyle. "Shut up."

A heavy set Sean raised his cellphone to them, "Beyonce just posted on Instagram. The Queen has graced us."

Damien laughed, "You better focus on winter exams and not Beyonce."

Sean put his phone away, "We have the Baking 101 exam together, right?"

"Yeah, so bake slow so I can copy your every move," Damien said.

Damien had met Sean through Jack'd. Originally, in his photo Sean had the body of a track star, but when they decided to meet Damien got the real version of him. Damien had nothing against dating a heavy set guy, but like most, he had a bit of shallowness in him. He also didn't like that Sean basically catfished him. Their friendship resumed once they both arrived to their first day of class and unexpectedly spotted each other. Damien liked Sean, out of all his friends, he brought the most positive energy.

"All I have to do is submit a black and white themed photo," Kyle said, "I can take that on my phone."

Kyle was at Arts & Crafts for modeling. Before Damien got a car down here, he would ride the shuttle bus to school every morning. Kyle was usually on the bus wearing headphones and looking ashamed to be on a bus. One morning, the bus was overly crowded, Kyle's IPhone went dead, and he and Damien had ended up sitting next to each other and connecting over their love of the show True Blood.

“Well some of us have to work for a good photo,” Sean said, “It takes me hours to get a decent one.”

Kyle rolled his eyes, “Because you trying to impress dumb ass dudes.”

“I don’t want to die alone,” Sean said.

Damien laughed, “Man, you’re twenty-one.”

Kyle got up, “I only take pictures for agents. If there’s no profit involved, I’m not striking a pose for shit.”

“Well I’m not you, men don’t flock to me. I have to meet them online,” Sean said.

“Then maybe you should find a way to change that and take those who flock to me because I don’t want them," Kyle said.

Damien sometime was tired of Sean’s dating issues. He looked up at Kyle, “You going to grab food?”

Kyle nodded, “Yeah, I’m not gonna sit here and starve. I’ll be back.”

Damien stood up, “I’m coming with you,” He looked over to Sean, “You want me to grab you something?”

Sean thought about it, “Just fruit...and some pancakes and chicken tenders.”

Damien smirked, “Alright, I got you.”

As they left the table Kyle whispered to Damien, “Next time make him get up and walk.”

“Be nice man, we all go through things.”

“I know, but he’s always going through things. Imma have to find new friends.”

Damien laughed, “But you can’t because every dude who talks to you is just trying to fuck.”

“I fucking know, I’m like the most wanted virgin in Georgia. If only I got paid for this shit.”

Damien could only laugh as they got in the buffet line. Besides exams and a hook up buddy who didn’t understand the concept of peace and quiet, it felt great having only a minor list of issues. His were nothing serious compared to what his friends sometimes struggled with.

43 - Trainer

When it came to choosing which one of his friend's apartments to chill at, Kyle's place was always the easiest and best decision. Unlike Harris, Kyle actually allowed them all to come over and didn't scold them if they weren't behaving 'straight enough', Sean had a roommate who always tried to jump into their conversations, and Damien's place was a studio apartment that barely had enough room for himself. Kyle had a two bedroom apartment all to himself with cable, internet, and food in his fridge.

There was a reason Kyle was able to go to school for something like modeling, his parents were wealthy. His mother was a fulltime RN and his father owed a mechanic's shop back in Kyle's home state of Tennessee. They were able to fund their only son's life while he learned how to pose and walk a runway. And their money wasn't going to waste, because even though Damien had come over tonight to actually hang with Kyle, the wanna be model was glued to his laptop at his kitchen table.

"What are you doing?" Damien, who sat on the couch channel surfing, asked.

Kyle kept his focus on the laptop, "I'm trying to set up my first professional photoshoot. The issue is that everybody with an

IPhone is claiming to be a photographer. And once I do find somebody decent they either charge a lot or sound as if they want the rights of my life signed over. It's giving me a migraine."

"Have you tried asking around campus?"

"I did, most dudes who said yes also just wanted to fuck on the low. I hate men."

Damien laughed, "Do you want to die alone?"

"Alone with the life of Tyson Beckford is all I want. Fuck the world of STDs and AIDs."

"There's also a lot of beauty in that world," Damien said, "I've had some magical relationships."

"No recaps," Kyle said as he dismissively fanned his hand at Damien. "I've heard them all, from Vincent to Zyan."

"Man, you're being a real bitch tonight. I wanna celebrate barely passing my exams."

Kyle kept typing at his laptop, "As soon as I get my situation straight over here we can."

There was a knock on the apartment door. Damien got up and answered to find Sean dressed in gym clothes.

Damien stepped aside as he eyed Sean up and down, "You look athletic."

Sean entered the apartment, "After being blocked on Jack'd once again, I've decided to make a change."

Damien shut the door, "Oh for real? What kind of change?"

Sean motioned at himself, "The most obvious one. I'm going to lose some fucking weight."

Damien shrugged as he looked Sean up and down, "I think you look fine."

"Don't lie to me Damien, I feel unhealthy so I'm sure I look unhealthy."

"But you're doing it for dick," Kyle butted in from the kitchen, "Not your health, don't lie."

“Fine,” Sean admitted, “I haven’t done shit with a guy since high school. And the only reason the dude hooked up with me back then was because I was the last nigga in the locker room after gym and he wanted a nut. I want somebody to make love to me, to adore me, to make me feel like I’m worth something.”

“As I said, I don’t think you need to lose much,” Damien said.

Kyle laughed, “No, you said he looked fine. Be honest Damien; just tell him to lose weight.”

“I can take it,” Sean said, “I’m a grown man, not some kid. If I can say it, you can say it.”

It hurt Damien to say this, “Alright, damn. You can afford to lose some weight. It doesn’t bother me though.”

“It’s not your body,” Sean said, “It’s not your dead sex life; of course it doesn’t bother you.”

“Okay, okay, okay,” Damien said, “I support you, damn.”

“Then come with me to the gym tonight, both of you. I signed up at Fit Planet.”

Kyle gagged, “Um, hell no. DL niggas go there to try to snatch up ass. All of them are fake ass personal trainers. Trust me, I know.”

“Me too,” Sean said, “That’s why I picked that gym. Call me thirsty if you want.”

Kyle rolled his eyes, “Very parched.”

Sean ignored Kyle as he looked to Damien, “Please, come with me.”

Damien figured the gym would be more entertaining than watching Kyle type, “Shit, there ain’t nothin else here to do.”

Sean excitedly bounced on his feet, “Hell yeah, now I’m ready to get my sweat on.”

Damien looked over to Kyle, “Aye, rich boy let me borrow some gym shit.”

Kyle nodded over to his room door, “Just grab whatever but not my orange New Balances.”

Damien headed into Kyle's room and dived into his closet of never ending clothes. He ended up finding some black gym shorts, kept on his white t-shirt, and borrowed a red hoodie. Damien fetched two bottles of water from the fridge and left with Sean, leaving Kyle to search for a legit photographer.

Damien was expecting to arrive to an empty gym, it being ten o'clock on a Friday night. Instead, he arrived to find about two dozens of dudes working out. Each area of the gym seemed to cater to different body types. In the area that included some weight machines, a lot of the more average Joe's were working out. In the heavy weights sections that had a vast selection dumbbells, you could find most of the chiseled men. Damien stuck with Sean in the cardio area, where most guys plus-sized or a bit older worked out.

While Damien had barely broken a sweat, Sean had looked as if he just came out of the shower only after doing about twenty minutes on the treadmill. Damien was proud of Sean making this decision to lose weight, but didn't agree with some of the reasons that were inspiring him. He couldn't bring himself to be as harsh as a critic as Kyle though.

Damien's cellphone started to vibrate in his pocket. The act of taking phone calls on the floor was forbidden and he didn't want to get Sean banned on his first visit. He let Sean know he was going to take a phone call and headed off to the locker room. Damien headed into the locker room area, checked his phone to learn his dad had called.

Damien hit redial and his father answered, "Dad, what's up?"

"I'm just callin to see how those exams went. I don't want you flunking out man."

Damien smirked, "I did alright, dad. Good enough to not fail out. Baking 101 really hurt my overall GPA."

"Alright, that's the shit I wanted to hear. We all rootin for you: me, Katrina, and Marion."

"How's Katrina doing in school?" Damien asked.

"She got a few more online classes."

"And Marion nor Vincent hasn't updated their Instagrams in a while."

Eric laughed, "That's good then. It means they still working like dawgs. Last thing I heard was that they gonna be workin with some rapper, traveling up and down the east coast hookin lil kids up with free cuts and school supplies. I don't know how Cut Up went from a strip club to a charity, but at least Marion's ass ain't living in here."

"I know that's right, but dad I'll call you tomorrow. I'm at the gym right now and phones aren't allowed."

"Alright, son," Eric said before hanging up.

Damien turned to leave the locker-room but ended up bumping into a toned guy who only wore a towel.

"Sup," The soap scented stranger greeted.

"Hey," Damien said.

"Aye man, if you ever looking for a personal trainer we can meet up at my place and discuss some stuff."

Damien knew exactly what this was. If he wasn't focused on school, he would entertain this guy. "I'm good."

His wanna be personal trainer, seductively bit his bottom lip, "You sure?"

"Yeah, I'm sure. Plus I'm sorta just here for my homeboy. Maybe you can train him?"

"The big dude on the treadmill who you were running with?"

Damien nodded, "Yup."

The guy laughed, "Nah, I'll pass on that though."

Damien could only shake his head and laugh as he brushed passed the guy and rejoined Sean who was just stepping off the treadmill.

Sean looked a bit dizzy, "Man, you driving back."

Damien put Sean's arms around his shoulders, "Alright, man. No biggie, I got you."

Damien was proud of Sean's overall goal to lose weight, but also of himself for not taking the bait of the so-called personal trainer.

44 - Practice

When Damien was a kid, Saturday mornings were all about cartoons. Once he got a bit older, it was all about watching Vincent and Marion play video games. And once his teenage hormones kicked in it was all about Saturday morning porn. And today, his Saturday morning was all about using his tongue to pleasure Mateo.

He had originally stopped by Mateo's to grab a hat he had left before going to watch Harris and his team practice. Mateo had answered the door only in some boxers and Damien couldn't resist him. They ended up on the living room floor, Mateo's legs in the air, with Damien eating his ass. This Saturday morning treat surpassed any bowl of cereal with a side of cartoons. After making Mateo as wet as he could, Damien figured he might as well get in a quick fuck. As he started to unbutton his pants, Mateo raised his palm to him.

"Nu uh, what are you doing?" Mateo asked.

Damien pulled out his dick, "I'm about to give you some dick, don't act special."

Mateo closed his legs together, "Nu uh."

"Well why the fuck not? You can't get me this hard and then not let me nut."

Mateo sat up from the floor, "I'm talkin to another dude. Like, it might turn into a relationship."

"But what about us?"

Mateo rolled his eyes, "You know the deal. We ain't nothin serious. You don't even listen when I talk."

"I do."

"What's my momma's name?"

Damien had no idea. He decided to go with the most cliché, "Maria?"

"Fuck you, papi," Mateo laughed, "Her name is Kim."

"Damn, so it's just over like that?"

"Yeah, this new guy and I might eventually start fucking. I don't fool around with two dudes, that's beyond messy."

Damien was going to miss getting in Mateo, "Well, can I at least eat your ass while I jerk off?"

Mateo parted his legs, "Yeah, but this is your last taste."

Damien finished what he had started and after nutting, grabbed his hat and left. He wasn't looking forward to getting back out into the hookup world, what he had with Mateo had been a good arrangement. The world of Jack'd and dealing with dudes who easily got emotionally attached was a stressful one. Damien set that thought aside as he pulled up to Harmon Park.

On the grassy football field, a rag tag group of men were gathered for football practice. Harris, captain of the Sharks football team, stood front and center. In the sun, his shirtless body glistened. And the dick print in the white shorts he wore was very apparent if you looked at it from the right angle. Damien didn't understand Harris' complaints about men joining the team just for sex, especially with how he was out there showing off the goods. Damien grabbed a seat on the bleachers.

A few other onlookers were on the bleachers, either here to support their friend or spouse.

One guy took a seat next to Damien and extended his hand out, "I'm Larry."

Damien shook his hand, "Sup Larry, I'm Damien."

"Who are you here for?" Larry asked.

"My friend is team captain, Harris."

Larry moaned, "Damn, the brotha with the thick dick? You fucking him?"

Damien laughed, "Nope, we're just friends. Who are you here for?"

"My boyfriend is the lil skinny dude with the glasses. He's trying to get into shape, bless him."

"Well, at least he's not out here just to stare at Harris."

Larry stared down Harris, "Oh, I told my man to get his attention. I would love a three-way."

Damien didn't feel like having an entire conversation with this guy about Harris. "Nice weather, huh?"

Larry ignored Damien and mumbled under his breath, "I'll catch his ball for sure."

Damien just decided to ignore Larry as much as he could and focus on the practice. The team had started running some drills and even played a little game against each other. Damien could only laugh as Harris walked around the field spazzing out and shouting every time one of the men screwed something up. A good chunk of them actually knew how to play, but still were no match for Harris when he would tackle them like they stole something. Damien just found the entire practice to be brutal. Harris was sexy, but not that much to come out here and break bones.

Harris brought the practice to a close and the majority basically limped off the field.

Damien left the bleachers and joined an angry looking Harris on the field. "Are you okay?"

"Did you see that shit? How can we win a game if they all play like bitches?"

"Half of them were good, better than me. And I'm sure the other half was distracted by you."

Harris furrowed his brows, "What the fuck does that mean?"

"Nigga," Damien said as he motioned at Harris, "Look at you. All your business is out."

"Oh, so not wearing a shirt is a gay shit now? Man, gay niggas always gotta twist shit into something else."

"I'm just saying...if you want them to focus...wear a trench coat," Damien teased.

Harris dropped his attitude and managed to crack a smile, "See, I can deal with you. You funny."

"Sean and Kyle are equally as funny. Yet you act like you can't stand them."

"I mean, they cool, but once Sean starts talking about that Beyonce shit I clock out."

Damien nodded, "Yeah, I get that, but what about Kyle?"

"He's cool, but that nigga too fucking pretty for me. Man, he makes a dude have unfaithful thoughts."

"I'm just saying, they like you, and I want all my friends to get along, so come around more."

Harris nodded, "I'll try, I'll try." He checked his phone, "Yo, my boy gonna be late. You wanna drop me off?"

"Man, when you gonna start calling him your boyfriend and stop the boy shit?"

Harris playfully shoved Damien, "Aye nigga, stop dictating my life and give me a ride."

"Whatever. Just make sure you dry off. I don't want my car smelling like sweat."

Damien had been surprised to learn mister masculinity had been in a serious relationship for four years with another man. It was interesting for Damien seeing somebody who was the same age as him, living the settled down life. He got close to that with Ford, but of course that didn't turn out so well. Damien had no plans to settle down again anytime soon though, school received all his focus.

They arrived to Harris' house to find his boyfriend Terrance on the couch watching the food channel. Terrance was one of those dudes who looked like your everyday corner street thug, but underneath it all he had an impressive resume. Not only was he ex-military like Harris, he was a popular college basketball player, but gave it all up to work at an organization that helped gay youth with their issues.

Harris dropped down on the couch next to Terrance, "I'm tired."

Terrance kissed Harris on the forehead. He looked up at Damien, "Was he mean?"

Damien nodded, "You know it. I was just stopping in to say hi. Enjoy y'all's black love."

"It's beautiful right? I can't wait to have his babies," Terrance joked.

Harris rolled his eyes, "Why you gotta say gay shit like that?"

The couple started to bicker back and forth and Damien took that as a sign to wave goodbye and leave. He could only smile as he walked back to his car, not sure how Harris could be so involved in the lifestyle yet ashamed of it.

45 - Pose

Damien started his morning trying to find a replacement for Mateo on Jack'd. So far, the search wasn't going so well. Most of the guys who messaged him were twice his age and he decided it was way too soon to go down that road again. He also got contacted by a bunch of profiles that lacked pictures, the guys simply claiming to be discreet. Damien also crossed them out as possible options, not ready to deal with the paranoia that came along with dating most DL men. All the guys who he thought were actually cute didn't even bother responding. It only stung his ego a bit.

Damien set down his phone and deleted the app. "I quit. I'll just jerk off for now."

His phone started to ring and Kyle's photo popped up on the screen.

Damien picked his phone back up, "Yo?"

"Do you feel like taking an hour long drive to Atlanta with me?" Kyle asked.

"Yeah, I'll go. What's going on?"

"I finally found a legit photographer. He's done photoshoots for a lot of dudes who do theater in the area and some popular models from ATL. I've checked his credentials, references, and everything. The combination of my looks and his skills can take me to the top. I might even get some acting jobs. I'm so nervous I'm shaking."

"Do you want to make this a road trip? I can invite Harris and Sean."

Kyle thought about that, "Yeah, do that. The more people around me, the less nervous I'll feel."

"Alright, I'll call them. I should be ready when you get here."

"Cool." Kyle said before hanging up his phone.

Damien dialed Harris' number first and he answered, "Yo, Harris, we're going on a road trip."

"We who?" Harris asked.

"So far just Kyle and I. We're going to Atlanta. He has a photoshoot."

Harris laughed, "You think I want to spend my day watching somebody take pictures?"

"It's called being supportive."

"Nah, I'm dealing with some shit with Terrance. He's been a moody bitch lately."

"Don't tell me you got this nigga pregnant," Damian joked.

"Fuck you," Harris said as he burst out laughing, "Enjoy your lil road trip. I'll catch y'all on the next one."

"Yeah whatever," Damien said before hanging up and calling Sean.

"Aye," Sean groaned out.

"Man, I thought you always woke up flawless," Damien said, "You sound wrecked."

"I went jogging this morning, threw up and now I'm feeling weak."

"Maybe you should take a break from this weight loss stuff and come to Atlanta with Kyle and me."

"Noooo," Sean groaned out, "I'm five pounds down. And I ain't going anywhere today, just in my bed."

"So both you and Harris gonna act stank like that?"

"Now, you know I'm always up for a trip. Don't group me with Harris and his standoffish self."

"Alright, alright, go rest those legs. And don't work yourself too hard."

"Bye Damien," Sean said and he ended the call.

Damien knew the trip would be a lot more fun if everybody went, but he got along with Kyle the best anyways. Unlike Sean, Kyle wasn't always whining and unlike Harris, Damien could joke around and make jokes without being told he was acting suspect. He got dressed for the trip and by time he was ready, Kyle was outside blowing the car horn.

Damien headed outside his studio apartment. The neighborhood he lived in was decent, the only flaw being listening to girls argue with their boyfriends all night or fighting each other out in the parking lot. He joined Kyle in the car and dapped him.

"Who else is coming?" Kyle asked.

"It's just me. Sean is down post-workout and Harris is having relationship issues."

Kyle rolled his eyes, "Did Harris finally realize Terrance is a man and that he's gay like the rest of us?"

Damien laughed, "I don't know. Let's not focus on his mess, today is your day dude. You ready for this."

Kyle gulped, "Yeah, it's all I ever wanted since I saw my first episode of Top Model. It's my boy hood dream."

Damien smirked, "Damn you must've been one hell of a gay boy."

Kyle laughed as he pulled off, "Shut up, modeling is an art not a gay thing."

Damien picked on Kyle a bit more throughout the ride to Atlanta. They also touched on the topic of Sean's new weight loss goal, Harris and his identity issues, the upcoming spring semester, and the decline of the show Dexter. They eventually arrived to the big city and drove to a shopping center where there was a bakery, soul food restaurant, discount clothing store and the photography studio.

Kyle parked, said a little prayer, and they both headed inside. In the lobby area, photos of the photographers past clients were hung all over the walls. Damien recognized some of the actors from small roles on TV. He wanted the best for all of his friends and only hoped this photoshoot was the start of Kyle's career in the modeling industry. It seemed to be all Kyle ever cared about, not sex, not searching for companionship.

Kyle hit a bell and out the backroom exited a bald man, who had the figure of a giraffe, narrow upper body, but an obviously surgically enhanced butt.

He smiled at Kyle, "I recognize that perfect face, Kyle, right?"

Kyle nodded, "Yup."

"I'm Anthony," The man introduced. He looked over at Damien, "Oh, and you're pretty yourself."

"Damien," He introduced, "Nice pictures."

"Thanks," Anthony said, "I've been shooting since the nineties."

"I've looked at almost everything you've shot," Kyle said, "I can't wait to work with you."

"My only rule is that you follow my directions, I make stars, the stars don't make me," Anthony proudly said.

Kyle motioned at himself, "I am yours."

Anthony led them to the back where his camera and lighting was set up. Damien took a seat on a leather couch and watched as Kyle was put through a series of challenging poses. He modeled everything from formal wear, to beach wear. At first Damien was enjoying the process, but he was starting to become extremely bored as Kyle was doing some headshots.

"Alright, clothes off," Anthony said.

Immediately Damien started to pay attention.

Without hesitation, Kyle started to strip down.

Damien had never seen his friend so eager to get naked for another man. "What are you doing?"

Kyle stepped out of his briefs and leisurely said, "Modeling."

Anthony laughed, "Exactly. This is the part when my clients usually regret bringing a parent along."

"I don't think you should have nudes floating around out there," Damien said.

"They're artistic," Kyle argued, "I know what I'm doing."

"If you're so concerned," Anthony said, "How about you join him? Help him cover up the parts you don't want exposed to the world. It'll actually improve the shots. It's very rare I can get an amateur male model to pose with another man. I know how to make stars. A duo photo will make Kyle standout. He'll become a star."

Kyle, who basically had dollar signs in his eyes, looked to Damien, "Yeah, what do you think?"

Damien couldn't believe Kyle was about to allow a man he just met to take nude photos of him. "Yeah, I'll do it."

Damien stripped down to his boxers and joined Kyle in front of the camera. Anthony directed them in how he wanted them to pose, Damien holding Kyle from behind as if they were posing for a prom photo. Damien's dick was pressed against Kyle's ass and naturally his dick started to get a little stiff, but not hard enough to make this moment an awkward one. The photographer requested hard faces from them both and once the scene was set, took a couple of shots.

Damien could feel Kyle's heart racing. He only hoped this extra step was enough to get his friend what he wanted. But today he saw another side of Kyle. Even though his friend was very conservative when it came to his sex life, today was proof that he was willing to do anything for his career. Damien could only think of one term as he held Kyle in his arms, ambitious.

46 - Bodied

Damien's morning had in interesting start. He woke up to some frantic banging on the door of his apartment. All sorts of thoughts were running through his head as he staggered from the bed to the door. Was somebody hurt? Were two of his neighbors fighting against his door? His questions were answered when he opened the door to find Kyle standing their glowing.

Kyle burst into his apartment, "Mother fucker shit damn, guess what?"

Damien rubbed his eyes as he laughed, "I'm guessing it has something to do with modeling?"

"Fuck yeah," Kyle said, "I've officially been asked to join Team Bodied."

Damien shut his apartment door, "What's that?"

"It's a local group of male entertainers. Now, I know your first thought was that they were strippers, but it's classier than that. People basically hire them to attend parties, host events; all while looking as sexy as fuck and being entertaining. I've been asked to join after Anthony shopped my portfolio around. This is a big stepping stone, because I will now get to meet so many higher ups in the Atlanta social world."

"Man, that's awesome."

"I've been invited to club Razor where Team Body is returning after being in LA for two months."

Damien yawned, "When?"

"Tonight, as in I need you to come with me to the mall right now because I need a shopping buddy."

Damien loathed the mall, knowing they would spend most of the time waiting in line. "Seriously?"

"Yes, and tell Sean and that asshole Harris they better show up tonight or I will cut them from my life."

"Fine, just give me a minute to get ready."

After he got dressed, Damien was dragged to the mall with Kyle. As he predicted, they either spent time waiting in line at the dressing rooms or to checkout. Kyle had finally settled on an outfit and they left. After getting dropped off, Damien had to focus all of his energy on getting Sean and Harris to come to club Razor. It was easy convincing Sean, glad to support Kyle, but it took a lot of arm twisting to get a yes out of Harris. Damien basically had to promise him that he would pay for all of his drinks.

Damien didn't count his mission as a successful one until he was actually riding in a car with all of his friends. Sean drove, bumping Beyonce the entire drive to Atlanta, Kyle was in the back texting away, and Harris sat beside him looking as if he wanted to jump out of the car and roll down the highway. They arrived to club Razor, one of the hottest gay clubs in Atlanta, to a crowded parking lot. Though just an hour away, the club scene here was a new world compared to the clubs in Tomorrow. Kyle being an invited guest tonight, him and his friends got direct entry.

Out of all the gay clubs Damien ever went to, Razor definitely took the cake. It was two stories high, there were exotic fishes swimming beneath the glass dance floor that brought the tropical theme of the club alive. Actual palmetto trees were covered with neon lights and a countdown clock to Team Bodied's return was on stage. Kyle and his friends were led upstairs to a VIP booth.

Sean kept tugging at the leather shirt he wore, "It's so damn hot in here. I'm sweating."

"It's because so much damn flaming punks up in here," Harris said.

"Stop it," Kyle scolded, "I will not let all your negativity ruin my night."

"Yeah," Damien agreed, "Let's focus on Kyle tonight. This is big for him."

A man in a dark suit approached the table, "Excuse me, but which one of you is Kyle?"

Kyle proudly stood up and shook the man's hand, "I'm me, all day."

"I'm Richard; I manage the ATL branch of Team Bodied aka a well-paid baby-sitter."

"It's so nice to meet you Richard," Kyle said.

"Listen, I want you and one friend to comeback and meet the guys before they hit the stage and join the party."

Harris quickly looked over to Damien, "Not you, you're staying with me. You have drinks to pay for."

Damien looked to Sean, "I guess you're the lucky guy."

"Me," Sean panicked, "Are you guys sure?"

Kyle did his best to yank Sean to his feet, "Just come on, Sean."

Richard led Kyle and Sean from the table, leaving Harris and Damien.

Harris waved over one of the VIP waitresses, "Yo, bring a bottle of the best vodka y'all got."

"Are you really that miserable?" Damien asked, "This club isn't that bad."

"It's not just this club, Terrance left me."

"What? After all these years? I thought you two were happy?"

Harris nodded, "We were. He wanted to meet my parents. That's not happening."

"Harris, you threw away something so great because you're not ready to come out to your parents? Dude, you're more involved in the gay community than I am. Hell, you fought in the Iraq war; you should be free to be whoever you want now. A big dude like you shouldn't be afraid to come out to his parents. Listen, I'll be honest, gay dating is a fucking task. When you find somebody good, somebody who makes you happy, you keep them forever."

The waitress delivered a bottle of vodka with two glasses.

Harris opened the bottle and drunk straight from it, "Man, you a good speaker."

"I'm trying to stop you from ruining a good thing. Keep your happy."

"Have you ever had a happy? That guy that made every day worth living."

Damien thought about it, "Many. But now that I look back on it, only one dude truly made me happy."

"Who?"

"His name was Zyan. It's weird cause out of all the guys I've been with, he was the type you didn't want to take home to dad but who I loved the most. We never actually dated; he was too much of a free spirit. And then after this situation I went through, he came off kind of cold but eventually apologized. The last time I saw him, he was behind bars and talking about joining the military. I let him get away and have yet to find somebody that's made me that happy on the inside. I'm telling you dude, fuck your parents, don't let Terrance go."

Harris took another sip as he thought about it, "I get what you're saying, but I have to think about it."

A siren went off and the lights in the club started to flash from red to black. Damien and Harris focused their attention down to the stage as they realized the countdown clock had finished and the curtains were starting to slowly part. A remixed version of a Rihanna song started to play as the first member of Team Bodied appeared shirtless and wearing some black jeans and combat boots. As the curtains kept parting, more members of Team Bodied were revealed. The fourth member of Team Bodied caused Damien's jaw to drop.

"Zyan," Damien said to himself.

As if his words had traveled across the noisy club and directly into his ears, Zyan's eyes met with Damien's. Team Bodied started a dance routine, well, all except for Zyan whose attention was still on Damien. Damien formed a smirk and simply waved at Zyan. Zyan's face lit up like a child's on Christmas as he waved back. It took a nudge from the guy dancing on stage next to him to snap him back into the moment.

Damien could not take his eyes off of Zyan. The moment was surreal. Inside, a familiar happiness was remerging.

47 - Happiness

It was a feeling he had forgotten. He thought it was with him all along, but its absence was only being overshadowed by his friends, school, a new town, and a stable hookup partner. Damien reconnected with his happiness. It felt good to have that happiness back in his life, him being given a second chance after foolishly letting it slip away.

After the club, he and Zyan went back to his studio apartment. The ride from Atlanta had been a quiet one. They only exchanged quick glances and smirks. But that was more than enough to let them know that they were glad to see each other. Damien didn't know what to say and judging by his silence Zyan was experiencing the exact same thing. Once they arrived back to his apartment, they made their way over to Damien's bed and lay down. They both just lied there, staring directly at each other.

Damien decided to say the first word, "Zyan."

Zyan laughed, "My nigga Damien."

"What happened," Damien asked, "How did we lose track of each other?"

"It's my fault. It's not like you coulda call me and shit.

"Still, I should've done more. But then of course you could've call me from boot camp."

Zyan laughed, “Man, I wasn’t in no damn boot camp.”

“But I thought you were enlisting? How are you out? Did you escape?”

“Nigga, I ain’t that crafty. I made the choice not to enlist after sleeping on that shit. Military niggas fine and all, but they be fucked up and shit. I ain’t never kill a nigga and I don’t plan on starting. So, I accepted my time and stayed in jail. Those niggas surprised me with a transfer and sent me down here to Georgia. The jail I was in down here had overcrowding so I got released about two years ago.”

“Man, luck was on your side.”

“Man fuck luck,” Zyan said, “Once I got out I was living on the streets. My momma aint even try to help me out.”

“Why not?”

“Man, if you had a son who kept getting locked up at some point you would get tired with that shit.”

“I guess but still-“

“-No, buts,” Zyan interrupted, “I had to deal with my situation and I did. So, I hustled, I did shit I don’t even want to talk about. Then one day this photographer asked me to take some pictures so I did it. Next thing you know, I was getting a call from Team Bodied and signed up. That silly shit saved me man; anything could’ve happen to me out there.”

“But you made it. You always seem to get back on your feet.”

Zyan nodded, “But the hard part is staying on my feet. When you were in my life, I managed to do that.”

“And you taught me how to live.”

Zyan looked around Damien’s apartment, “Man, it looks like you doing alright and shit. Why you in Georgia?”

“I’m in Culinary School now.”

“Yo, that’s good. I thought you were down here being stupid once I saw you at Razor.”

"Nah," Damien said as he laughed, "I was supporting my friend. Kyle, he's joining you guys."

"Oh, that dude is gonna go far," Zyan said.

"He's only been in the group for a couple of hours."

"I know, but when him and the big dude came back there to meet us, he only talked to Chance."

"Who's Chance?" Damien asked.

"Oh, he's like the lead member. He's a fucking jackass. But Kyle was kissing his ass hard."

"Not surprising, I just sorta learned that Kyle goes in hard when it comes to getting fame."

"He might get promoted quick because imma tell them my momma died or some shit and take a lil break."

"Why?"

Zyan gently punched him, "For you my nigga. I ain't leaving, I just found you. Unless you got a new nigga."

"Nope. I'm all on my own, besides my friends."

Zyan scooted a little bit closer to Damien, "Alright then, so can I stay?"

Damien leaned in a give him a kiss on the lips, "You know my answer."

Zyan reached down and started to unbutton Damien's pants. It had been a long time since Damien was so excited about sleeping with somebody. The moment he started to get hard, loud banging started on his apartment door. Zyan quickly sat up as the banging got louder. Damien checked his phone to learn they had been talking for nearly two hours and he had a ton of missed calls from Harris. He got up to go answer the door and Zyan went along with him.

Damien opened the door and a teary eyed Harris barged in, his face bruised.

Harris got up in Zyan's face, "Yo, who the fuck are you?"

Zyan raised his fists to Harris, "Big nigga you better chill out before I break your jaw?"

Damien shut the door, "Harris man, calm down. What's wrong?"

Harris was still focused on Zyan, "Aren't you the nigga from the club? Yo, you gotta roll out right quick."

"Man, Damien get this nigga out my face before I knock him out," Zyan threatened.

Damien stepped in between Harris and Zyan, "Everybody chill out."

Harris backed down and started crying, "I went to see Terrance."

Zyan calmed down and took a seat on the couch. "Imma just mind my business before I beat his ass."

Everybody somewhat cool, Damien focused on Harris, "Did you do something to him?"

"I tried to explain to him why he couldn't meet my parents and shit. So, he started telling me to get out, whining about how his family was coming down and he wanted everybody to all meet at once. I don't want to meet his fucking family, Damien. I ain't ready for that shit." Harris wiped some tears from his face, "So I let that nigga know that my name was on the lease and I wasn't going anywhere and his family had better change their plans. He got in my face, I pushed him, and that bitch hit me with an Xbox controller."

Zyan tried to hold in his laughter, "Well damn."

"I was about to kill that bitch, Damien," Harris said.

"You're drunk and a big dude; he probably had no choice but to use an Xbox controller."

"Are you taking his side?"

"No," Damien said, "I just think you both need to talk when you're not drunk."

"No, I can't. He wants me to be something I'm not."

“Gay?” Damien said, “Because you are.”

“I know that, but I’m discreet. I’m not having no family Thanksgivings and shit.”

“Harris when you’re dating another man for so long at some point you have to meet his family.”

Harris got in Damien’s face, “You doing that shit again, taking his side.”

Zyan got back up, “Aye big man, back up out his face.”

“Damien, tell this dancing ass faggot to shut the fuck up,” Harris said as he motioned at Zyan.

Zyan charged forward and with one straight punch, knocked Harris out.

Damien never saw somebody get dropped, “Holy shit!”

“I’m sorry,” Zyan said, “But that nigga needs to sleep that drunk shit off.”

“Yeah, I guess. You wanna help me put him in the bed?”

Zyan smirked as he massaged his fist, “I thought we were going to fuck or something.”

Damien laughed, “I know right, but I actually have a social life now and shit like this happens.”

Zyan and Damien lifted Harris up and put him in the bed. Even though anybody would consider this night a disaster, Zyan being here made it all good for Damien.

48 - Game

Harris was usually spot on in the looks department, but this morning he missed the mark. His jaw was a bit swollen thanks to Zyan and he had some bruising on his right cheek thanks to Terrance. While he had slept off his drunkenness in bed, Zyan and Damien slept cuddled up on the couch. They both had gotten an early morning start before Harris. Damien was getting dressed to go meet Sean for an early more gym session while Zyan and Harris were talking it out over some cereal.

Harris' mouth hurt so bad he barely could chew, "Fuck, you hit hard for a stripper."

"Nigga, if you call me a stripper again imma have to drop you one more time," Zyan threatened.

"Oh, it won't go down like that brah, you caught me off guard."

Zyan thumbed over his shoulders, "We'll we can go outside right now."

Harris shook his head, "Nah, let's postpone that, my face hurtin all over."

"I didn't want to hit your ass, but you were all up in my boy's face," Zyan said.

"Damien," Harris voiced, "You never told anybody that you had a boyfriend?"

Damien stepped out of the bathroom dressed for the gym, "I've told y'all about every guy I've been with."

Harris looked to Zyan, "Oh, you the dude who went to jail and shit then enlisted."

"Yeah, that's me."

"I served in Iraq. Where you serve at?"

Zyan laughed, "In county, about two hours outside of Atlanta. I didn't enlist, I served my time."

"Oh, so y'all back together now or something?" Harris asked.

Damien stalled to answer, "Well-"

"-Yeah," Zyan answered, "I ain't letting him out of my life this time."

Damien was glad to hear some assurance of their relationship status.

Harris nodded, "Enjoy that shit man. I love Terrance, but he wants too much right now."

"Aye, man," Zyan said, "Love hurts my nigga. Fill that void with some ass."

Harris formed a smug grin, "That shit won't be hard. I got a whole football team to run through."

Zyan dapped him across the table, "Aye that shit sounds hot."

Damien cut in, "But I still think you'll go back to Terrance. You two were good together."

Harris stood up, "Yeah whatever. Aye, is it cool if I chill for a while? I'm still tired as shit."

Damien nodded, "Yeah, I'm going to meet Sean. Zyan, you coming?"

Zyan got up, "I guess I can do some cardio, I'm starting to feel a lil thick anyways."

"As long as you don't jog that ass away, I'm cool," Damien said as he seductively bit his bottom lip.

Zyan playfully shoved him, "Aye nigga, respect my temple, I ain't no piece of meat," He said as he laughed.

Zyan and Damien left the gym and drove down to the gym. To Damien, Tomorrow, Georgia just seemed like a more vibrant town now that Zyan was there with him. He was all excited about introducing Zyan to everybody, taking him around town, and overall seeing how them officially being together would play out. They arrived to the gym and Sean was in the cardio area doing some stretches.

Damien introduced Zyan as he approached Sean, "Yo, this is Zyan."

Sean smiled, "The guy from the club, man I envy your body. What's your workout plan?"

Zyan patted his flat stomach, "Nigga I'm hood fit, spent many nights starving."

Sean laughed, "Still, I can't wait to reach where you at."

"Ain't nothin wrong with being a big nigga."

"I gotta disagree with you on that one," Sean said, "There's no fun in being a gay fat man."

"Aye, there's plenty of lonely skinny gay niggas out there. It's all about having game."

"Still, being fat gets you ignored on Jack'd and shit."

Zyan rolled his eyes, "Man, go to a club or some shit. Walk up to a nigga and spit game."

"I'm not good at stuff like that."

"Cause you so down on yourself big dude. I've done seen some of the ugliest niggas get numbers. And you cute as hell."

Damien could tell by the look on Sean's face that he was not buying what Zyan was selling.

Sean checked his fitness watch, "I guess, but I still need to work out. Y'all ready to start."

Damien clapped and rubbed his hands together, "Yeah, let's hit the treads."

On the treadmill, Damien jogged at a slow pace, not really trying to work out just here for support. Zyan was mostly joking around or rapping a bit too loud every time a good song came on over the gym speakers. As for Sean, he was jogging as if his entire life depended on it. Damien was starting to feel bad watching his friend jog through pain and misery. All of sudden, Sean staggered off the treadmill, jogged to the nearest trash can and vomited.

Damien rushed over to check on him, "Sean, you okay?"

Sean wiped his mouth clean using his hands and looked around the gym, "They're all looking at me."

Zyan joined them, "Aye, Damien all your friends kinda fucked up."

"They still looking," Sean said as he tried to stay on his feet, "Acting like they've never seen a fat dude."

"Nigga, they lookin cause your ass throwing up," Zyan pointed out.

Damien rubbed Sean's sweaty back, "Dude, it's time to hit the showers. You can barely stand."

Sean shook his head, "I'm not showering in here, I'm going home."

"Do you want me to drive you home? I don't think you can do that yourself."

"I just need some water," Sean said, "I'll be alright."

Sean walked off to go buy a water in the gym lobby area.

"Aye, let dude get himself together," Zyan said, "I'm going to shower."

Damien hesitated on leaving Sean alone before deciding to join Zyan, "Alright, I'm coming."

As they entered the locker room area, somebody grabbed Damien's arm.

Damien jerked his arm away as he looked to the right, "Yo."

It was the same dude who had tried to become his so-called personal trainer, "My offer's still open."

Zyan cut in, "Aye, why you grabbing on my nigga like that? What you want?"

"I'm Ashton man, I'm a personal trainer, relax."

"The answer is still no Ashton," Damien said as he walked off to go get undressed.

Zyan mean mugged Ashton, before he joined Damien and also started to slip out of his clothes, "Nigga was trying to fuck, huh?"

"He'll be alright, I'm sure he's already fucking a couple of dudes in this gym anyways."

Zyan and Damien headed into the steamy shower area and found a spot in the rear. The entire shower, Damien was fighting off an erection as he watched Zyan soap himself up. Through the steam, Damien spotted Ashton across from them doing more staring than showering. Damien got Zyan's attention and nodded over to where Ashton showered. Zyan started to laugh.

Zyan kept his focus on Ashton as he started to grab at Damien's soft dick. It didn't stay soft for long, Damien dick getting hard the more Zyan played with it. Zyan leaned in closer to Damien and started kissing on him. Ashton kept on watching, his dick hard also. Damien knew exactly what was going on, he was getting his chance to show off Zyan.

Damien started kissing on Zyan and rubbing his dick against his thigh. Zyan took things bit further as he forced Damien down on his knees, turned around, and shoved his wet hole in his face. Damien dove in and started to eat Zyan's ass. Zyan's moaning and groaning was joined by Ashton's who was now over on his side of the shower jerking off. Zyan started jacking his own dick as Damien sunk his tongue into him.

In unison, both Zyan and Ashton started to nut on the shower floor. Zyan forced Damien back up to his feet and they continued to makeout and teasing Ashton until he finally left the shower looking frustrated. Along with the indescribable happiness Zyan brought into his life, Damien was glad to welcome back the risky sex.

49 - Touchdown

Damien found himself settling into his happiness. Zyan had been back in his life for nearly two weeks now and he only improved everything. Damien started the spring semester with more of a drive, always excited about preparing the perfect dish in class and taking it home to Zyan to sample it. They both had even started searching for a better place to live together. Zyan was also shopping around his resume to some local male entertainment groups. They didn't offer as much as Team Bodied, but his main goal was trying to work as close to Damien as possible.

As for his friends, Damien was starting to notice that Kyle barely came to school anymore, too busy training with Team Bodied. Sean was officially fifteen pounds down, but for some reason the extreme working out was making him look tired in the face and almost sickly. As for Harris, Damien decided to go stop by the football field to see how his team was progressing. When he arrived, practice was ending and everybody was leaving. He didn't spot Harris but was pointed toward a building that contained a locker room and public restrooms by one of the players who last saw the team captain heading in that direction.

Damien made his way across the field and headed inside the locker room area. He walked around and didn't spot Harris, only his duffle bag. Through the vents, Damien could hear some faint moaning coming from the restrooms. He made has way out of the locker room and around to the men's restroom. As he tried to enter, the door was jammed. He pushed harder to learn a trash can was blocking the door. Sure it was safe to open the door; he pushed harder until he now had a clear view of Harris fucking a guy on the sink counter.

A shirtless Harris' pants were around his ankles, revealing his dark muscled butt as he aggressively stroked into a guy who wearing nothing but Nike Elite socks. Harris started cussing and pumping even harder as he nutted. He pulled his dick out of his sex partner and slipped off the nut filled condom and tossed it in the sink.

Harris quickly turned and face the door, revealing his curved dick, "Damien, what the fuck?"

Damien pushed his way into the bathroom, "Sorry to interrupt your fucking freak fest."

Harris pulled up his shorts, his dick outline still visible, "Aye, don't hate on my stroke."

"I was just coming to see how the team was doing."

Harris started to finger the guy on the sink, "They good. He's being awarded for getting a touchdown."

Damien looked away from the scene, "Well, I'm going to leave. You should really call Terrence."

Harris laughed, "Maybe, but right now I'm getting ready to get back into this ass. Peace."

Damien left the field upset with what Harris was becoming. He was once doing good for the gay community, but was now only poisoning it. This is why Damien was really starting to only enjoy the company of Zyan. He was getting tired of watching Sean kill himself, not impressed with Harris' new ways, and slowly was becoming disconnected from Kyle who only seemed to now care about Team Bodied.

He arrived home to find Zyan in their room, still in bed; the sheets only slight covering his butt. Damien started to go over and give it a nice smack then burry his face deep in it but there was a knock on his apartment door. He could only wonder which one of his friends it was and what drama they were bringing along with them. He exited the bedroom and went to go answer the apartment door to find Vincent and Marion looking like new money. They both wore black t-shirts with the name of their barber shop Cut Up on the front and jeans. You can tell by their bodies and clean skin that they were investing a lot of their new funds into themselves.

Vincent dapped Damien, "Surprise motherfucker!"

Marion brushed passed Damien and surveyed his apartment, "Man, they got you living like a bum down here," He said loudly as his eyes shifted in every direction.

"I like my apartment," Damien defended. "What are you two doing here?"

Vincent entered the apartment, "Cut Up is in ATL doing some hair cutting for a bunch of kids in the school district. We decided to stop by and come see you since it's been awhile and officially invite you to come to the event tomorrow. Marion wanted to go straight to a strip club, but I tried to tell him that only the dirty strippers go on before dawn."

"Tits and ass look good on any stripper," A hyped up Marion said, "Not that you two would get that."

"Nigga, I thought you had to shit," Vincent said.

Marion rubbed his stomach, "I do. That ATL soul food is nasty. Where's the bathroom?"

Damien pointed over his shoulder, "Over there and use some spray."

"Nigga, I'm the oldest, I can shit in the tub and you would still have to clean it up," Marion said.

Damien rolled his eyes as his brother entered the bathroom, "Well he's gotten worse."

Vincent laughed, "Actually, he had a ton a red bull and I think he did some coke this morning. Don't let him know I told you that. We're trying to work that out in private. But when he's not like that he's all business. Cut Up has really brought us together. And the fact that we're doing good overall betters the soul."

"I heard you guys are traveling with a rapper."

Vincent laughed, “I bet Eric said that. We’re working with Tristan Tunz. The R&B artists.”

“Oh,” Damien said, “How did you guys go from sitting in my dad’s house to this?”

“Marion came up with the free haircuts idea mainly to promote our barbers. We started locally back home. He then got other barbers from all over to join in on the idea and used a loan to get the bus we travel in. I returned to social media and used the few connections I had to get us a bit more popular. One day I got a message from Tristan, well...a dick pic. He claimed it was a mistake, but I knew he was just trying to bait me in. I sent a pic back and we linked up and I got him to join the tour after I gave him some dick.”

Damien’s jaw dropped, “He’s gay? Every song he writes is about fucking bitches?”

“They’re just songs man. He knows how to please a nigga in bed. But, he’s only second compared to you.”

Zyan stepped out of the bedroom, butt naked, and rubbing his eyes, “Yo Damien.”

Instantly, Damien could since a change in Vincent’s attitude as he watched him tried to resist a snarl.

Zyan noticed they had guests, but didn’t even both to cover up his semi hard dick, “Oh, my bad.”

Damien eyes widened, “Um...Zyan...”

Marion strolled out of the bathroom and stopped as he spotted Zyan, “What the hell?" He quickly looked away from a nude Zyan.

Zyan looked from Marion to Vincent, “Aye, who are these fine ass dudes?"

“Um, this is Vincent and my brother Marion,” Damien awkwardly said as he pointed to them.

Vincent gave out the fakest, “Sup,” As he continued to eye Zyan up and down.

"I need to see some titties ASAP after all of this shit," Marion said as he walked toward the apartment door.

"It was nice meeting y'all boy," Zyan said.

"For sure," Marion said as he was shoved out the door, "Don't kill my bro with that dick!"

Vincent didn't even give Zyan a response. And judging by the way Vincent slammed the door upon leaving, he was upset.

50 - Ignorance

Marion and Vincent rented out a local park in Atlanta for a Cut Up charitable event. Children and teens from surrounding areas were invited down to get free haircuts. A lot of local barbers volunteered their time to come out and pitch in. Along with free haircuts, food was being served and school supplies were being given out. As Damien arrived with Zyan he was surprised his brother and Vincent managed to put together such a big event.

Damien spotted some local celebrities from Atlanta based reality shows and the radio station was doing a live show and blasting the greatest hip hop and R&B tunes. Also Tristan Tunz was scheduled to perform in a gazebo area they had set up like a stage. In the rear of the park was an all-black bus with Cut Up painted on the side of it in red and white patterned lettering. A lot of free t-shirts were being handed out with the same logo on the front of it to the sponsors and celebrities in attendance. Damien and Zyan's first stop was over to the bus to receive their free shirts.

Zyan spotted Marion as they started towards the bus, "I hope your brother doesn't run away from me this time."

"He wasn't being himself and plus you're actually not butt ass naked this time," Damien explained, "But trust me, you met a different Marion."

"What you mean?"

"I mean that he was high on coke but let's just keep that between us."

Zyan sucked his teeth, "Man, he should be the happiest nigga in the world. Why he on that stuff?"

Damien shrugged, "I don't know. If my dad knew, he would fucking kill him though."

They arrived at the bus and were spotted by Marion.

Marion grabbed them two shirts from a box and formed an awkward smile, "You late."

Damien grabbed the shirts and passed one to Zyan, "Because there was a ton of traffic. How you feeling?"

"Oh I'm straight," Marion said, "Why wouldn't I be?"

"I'm just asking," Damien said.

"Dude don't worry about me," Marion said, "Matter of the fact, who is this nigga with you?"

"I'm Zyan," He reintroduced, "I'm your lil brother's dude...you met me yesterday."

"His dude?" Marion repeated, "Like his boyfriend and shit?"

"Yeah, you got a problem? You don't approve?" Zyan asked.

"Nah, I guess you cool. Thought his nerd ass would end up with a white boy or some shit," Marion said.

Zyan laughed, "That's why I fuck with him though. He's different."

"I'm not an alien, damn," Damien said, "I'm just as messed up as the both of you."

Zyan laughed, "True, true."

Marion clapped his hands together and then pointed at them, "Aye, put them shirts on and represent Cut Up."

Both Zyan and Damien slipped their shirts on over what they were wearing.

Zyan thumbed over his shoulder, "Aye, imma go take a piss right quick."

Zyan walked off through the crowd and left Damien with Marion.

"He seems cool," Marion said. "But at least I know you with a dude whose ass I can beat."

Damien knew they had more important matters to discuss, "So, why were you acting like that yesterday?"

Marion let out an awkward laugh, "Like what?"

"I'm not stupid Marion, you were clearly on something."

"You saying I'm a crackhead or some shit?" Marion asked.

"Or a coke head. No matter what it is, just stop doing it before you mess all of this up that you've built."

Marion rolled his eyes, "Nigga, I don't need your protection. That's my job."

"I was cool for a long time having an asshole as a brother, but I'm not going to tolerate a drug addict."

"Please, I tolerated your ass being a faggot. I was nice to your boyfriend and shit."

Damien knew Marion didn't mean that from the heart. "Marion, just remember. If you need me, I'm here."

Marion laughed, "Nigga, I'm cool. Aye, I don't have time for this. I have some interviews to go do anyways."

As Damien watched Marion walk away through the crowd, he knew this was only the beginning of his drug issues. He knew his words alone weren't enough to help his brother and that at some point he was going to have to bring their father into the discussion. Damien was going to give his brother a chance to possibly hit rock bottom and repair his own ways, but if that wouldn't work he was definitely telling everything to his father.

Damien headed through the crowd to go find Zyan but instead ended up bumping into Kyle.

"Yo," Damien said, "You came stranger."

"I got the group text, I figured I should show up to give you a legit goodbye," Kyle said.

"Goodbye? Where are you going?"

"Well, the Team Bodied brand is officially expanding to LA and they want me on the team there."

"But what about school man? Modeling?" Damien asked.

"I've sorta made it without school. And with Team Bodied on my resume, I can get plenty of modeling jobs."

"Man, that's not cool that you're leaving."

"I've been a southern boy all my life. It's time for me to go west coast."

Damien knew nothing he could say would stop Kyle from chasing the spotlight, "Promise me one thing."

"And what is that?"

"That you won't work yourself to death and go on at least one date."

"Maybe," Kyle said, "Hopefully west coast dudes aren't as ratchet and thirsty as these southern boys."

Damien playfully nudged Kyle in the arm, "Yeah whatever mister married to work."

Kyle pointed through the crowd, "There's Sean over there looking uncomfortable in his own skin as always."

"Yo Sean," Damien shouted as he waved him over.

Sean made his way through the crowd doing his best not to bump into anybody, "Man, it's crazy out here."

Damien pointed at Kyle, "Do you know this fool is moving to the west coast on us?"

"What?" Sean exclaimed, "I'm jealous. I heard they got some bomb dot com personal trainers."

"Are you still on this weight loss thing?" Kyle said, "You look fine."

"I look fine because I've been working out, I'll look better after I lose some more," Sean said.

Damien did not want this topic to be stuck on Sean's weight issues, "I'm glad you two came."

"I had to," Sean said, "I need to redeem my image in front of your lil thug husband."

"What embarrassing thing did you do, Sean," Kyle asked with a sigh.

"Last time I saw him he was standing over me while I threw up in a garbage can," Sean revealed.

Kyle sympathetically placed his hand on Sean's shoulder, "You need to get it and then keep it together."

Sean brushed Kyle's hand away, "I will once I'm in shape."

"Well, while you starve, come with me to grab a burger from the grill," Kyle said, "I'm hungry."

Sean nodded, "Alright. But walk fast cause I wanna be by the stage when Tristan Tunz performs."

Damien surveyed the crowd, "I'll see you two later, I'm trying to find Zyan."

Damien separated from his friends and once again found himself maneuvering through the crowd as he searched for Zyan. A lot of people kept showing up and from what Damien could hear, they were all excited for the Tristan Tunz performance. Instead of Zyan, Damien found himself spotting Terrance who wore a shirt promoting the LGBT youth group he worked for.

Terrance dapped Zyan, "Thanks for the invite, I brought some teens from the group down."

"That's awesome. I figured you would do that."

"I'm surprised you even invited me, especially with Harris and I being on a break."

"A break? He's acting as if you two were done," Damien said.

"I still love him, but he's being stupid. He drunk dials me often. I'm not taking him back though until our relationship grows. I'm tired of hiding and sneaking around, I'm to grown for that," Terrance declared, "He's twenty-six years old, it's time for him to let his parents know what's up. I want a wedding and for both of our families to be there, not just mine. If I find him out here, I'm going to smack him upside his head again."

Damien laughed, "You do that. I'll talk to you later though. I'm trying to find somebody."

Damien continued his search for Zyan, getting annoyed with the crowd slowing down the process.

Out of nowhere somebody snatched him by the arm and pulled him inside.

Instead of Zyan like he wanted, it was Harris who wore a snarl, "So, what he say?"

"He who?" Damien asked, a bit upset with the way Harris nearly yanked his arm off.

"Terrance. I saw you talking to him. What did he say?"

"That he still loves you and just wants you to meet his family so you guys can have a nice wedding."

Harris rolled his eyes, "Wedding? We agreed to sign papers at the court house and that's it. Now he's trippin."

"Nah dude, you're trippin."

A guy who looked as if he was sixteen with a fresh haircut walked up to Harris, "Alright, my cut is done."

Harris motioned at the guy, "Damien this is Jaden. J, this is my friend Damien."

Jaden smiled at Damien, "Hey."

Damien noticed Jaden wore one of the LGBT youth group shirts that Terrance was wearing, "Hey."

Jaden refocused back on Harris, "I'm ready when you're ready."

Harris seductively licked his lips at Jaden, "Yeah, just wait by the front gate. I'm coming."

"Alright, cool," Jaden said before he walked off.

None of this seemed right to Damien, "Please tell me you're not doing what I think you're doing."

Harris laughed, "Aye, lil dude is eighteen. His birthday was last weekend, I checked out his permit."

"Dude, you're going too far. He's one of Terrance's group members."

"And? I'm a single man and I'm enjoying it. Now, imma go flood his virgin ass at the nearest hotel."

Damien stood speechless as he watched Harris leave. He didn't agree with Zyan's belief that a lot of military dudes were messed up, but Harris wasn't doing them any justice. He was supposed to be an American hero, a gay black man in a great relationship challenging the stereotypes. All of that was being washed away as his list of sexual partners grew longer.

Tired of searching the crowd, Damien went back to where he started and found Zyan by the bus.

"I walked all over looking for you," Damien said.

"Aye, my momma taught me that if I get lost to return to the last place I saw the person I was looking for."

"My dad taught me not to get lost or he'll cut my ass," Damien said.

"He needs to cut your brother's ass with his coked up self," Zyan said.

The bus door opened and Vincent exited. His face dropped upon spotting Zyan, "Sup bitches."

"Whoa," Zyan said, "I'm not your bitch, bitch."

Vincent shut the bus door, "Don't take it personal man. Damien, check your bitch, he likes to bark."

"Vincent, stop showing off," Damien said, "We get it, you're cool."

"I'm cooler than cool," Vincent boasted, "Cool people don't have events like this."

Damien wasn't going to feed into his mess, "This is a nice event so don't ruin it."

"It won't be ruined unless your bitch tries to start a gang war or something."

"Yo," Zyan said, "Why so many of your friends try to test me Damien?"

Vincent laughed, "I'm not his friend. We've got a lot of history, we're more than friends."

Zyan laughed, "Nigga, are you serious right now? Damien, can we go?"

"Y'all can't leave now," Vincent said, "My dude Tristan Tunz is about to shut it down."

"Where is the big star anyways?" Damien asked.

Vincent nodded at the bus, "He's getting dressed. I had to give him some pre-show dick."

"He's fucking you?" Zyan asked in shock, "I wonder why his track list sucks. He makes bad choices."

Vincent let out an overdramatic laugh and out of the blue suckered punched Zyan. Zyan stumbled but used the bus to quickly regain his balance. He charged at Vincent but not before Damien could step in and hold him back. Zyan started up a cussing storm while Vincent just stood there laughing. More people rushed over to create a barrier between Vincent and Zyan.

Tristan stepped off the bus with a mic in his hand and approached Vincent, "What's going on out here man?"

Vincent motioned at Zyan, "You know how thugs act in public. I know we should've booked security."

The crowd started to get distracted by the fight.

Tristan turned on his mic and spoke into it, "Ignore the ignorance, today is about our promising youth."

The crowd started applauding and some yelled for Zyan to be escorted from the park. Damien didn't think twice about what to do next. He went over to Zyan and talked him into calming down. Once Zyan composed himself, they both started to leave through the crowd. Damien looked back at Vincent who just smirked at him and shrugged as he followed Tristan Tunz to the stage.

51 - Four

After the drama of the Cut Up event, Damien wasn't expecting an apology call from Vincent. In fact, he didn't want to speak to Vincent at all but somehow at the end of the call had ended up agreeing to have him and Tristan over for dinner. As expected, Zyan didn't take the news well. Damien was surprised Zyan could actually get mad at him, used to the roles being reversed. Zyan sat in the bed watching ESPN all day and ignoring Damien.

Damien was tired of being the bad guy in this situation. He sat on the bed, "Seriously?"

Zyan kept his focus on the television, "What?"

"You're still mad."

"I told you. I'm not participating in no whack ass double date with Vincent's bitch ass."

"Believe it or not but he's a part of my life, a very close friend to the family."

"And y'all used to fuck around with each other and he still wants too."

Damien shrugged, "And? It's not going to happen. I can't make him stop liking me."

"I get that, but he fucking takes all his frustration out on me. I still owe him an ass beating."

"Why do you have to fight everybody?"

"Because gay dudes need to stop running their mouths like bitches and learn that real men throw fists."

Damien rolled his eyes, "So being gay makes you a bitch?"

"Don't try to twist my words. You know Vincent was being a bitch ass yesterday."

"He was but you get used to him. You have to know how to deal with people."

"Oh, so if he punches you in the face you just gonna laugh and roll with it?"

"Alright," Damien said, "That was uncalled for but he apologized. Beating him up won't make things even."

"It would for me."

"No, you have to hurt him where it hurts. The heart."

"Huh?" Zyan said as he raised his right brow.

"Tonight is your chance to rub in his face that you got all of this," Damien said as he rubbed his hands at his chest.

Zyan laughed, "Oh, so you wanna fuck with him on an emotional level. Make a nigga suicidal and all."

That statement took Damien back to Kendall's suicide. "No, I mean, just make him a lil jealous."

Zyan shrugged, "I guess so. But the minute he lays a finger on me, he's losing some teeth."

Damien crawled closer to Damien and snuggled up to him, "Deal."

A story on ESPN caught Damien's attention as they started to air some clips of football star Max who had an interview with Wendy Winfrey. It was being billed as her big exclusive, an inside look at the first openly gay football player to play in the Superbowl. The woman wore more makeup than a clown and Max wore a suit only a millionaire like himself could afford. Most of the questions focused on his career, but Wendy finally brought up his private life.

"Have you ever been in love Max?" Wendy asked.

Max thought about it for a moment, "At the time it was lust, companionship, but today I'm mature enough to accept that I was indeed in love with a man. I think mainly fear, the idea of only being famous for my sexuality instead of my talent, is what kept me in denial of this love I had for this man."

"So, this was before you signed your contract?" Wendy clarified.

"Yeah, I was with this man when I was in college."

"And are you still in contact with this man that you supposedly love?"

Max shook his head, "No, he cheated on me and I cheated on him at the same time."

"Why cheat on a man you love?"

Max chuckled, "Sex."

"Pretend as if this man you loved is watching, what would you say?"

Max looked in the camera, "Damien, what happened to us? I love you. Tweet me."

Wendy started to wrap up the interview.

Zyan looked to Damien, "Is that nigga talking about you?"

"Um," Damien was finding it hard to believe it himself, "I think so."

"Damn," Zyan said as he laughed, "Are you gonna tweet him?"

"I don't even have a Twitter and I'm already in a relationship."

"Wait, you're choosing me over a nigga who has a Nike deal?"

"He's a strict top, of course I'm picking you," Damien teased, "Oh, and because I love you."

"Nigga what?"

"I said I love you."

"Over him? The nigga with a Nike deal? Well, damn." Zyan kissed Damien, "I love you too."

It completely skipped both of their minds that this was the first time they both officially declared their love for each other. No more tension between them, the couple spent all afternoon just cuddling in bed and watching reruns of Martin. They had to breakup their love fest and get dressed for tonight because they had company coming over. While Zyan straightened up the place Damien threw together a quick dinner of turkey chili and cheese biscuits. Vincent and Tristan arrived around eight.

Tristan entered carrying a bottle of wine, "It's a peace offering, a one thousand dollar one."

"It was all Tristan's idea," Vincent said, "I figured my apology was enough."

Damien took the bottle of wine, "Thanks Tristan."

Zyan dapped Vincent, "Aye man, let's start over like men. None of the bitch ass shit."

"I'm all man," Vincent said.

"Not the way you threw that cheap shot," Zyan said.

"I was defending myself. Never know when you thugs can snap."

"Enough," Damien said, "Dinner is on the table."

"I'm ready to eat, it's been a while since I've had a meal cooked by a normal person," Tristan said.

Zyan looked Tristan up and down, "Normal? My nigga is above normal."

"I mean normal as in not my private chef," Tristan clarified.

"Are we ever going to sit down?" Damien asked.

They all made their way over to the table and started their meal. Tristan was mostly going on and on about his career while Zyan tried to combat it with stories of his Team Bodied career. The conversation during the entire meal basically consisted of

Vincent and Zyan trying to one up each other. At some point Vincent even decided to kiss Tristan because of how proud he was of him.

Zyan softly laughed, “Damn that’s how y’all makeout?”

Vincent rubbed Tristan’s chest, “Sometimes I just can’t resist him.”

“I know how you feel. My nigga never know when I’m about to tackle him,” Zyan said.

Zyan turned to Damien and aggressively started kissing him, shoving his tongue deep into his mouth. Vincent sat boiling the longer they went on. Not to be outdone, Vincent grabbed Tristan and started kissing on him again. All of this action was getting Damien’s dick hard.

Zyan stopped kissing him, “And I always get access to his mushroom dick, no questions asked.”

Zyan dug into Damien’s pants and started to play with his dick.

Vincent continued kissing Tristan and dug his hand into his pants.

Zyan whispered in Damien’s ear, “This jealous nigga gonna learn tonight.”

Zyan got up and pulled Damien to his feet. He led Damien over to the bed and pushed him down. Zyan stripped from his clothes revealing his heavily tatted body. He joined Damien on the bed and started to strip him naked. Damien didn’t even bother to stop him, always up for any craziness Zyan had planned. Zyan started sucking his dick, making sure Vincent had a clear view.

Vincent snarled, “Man, your head game ain’t shit.”

Vincent dragged Tristan over to the bed and they both started to strip naked.

Tristan lay down on his back beside Damien. “Man, y’all dudes wild.”

Vincent got down on his knees and started to eat Tristan’s ass.

Zyan stopped and watched, “Man, eat that ass like you want it.”

Vincent looked over to Zyan, “Nigga, fuck you.”

Zyan mounted Damien, “Nah, that’s Damien’s duty.”

Zyan slid Damien’s dick into him and slowly started to ride him. Vincent could only watch in complete disgust as Zyan moaned and groaned atop of Damien. No longer into to playing this silly game, Vincent once again threw a cheap shot and punched Zyan and sent him tumbling to the floor.

“What the fuck?” Damien said as he sat up.

Zyan let out a cynical laugh as he slowly rose to his feet, “Another bitch shot, huh?”

Vincent raised his fists, “Nigga come at me.”

“Oh, I’ll come at you,” Zyan said.

Damien didn’t want to see any bloodshed, “Zyan, relax.”

Zyan looked to Damien, “I’m not going to hit him, but I’m going to hurt him.”

A confused Vincent kept his fists raised, “Nigga what?”

Zyan got down on one knee and focused on Damien, “I want you to always be my nigga, will you marry me?”

Damien definitely knew that was a punch in the gut Vincent wasn’t expecting. He had never seen Vincent look so genuinely distraught. He actually felt bad for him, almost feeling guilty for putting the idea in Zyan’s head to go after him emotionally. As for the proposal, Damien never envisioned the question being popped midway through a foursome and especially by Zyan out of all the men he had dated.

“Damien don’t do this,” Vincent said. He got down on one knee, “Fuck him, please, marry me? I’m begging.”

“Um, I’m right here,” Tristan said as he raised his hand.

Damien was ready. He was ready to commit and live happily ever after.

Damien looked to the man who he felt the strongest bond too. "Yes, I will marry you."

One man's heart was left broken, another's heart now officially tied with Damien's. It was no longer just about him, but instead about them.

52 - About Them

After officially signing the documents following their courthouse wedding, their families went to setup the wedding party. The Georgia sun blazing hot, Damien and his husband refused to stay in their dress clothes any longer. They didn't put their guests through the suffering, allowing everybody invited to wear casual clothes. Both Damien and his husband wanted to keep some kind of tradition and figured wearing dress clothes to the courthouse had been just enough.

The moment Damien and his husband got back to his apartment they stood in the center of the place. It felt different. Though this was the apartment they had did all their planning and had merged together as one, they had out grown the place. This was a place for two married men. Damien now an assistant chef at a local restaurant, he could afford a new job. As for his husband, Zyan's solo male entertaining career was expanding as he somehow got Harris to team up with him to become a duo.

Damien loosened his tie, "Husband, I need a shower."

Zyan laughed, "Husband, I like you all hot and nasty."

Damien kissed Zyan, "Aye, save all that talk for the honeymoon."

Zyan laughed, "I can't believe your daddy back tracked on sending us to Hawaii."

Damien shrugged, "I'm surprised he even offered."

"Man, if him and Katrina hadn't have their expensive wedding we could be on our way to a beach right now."

"I don't care where I'm at as long as my husband is close."

Zyan smirked, "Damn nigga, that shit make my dick hard when you call me your husband."

"You think you can hold on to that nut until after the wedding party."

Zyan grabbed at Damien's crotch, "Nigga, I won't even make it through the toast."

Damien leaned in and dug his tongue into his husband's mouth. That was enough to let Zyan know it was time to start stripping out of his dress clothes. He had managed to get butt naked first and then got Damien out of his clothes. They stood in the center of the apartment kissing as their hard dicks sword fought with each other.

Damien figured they were warmed up enough. He got down on his knees and started to lick Zyan's dick. He traced the tip of his tongue along the veins of Zyan's dick before finally shoving the head into his mouth. His dick was a bit sweaty, but Damien didn't care. He loved all the scents and tastes of his husband's body. Damien fingered Zyan's damp hole as he bobbed his mouth up and down his husband's dick.

Zyan tore his dick out of Damien's mouth and beat it against his face. "My turn."

Zyan forced Damien to his feet and got down on his knees. He went in hard, sucking at Damien's dick and even sticking his balls into his mouth. Zyan even managed to stick his head in between Damien's leg and eat his ass out a bit. It felt so good that he had Damien moaning and nearly on his toes like he was a ballerina. Zyan got back to working on Damien's dick until he nutted in his mouth. Damien dick was still hard as Zyan kept on sucking and swallowing.

Zyan stood up and Damien led him over to the bed and they both lay down. Damien mounted Zyan and slowly slid his stiff dick into his hole. It had took a lot of preparation for Damien to take a dick, especially one so big. But he was willing to do anything for the man he was going to spend the rest of his life with. As he slowly rode Zyan's dick, he regretted holding out so long because it felt good even though he still preferred topping. It wasn't just all about his preference anymore, but also Zyan's.

Into the apartment strolled Vincent, "Ugh, I figured you two would come back here and fuck.

Damien paused on Zyan's dick as he looked back at Vincent, "What the fuck?"

"I had to come grab the wine bottles we forgot to pack. It's my duty as the best man."

Damien went through an entire list of names before landing on Vincent's as the best man. Marion didn't want the attention, especially after the web famed he had garnered when he screwed up some little boy's haircut while high on drugs. And Leon was back in North Carolina, Megan's second child due at this time. Harris stuck with his new business partner and was Zyan's best man. Sean was in Boston running a marathon; a lifestyle that he had become addicted too. And Kyle wasn't paying for a ticket from California especially after shipping a TV as a wedding gift.

By default, Vincent was labeled the best man. It turned out to be a really good decision because Vincent really took the role seriously. And it not only strengthened him and Damien's relationship, but it sorta made him and Zyan okay with each other. Sure, they still fought like cats and dogs, but at least the fights didn't involve any sucker punches.

Vincent snapped his fingers at the newlyweds, "Put on some damn clothes and let's go."

Damien slid off of Zyan's dick, "You're just jealous, Vincent," He teased.

Zyan sat up and kissed Damien, "But he's right. Let's go tear the house down."

"And I'm not jealous," Vincent said, "Just patient. He'll come running back to me eventually."

Zyan and Damien burst out laughing and started to get dressed.

They all left the apartment and arrived to the wedding party that was a small gathering on the roof top of a local bar. Damien's brother, father and step mother came along with Zyan's mother and sister. The rest of the guests were either friends from school or work. Some panels on the roof provided enough shade to keep the blazing sun from melting everybody.

A now clean Marion was over at a table with his pregnant girlfriend, the blonde bombshell, and ex-stripper Alana. Marion met Alana during one of his coke binges and of course got her pregnant that night. Alana wasn't about to be a single mother or the baby mother of a coke head. She did everything she could to make Marion into the man she wanted to raise a child with. Alana still had some work to do, but Marion was becoming a much better man overtime.

As Damien and Zyan made their way to their table, Harris stepped before them.

Harris dapped Damien, "Aye man, congrats again." He looked to Zyan, "And thanks for the opportunity."

Zyan shrugged, "No problem nigga. I might be able to retire and just manage you, the ladies and men love you."

Harris looked over to Terrance, "They can love me all they want but they can't have me."

"And maybe you and Terrence can get married next," Damien said.

"He said as long as we can do it in the Bahamas I wouldn't have to introduce him to my parents for another two years," Harris said.

Damien didn't like their compromise, upset Terrance didn't hold out on Harris longer. "Alright, then. Good luck."

Damien and Zyan finally made it to the table with their parents. The entire time, Zyan's mother and Damien's father bickered back and forth. It was funny seeing them trying to out parent each other, giving out all types of common sense advice. Damien took a moment to step away and go stand on the balcony. As he glanced over his shoulder at his family and friends, he still wished his mother could be there. The moment he started to shed a tear, Zyan showed up and wiped it away.

"Don't cry, I know your mom is here in spirit," Zyan said.

"How do you know I was thinking about her?"

"Because I just know it, I can feel it. That's why I know we were made for each other."

Damien smirked, "To borrow your words, you my ride or die, my nigga."

Zyan laughed, "Exactly. Now let's go before my moms have to drop your daddy."

The couple shared a kiss. Forever and forever, it would be about them.

About Him
www.tysonanthony.com
Thank You